A Real Love At Last

A Real Love At Last

*A Romance in Williamsburg
and Places Beyond . . .*

Victoria Leigh Gabriella

Copyright © 2014 by Victoria Leigh Gabriella.

Library of Congress Control Number:		2014917758
ISBN:	Hardcover	978-1-4990-7869-5
	Softcover	978-1-4990-7870-1
	eBook	978-1-4990-7871-8

All rights reserved. No part of this book may be reproduced or transmitted in any form or by any means, electronic or mechanical, including photocopying, recording, or by any information storage and retrieval system, without permission in writing from the copyright owner.

This is a work of fiction. Names, characters, places and incidents either are the product of the author's imagination or are used fictitiously, and any resemblance to any actual persons, living or dead, events, or locales is entirely coincidental.

Any people depicted in stock imagery provided by Thinkstock are models, and such images are being used for illustrative purposes only. Certain stock imagery © Thinkstock.

This book was printed in the United States of America.

Rev. date: 10/28/2014

To order additional copies of this book, contact:
Xlibris
1-888-795-4274
www.Xlibris.com
Orders@Xlibris.com

670012

Contents

Chapter 1	First Stare: Impulsive Rescue	9
Chapter 2	Our First Date? Please!	26
Chapter 3	Movie Time: Our Second Date	38
Chapter 4	Baseball Games	49
Chapter 5	Incredibly Idiotic Error in Judgment	56
Chapter 6	I'm Trapped in Purgatory: The Week from Hell	62
Chapter 7	The Perfect Picnic at the Winery	74
Chapter 8	I Am Trying to Be Civil Here	79
Chapter 9	Racing Horses and Racing Hearts	90
Chapter 10	The Williamsburg Inn: I'm Going In	99
Chapter 11	I Love Making Love with Her	106
Chapter 12	Sweet, Sexy Seductions	119
Chapter 13	Family Matters	128
Chapter 14	Just Getting to Deeply Know Her	143
Chapter 15	My House is Our Home	153
Chapter 16	I've Got a Fucking Life Now	165
Chapter 17	Career Crisis Coming On	178
Chapter 18	Falling More in Love in the Fall	185
Chapter 19	Thankful Celebrations	199
Chapter 20	Grand Illuminations	210
Chapter 21	My Marriage Proposal	220
Chapter 22	Marry, Marry Christmas to Me	227
Chapter 23	A New Year, a New Life	235
Chapter 24	I Learn My Lessons Willingly	241
Chapter 25	Super Wedding Preparations	249
Chapter 26	You're Mine, I'm Yours	256
Chapter 27	Oh, What a Night!	268
Chapter 28	Romantic Honeymoon in Switzerland	280

Chapter 29	She Gets My Motor Running	298
Chapter 30	I Bet I Can Win in Vegas	304
Chapter 31	March Madness in the Mountains	315
Chapter 32	Fun Fucking with Food	327
Chapter 33	Sensual Spring Flings	338
Chapter 34	Charming Southern Hospitality	351
Chapter 35	Hot Savannah: We Need Ice to Cool Off	364
Chapter 36	Sizzling, Steamy Summer Sex	372
Chapter 37	Blow Out My Birthday Candle	379
Chapter 38	What a Trip to Ireland	385
Chapter 39	A Gorgeous Game of Golf	389
Chapter 40	Mountain Meadow Mating	396
Chapter 41	Just Call Me Worry Wart	400
Chapter 42	Beach Blanket Bingo in a Bikini	405
Chapter 43	Tripp, the Asshole Ex	412
Chapter 44	Holy Hell! I'm Hospitalized!	419
Chapter 45	River Walk in San Antonio, TX	425
Chapter 46	Tied Up in Knots? Not Me!	431
Chapter 47	Cinderella's Castle	442
Chapter 48	Real Love at Last—Really!	448

Author's notes 463

A mature love story between a man and a woman who fall in love with each other for the first and last time in their lives.

"A Real Love at Last" is dedicated to ReBecca Richardson, my beautiful tattooed friend in Williamsburg who keeps me young at heart. Even though there is a significant difference in our ages, she never makes me feel like I am a senior citizen with an AARP card. She was the first to hear me tell her about a dream I had in July 2014 I couldn't forget. Becca is a writer herself and is an extraordinarily bright, articulate, and gifted idea partner and editor genius. She encouraged me to write more and our friendship blossomed into something very special to me. I am sure none of this would have happened the same way without her support and encouragement.

"I love you, Gothic Warrior Woman and my own personal hair fairy, my fantasy little sister, and real true friend at last. I will be forever grateful to you from the bottom of my heart."

Victoria Leigh Gabriella

CHAPTER 1

First Stare: Impulsive Rescue

I see her the moment she walks into the Second Street Bistro. She immediately grabs my attention. The young blonde hostess leads her to a small table for four directly in front of the bar where I'm sitting. I can't seem to take my eyes off her. Tall, with soft chestnut-colored hair just below her shoulders, and a figure that takes my breath away.

Her beautiful eyes are carefully made up, with only enough makeup to enhance her natural loveliness. She is wearing tight jeans, low heels, and a blue blouse that hugs her curves perfectly. I think I can see just a hint of her full cleavage, attracting my eyes. The beautiful brunette is a sexually tempting woman. I catch my breath as I watch her walk closer toward me. I try very hard not to stare, but my eyes keep flickering back to her.

Oh, shit. I could get lost in that body. Just how I'd like. Made perfectly for me. Full yet perky breasts, a slender waist, curvy hips, and a sweet, tight round ass.

She sits gracefully and slowly removes her sunglasses, placing them on the table in front of her. A nice full-grown woman. Not a girl—maybe in her early to mid-forties, I hope.

Even though she still looks young to me, she has the air of an experienced woman. The thought crosses my mind . . . just right for me. Yeah, I've had my fill of "girls" in their twenties, thirties, and even some in their forties. Too young or silly, I guess, for me now. They just don't have anything in common with me other than having momentarily stiffened my cock. I'd like a real woman who's had her share of life experiences. We'd have some similar memories of growing up if we are nearly the same age. I could actually fucking talk to her.

Turning back to my gin and tonic, I take a big gulp and almost choke as the fiery liquid slides down my throat. I need to get out of here because I don't want to make a fool of myself over a woman I can't have by staring at her beauty.

I recently moved to Williamsburg, Virginia, after serving in the Marines for thirty years. It seemed a good place to settle in since my sister and her family live only an hour away in Richmond. It feels as though I am still finding my way around and have met a few people in my immediate neighborhood.

I need to make some friends here. Could I be friends with her? Would she want to know me?

I'm used to being in new places after being stationed all over the country as well as in multiple tours in Europe, Iraq, and Afghanistan. It is taking me a while to adjust to no longer being on active duty, surrounded by just a bunch of tough guys and giving them orders. It is never easy to meet new people and become friends with them.

I feel like a stranger here, but I want to fit in and feel at home. This is where I plan to stay. I am tired of living in places for only a few years and then picking everything up and starting all over again. It gets old pretty fast. I already have a few good friends who I know will be my friends forever. The problem is none of them live near me.

I can count on them. Good Marines, good men.

My best friend Keith Jones settled in Norfolk, an hour southeast. Therefore, I am not completely alone. It's just I know few people who actually live here in Williamsburg.

New place, new life, new house, new woman?

Would she let me in her life? Maybe more? My consciousness keeps whispering, taunting me with possibilities.

I continue to keep my eyes on her while she sits alone and glances at the door every so often. She is obviously waiting for someone. I ponder her situation as I ponder my own. She is unaccompanied for the moment while I am alone for real. I hope to change that now that I have decided on a place, settled and ready to build a life.

I need a change since I'm no longer active duty. I need a fucking real life. Perhaps even a wife to share it with. Part of a loving couple. My own wife.

I am happy with my decision to retire from the corps because I need to get that fucking life. I gave my everything to the military and want to have my own stability, apart from the service. Moving around as often as I did wrecked any potential social life. I've been on my own most of my existence. I'm tired of being alone. I need more than Marines around me.

I need a woman to love me and who will let me love her back.

Here I sit, alone in a strange bar, in an unfamiliar town, and barely knowing anyone on this warm June night. I drink my gin and tonic as I look around the restaurant, killing some time before going home to my lonely new house. My eyes rise to take a quick glimpse of her.

She is still alone. Waiting. I think.

I watch the green-eyed beauty, but then I look away so she doesn't catch me staring at her.

Staring at her like I'm some kind of scary pervert or something. I don't want to frighten her, being a stranger in a bar.

Who is she? I don't have a chance with this gorgeous woman. She's probably already married. Fuck it. I can't take this shit.

I try to see if she is wearing a diamond wedding set, but I can't see her hands.

Just give it up, Stevens.

I'm trying to think of something else. I can't, for some reason. My stiff gin and tonic is almost gone now; I didn't realize I was practically gulping it down.

Should I get another one? I think I need another one, for various reasons. It will give me a reason to stay here. I would look suspicious if I sit without something. I am not ready to stop watching this woman in front of me.

Glancing back over at the woman who is still at her table all alone, I find myself wondering how I can meet her. Different scenarios drift through my mind, trying to think of some way to get to know her. She is still by herself when the waitress comes over to her table. I hear her order a glass of Riesling, my favorite wine. Her voice is sweet, slightly husky, and low. I want to hear her speak more. The early evening sunlight burnishes her glossy brown hair, picking up a few red highlights.

Why is she alone? Perhaps I could get up my nerve and go introduce myself.

No, a stranger in a bar coming up to her out of the blue: not a good situation. I might scare her. I don't know how I can get to talk to her without going over there. She must be waiting for someone, a beautiful woman like that. She won't be alone for long. What man in his right mind would ever leave her alone?

I begin to watch her closely, fearing the sight of another man coming up and kissing her hello. I'm scared of her leaving the restaurant without me ever having a chance of finding her again and knowing her name. I hope she is just here to meet some friends instead of a husband or lover.

I keep my eyes on her, glancing away enough to not be caught with obvious lust in my gray eyes.

I wonder, 'What's her story?'

My mind wanders briefly to my own situation as I ponder on the intriguing woman, sitting and waiting, in front of me.

It's been so long since I've been with a woman. A few friends with sexual benefits along the way, but I haven't found any woman with whom I want to spend the rest of my life. My career has made it almost impossible to have any kind of lasting, loving relationship. I was too busy, dedicating myself completely to being a Marine. It took a lot out of me: living in foreign countries, working my way up the ranks, becoming a commanding officer, and the overwhelmingly tense experiences in Iraq and Afghanistan for all those years. Being a Colonel is an intense full-time job when it is done right, especially during warfare.

I ended up with fleeting one-night stands and short-lived relationships, solely for sex. Meaningless experiences. Just fucking as a means to an end. I imagine often what it would be like to fall in love. Many of the Marines I knew through the years went through woman after woman, wife after wife. That just isn't me. Real love requires a lasting commitment and a complete devotion to another person's welfare.

My thoughts drift although my intense stare rarely does. I can't stop looking at her for more than a few moments at a time.

I believe real love must exist for some people if all the romantic books and movies are based on someone's true story. I hope perhaps I can find and experience such love. I feel I have it within me to love someone with all my heart. I haven't found the right woman, the one I can't live without. I feel time slipping quickly by. I don't want to waste any more time.

Will it happen to me, or is it too late to hope?

I suddenly realize I have been staring at the lovely woman like a thirsty man who sees cold water in the desert. People are going to start to notice if I don't take my eyes off her. I want to watch her, but I don't want to frighten her if she or others become aware of a strange man staring from behind the bar. Taking a deep breath, I try to get myself under control. I have to shift around in my seat to ease my aching cock. It's starting to have a life of its own because of a beautiful unknown woman.

Jesus Christ, Stevens. Get a grip. You don't even know her. She's probably married or, at the very least, has a lover. Someone who looks like her is bound to be involved.

Suddenly, I see her eyes dart to the door as a man about my age, late forties, comes in.

Is that fear and pain in her eyes?

The man runs his hand through his graying hair as he scans the restaurant. He's a little less than six feet tall, a bit stocky, and soft around the middle. He's got the look of a middle-aged man who doesn't really give a fuck about his appearance anymore. He is dressed in a red golf shirt and tan slacks. He has no muscle definition I can see, but maybe he is stronger than he appears. I make note of him out of the corners of my eyes, but I can tell by her face she knows him. Therefore, he must know her.

Goddamn it! Shit! She won't be sitting there alone much longer.

He sees her and hones in like a heat-seeking torpedo fired from a nuclear submarine.

Who is this fat fucker? And who is he to her? Is he a friend? Is he her lover? Is he her damn husband? Fuck, no. I can't believe she belongs to him. Shit, shit, shit. Well, that's it then. So much for imagining I can get to know her. I might as well go since I don't want to see them together. Women like her are always taken.

Before I have the chance to summon a waitress and pay for my drinks, I can't help but watch as he approaches her, looking as though he's going to lean down for a hug or a kiss on her cheek. I cringe thinking of his hands or lips on her.

Don't. You. Fucking. Touch. Her.

"Stay away from me. Don't touch me," the woman says quickly, but quietly.

What the fuck? What did she just say? Did I imagine her saying that? Is she afraid of him? Who is this asshole? Does she need protecting?

I can't stop myself. My whole body tightens as I focus on their conversation. He sits across from her, thanking her for coming. She's looking down, not meeting his eyes. Her hands twist nervously in her lap.

"I could have just mailed the bracelet back to you if you had told me your address. I don't understand why you insisted we meet in person," she says softly.

She reaches down for her purse and pulls out a gold braided bracelet, placing it in front of him on the table instead of his outstretched hand.

He's not her husband then. I don't see a wedding ring on her left hand. Not married to anyone else either.

Excellent.

Are they dating?

No, she said stay away from her. She doesn't know where he lives. She said he hadn't given her his address.

I let out a calming breath.

All good so far.

"I wanted to see you again. It's been such a long time," the man murmurs as he slips the bracelet quickly into his pants' pocket.

He's staring at her like he's got his own hard-on for her. I know that look. He said he hasn't seen her for a long time. He looks as though he could eat her alive.

Umm.

I don't like that look in his eyes. Get away from her. She said not to touch her.

Stay back.

"Well, I agree your daughter should have Granny Ruth's bracelet, not me. It did belong to her great-grandmother after all. Her name is Ruth, isn't it?"

He nods affirmatively.

I become aware of the waitress. I throw my credit card at her to pay for my drinks.

The woman continues, saying, "She should have it as a family heirloom. I hope she treasures it as much as I once did. I loved Granny Ruth, too. Now, you have what you came for. Please leave. I have nothing else to say to you."

"I was hoping we could go to your house and catch up. It's been years since I've seen you. You look great. I've never seen you look like this before. If I had known, I would have tried sooner to look you up," he says, leaning toward her and reaching for her hand across the table.

I think he is trying to grab one of her hands. The fat fucker is practically staring at her with clear lust in his eyes.

I see her physically move back, away from him.

She flinches. "But you said you're married when you called me. You said you've married for a third time. There is nothing for us to catch up on. You made yourself quite plain you wanted nothing to do with me when you walked out on our marriage with little to no warning. Go back to your third wife. I wasn't good enough for you to stay, remember?"

What the hell? Is this some kind of trip down memory lane? Memories of a past love?

"Well, sweetheart, you certainly look good enough now. Let me come over, and we can talk about old times," he says, leering at her in front of everyone in the restaurant.

He isn't hiding his intentions from her. He wants her. I can see her eyes slightly panic.

Don't call her sweetheart. She's not your sweetheart!

I almost get up to go over to them, and then I stop, because I don't know what to do, what to say. It's not my business. I can't intrude. Can I?

I suddenly want it to be my business.

"Come on. I remember how you used to love me. Let's go to your house while I am in Williamsburg. I drove all the way down to see you and get the bracelet. I want to get to know you again. We were married for almost ten years. I could be good to you. It was once great between us."

He seems to want to reach over and touch her. He only stops when she holds her hand up to warn him.

Don't you fucking talk to her like that! Oh, shit. They were once married. He's her ex-husband. Thank God he's not her husband now. I'm glad he's an ex. Judging from the tone of her voice, he hurt her when he left. She loved him once. Is she still in love with him? Shit, I hope not. She can't be. Fuck that! She looks like she's about to crawl out of her skin. He just stares at her, and I can't take it anymore.

"No. I need you to leave. The bad times far outweigh any good memories I have of our life together. It is over and has been for many years. You moved on with other women. Leave me alone. If you won't leave, I will," she says as she reaches for her purse.

It is flight-or-fight time for her.

It's clear he came here, hoping for something more. After all, I'm a guy. I know what he's thinking. He can't wait to get into her panties again. He wants a quickie, for old times' sake. After all, they used to be married. He feels as though he still has some kind of ownership over her. I can tell by the way he's looking at her. It's like he's remembering when he last fucked her.

Does he know where she lives? Or is he planning to follow her home? Can't he see she is way out of his league? Obviously, she's a classy woman, a lady. I suddenly feel a little sick, thinking of his hands on her. No, damn it. No!

The asshole replied, "I'm not leaving and you aren't either. Stay here and talk to me. I can make you stay. You know I will."

I won't have it. I just can't. She needs help. She shouldn't be facing this alone. Why isn't someone with her? No one else seems to be coming. She met him alone. In public, yes, but still alone with him. No boyfriend to protect her.

What can I do? I've got to think of some way to make him leave.

The receipt and my credit card appear in front of me. I scribble my signature and put away the card without acknowledging the waitress.

I see her eyes fill with panic as she realizes he isn't going to leave her alone. She is thinking he may even follow her out of the restaurant if she leaves first. I almost feel her anxiety, the indecision crippling her and freezing her in place. It is like watching a defenseless baby rabbit about to be devoured by a king cobra.

A sudden thought crosses my mind, teasing me with its possibilities. Yes, that would work. I can help her and get to know her at the same time. The more I think about it, the better I like it. No one ever said this Marine wasn't fast on his feet. I can think fast. Well, here goes nothing. I make the decision on impulse. I'm going in. I pray she'll cooperate, or this could blow up in my face.

Very badly.

Getting up suddenly from the bar stool, I make my way to the front of the restaurant and then turn back toward their table. I hope they will think I have just come in and didn't notice me sitting at the bar before. I swiftly walk down the aisle and slide into the chair closest to her, putting my arm around her shoulders as if I do this every day.

Leaning in, I barely breathe softly into her ear. "Let me help you."

Without thinking, I automatically press a brief kiss to that tender spot right below her ear.

It's one of my favorite places to kiss. I can't help but breathe in her slightly vanilla scent. She smells fucking good.

God, so incredibly good.

Suddenly, I'm having trouble breathing normally. What's happening? It's as though I feel a sudden charge from her skin to mine. I am completely aware of her in my arms. She's so close to me. I can feel her body pressed against mine.

"Hey. I'm so sorry I'm late, baby. I got here as soon as I could. I didn't want you to have to deal with this," I state boldly, looking her in the eyes and pleading with her to go along with me.

She's staring at me in shock, her olive green eyes wide and her mouth slightly open. She's not screaming or pushing me away yet. I surprised her so much she is frozen. I smile at her, my million-dollar smile, and grab her hand, raising it to my lips and kissing her knuckles. Her hand looks small in mine, and her skin is soft against my mouth. I don't let go of her hand, squeezing it gently.

Good. She hasn't pushed away from me yet. Maybe she'll cooperate with me, acting out the pretend-boyfriend scenario. I know I'm a stranger, but I want to help. Please. Let me help. I can protect you from this prick, your asshole ex-husband. I'm big and strong. Bigger and stronger than him.

I turn to look at the asshole ex-husband who hasn't left yet. I know now he wasn't planning on leaving without her. He's looking at me as if he can't believe I'm there, wondering who the hell I am.

Yes, I am now her boyfriend. She's taken. No longer available to you or any other man.

I just stare at him impassively. He says nothing and continues to look at me, obviously wondering how to make me leave. My sudden presence is spoiling his plans for the evening. He narrows his eyes. In turn, I narrow mine back at him.

I want to intimidate him to death. He needs to get the hint. No one wants him here.

It's still obvious I have a military background from the way I look and carry myself. I'm hoping it would be enough although I know I'm also a good-looking guy. Maybe my build will make him back off. Dark brown hair with just a touch of gray at my temples, gray eyes, 6'3", and covered in muscles. Not a muscle-bound ape, but strong.

Yeah, right. Tall, dark, and handsome. That's me.

Since retiring, I've let my hair grow, so I now no longer look quite so military. I love having hair again and have even let a bit of stubble grow on my face. Not a full beard, but more than a five o'clock shadow. It helps me remember I am no longer serving. Yeah, I'm not practically bald and clean-shaven. I was happy when my hair grew in still mainly brown because I really didn't know for sure.

Being in the Marine Corps means I'm built with muscles in all the right places, and I am at least five inches taller than him. I take good care of myself—lots of lifting weights and marital arts training.

He, on the other hand, is a sorry excuse for a middle-aged man. Pudgy around his waist, with graying hair that is thin at the top. Full face, double chin. Sloppy attire. I could take him in a heartbeat. How could he even think he still has a chance with her? Just because they were once married? She can't still be in love with him. Not years after he walked out on her. He is delusional. Crazy. Why doesn't the fucker leave her alone?

"So I see she's given you back the bracelet. Good. I don't want her to have anything that will remind her of you. She only wears what jewelry I give her. I think it's time for you to leave. We plan on having a bite to eat, isn't that right, honey?" I say smoothly as the boyfriend, realizing that I mean every word I'm saying.

Will you allow me to buy you dinner later?

I look at her, willing her to say yes. Her eyes widen a bit before she murmurs, "Yes, I'd like to eat something."

Good. She agreed. She's catching on and playing this lying game with me.

The fucker looks at me with his eyebrows raised. "And you are?" he says coldly.

I can't cope with the fact this fucker hasn't left yet. Can't he see she doesn't want him here?

Believe me, neither do I.

I stare at him, my eyes narrowing slightly with as hard a look as I can give him. "I'm Michael Stevens, the boyfriend and lover. Since your business is finished, I don't see the need for polite introductions. Good-bye."

He doesn't get up to leave. Instead, he replies, "I'm Tripp Richards and I'm looking forward to catching up with my ex-wife. Perhaps you could give us some privacy."

He stares at me and I stare back.

I can see he isn't even remotely thinking of leaving. He is trying to get me to leave just as much as I am him.

Turning my head to the woman next to me, I look at her softly as I say, "No. I don't think so. This lovely woman and I are dating. I think it is time for you to leave."

I look back at him intently, the message clear in my eyes.

Get the fuck away from her and never come back.

He glances at the woman, his narrow eyes disbelieving. "Becca, I didn't know you were seeing someone."

Great! Now I know her name. I was wondering how I was going to figure that out.

Her name is Becca.

She looks at me before turning toward him. "Why would you know? I haven't seen or talked with you since you left me. I thought you moved to Maryland when you left me. Please leave, Tripp. We're done. I don't want to see you anymore," she states firmly.

Good girl!

Wait, she said his name. His name is Tripp? That's a "vacation," not a fucking name. What an asshole name.

My God. He's a stupid prick with a stupid name.

A nickname? Yeah, he's a fucking trip, all right.

Unbelievably, he finally stands up. He runs his hands through his hair, looking thoroughly frustrated. His mouth is in a thin straight line as he snarls. "Good-bye."

Yeah, go away, Tripp, and take your trip down memory lane with you.

He turns and strides toward the front of the restaurant, anger resonating all through his body. I think I hear him slam the door on the way out.

Yeah, go the fuck away. Finally. But I need to make certain first.

I take a deep breath, looking over at Becca. She appears stunned but relieved he is gone. I lean over and whisper gently to her, "You okay? Stay here, please. Promise me. Say it."

She looks as though she's still scared. I hate seeing that look on her face, knowing that I would do anything to make it go away. She looks down and softly whispers, "I promise."

I stand up, looking down at her. I lift her chin and then run my fingers down the side of her cheek. "I'll be right back. Don't worry. I've got this."

I walk swiftly out the restaurant, seeing the asshole ex-husband about to open the door to a car. I catch up with him and look him straight in the eyes.

My voice is cold and deep as I say, "In case I wasn't completely clear in there, make sure you leave Becca the fuck alone. You've obviously hurt her enough. She's mine. Leave her alone. Go back to wherever you came from and don't come to Williamsburg. Believe me, I'll be here if you do."

I think for a second he might challenge me. It surprises me when he chooses to say nothing back. I would welcome the chance to really let him have it. I know my height and build can be intimidating, so for a moment, I see doubt flicker in his eyes. I want to make sure he leaves although I am also in a hurry to get back to Becca. I don't want her to leave yet.

He angrily gets in and starts his car. He is backing out of his space as I hurry back in Second Street.

She's sitting at the table, looking down at her hands when I sit down next to her. I wait until she looks up at me, and I smile, chuckling softly under my breath a little.

"Well, that was *fun*." Her olive green eyes sparkle slightly as I gaze at her. She is smiling at me.

What a lovely, sweet smile.

I smile back.

"Who are you? Why did you do that for me?" Her voice is low and hesitant.

"I'm Michael Stevens. Weren't you paying attention? All I know about you is your name and that your ex-husband is a jerk. You are Becca. Is that short for Rebecca?"

"Yes. I'm Rebecca Connelly. It's nice to meet you, Michael. Thank you for making him leave me alone. I wasn't sure what to do."

"It was my pleasure. As for why I came over, I could tell you needed assistance. I wanted to be the one who took care of it for you."

Suddenly, out of the corner of my eye, I see that bastard ex-husband come back into the restaurant's foyer. He comes in through the front door near the hostess desk and is looking intently at us. He is about to pass the hostess and head our way, I can tell.

Goddamn it! He came back, really?! Are you kidding me? What the fuck does he want now? Obviously, he still thinks he has something to say to her.

Well, I'll convince him to leave her alone. I want him to completely see that she no longer wants him. She's mine.

Leaning toward her, I put my arm around her and pull her close to me. I take a deep breath first. I look into her eyes and whisper, "Trust me, please. I won't hurt you. I promise. Let me do this."

I slant my head slightly before slowly lowering my open mouth down, touching her soft lips. I pause hovering over her barely open lips, testing to see if she will turn from me before I can press her lips with mine gently. Her mouth opens a bit in surprise and I taste her sweetness, a slight minty freshness. My mouth moves over her lips, licking her bottom lip and pulling it slightly with my teeth. She's breathing quickly but not pulling away as I feared. I press against her a bit more, feeling her lips give way under me, in surrender.

Oh my God, I think she's kissing me back just a little!

Hesitantly, she moves her slightly open lips under mine.

I open my mouth a bit more, wanting so much to taste all of her. I forget where we are and can only concentrate on her sexy mouth, feeling her lips slowly move against mine. My heart starts to beat fast, and it's all I can do not to groan out loud. I want to feel the inside of her mouth with my tongue. It's been so long since I've had a kiss like this. She must trust me if she's not pulling away. It is all I can do to stop my tongue from slipping inside to see how warm and wet her mouth is.

I know I surprised her by suddenly kissing her, taking full advantage of the situation. I am a stranger to her, and I must remember she doesn't know me yet.

Who am I kidding here? I've never had a kiss this hot. I want her, and I want her now. It's amazing, this complete need I have of her, so fast. I feel as though we're meant to be together somehow. Like I've known her, I mean really known her. Surely, she must feel it too. It's so strong I can't breathe. It almost feels as though a hot, electrical charge is racing between us.

Gradually, I become aware the fat fucker is standing next to us, glaring down.

Looming over us somehow.

How dare he interrupt? Not only is he an asshole, but he is a rude asshole. Can't he see we're busy? Doesn't he see I'm here? Does he really believe he can take her away from me? I'm kissing her, so get the hint and leave. I thought he wouldn't even dare come over here when he saw us kissing. He should have just turned around and realized she was no longer his for the taking. He's a stupid man with a stupid name.

Fuck it. I have had enough of his shit.

I pull back slowly, not wanting to break the connection I have with her. I quickly kiss her temple and sweet-smelling hair before I turn to face Tripp, with a stern but questioning look in my eyes.

What the hell does he want now? He can't have her again. He left her. They are divorced.

I can see him looking at me and assessing the situation. What does he still need to say to her? I decide to nip this in the bud. Becca doesn't need to hear any more of his shit.

I'm going to put a stop to this and make him leave her alone even if I have to carry him out of the damn restaurant.

Before he can get out one word to her, I stand straight up, looming back over him. I am much taller than he is, and I know I am stronger and quicker. I can bench-press 250 easy.

I practically growl at him, "I guess I didn't make myself clear. Or maybe you're a damn idiot. She's mine now. She belongs to me. Get the hell out of here, or do I have to make you leave us alone?"

And believe me, I can and I will. My right hand automatically opens and then clenches at my side. Don't mess with me, you fucking prick. You won't even see what hit you. I'm that fast. Better men have tried to take me on and failed.

I start to visualize my first move. I have trained extensively in all of the martial arts. It helped keep me alive many times. I'm a God Damn Marine, for fuck's sake. I'm too tough for you to handle. I swear to you, asshole. Just give me the opportunity to prove it to you. Do it. Do it now. I want to hit the fuck out of you.

Tripp's eyes widen, but he still doesn't back down fast enough for me. He stares at Becca. I can see him struggling with the words, but in frustration, because he didn't get to say what he wanted, he finally spits out, "I'll call you. Good-bye, Becca. Expect to hear from me." He cuts his furious eyes toward me, the anger clearly showing.

Take a good hard look at me, bastard. I earned every single one of these muscles in the military. Try it. Just try me.

I stare right back, "I don't think so. You better not call her."

He smirks at me, as if thinking how I could stop him from contacting his ex-wife.

"I'll talk to you soon, Becca."

The fuck you will. Over my dead body. You're never calling her again.

I hate thinking he knows her number. That has to change. I don't want him to contact her at all. How does he know how to call her? I guess he could have just looked it up if she is listed. She needs an unlisted number now so he can't bother her.

She said she hasn't seen him since he walked out on their marriage. He has been investigating, finding out about her life now. Her number and address. I don't think she would have given him her number or address voluntarily, judging from how she is acting. He said he wanted to go to her house, so yes, he probably knows where she lives.

He must have called her to set up this meeting to exchange the bracelet. That was just a pathetic excuse to see her once more. I doubt he even gives the gold bracelet to his daughter.

Why is he really here after all these years? I suspect he must not be happy in his current marriage with wife number three if he's looking around for his gorgeous ex-wife. He's not hiding his desire for her.

Perhaps he thinks he can have his marriage and more on the side. He's had her once before, so he remembers what it was like to fuck her. He's trying to seize an opportunity.

Jerk. I mean, look at him. Again, I just see a sad, fat middle-aged man, soft around the waist with gray, thinning hair. Give me a break. Does he really think she will want him? Are you kidding me? Maybe he was okay when he was young, but that's all gone now.

God. He's nuts. A beautiful woman like her? Asshole. Go away. Go away now.

Becca looks up at him and whispers, "I told you. I never want to see you or talk to you. I shouldn't have come. It was a mistake to see you. It's been too long. I hate you for what you did. You can't take away what you did to me when you left. So go, forget we were once married, and forget you still know my number. In fact, forget you even know my name.

I wish to God I had never married you. It only brought me heartache instead of real joy."

I can see a brief flash of pain in her eyes before she looks down.

I look at her, wanting to take the pain away. I hate that he hurt her, but thank God he's no longer her husband. This is a good thing, as far as I'm concerned.

Damn it! I hate the thought of her being with him even though it was a long time ago. The thought of his hands on her, having intimate sex with her, and claiming her as his wife is almost more than I can take. It makes me feel sick inside somehow, a deep, almost twisting pain, like a sharp knife stabbing me.

Doesn't she see he's the one with commitment issues? He's on his third wife, for fuck's sake! How the hell does he get women to marry him? How did he get so lucky to have this gorgeous woman?

If she were mine, I'd never let her go. I feel very protective of Becca, wanting to make her happy. I mean, like really forever happy. I want to be the one to make her smile and giggle. I don't even know her yet. I can't believe how much I feel for her so fast, so hard. I want her to actually be mine. Not a pretend boyfriend, a pretend lover, but for real.

Tripp starts to protest. "Becca, I . . . I . . ."

I make up my mind. I have no problem being decisive. Once I've decided something, I never change it. I learned to follow through on my decisions during all those years in the Marines. Not standing by my decisions could have easily gotten me or others killed, particularly when I was in the war.

I always get what I want. I want her, all of her, completely. I'll do whatever it takes. I'm going to be in her life. I will be intimately involved with her. She just doesn't know it yet. I have to convince her she can trust me with her life.

I interrupt his inability to form a coherent sentence by snarling at him. "I believe she said *no*. Now leave! Go! Get in your damn car and drive away this time."

As I stare him down, Tripp finally seems to get the message and storms out, muttering "Fuck!" under his breath. I can see him rake both of his hands through his graying hair in total frustration as he walks furiously out of the restaurant. I sit back down, putting my arm back around her. I squeeze her shoulder reassuringly.

I whisper to her, "Wait until we're sure he's really gone this time. I'll watch for his car leaving the parking lot."

We sit silently for a few minutes until I see his light-colored car pull quickly out into the street. He speeds away into the dark night, clearly taking his sexual frustration out on the accelerator.

Thank goodness he's gone. Now I can have her for myself.

I remove my arm from around her though I don't want to let her go. But I no longer have a good excuse to keep it there, touching her. I shift slightly in my chair to give her room but stay as close as I can without crowding her.

She has been hurt. I can fix that, I know. I am good at fixing things. All she has to do is let me in close enough to get the job done. The song "Fix You" by Coldplay is one of my favorites, and it is now playing over and over in my head.

"Are you all right, Becca?"

She can only nod at me right now.

I don't want to scare her by being overly familiar though I just pretended to be her boyfriend to help her.

I kissed her.

She kissed me back.

CHAPTER 2

Our First Date? Please!

The fat fucker is finally gone.

I expectantly gaze at the stunningly sexy woman I rescued from him. Becca turns to me and says politely as she thanks me, clearly dismissing me, "Once again, I must thank you for helping me. I don't know you, Michael, and I've imposed on you enough tonight. I'm not sure where you came from. You appeared suddenly here, rescuing me from an unwanted situation. I've got to go. Good night, and thank you very much."

Becca leans down to collect her purse before standing up to walk away, out of the restaurant, out of my life.

Inside my head, I'm screaming, "No, baby, no! Don't go yet! Don't leave me!"

There's nothing I can do to make her stay. I realize she's about to go, and all I know is her name. That's not enough. She'll slip through my fingers, and I'll have no way of finding her again.

What can I do to make her stay? How can I convince her to stay long enough for me to get to know her? I need time.

"Becca, you said . . . you said you'd eat with me. You said it. I heard you agree to dinner. Please stay. We're here together in a nice restaurant. Let's eat something. I want to get to know you. I want you to get to know me. I rescued you. You owe me a little of your time. This is the fun part. I won't hurt you. You can trust me even though we've only just met. I promise. Besides, I've kissed you five times already. The least you can do is enjoy a meal with me. I don't want to eat alone. Stay. Please. We need to celebrate that he's gone."

I look intensely into her beautiful green eyes, willing her to stay with me.

I need more time with her. I'll beg over and over if I have to.

She looks at me shyly, considering me. I see her swallow and take a deep breath before finally nodding yes.

Thank fuck.

Before she can change her mind, I motion quickly to the waitress for menus and order two Rieslings. Becca looks at me in surprise, but she doesn't say anything.

Yes, I know, I was paying attention earlier. Don't worry. I am not some kind of stalker. I would never do that. Scaring women is not my thing though my height and strong build can make me look somewhat overwhelming. It was a good thing as a Marine, though. My muscles came in handy many times.

We look at the dinner menus, and I tell her to get whatever she wants. After the waitress takes our order, I clink my wine glass to hers, saying softly, "To our first date."

I hope I haven't overstepped her boundaries; however, she needs to know from the very start I want to date her. A lot.

Becca laughs softly but doesn't reply.

We're going to know each other. I hope very well, in the not-too-distant future.

"So, Ms. Connelly, tell me about you. I want to know everything. Spill it."

I guess I might as well jump into it. Besides, I can't wait to know all there is about this beautiful woman. I want to know what she looks like when she's happy, when she's laughing, when she's pissed, when she's in love.

Fantasies of us making love drift through my mind. I visualize quick images of me on top and inside of her.

Wow. Shit, Marine, pay attention. Stop it. You need to focus. Don't want to screw this up right at the start, before you even get the chance to state your case. It is surprisingly important to you. You need to know her.

Becca takes a deep breath. I can tell she doesn't like talking about herself. "I'm not very interesting. I live quietly. I grew up in Virginia and went to William and Mary. I guess that's why I am happy in Williamsburg. I fell in love with the place when I was a student. I no longer have my mom and dad, but I'm close to my older sister and brother. We do a lot of things together. I've taught fifth grade for many years but recently decided to try fourth. I'm on summer break from school right now."

She pauses, thinking back, before continuing. She decides to share a bit more information with me. "And yes, I was married to Tripp for many years ago. He was in the navy then. We lived in California, Florida, and South Carolina before coming back. Virginia is home for me, and though I enjoyed living in other states, it was nice for me to be back home and closer to what is left of my family."

"Do you mind me asking about him? I am curious now since I just kicked him out of here."

"Tripp and I were married for almost nine years when he left suddenly. It was all over in a matter of several weeks. I didn't see it coming. Not really. A few clues now that I look back. I was still dealing with Mama's death and trying to finish out a school year. Divorce never entered my mind as an option. Too naive and easily fooled, I guess."

She tucks her hair behind one ear and looks down at her hands in her lap. I wait, wondering if she will go on sharing. Finally, I ask, "Do you have any children? Why were you with him?"

"We didn't have any children because... well... I can't have any. I got an infection and... there were complications... and one thing led to another. I think that's part of the reason why he left. I must have been a disappointment as a wife, not being able to give him a family. He mentioned he has three children now, so I guess he got what he wanted. But he didn't love me enough to stay. I was hurt because I thought I had been a good wife to him. I'm not perfect, but I loved him. It wasn't enough to make him stay with me for the rest of our lives. He certainly couldn't have gotten away from me any faster than he did. I've been alone ever since."

I interrupt. "I just don't believe that. There must have been more than the fact you could no longer have children. There are many other options. If he loved you, he would have been willing to try alternate methods for having a family. He is the one with the problem, not you. He wasn't the right man for you. He couldn't have completely loved you the way you deserve to be loved if he walked away. I'm glad you didn't waste your whole life on him. I know it was a hard time for you, a big adjustment, but it was the best thing for you. You should have a better man, a man who loves you."

Love, real love. From a man who can't live without you. Who adores and loves you and only you.

I ask gently, "Why in the world did you agree to see him? Was it important to give a bracelet back to him?"

"Since we haven't been in touch for so long, I was shocked when Tripp called to tell me he wanted his grandmother's gold bracelet back. It is evidently for his daughter Ruth's birthday. I think he has two daughters and a son, but it is for his daughter Ruth. I wore it for many years and loved it. It felt as though it was all I had left of him. It's worth a lot of money, and I have felt guilty for years I kept it when we divorced. It belongs to his family as an heirloom."

She pauses for a long while, and I fear she is going to stop sharing her life to me, the stranger. But then she shrugs slightly and goes on to explain more.

"I didn't know how to get it back to him, not wanting to contact him or knowing how to find him. I don't wear it anymore because now I don't want to be reminded of him. I would have mailed it to him if he had given me his address. I thought he was living out of state, a long way away. I had no idea and didn't want to know where he was. There was no need. That's about it. I don't like to talk about it."

She pauses before adding, "I'm sorry, I'm rattling away for some reason. I think I'm still in shock a little."

She shakes her head at herself, realizing that she has told me something extremely personal about herself. She seems embarrassed she blurted out her personal life to me.

To a stranger. But I don't plan on being a stranger any longer than I have to be.

I can see the pain these memories bring her. That asshole left her and made her feel like she was defective or something. Worthless, like a piece of meat he threw away and never thought about again. I wish I could have hurt him when I had the chance.

I think about her confession.

Wait, wait! Did she say she's been alone? She's been alone all this time?

I hope that means there's no one she loves now. But how has this gorgeous woman stayed alone?

Oh, I get it.

Her marriage failed, and she blames herself. She doesn't trust herself to love. She doesn't trust to let someone love her. She won't risk her heart, fearing the pain of another heartbreak.

Oh, baby, if you only knew. Let me. Let me into your life. I'm right here in front of you. Look at me. I am looking at you, trying desperately not to stare. Pay attention to me. I won't break your heart.

Oh gosh, I'm getting a bit ahead of myself here. I barely know her name. Calm down, damn it.

"I'm glad you told me. It helps me understand more about what happened tonight. Thank you for sharing that with me. I understand how you feel."

I change the subject to something less personal, hoping she will continue to feel comfortable with me.

"Becca, do you actually live here in Williamsburg? I bought a house in Two Rivers out on Route 5 heading toward Charles City County," I ask, hoping she'll say yes.

I want her living close to me. Who am I kidding? It wouldn't matter. I'd drive all over Virginia if I had to in order to see her.

"Yes. I know where Two Rivers is. I think it's beautiful. I once attended a wedding at the country club. The wedding was held outside, overlooking the rivers. It was a lovely sunset ceremony."

Okay, that's not much information about where she actually lives. How do I get her to open up about that? Does she live far away from me?

The waitress comes over with our orders. She has ordered a chicken Caesar salad while I have my standard sirloin steak, medium rare, and potatoes. Our meals look great, and we both dig in.

I look at her and laugh. "I guess we're hungrier than we thought. I was afraid all that drama would spoil your appetite."

She giggles softly to herself before eating her salad.

I like that sound.

We sit quietly for a moment as we eat, me racking my brains for something normal to say to her. "So what do you like to do for fun around here? I've recently moved here and would appreciate knowing someone with whom to do things. New experiences for me. Maybe we can go out, you know, like on a real date?"

I broach the subject lightly, hoping she'll pick up on the fact that I want to see her.

I am asking her for a date.

And soon.

As soon as damn possible.

I want to know more about her.

She glances at me under her lashes. I can't stop looking at her, and I want to touch her again so badly. That scorching hot kiss keeps popping in my head. It's a good thing I'm sitting down, or she'd see I already have a hard-on. One look at her, and that was all it took. My dick is saluting her smartly under the table. It rises, snapping to rigid attention without my command. I carefully make sure she can't see the bulge in my tight crotch, keeping it hidden by the table.

What is she doing to me? I'm not fourteen anymore. I try to control my thoughts and calm down so it will go away. The last thing I want to do is scare her away from me. She doesn't need a stranger with a hard-on staring at her. I could end up in jail or something. Who knows? She'll think I'm a sick pervert trying to pick her up. Trying to force her into a situation she doesn't want. Just another jerk like her ex-husband.

"Well, I like a lot of different things, I guess. I love movies, reading, the beach, historical places, and many sports such as football, baseball, and golf. I go for walks in Colonial Williamsburg and visit wineries around the state. I love to travel, especially with my sister and brother. Last year we visited Italy but recently got back from a trip to Scotland during my spring break," she murmurs.

I comment, "I have traveled quite a lot in Europe. I've been to Italy but not Scotland yet."

"What about you, Michael? Tell me the abridged version of your life story."

Becca takes a sip of her wine as I consider where to begin.

She said my name. I like that.

I've got to stop looking at her mouth, her lips closing around the edge of the wine glass. I know how soft those lips are and how sweet she tastes. It's too distracting.

Focus, Stevens. You've got to concentrate here.

"I was born in Jackson, Mississippi. You can hear my Southern accent more when I'm tired. My parents are deceased, but my sister and her family live in Richmond. I have one nephew. I'm close to them since they are the only family I have left. They're the reason I've decided to settle in Virginia now that I've retired from the corps. I joined the Marines right out of high school. My dad was in the army, and I grew up as a military brat, moving with my family from base to base as my dad was reassigned jobs."

"When I was eighteen, I decided the Marines were it for me. I stayed thirty years and lived at bases all over the country. I earned a degree and a master's in engineering along the way. I did a couple of tours in Europe, three in Iraq, and three in Afghanistan. I finished my career as a colonel. I have retired. I've never been married. No children, of course."

She's listening attentively, so I continue.

"My career kept me busy, and it was too hard to think of having a wife or family while I was overseas for much of my time. I was gone, working in foreign countries for many years. It wouldn't have been fair to any wife or possible child and too hard on me as well. I knew many of my buddies went through multiple marriages and divorces, leaving behind children as collateral damage. Heartbreak and affairs. I watched it tear them to pieces. That isn't for me. I couldn't see doing that to a wife and family. Well, I guess that's me in a nutshell, so to speak."

Yeah, I'm a funny guy. Did she get it? I can be a nut with a nutty sense of humor.

I've actually got a nutshell here. Pay attention. I'm a man.

She looks at me but doesn't say anything. No smile or even a slight lift of the corners of her tempting lips to let me know she got it.

Nuts.

I decide to give it a shot. "Becca, I've been alone, too. For many years due to my job and choices, I know. I am planning on settling down here in Williamsburg and looking forward to my new life outside of the corps. I've been lonely. But I am hoping to change that," I tell her softly, hoping not to frighten her away.

Did I go too far?

She has been watching me talk, sometimes glancing shyly down, but still her eyes come back to my face and mouth.

I hope she likes what she sees, because I sure as hell do. Please, baby. Like me. Like me now. A lot.

Because I plan on you loving me someday. Me loving you in return.

I think I could love you. Give me the chance to find out for certain.

She looks straight at me and says quietly, "Thank you for your service, Michael."

People rarely say that to me. I guess most of the time they don't know what to say when I tell them I fought in a war. And I fought hard because I did not want to die there. I spent way too much time in lawless, dangerous countries where I could only trust the other Marine by my side. Everyone else and everywhere I went was a threat to me, a possible danger. I had many close, too close, calls.

I tried hard to be brave and never let my men down. I never, ever let my guard slip when I was in country. Realizing what Becca said to me, I am touched by her honesty. She seems to mean it.

I reply gently, "It was my honor and privilege."

We sit quietly for long moments, lost in our own thoughts. Taking a deep breath of steely courage, I decide to take the chance.

She can only say no, right? Please don't, though.

"I've only been here for a month, and I haven't met many people. I am getting to know a few of my neighbors after meeting them out working in their yards. Some of the things you say you like to do are the same for me. Would you like to go to a movie with me tomorrow? I'll let you pick a good one."

Please say yes, please say yes, please say yes.

Becca looks at me startled.

Hasn't she been paying attention? Can't she see I want to be with her?

She swallows, and I can see her trying to make up her mind. Her eyes narrow slightly as she considers the idea.

I am asking her for a date. Should she or shouldn't she? She has trust issues. She's wondering if she can trust me.

Finally, she says, "What would you like to see?"
I think that's a yes.
Yes! Oh my God! Step one completed.
I quickly pull out my phone and check out the movie schedule at New Town Regal, the only good theater in town. I tell her the different movies, and of course, we want to see the same one. I don't fucking care which movie we see together. I think I remember this is supposed to be a romantic movie. That seems to be the kind of movie she likes because I can see her eyes light up and sparkle at the sheer mention of the title.

Umm. Not an adventure movie, suspenseful murder mystery, science fiction, or superhero flick.

A romance.

Umm.

This might work in my favor.

Hopefully, I can hold her hand or put my arm around her. Maybe steal another kiss. I want another one, more on her mouth. Any movie would be fine with me, as long as we're together in a dark theater. I pick the earliest matinee time, so we can go early in the day and have lots of time to spend together afterwards. I don't want her to go home right after the movie is over like she would if we go at night.

While I have my phone out, I suggest we exchange phone numbers so we can contact each other. Becca hesitates for a moment but then thankfully gives me hers. I immediately call her and am happy to hear her phone in her purse start to ring.

Thank goodness she gave me her real number.

Just checking.

Can't help being cautious because I don't want her to slide away from me. Slip-sliding sexy woman.

I hear a Goo Goo Dolls song, "Slide" playing as background music in the restaurant. It is one of my favorites. John Rzeznik sings:

Could you whisper in my ear
The things you wanna feel
I'd give you anything to feel it coming

She answers it curiously, not knowing that it's me. It is obvious to her when I put my phone up to my ear.

Yes, please.

Becca, so why don't you slide?

Slide into my arms, my heart, and into me. I want to slide right into you as well, baby.

"Hello, Ms. Connolly? This is Mr. Stevens calling to give you my phone number. It's even an easy number to remember. Save it on your phone in your contact list."

I laugh at the look on her face. "I'd like to pick you up at your house for our date tomorrow. I can be there at noon since the movie starts at quarter after. Good-bye."

She giggles and smiles at me. "I'll just meet you in front of the theater, Michael. It's okay. I go to the movies there all the time. It's very close to where I live. I'll meet you out front at the ticket booth."

Okay, that means she doesn't trust me with her address yet. She says she lives close to the theater, but that covers a lot of area.

Be patient, Stevens. She only met you. Give her time.

We continue to talk over dessert (chocolate fudge cake for me and peach pie with whipped cream for her) and coffee. Becca is starting to calm down, and I wish this night would never end.

But I see her glancing at her watch.

She's getting ready to leave me. It's getting late, and I worry about her going home alone in the dark. Does she have a good car? What if she breaks down or something, and I'm not there to help?

Shit. Still, I got her phone number and her promise to see me tomorrow, so I'm feeling hopeful that she won't disappear off the face of the earth. If something happens to her car on the way home, she has my number now. She can call me up to help her. I'm good at fixing some things on a car. I can definitely change a tire; no problem there. I want to be there for her if she has a problem. She can't disappear from my life now.

Because I will find her again. I have to. I wonder absently if there is some way to determine her address from her phone number. Maybe on the Internet, but I don't know how. I'm not a stalker who will follow her home to see where she goes.

Get a grip, Marine. Wait until she tells you herself.

The waitress comes over with the bill for our dinner and drinks and hands it to me, of course. I'm the man, so I get the check. It's my privilege to pay for her meal. I become aware Becca is arguing about paying her part of the check.

"Please let me pay for my salad and wine, Michael. I feel as though I should, considering what you've done for me tonight. It's not a problem.

I am perfectly capable of paying for my own meal. We've just met. You don't need to pay for me."

"No, I've got this. It's my pleasure," I say quickly, giving the waitress my credit card and staring Becca down with my impassive face.

Don't argue with me. There is no way in hell I'm letting her pay. This is our first date as far as I am concerned, and I am the man. I will take care of her. She needs to get used to this. Not matter how independent she is, she has to let me do this. I am not about to go Dutch with her. I will not be placed anywhere near the friend zone. Hell no.

Even from the very start. I want her to feel taken care of and cherished. She doesn't have to pay. We're going to be each other's best friends, but we're also going to be much more if I get my way. Lovers. I can be very charming and persuasive when I want something.

I walk her to her car in the parking lot behind the restaurant. On the way out, I grab her hand and hold it as we reach her car.

Yes, I get to hold her hand.

She doesn't try to pull away, and I want her to get used to my touch. I want her to feel comfortable when I touch her. We're standing next to her dark gray Acura TSX.

Fairly recent model. Not new, but well taken care of by her. Nice. I like the look of it. It's sophisticated and elegant in its own way, just like its beautiful owner. I'm glad to see she's driving a safe vehicle.

"Thank you for letting me get to know you today, Rebecca. It's been an unforgettable experience. I've enjoyed it. I can't wait to find out more. I look forward to our date tomorrow," I tell her softly as I raise her hand to my mouth. I kiss her knuckles, looking into her eyes. Kissing her hand is one of my most romantic moves. It's all I can do to let go of her hand and open her door for her like a gentleman. She shyly tells me good-night before sliding behind the steering wheel.

Before I shut her door, I lean in and whisper to her, "Six."

Her eyes question me until comprehension finally dawns on her when I say, "Kisses. Six kisses now. Good night, Becca. I look forward to seeing you tomorrow."

I've managed to kiss her six times. If I have my way, it would be in the fucking billions someday. And I plan on getting my way. Now if I could only make it until tomorrow. Movie time. Romantic movie time.

On the drive home, I put on a CD of my current favorite band Kings of Leon. The familiar song "Use Somebody" comes on. I have listened to this CD so much I know the words by heart. I say them along with Caleb as he sings the lyrics:

I hope it's gonna make you notice
Someone like me
Someone like me
Someone like me, somebody.

CHAPTER 3

Movie Time: Our Second Date

I toss and turn all night long, filled with thoughts of Ms. Rebecca Connelly. By sunup, I've had so many hard-ons I had to take matters into my own hands. This is ridiculous. I usually have more control than this. Serving in Iraq and Afghanistan has made me an expert on jerking off quickly and quietly. Being around testosterone-filled tough guys and having to be constantly in control is difficult. Everyone has a fucking hard-on all the time, and someone is always trying to come without everyone else knowing what they're doing. Living in such close quarters makes privacy impossible. Of course, we all know what's going on. It soon becomes a part of everyday life.

In fact, I hold the record for fastest jerkoff—not that I am at all proud of that. What a contest that was. The things Marines do to kill time. I definitely could beat everyone else by a mile, pun intended. But now that I have a home, making myself come just feels so empty and alone. I used to be able to get off just imagining a pair of tits, an ass, and a wet unidentified pussy.

This morning all I can think about is a pair of olive green eyes. Sex is obviously so much better when I'm actually sharing it with another person, for Pete's sake. I realize that when and if I ever get the privilege of being with Becca sexually, I don't want to come quickly with her. My ultimate goal is a long-lasting, loving sexual experience for us both. I want to make it last forever.

Forget about being quiet anymore. I did that for years. I won't be able to do that shit with her. I am naturally a bit of a talker during sex with an actual woman. I can't help whispering about everything I am thinking and feeling, for goodness' sakes. I'm strong but not the silent type. I'm afraid I'll be shouting to the rooftops with her. I tend to be a verbal guy while making out. I can't control it very well.

The morning seems to drag on. I eat my regular big bowl of Honey Nut Cheerios and get dressed in my gym shorts and T-shirt for a run. Maybe if I get outside and exercise, I can clear my head. I run like a crazy person through my neighborhood, pounding out six miles easily. I come home, and I shower quickly and then spend an inordinate amount of time debating what I should wear to the movie. After many false starts, I decide on a pair of khaki chinos and a button-down white shirt with a pair of brown loafers.

This is damn annoying. I feel like a teenager again. What is wrong with me?

At long last it's time to go. I drive quickly to New Town Regal and end up getting there a half hour early. That's fine with me. I buy two tickets for the movie as a preemptive strike.

Hopefully, that would keep her from arguing about who is paying for the privilege of taking her to a movie. This is our second date. It is not two new friends meeting at the same movie at the same time.

I wander around a bit outside looking at the different stores, but it has gotten warm and slightly humid. Since I'm still having trouble adjusting to the summer humidity here, I decide to wait for Becca in the theater lobby. I am past the ticket booth. If I wait inside, she'll have to pass by it. I need to make sure she doesn't buy her own ticket since I've got that covered already.

At a little before noon, I send her a quick text to let her know where I am:

Becca. I'm waiting for you inside the theater lobby. Don't buy a ticket. Come in and find me. Michael

Find me, find me. I'm waiting. Where is she? Is she coming or standing me up?

I am surprised when I hear back from her immediately:

Michael, I'm coming. Ok, but I can buy my own ticket, you know. I won't though, so Thank You. See you in the lobby. I'll be there soon. Becca.

I can't help myself. Yes, baby. That's what I want. You coming over and over and over again. And I'll be the one to get you there. I promise. Oh, damn it.

Stop it, Stevens. Control your fantasies, your sexual thoughts of her. You barely know her and she barely knows you. You're imagining too much too soon. Stop getting ahead of yourself. You scare the shit out of her, and then what will you be left with? With nothing, that's what. You can't let that happen.

I'm looking down at her first text on my phone over and over again when I get a funny feeling. I know she's here without looking. My eyes dart up and there she is, walking through the front doors. She sees me and smiles.

Goddamn, she looks good. That smile is for me.

She has a blue skirt on and a soft pink camisole top under a button-down white shirt. My eyes are immediately drawn to her tempting cleavage. She walks quickly over to me.

Oh, here I go again. Unbidden thoughts come on. God, I wish I could see her. I dreamed last night of taking her nipples in my mouth and sucking them gently. I wish I could see a little pucker where her nipples are. I want them to get hard and pout for me. Maybe it will be cold in the theater. She doesn't seem to have a jacket, but she does have that shirt on. It could be a problem.

Come, air conditioning. Work your magic. It's summer. Isn't it always freezing in a movie theater in the summer? I want to feel those nipples hard under my palms. I know her tits will fit my hands perfectly. They will swell inside her top, full and round and waiting for me.

Thankfully, of course, she has a short full skirt on. It's going to take all my willpower to keep my hand from sliding up her thigh, especially when I know the only thing between us is a little slip of silk (I hope silk!) panties. Her tan legs are long and everything I could ever want.

Calm yourself down, Stevens. The way she walks just about does me in.

As she approaches me, I raise my eyes up to her face instead of her breasts, trying hard not to look at her with too much obvious lust.

There's that amazing spark between us again. She has to feel it as strongly as I do. I hope so anyway, or I think I might go out of my mind.

I immediately reach for her hand and give her a quick peck on the lips.

Good, Stevens. That wasn't too long a kiss. She needs to know you're going to touch her and kiss her like you did last night, keep it light and casual. Don't scare her.

"Hey. Are you ready? Thanks for coming. I've been looking forward to this movie all morning. It looks like it will be good."

Hell, yeah. I'm glad you're here with me.

"Hey. Sure, Michael. It's good to see you again. Thank you again for last night. I really appreciated what you did for me. I wasn't sure what to do. I hope you will like the movie. I saw it during some previews not long ago and thought it looked sweet. I hope you don't mind sitting through a chick flick with me. I think it may be beyond the call of duty on your part."

"It is my pleasure. You don't need to thank me at all. I am happy to do it. Well, let's go see the movie then. I want to see it as well. It is about to start soon, so let's go and find a seat. I like to watch the previews of coming attractions. I already have our tickets. We're in theater 7."

Don't argue about the tickets. I have them. I told you.

Umm. Coming attractions?

Previews? I know what I want to view. I could come just thinking about it.

"Okay."

Such an inane, simple conversation, but normal.

I'm trying for normal here. She graciously thanks me for paying, saying I didn't have to do it. She doesn't want a drink or popcorn though I offer. We make small talk as we take our seats in the theater. Of course, I wish we could sit way at the back in the dark and possibly make out and have a little privacy, but we end up front and center to my dismay. My imagination is running away with me. She doesn't know me well enough to make out in the dark theater.

I try to pay attention. She tells me about her morning and that she's wanted to see this movie for a while.

I'm happy she's happy. Always, I think. My own thoughts suddenly shock me. Gosh, I am moving a bit fast, even for me.

When the lights go down for the previews of all coming attractions, I decide to make my classic move in a theater. Making sure the cup holder armrest is the hell out of my way, I put my right arm around her, pulling her as close to me as I can get in these seats. Male thigh pressed against female thigh. My other hand pulls her left hand into mine and places it on my thigh, fingers locked in mine. Now I'm glad there is not even popcorn and a drink to get in the way. I can feel her left breast squeezed slightly against the side of my chest. I swallow and exhale slowly.

Now I can watch the fucking movie. I may not be able to concentrate, but at least I have her where I want her for now.

She looks at me for a moment before giving in slowly. I feel her relax against me. I think she was a bit shocked to suddenly find herself pressed up so closely to me. Her whole body was rigid at first, but she settled into me softly as she sighed. She snuggles a bit under my arm, getting comfortable. I place my lips gently on her temple, not kissing and yet so close.

I can breathe her sweet scent. What shampoo does she use? It smells so good. Or maybe it is just her natural scent.

Trust me, honey. You can trust me. I swear. This is feels great, getting to hold you so close again in my arms. I know my arm will have to fall off before I move it again. Not even losing all circulation and going numb will stop me from holding her. I hope I can get her to put her head on my shoulder, but maybe it's still too soon.

During the previews, she tells me which ones look good. I make a mental note so I can make that happen in the future. And then the movie begins. I try, really try, to watch. I know I should so I can talk to her about it intelligently later. After a while, I calm down enough to actually enjoy it. The movie is a chick flick but is surprisingly good. It has several appealing actors, good dialogue, and is very funny in places as well. I actually like romantic movies. I like other kinds of movies, too, but I don't mind a romantic comedy or chick flick at all.

Yeah, I know I'm a little bit of a sap. I enjoy love stories. The problem is they often seem almost too good to be true. Only in books and movies could love really be that good.

But then, somewhat to my surprise, there is a love scene. I should have realized since this is supposed to be a romantic movie. I knew it coming in, but didn't really think it through far enough in advance.

A sex scene, I should say. A pretty fucking amazing, sexy love scene at that.

I'm a little shocked. Watching sex on the screen while holding my woman is a real turn-on. Was this R-rated, and I didn't pay attention? The attractive actors start to get into it, hot and heavy and amazingly sensual. It becomes hard to watch as I realize I can't control my physical response. I can feel the heat travel all through my body. My hand starts to run softly up and down Becca's bare arm, fingers stroking her soft skin over and over.

My God, this is practically soft porn. It is somewhat graphic in places. What happened to using your imagination? I had no idea this was going to be in the movie.

I break out into a slight sweat, trying hard not to breathe too loud or fast. I glance over at Becca and realize she's as turned on as I am. Even in the dark, I can see she's blushing a sweet pink. I have to shift a little in my seat, trying to adjust to the hard tent forming in my pants. I hope she doesn't notice. Our hands are both damp, but I refuse to let go. Finally, the scene is over, and I can breathe again. That was the longest lovemaking scene ever, or at least it felt that way to me.

Happy, happy ending. For the fictional characters in the movie, that is.

I know Becca is bound to be wet between her legs. She has to be, after watching that sex scene. It's all I can think about now, wondering what if.

Is she or isn't she?

I'd give anything to know for sure. My legs are still trembling.

I wonder if I'll be able to walk out of the theater. Please, God, help me find the strength. I can't believe I only saw her for the first time yesterday. I am finding many sudden and surprising feelings to deal with now.

The movie ends, and I lead her out of the theater. She says how much she enjoyed the movie when I ask her about it. We talk briefly about it:

the actors, the plot, the scenery. Neither one of us even mentions that sex scene, the one that gave me a heart attack. I might dream about it tonight, only it will be Becca and me in place of the actors.

I've got to think of a way to keep her with me longer. To my delighted surprise, she tells me she's hungry. For food, I assume.

Good-that I can do.

She suggests going down to Merchants' Square in Colonial Williamsburg. I've been there before, and it's a quaint area filled with shops and restaurants. It seems this is one of her favorite places, and she wants to share it with me.

Okay. Good. I like this.

We walk toward the parking lot as I grab hold of her hand in mine, and she offers to drive since she knows the way better than I do. However, I want to be alone with her in my car, so I tell her to tell me where to go.

I think she's surprised to see my car. I own a black 7 Series BMW. It's a really great sophisticated car that I treated myself to when I got out of the service. I love its elegance and the way that it handles when I drive it. It is loaded with everything I wanted: GPS, backup camera, DVD player, heated steering wheel and seats, sunroof, leather seats, etc. I open the door for her, and she pauses before hesitantly sliding in. Her skirt hikes up just a bit as she swings her long legs inside.

I know I'm just torturing myself, wondering what color her damp panties are. I hope they have the scent of an aroused woman clinging to them.

I walk around to the driver's side and start the car quickly. We make our way to Merchants' Square. The Kings of Leon song "Sex on Fire" comes on the radio. I ask her if she knows this song. She says she has the CD.

I like the words. A LOT.

I glance at Becca sideways.

Yeah, your sex is on fire. I am burning up already as well.

I park my car in the lot behind the Craft Store, just talking casually. After turning off the car, I turn in my seat and look into her eyes. "Are you hungry, Ms. Connelly? Because I certainly am hungry. Let's get something to eat together."

I don't let her out of the car yet. I reach over and stroke my fingers down her cheek, with my hand curved around her jaw and neck. I keep looking at her, judging her reaction and pleading with her with my gray eyes. Slowly, I lean forward, making sure I'm giving her time to say no.

She continues to stare into my eyes, so I take this as a good sign. I can't seem to stop myself. I lean more, pausing with my lips hovering hers, giving her the time to really decide. I wait but then can't anymore. My open mouth lowers as I slant my head. My hand goes up to cup her cheek without thinking. I need to hold her in place for me.

I have to feel her lips move under my mouth like they did yesterday. I start to kiss her slowly and gently, but the touch of her lips parting beneath me is too good to be true. I stroke my tongue in and out of her mouth, exploring as much as I want for now. I hear her moan softly in the back of her throat.

Good, she's responding to me.

I gather her up in my arms, getting as close to her as I can in the front seat. When I've had about as much as I can take without hauling her over the front seat into the backseat, I pull slowly away from her mouth. My fingers reach up to caress her bottom lip before I take a deep breath and force myself to get out of the car and open her door.

I got another kiss, a small taste. I want more.

Becca leads me giggling to the Cheese Shop in Merchants' Square, telling me they have the best sandwiches in Virginia. She laughs, remembering that when she lived in California, she used to dream about these sandwiches. I guess they must really be good. She orders a Virginia ham and provolone cheese sandwich on fresh French bread with extra house dressing. I end up with basically the same thing, except I wanted turkey. Virginia ham is a bit too salty for me. This time she doesn't argue with me about paying.

Maybe she's starting to see I am serious, she can depend on me, and I treat her like a lady.

We go outside to sit under the tables with umbrellas and watch the tourists walk back and forth in front of us. I find she is starting to relax, and our conversation starts to sound more and more like we're becoming friends, comfortable with each other.

After we eat, we decide to walk down Duke of Gloucester Street. She lets me hold her hand as we walk down the middle of the street and dodge manure and horse-drawn carriages. Becca tells me all about the history of Williamsburg and points out the different buildings, explaining to me what they are. One of the houses actually once belonged to an ancestor of hers on her mother's side. She has a love for history, and I can tell she knows a lot. Not only is she beautiful, but she is intelligent as well.

She takes me on a quick walking tour of the campus of The College of William and Mary. Since she graduated from there, I can tell this campus is special to her. I get her to tell me about her college friends and experiences. One of her best college friends was a woman named Courtney Young from Roanoke. They were roommates senior year, both majoring in elementary education, and have been friends since college.

I also notice Becca has been receiving texts because I hear the beep going off from her phone. She doesn't check the texts but tells me she knows whom they are from. Her best friend Mackenzie Grayson lives in Portsmouth, and they've been friends since high school.

I have no doubt that they tell each other everything. Having a sister has taught me that women talk to each other a lot. I'm guessing some of the texts must be about me. I only hope they're good. I plan on asking Becca if we can meet Mackenzie for lunch sometime so I can meet her. If there's one thing I know, if a woman's girlfriends don't like me, I don't have a chance in hell of making anything permanent work. I'm thinking not only do I need to win Becca over but her friends and family as well.

I know I can do this. I hope it isn't too soon for her but I want to get things started. I have to win them over. I'll charm their pants off—not literally, of course. I'm only interested in charming Becca's panties off.

By this time, it's early evening. I could happily spend the rest of the evening with her, but I know she isn't ready to have me in her house yet. I've got to earn her trust and work for it. Today's been such a good day; I don't want to push my luck. I reluctantly drive her back to her car at the theater. We listen to my CD from a band known as The Calling. My favorite songs are "Wherever You Will Go" and "Anything." Becca says she likes them, too.

As I park the car next to hers, I turn to her and say, "Have I told you how lovely you are today?"

"No, sir, I don't believe you have."

"Obviously I have certainly been remiss in my duties as your date today, haven't I? I must make up for it as soon as I can. Today has been so much fun for me. Thank you very much for spending the day with me. I hope you've enjoyed it at least half as much as me."

"Yes, of course I have, Michael. Going to the movies and having lunch out are some of my favorite things to do."

"Will you let me take you out again tomorrow?" I ask hesitantly.

Let me see you again. We've only just begun.

"I'm sorry, but I have plans with my sister and brother-in-law tomorrow. They're driving up to spend the day with me. Perhaps on Monday we could do something."

I have to wait until Monday? Two days?

"I want to meet your family sometime if you'll let me continue to date you." She looks at me slightly surprised.

Don't you get it yet? I want to be part of your life and that means knowing the people you love.

I can see in her eyes this is too fast for her. She's thinking we've just met.

Pull back and regroup. Don't push too hard. Even though I know what to do, it is difficult to hold back. I need to be patient; I can't have what I want immediately when I want it, like it was when I was commanding Marines. She's not a Marine.

"Well, I'll think about it. Maybe sometime down the line, I don't know." She sounds hesitant.

"Okay, when you're ready."

Anytime, baby. I'm ready. I'm ready for you.

She starts to unbuckle her seat belt to get out. I tell her to wait while I get out and come around to help her out of the car.

I don't think she's used to someone doing that for her. Well, she's going to have to get used to it because my mother raised me to be a gentleman.

Most of the time, that is.

Now there's nothing left for me to do except say good-bye. I lean toward her. I desperately want to kiss her good-bye but don't want to push her too much.

Instead I whisper in her ear, "Eight. Those eight kisses belong to me. I'll see you on Monday. I'll plan something for us to do together and call you Sunday night." I watch as she drives away, leaving me wondering where she lives.

I remember a sweet love song from my childhood called "If You Could Read My Mind" sung by Gordon Lightfoot. The words circulate in my head as I head home.

If you could read my mind, love
What a tale my thoughts could tell
Just like a paperback novel
The kind the drugstores sell

I drive dark and twisty Route 5 home to my big empty house. I hardly even notice the road but find myself pulling into the driveway. My mind has been full of Becca, the song, and our coming date to notice the drive home. It's a wonder I found my way home or did not wreck the car.

Autopilot engaged, sir. Apparently.

I unlock the door, flip on the light switch, head straight to my bedroom and fall onto the bed fully clothed. I don't think I moved the rest of the night.

Monday. I have to wait two days. Tomorrow's going to be a long day for me home alone. I hope I can do this. I may end up calling her or texting her just to make sure she doesn't forget about me. Monday. What can we do together on Monday? I have to think of something good. It needs to be fun.

What did she say she liked?

Umm.

Baseball. She said she liked baseball, didn't she?

CHAPTER 4

Baseball Games

By the skin of my teeth, I manage to make it to Sunday night. Since I knew she was with her family, I texted her *once* to let her know I hope she's having a good time. I wonder what they are doing together. Of course, I think we could be having an even *better* time together if she'd only let me. But it's too soon, date number three.

I thought of what I wanted us to do. I spent a great deal of time on the Internet checking out the area attractions. She told me on Friday that she liked baseball, so I plan to take her to Norfolk to watch an International League baseball game with the Norfolk Tides. I found their website and game schedule. There is a home game starting at six Monday evening. They're playing the Durham Bulls.

Bull Durham? Wasn't that a movie? Kevin Costner? A baseball fantasy? Build it and they will come? A baseball field in the middle of an Iowa cornfield pops in my head. A slice of heaven on earth in Iowa. Have a catch, Dad?

We can spend the night at Harbor Park enjoying a baseball game. I call her to tell her the details.

"Hey, Becca. It's Michael. Would you like to go to a baseball game with me tomorrow? The Tides are in town. I can pick you up around four-thirty so we can get there on time. It's a night game. The weather is supposed to be good, so it should be a beautiful evening at the ballpark. What do you think? Will you let me take you?"

I want to take you any way I can get you. Maybe this time you'll let me know where you live.

"Hi, Michael. It's good to hear from you. Thanks again for the movie. I really enjoyed seeing it with you. Actually, I'd like to go see the Tides play a game. I love Harbor Park and haven't been to a game yet this season. That would be really fun. Are you sure?"

There's that sweet, slightly husky voice haunting my dreams lately.

"Of course, I'm sure, baby. What's your address? I'd like to pick you up so we can get there in plenty of time." I hold my breath, hoping she'll just go with it.

I won't even come in if she doesn't want me to do that yet. I'll just pick her up at her door. Like a fucking gentleman.

Unbelievably, she gives me her address.

Yes! My plan in action.

"Okay, I'll be there tomorrow. I've missed you. See you soon," I add softly before hanging up.

Hell, yeah, I've missed you. I can't stop thinking about you. This woman has gotten under my skin big-time.

Tomorrow can't come soon enough for me. It's a long night, but I know I need to be patient. Before I see her, I know I'll have to take matters into my own hands again so I don't show up at her door with a hard dick. This is getting to be a habit I have to stop. My cock won't settle down. I don't want to scare her away.

I think it's because I know she hasn't let any men get close to her in such a long time. It's like she's almost a virgin all over again. I need to take my time and get her to trust me. She'll be mine, only mine. The problem, though, is coming alone only lasts until I think of her or see her and then my dick gets hard all over again. It's a never-ending cycle. I only hope she doesn't notice it as much as I do. I am completely and totally aware of how she makes me feel.

I show up at her door promptly. Becca comes to open it but doesn't invite me up the stairs. It seems her condo is on the second floor. The front door only opens up to a small foyer and closet. She looks so sexy I can hardly speak at first. She has on her tight jeans and a little green top that stretches across her full breasts. I can definitely see the small buds of her nipples.

Is she cold? Air conditioning?

I wonder if she has a lightweight jacket or something; not sure I want other men to be able to see her like that. But it's really warm tonight, so I don't think she's going to bring one with her no matter what I suggest. Hopefully they will go back down, or I might wreck the car trying to keep my eyes on her. I take her hand and kiss the back of her knuckles.

That's nine as far as I'm concerned. I have big plans for ten and more. That's double-digits time, and it should be memorable for me and her. I want her to dream about me tonight. I almost can't wait, but I decide it will be better if I show a little patience.

We drive to Norfolk, making our way through the Hampton Roads Bridge Tunnel and downtown. The songs sung by Lady Antebellum fill the silence between our words. I hear "I Need You Now" and "Just a Kiss" softly playing as we talk about the baseball game we are going to see tonight.

Harbor Park is an excellent ball field near the Elizabeth River. We quickly get our tickets and head for the third-base side. On the way to our seats, Becca asks for a program and a pencil. It appears she plans on keeping score by herself. She seems to know what she's doing while keeping track of all the plays.

I admit I'm definitely impressed. My woman knows her baseball. I only hope I can keep up. I try to watch her and the game at the same time.

It's the bottom of the second inning. Rodriguez for the Tides comes up to bat. He quickly goes down swinging. Out. Becca writes a K and circles it. The next player, Juan Baxter, comes up and pops a fly ball to center, which is easily caught by the center fielder for the Durham Bulls. Second out. She writes an eight and circles it.

The next Tides ballplayer at bat makes it safely to first, and she draws a small diagonal line from the bottom center of the square to the middle right, indicating he is now on first base. Randall walks to first, and she draws that same line, only this time, she marks it with a *w*, indicating a walk. She goes back and draws a line to move the other runner to second base. When the next Tides player hits the ball to the pitcher getting thrown out at first, she jots down a quick 1–3 and circles it. Pitcher to first base. Three outs. End of the inning.

Yep, she knows how to keep score. She doesn't miss a thing.
How the hell does she know this?

Comprehension finally dawns on me. I'm so slow tonight. She has mentioned she has an older brother. From what little she has said, it is still obvious she adores him and looks up to him. He seems to have taken a great deal of time with her when they were growing up though he was older. I think she worships the ground he walks on.

An older brother with a little sister. There is a special relationship there. He is the reason she likes, understands, and enjoys sports so much. She learned it from him, wanting to share his interests.

Thank you, thank you, older brother.

We enjoy the game, having hot dogs and sharing a beer to cool off although I can tell she doesn't like beer that much. I know she's a wine woman. The Tides are winning, making it a relaxing summer evening. At least I hope she is having fun. She seems to enjoy herself, talking excitedly about the game. I could watch her all night. She makes comments when a Tides player hits a long ball to center field or strikes out swinging. She watches each pitch thrown into the catcher's leather glove and keeps count of all balls and strikes.

Umm. Balls everywhere. Baseballs and my hard balls.

And bats. Hard wooden or aluminum bats swinging away. Me, feeling quite attached to my own personal bat. Balls go nowhere without bats.

Umm, I have a very special hard wooden bat just waiting to swing her way. Doesn't she know I need to hit a home run soon? Third base? Right this moment I would gladly settle for second or even first as the last resort. Any base with her anytime, anywhere, anyhow. Just please, please let me be a ballplayer, too, tonight. I have a game I need to play.

A Real Love At Last

The Tides win, but I have lost all concentration on baseball. I want to play my special ball game with her. I realize I am thinking about sex with her so much anything reminds me of it. Her most innocent comments and observations are so damn sexual to me because I am reading into them what I want to hear in her voice. The competition between two opposing teams, the game itself, the warm humid night air, the feel of her next to me all combine to turn me on as hell.

She keeps her feet propped up on the empty seat in front of us. The sight of her bent legs spread slightly at the knees makes me want to stand up to the plate for my turn at bat.

I want a shot at this. My arms are strong, and I am fast on my feet. It won't take much effort to hit the ball, run the bases, and slide into home plate, scoring. Perhaps if this game lasts long enough, I can come up to bat several more times before the game is over.

I become aware she is talking to me. She has spilled her large ice-filled Sprite down the front of her top and on her lap. I sigh at the sight of a wet T-shirted Becca, now damp in all the right places.

Is this torture never going to end?

She is embarrassed and gets up to head to the ladies room, saying she will use the hand-dryers to dry herself.

Blow-dryers blowing warm air. On her nipples. Between her thighs.

I groan out loud and receive a few strange looks from nearby fans.

I watch her climb the stairs back up to the concession level until I lose sight of her. I turn back to the game, but my mind is not on the ballplayers right in front of me.

I am a good athlete. I can score easily. My ERA is excellent. I rarely miss and hardly ever strike out. I keep my eye on the ball and connect my hard wooden bat with the fast pitch every time I swing at a ball in the strike zone. I don't waste time if the pitch isn't where I need it to be to hit it out over the centerfield fence. A hard fast line drive or a fly ball hit so high and deep it is uncatchable by the outfielders. I score a run to win the game.

I need to score with Becca.

I hear the crack of a bat and watch a Tides player run around all the bases as he scores a home run.

I need to get a grip. Yeah, I know. A good solid grip on my hard wooden bat would feel great. Fingers wrapped tightly, squeezing hard enough so the bat doesn't fly out of her hands. Swing hard, Becca. Hit it out of the park for me. Over the centerfield fence home run with all the bases loaded would be great.

I definitely am loaded here, so to speak. Unload me, please.

It's a little late by the time the game is over. I help her into the car, touching her as much as I can get away with. She's quiet on the way home, but I can tell she's just relaxed. It's like we're in our own bubble, traveling through the darkness. Even though it's dark, I can still see her. I put my hand on her thigh, wanting somehow connect with her as I drive her home on the interstate. We pass Ocean View and head northwest toward the Peninsula on the crowded I-64.

It is dark in the car on the long interstate. David Cook, an American Idol winner, has a CD I really like. The songs "Fade into Me," "The Time of My Life," "Forever and for Always," and "Take Me as I Am" are really good with emotional melodies and lyrics. I pay attention to the headlights and brake lights in front of me, but my mind is on my plan for when we get home.

My ball game comes to mind. I don't know if she will let me play this game yet though. I have a set of balls that need to be played with as well.

I have a hard thick bat she can swing. I need to make my fast pitch to her. I can throw a 96 mph fastball straight into her soft, smooth catcher's mitt. The twack of the ball hitting the leather glove is satisfying and right on target.

There is no other sound like that, when the pitcher knows he has conquered the batter. The ultimate contest in a baseball game is between the pitcher and the batter. His skill as a pitcher against the other's skill as a batter. A strike. I need to throw as many strikes as I can over her home plate.

The umpire calls, "Three strikes, you're out." I win.

The second ball game on this warm summer night is about to happen if I can make it.

We are definitely having fun getting to know each other so far. I want to know all of her. It is all I can focus on. I know it is partly because I haven't been intimate with a woman for several months now. The last time was when I was stationed at Quantico where I retired. It was nothing serious at all, just someone to fuck and who wanted to fuck me back.

I know it is different with this woman. I think about her. I want to hear her giggle. I need her to be attracted to me. I desire her so much it is killing me to not have her. But she hasn't agreed yet. So far, all I have gotten are kisses and hugs. That's a great start, but I want much, much more.

True, complete intimacy with a woman is my goal. With this particular woman. Something I have never had before but have hoped for in the deep recesses of my heart.

We drive silently back to Williamsburg, Becca gazing out of the window and me lost in my thoughts of her. I hear Chris Brown's song "With You."

Oh, I'm in to you, and girl
No one else would do
'Cause with every kiss and every hug
You make me fall in love

And then I hear Nelly's "Just a Dream" taunting me on the radio station 94.9 The Point. I crash back down to unyielding hard earth, to the reality of my situation with this lovely, desirable woman. We have only been out a few times, and she is still getting to know me. The song's words remind me this could all just be a dream I have conjured up in my own head. The dream I now have that she really could be mine forever.

We arrive at her condo. Before she could say good-bye, I nuzzle her neck for a long quiet moment as I pull her across to me in the driver's seat. I finally let her go, and I get out the car to open the door for her. I take her hand to pull her out of her seat.

I don't know I am about to make the absolute biggest, stupidest fucking error of my life. The worst part is I knew better and didn't stop to consider the full consequences of my actions. I scared her away from me. She ran.

CHAPTER 5

Incredibly Idiotic Error in Judgment

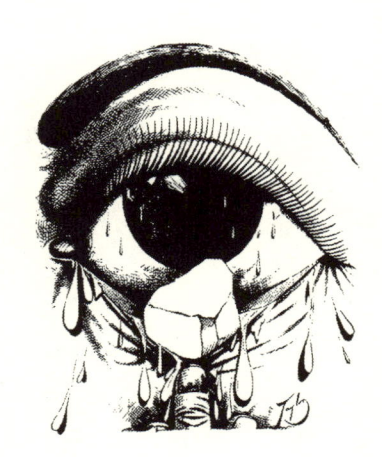

    Becca gets her keys out of her purse. I start to panic she's going to rush inside and shut the door in my face. I walk her to her door, holding on to her elbow to guide her. Standing in front of her door, I step right in front of her and put both of my arms around her.
    It's time for my tenth kiss (and hopefully a few more), and time for her to realize how serious I really am. I can't wait anymore. I need her to know how I feel.

I lean down and push her hair behind her ear, whispering to her, "You are so beautiful. Let me kiss you."

I look into her eyes before pushing her back against her front door and swooping down, covering her open mouth with mine. My right hand is cupping her jaw, holding her in place, while my left arm is pressing her tightly against me. I kiss her deeply, passionately. I can't hold back anymore. In between breaths and kisses, I groan out how much I want her, how much I need her.

She doesn't pull away from me. In fact, she puts her hands around my neck with one hand caressing my hair. She's responding, and I lose it. Next thing I know I twist her in my arms and push her even more firmly up against her front door. I want her to feel me, all of me, so I push my hard thigh between hers, spreading them apart. My mouth swoops down on her open lips again, pushing my tongue inside. She's gasping under my lips. I hold her as tight as I can as I thrust my aching cock up and between her thighs. My right hand grabs her breast, cupping it. My other hand is holding her close.

I want to unzip her jeans, pull them down, rip her panties off, and bury myself into her. But I can't. We're outside, for fuck's sake. Anyone can see us. I know it's too soon. I don't want to take her like this.

She tears her mouth away from my lips, gasping, "Michael, Michael, stop, stop, let me go. Please. Let me go. I don't want this. Let me go."

I can't, not quite yet. My whole body is hard, plastered against her and aching. I thrust at her once more, letting her feel how much I want her. I'm so close to where I want and need to be. A few layers of clothing are all that separate me from her.

Maybe if I tell her, she'll understand and not push me away.

I start murmuring to her, "Oh God, baby. I have so many feelings, feelings for you. I can't stop thinking of you. Please say you think of me too. You feel so good to me, so good. You are mine, and I want you with everything there is inside of me. I am yours. Feel me wanting you. Touch me. I ache for you to touch me. I want to be with you, inside of you, more than I want my own life. Don't you know you belong in my arms? And I belong with you."

I go on, barely able to breathe, "Can't you feel how good it's going to be between us? We're going to be so good together. Let me love you. Let me love you every damn day and every minute of the night. Do you want me, baby? Are you wet for me? Only for me? Only I get to touch you, be deep inside you, and see you. I don't know if I can wait much longer. Please, baby, please. I need you, I need you so much."

The words just keep pouring out of me, in between kisses on her mouth, her cheeks, and her neck, anywhere I can reach with my mouth. I can't seem to shut up, all the frustrations of the past few days welling up inside of me and coming out.

It's too soon, too soon for her to hear all this. I'm afraid I'm overwhelming her.

I bury my face in the curve of her neck and shoulder, trying to find some reason, some logic, some will to stop. I know I need to stop before I frighten her with my sexual needs, but my dick feels so right nestled between her thighs. I can feel her moist heat seeping through me. She feels warm and ready to me. My whole body heats up rapidly from my head to my toes. I know she can feel me burning against her. It's like I have a fever.

Somehow I find the strength to loosen my hold on her. I step back shakily, looking to see her reaction. At first, she sways a little, and I reach out to steady her. Her eyes are wide and slightly scared, dark, and overwhelmed.

Oh no. That's not exactly the response I hoped to see. I know my gray eyes are burning into her, willing her to let me in, into her life.

If I stay here much longer, I'm going to lose my head, sweep her into my arms, and carry her upstairs. The thought of her being unwilling stops me. I better leave while I still have enough strength to do so. I pick up her purse and keys on the porch and hand them to her. I'm still having problems managing my heart and my breathing. She seems to be having trouble, too. I can see her face in the dark with a little light from the streetlight shining on her.

She whispers huskily, "What . . . just happened? What . . . what do you want from me? Don't you see I don't know enough about you? We can't, we can't make love, and it's too soon for me. I don't know you. Would you hurt me? I don't know you very well. You could have a disease or something. I don't know if I can trust you. I don't know you. Please, I just don't know you well enough. Not yet, not yet."

I stand in front of her, not touching her this time. I'm radiating so much heat; I know she must feel it. I stare into her eyes.

"Would you like to know me, Rebecca? Really know me?"

She hesitates so long I stop breathing waiting for her answer. I can see her question me with her eyes.

"Can I trust you?" she murmurs almost to herself.

I softly whisper, "I'd never hurt you. I swear on my life. And you can be sure you are safe with me in every way. I have nothing for you to worry about."

"The Marines have tested me to death, and I'm clean because I've always been careful. There's nothing. I promise you. I would never endanger you like that or any other way. I swear. I'll do anything to make you feel comfortable. You want me to wear a condom? No problem. I'll show you all my test results. I'll get tested as often as you want so you will have no worries on that score. I'll do anything you want because I want you. Very, very much. Let me love you. I need to love you. It's really that simple."

She doesn't say anything, but she is looking me in the eyes. I don't think she knows what to say to me. She has a slight frown between her eyebrows as she considers my impassioned plea. I look deeply into her in the dark, willing her to believe me. She starts breathing rapidly and then looks down, her lashes lowering as if she can no longer meet my intense gaze on her. I can't see her expression now.

Oh God. Is she going to push me away? Kick me out of her life completely? Have I blown any chance I ever had with her? I can't breathe with the uncertainty of her thoughts.

"Now you know where I stand. I've put my heart and soul in front of you tonight. I am fucking serious where you're concerned. Think about it. Think about me long and hard. Because I'm going to do everything I can to convince you we belong together. I know we've only known each other a few days. I knew the first moment I saw you. I couldn't stay away, even then. I find I am incapable of staying away from you. I don't have the strength to do so. I have no doubts about us. Let me know if you want me the way I want you. And by the way, that was the *tenth* and *eleventh* time I've kissed you. We're in the double digits now."

Becca stands there, only looking at me. She has calmed down faster than me. Long moments pass while I wonder what's she thinking and feeling.

She looks at me under her lashes. "Let me think . . . give me time to think. It's too much, too soon. We've just met. I don't know you. Yes, we've gone out a few times and I enjoy being with you, but I don't know how I feel this fast. Michael, give me time. I need to decide if this is what I want. I don't let people in, only family and close friends. I'm not sure how I feel about you, about this."

"Okay, Becca, I'll try. Please promise me you'll think of me. Give me a chance. Let me in your life."

We stand together, looking at each other. I'm no longer touching her. I don't want to leave her. I barely hear her ask a question.

"Is that really what you want? You want to be in my life as what? My real boyfriend and lover? No longer pretending, but for real?"

"Yes, for real."

"Do you expect us to have a sexual relationship this soon after meeting each other? Is that what you want? Sex with me? I don't know. I am sorry, but it has been a long time for me. I am not used to receiving such an intimate proposition so quickly from a man, especially one I know so little about."

She pauses but then continues. "I usually don't let it get this far, but you seem to have made up your mind about me very quickly. Do you often do this? Proposition women you have just met for sex? Is it because you have recently moved here and haven't had time to meet a woman willing to fulfill your needs? If that is all you want from me, I am not interested. Sex without love is meaningless to me. It makes no sense to me to be so intimate with another person if I do not love them and I know they don't love me. I don't share myself that easily. I never have."

I try to find the words to reassure her I am not a sex-crazed man though that is exactly the way I have been feeling and acting with her.

"I am not just looking for sex with you, Rebecca. I want more from you when we have a relationship. I need to feel the connection we have for one another and find out if it is as real as I think it is. I promise you I am not using you for sex. Yes, I do want you that way, but only when you are comfortable enough to let me have you intimately. I want that very, very much. With you and only you."

She hasn't turned to shut the door in my face as of yet. She is thinking about what I said to her.

"Don't worry, honey. I will give you time to know me, really know me first. I am a regular guy with regular needs. Nothing scary, I swear to you. I'll be good to you if you let me in."

Her eyes hold a question. "How long are you going to keep counting kisses, Michael?" she asks me huskily.

"Don't you know, baby? Until the number is too high to count," I tell her, gritting my teeth. "Good night, Becca. Please think about what I said. I need to hear your answer soon."

It is taking me everything I have to wait for it.

I pull her hand up to my lips and press them against her knuckles for several long beats of my heart. Then I force myself to turn and walk to my car. She stands there alone by her door, watching me before turning and going inside. I watch to see a light come on in the windows to be sure she is safe indoors before I leave.

I'm barely able to drive home. I am startled when I find myself in my own driveway. My mind was so filled with thoughts of her I do not remember driving down Route 5 at all.

Please, God, let her dream about me tonight. Because I can't stop dreaming about her.

I angrily turned the damn radio off on the drive home.

No taunting love music for me tonight.

CHAPTER 6

I'm Trapped in Purgatory: The Week from Hell

The next morning, I haven't heard a word from Becca. Long hours drag by slowly. I keep checking my phone hoping against hope she's been thinking about me and what I said.

No phone call, no text, nothing from her. I wonder if I should call her, but I want to give her time.

She said she needed time to decide about me and whether I will be allowed in her life.

How long? Hours? A day? Two days?

I eat, go for an exhausting run, take a cold shower, and just basically piddle around my new house, trying to kill time instead of brooding and driving myself crazy with worry.

This is my own fucking fault. I brought all of this down on me because I acted like a horny teenager with no control. This thought is making me angry at myself. Desperate rage because there is no one else to blame but me. I mentally beat the shit out of myself.

I bought this beautiful brick colonial house in Two Rivers. It's in a lovely tree-filled neighborhood with a golf course and country club nestled between the James and the Chickahominy Rivers. The thing is my house is basically empty. It's big and empty. My footsteps echo on the wooden floors in the great room as I pace back and forth in frustration.

Why did I buy such a big house, for a life I don't have yet?

I have what I need to survive, but it definitely does not look like a home yet. The walls are white, and the rooms are empty, except for a few things in the great room and my bedroom. I have my bed. It definitely looks like a bachelor lives here.

I know exactly what it needs: a woman's touch. And I'm working on that. I want her to come over and see my house sometime. I don't want to push her, though. Maybe I'll save that for later, way later.

Finally, by the late afternoon, I can't take it anymore. I realize suddenly I shouldn't expect her to call me first; she's the lady and I'm the gentleman. I'm afraid I might scare her with an actual phone call. I can't breathe, fearing the words that will shut me out of her life forever. I send Becca a text, hoping she'll respond to me at least that way. The fact she's not saying anything to me is driving me nuts.

Not funny right now.

I run my hands through my hair.

She has to understand I lost control for only one night. I'm sorry, but it doesn't mean she can't trust me. I am a man with normal desires after all. Doesn't she feel anything for me? She seemed to be enjoying it at first before I practically attacked her against her front door. Shit.

Becca. Thinking of you. Are you thinking of me? Please say yes. Michael.

Now that I've sent it, I feel like an idiot. What is she going to say? I really have no idea what she's thinking. She doesn't say much about how she feels about me while I've poured my whole heart out to her.

I've tried to look for all the little clues that let a man know when a woman is interested in him. I thought she was, but I could be reading into it what I want to see. Maybe all of this is just wishful thinking on my part.

I spent years in the corps, following orders before making colonel in the Marines. Then I was the one giving all the orders. I liked that a lot. Having control. I am used to getting what I want, when I want it, because that's the way it works when you're the commanding officer. But that's no way to treat a woman. I think I need to apologize. I got carried away. I know it.

My phone dings with a text message:

> **Michael. You've given me a lot to think about. Give me a little more time. Don't push me. Becca**

Now, that does not sound good to me. How could I have been so wrong, so stupid? Shit, shit, shit. I've overwhelmed her. Becca's not ready. She needs more time to decide. Time I need to give her. I'm so afraid that I've lost any chance with her that I might have had. God, I've rushed her with my demands.

Women need time to adjust. They need romance. Hell, everybody knows that. What is wrong with me? I guess I wasn't very romantic, thinking only about what I want and what I need. I was so damn excited about kiss number ten (and then eleven) I forgot the woman I was doing it for. I need to give her time to want me, too.

> **Becca. I'll do anything you say. Please don't pull away from me. Not from me. I never want you to be afraid of me. You can trust me. I swear it. Michael**

And then she says what I've been dreading all day.

> **M. I'm not sure I can give you what you want from me. B**

Yeah, I know. This man you just met wants to be in your life, in your house, in your bed, in your heart, and in you, period. No wonder you're having doubts about me. No wonder you're about to run from me.

Fuck it.

I pick up the phone, before I change my mind, and call her, needing to hear her voice. She answers hesitantly after six rings.

"Hello, Michael."

She has caller ID. She's not sure she wants to talk to me yet.

The words rush out of me. "Becca, let me try again. I'm so sorry. I don't want to rush you, but I'm going crazy, wondering how you feel. I'm not apologizing for wanting you, but I am apologizing for pushing you too fast. I'm sorry. Please forgive me."

"I . . . I forgive you, but I need . . . some time to decide if I can let you into my life or not. You're rather a lot to take on. Intense, if you know what I mean. Give me a week and I'll let you know. I'll consider it and let you know then."

A week?! FUCK! I really fucked this up if she needs a whole week to decide if she wants me or not. It took me minutes. Damn it. Damn it all to hell. I'm a fucking idiot.

"Are you . . . are you breaking up with me?"

I can't seem to catch my breath.

"Michael, I'm not even sure I know we're a couple. It's been too fast for me. You rescue me, we go out twice, and then all of a sudden you want a sexual relationship with me. I guess that's what I need to decide. I need to be sure I want to be in that kind of a relationship with you. I don't know. It's been so long. I'm out of practice with all of this. Is that what you want from me? A sexually exclusive relationship? You said all those things. Is that what you want with me?"

"Yes! Look, I'll give you whatever time and space you think you need. Today's Tuesday. Do you really need until next Tuesday to decide? What if we say Friday?"

Please. Tuesday sounds like forever. It may get ugly.

"No, Michael. Next Tuesday."

Shit. She's not giving in. I can't bargain my way out of this.

"Do you have any idea the effect you have on me, Rebecca? I'll do anything you want if you will only give me a chance to be part of your life. Please don't make me leave you alone. I can't—I don't have the strength to stay away from you."

"I need time to think this through. I am not used to letting anyone get close to me. Give me time to decide if I want you to really know me. Things have progressed too fast for me. I'm not comfortable with this."

"So I can't see you, or touch you, until next Tuesday. Can I at least call you?"

God, please say yes. Give me that much or I'll lose it.

"Yes, I guess we can talk on the phone."

"Well, expect my phone calls then, Ms. Connelly. Something which feels this good can't possibly be wrong. I know you have to feel it, too. I feel it so strongly. It can't just be me, imagining this spark we have between us all by myself. You have to know we have a definite connection. I want to explore it with you. I have never been so sure of anything. I'll talk to you soon. See you Tuesday. Good-bye, Becca. I will be back. Count on it."

I hang up, feeling like shit. I've scared her and she's running. Away from me. I brought this pain all on myself. There is no one else to blame but me. I'm an idiot. A real self-centered idiot, only thinking about myself. I am no better than Tripp. Another man wanting what she is not ready to give.

I've got to think what to do. She didn't forbid me from sending her anything. I can be the romantic guy of her dreams if only she'll give me the chance. I'm a Southern gentleman. Yes, maybe a wolf who is patient, but a gentleman nonetheless.

Day 1: Six days to go. The Week from Hell has officially begun. The darkness descends upon me. No light at the end of the tunnel, no light in my future. I'm in purgatory. Can't sleep, can't eat, and can't breathe. I don't call her. Maybe then she'll start to miss me. I'm afraid my voice will shake if I actually try to talk to her. I find a card to send her, writing to her about me, my family, and my childhood. Maybe it will help her feel as though she knows me a little better. I listen to my 3 Doors Down CD with the song "Here Without You."

It doesn't help. I only feel worse.

Day 2: Five days to go. I need to get out of this goddamn house. Jerking off isn't helping at all. I spend the whole day running around my neighborhood, going for runs in the morning, the afternoon, and the early evening. I wonder if anyone in the neighborhood keeps seeing me out there and can't figure out why I am exhausting myself. I don't think I have ever run so much in one day. Not even in basic training. If I wear myself out, I hope I can sleep tonight. I feel so alone. Without her, there's no life, no peace of mind. I send another card, listing all my favorite things for her. I hope she sees we have some things in common.

So far, my first card has not been returned to me shredded into little pieces. I am encouraged a bit she accepted it.

I don't sleep well at night, tossing and turning in potent frustration. Somehow I end up listening to Matchbox Twenty's song "3 AM" at 3 a.m. The words mock me.

She says, baby
It's 3 a.m., I must be lonely
When she says, baby
Well, I can't help but be scared of it all sometimes

Day 3: Four days to go. I take a chance and call her. Her sultry voice is enough to bring me to my knees. I need to sit down to be able to talk. She sounds fine, and she even says she misses me.

A small victory, but I'll take it.

She still gives me no clue what her decision is going to be. Today's card is all about my experiences in Iraq and Afghanistan. The clerk at the Hallmark store is starting to recognize me and stares at me curiously.

Yeah, I know I was here yesterday too. I'm buying another damn card. Isn't that your job? We're in a Hallmark store, for Pete's sake. Don't look so darn surprised.

In this card, I don't tell her everything about those countries because some of it was just too hard to stand. I know I will always be haunted by the things I had to do and the horrible things I saw, especially during the war. I still have nightmares about it at times, but I am trying to work through it now that I know I am safe and have a secure home.

I tell her because I want her to know about me being a Marine and what it was like for me there. It's a large part of my life, so I want her to know. She needs to know about me.

I am going crazy trying to make it to Tuesday. I call my Marine buddy Keith in Norfolk. I haven't spoken to him about meeting Becca. He answers the phone, and we exchange small talk. I can tell he is drinking a beer while talking.

"What's up, Michael? I can tell something is bothering you. You sound strange."

"I don't know. A woman I met recently has gotten under my skin. We've been out a few times, but now she has kicked me to the curb big-time."

"She is just another bitch in a long line of fucks. Forget about her and move the hell on. There are plenty of other pussies for you to explore."

I get angry at him. "No, she's not like that. I really like her."

"Yeah, you like her tits, ass, and pussy. I know you, dude, remember?"

"Goddamn it, it's not like that with us."

"Dude, you haven't tapped that yet? Is that the problem? Your hard dick has no place to go?"

"Shit! I don't know what to do. She is driving me crazy."

"Let it go, dude, let her go. If she doesn't want to fuck you, she isn't worth the effort. Trust me."

I hope this is the beer talking. He's not helping at all.

"Talk to you later, dude."

"Yeah, good luck with that bitch. My advice is to forget about her, but do what you have to do."

Day 4: Three days to go. I send her a dozen long-stemmed yellow roses tied up with a big pink satin ribbon. I watch from my car in her parking lot to see the florist truck deliveryman give them to her. I simply wanted to see she got them. I couldn't catch a glimpse of her as she signed and accepted them. I was parked on the other side of the lot so she wouldn't know I was there.

She mentioned once that her favorite flower is a peace rose because her father grew them when she was a child. There was a large peace rose bush right below her bedroom window, and she could see them when she awoke on the mornings in the spring and summer.

I looked up images of peace roses on the Internet. They are yellow roses edged in different shades of pink. I think they are perfect for her. Soft yellow petals like the color of sunlight and warmth. The pink edges remind me of her lovely blushing cheeks when I kiss her. Both of them have a natural sweet scent. Petals furled tightly around each hidden center just like a woman's secret places.

I want to see her petals bloom wide open for me under the warmth of my love for her. I just need to get past her defenses. This particular female peace rose has many very sharp thorns protecting its fragile but quietly courageous heart. I need to break each thorn off its long stem. One by one, those thorns need to get out of my way.

But I couldn't find a dozen peace roses to send her even though I called every fucking florist in Tidewater. This is as close as I can get. Yellow roses tied with a pink satin ribbon.

I write a brief message to her on the card at the florist:

Thinking of you every minute, every day. Michael.

I hope that's not too much. It's true.

Should I send her chocolates next? She must like chocolate, right? Everybody does. What's not to like about chocolate? Don't women think flowers and chocolate are romantic? Yeah, I am all about the romance now. I'm starting to be able to breathe a little better. The end is in sight. I have to be patient. Help me, God.

I send her the most romantic card I can find in the Hallmark store. Hopefully, these words will say it for me.

Should I make her a playlist too? The words in some of my favorite songs could answer her questions as well. I think about it. Does she have an IPod or whatever those things are that hold a music list? How do I do this? How about a CD? I am not good with some of the new technology. It comes out so fast; it is hard to keep up with all of it. Maybe I can get Keith to help me. He might know how to do it and not tease me about it. He's alone too, so I know he will get where I am coming from. I think about it, not sure what to do.

Day 5: Two days to go. I send her the biggest box of milk chocolate candies I can find. Milk chocolate–covered caramel and pecan clusters.

My favorite candy. I like sweet, chewy, nutty candy. I hope she likes them too.

I also send her a text message:

> **Ms. Connelly. I am inviting you to go on a picnic with me to the New Kent Winery on Tuesday. Please let me know if you're available. I anxiously await your reply. Michael**

No card today. I mail her a handwritten love letter. I try to write the sweetest, most romantic things I can. I hope she loves it. I pour my feelings out on the paper, trying to be romantic instead of overwhelming her with naked need and desire.

I quietly but steadily go out of my mind all day. At the end of the day, as I am losing all hope, I get this from Becca:

> **Michael. I would love to go on a picnic with you to the winery. See you Tuesday. Becca**

Thank you, God. I admit I was praying. Maybe I'll be able to breathe again on Tuesday.

Day 6: One more day to go.
THE WEEK FROM HELL IS ALMOST OVER NOW!

What is this woman doing to me? This can't just be about sex. I could have sex if I really looked for it. The thought of making love with Becca is almost more than I can bear. Yes, I want her, but I'm beginning to think she means more to me than that. Am I too old to be falling in love for the first time in my life?

I want to be with her all the time. I think about her most of the day, wondering where she is and what she's doing. I want to share my life with her. I want her to share her life with me. I finally have to admit to myself I am falling in love with her. So fast and so hard.

This is love. This is what it feels like. I know it now. Please let her feel the same way. She has to make the right decision. I'll give her the time she needs to learn to love me. She has to. I try to be positive in my thoughts, knowing I might not be able to handle it if she pushes me completely away, banned from her life forever.

I spend the day showerless, deodorantless, unshaven, with messy hair, a torn T-shirt, and stained shorts, staring unblinkingly at the television but not seeing it or paying attention. I think about getting drunk, but I do not have any beer in the house. I don't have the energy to drive to the store to get a six-pack.

The hours, minutes, and seconds pass by painfully, hopelessly, depressingly, despairingly, and alone. She isn't going to let me into her life. Some other man will come along and take her. He will be the one she loves and lets in, not me. A vision of another man kissing her, making love with her, is too much for me.

Sudden sharp pangs of irrational jealousy toward this future unknown man almost make me double over. Or maybe there is someone else she already knows just waiting in the wings for the right time to make his move on her. I have no idea if she is interested in another man she already knows. I only know she wants nothing to do with her ex-husband. At least he is one less man I need to worry about taking her from me.

She is so delicate, so easily sliding through my fingers. I am trying to hold on with everything I have. I am worried what she is going to say to me tomorrow. I can't eat or breathe very well. I can't go for a run. I can't think about anything but Becca's decision. It's a form of torture.

I sit and watch the music video by Nelly featuring Tim McGraw of their song "Over and Over." The words fit me perfectly right now. I watch this damn video over and over as well.

'Cause it's all in my head

I think about it over and over again
And I can't keep picturing you with him
And it hurts so bad, yeah

Tomorrow is the day I find out if I am going to have her again in my life or spend the future in darkness. My eyes are red and dry, and I don't sleep all night. I stare at the ceiling all night long as I lay on my big empty bed.

Will she give me another chance? What will I do if she completely disappears from me? Slips through my fingers?

Day 7: It's Tuesday.

Fucking finally.

I get up early and clean myself up. When I think it is not too early to disturb her, I text Becca to tell her I'll pick her up at eleven-thirty. She simply replies "ok." I already have the car packed with all the necessary picnic items except the food. It's a beautiful, cloudless day and just the right temperature for being outdoors. I can't believe I'll be able to see and touch her today. That is, if she makes the right decision.

Please.

I need to remember she hasn't told me anything yet. But the fact she agreed to this picnic at the winery must be a good sign. At least I hope so. I arrive at her door and ring the doorbell on time. She opens the door and gives me a quick hug and smile. I want to kiss her, but I manage to stop myself.

So far, so good.

She has on a cute blue summer dress with sandals. Her neck and shoulders are exposed, and the only things holding up her dress are two small thin straps. I know she must be braless although there may be some kind of strapless bra under her dress.

Hope not. How can I find out for sure? I'm extremely curious.

I am surprised when she grabs my hand and takes me up the stairs. Her two-bedroom condo is modern, attractive, and colorful. It's cute, like her, with high ceilings and an arch with two columns. She has comfortable furniture and nice artwork. I like her taste. She shows me things she's collected from her travels around the country and Europe. I can see that she is surrounded by things she loves and holds memories for her.

I notice she never takes me down the hall to where I presume is her bedroom. It's apparent to me I'm not allowed in there yet, not even to look. I don't say anything because I'm trying very hard not to fuck this up. In the great room, I sit with her and ask her how her week has been. She tells me all of her activities and mentions again she had missed me. I don't tell her about my week.

The Week from Hell.

The suspense is killing me. I have to know what she has decided about us. I look into her eyes and finally get the nerve to ask her the question I've waited all week to hear the answer.

"Have you thought about us, Becca?"

"Yes, Michael. I have. I can't help but think about you. Every day there was something about you that made me think of you. Thank you for all your thoughtfulness this week. It meant a lot to me. I can see you put much thought into each thing you sent me. You're very sweet. I do feel as though I know you a bit better now."

Good start as far as I'm concerned.

"Have you . . . decided anything yet?" My voice is gentle but strained. *I'm holding my breath here.*

She holds up her hand in front of me, like a stop sign.

I think she's trying to tell me to stay back. Oh no.

"I need to say this without you interrupting me. I can't think when you're close to me. You can be a bit . . . intense. So stay where you are. I've thought long and hard about what to say to you. To be perfectly honest with you, I . . . have never felt like this before. I've never felt such a strong attraction to a man, especially one that I've barely just met. I am a bit stunned by it all. I am not sure what to think."

"Even when I was married, I certainly never felt the way I already feel about you for Tripp at all. I was young and thought I was in love with him. He was all I knew, so I thought that's the way it was supposed to be. But when I saw him again, I realized how much we've both changed, and he is not the man I once loved. He scares me a bit. Then you suddenly showed up in front of me, so . . . so gorgeous, so sweet." She pauses, and I hold my breath.

"I didn't tell you to go away because it was all I could do to look at you. You are an incredibly handsome man, Michael, and I could barely talk. And since that night when you pretended to be my boyfriend to rescue me, I find myself wanting you to really be my boyfriend. When you kissed me, I basically couldn't breathe. I've thought of little else but that."

"So, if you think you can be with me exclusively, I'm willing to give it a try. I will risk trusting you. I am out of practice with all of this. I know I . . . want to be with you and think I'm falling for you. Already. It's too fast, but I'm just not strong enough to stay away from you for very long. This week certainly proved that to me. It's been a . . . difficult week for me. But Michael, you have to give us time to get to know each other. It's been very fast. We don't know each other. We haven't spent enough time together. I need that before I can feel really comfortable with you."

I sit there and look at her, not blinking but breathing deeply. This is more than I could have hoped for. She is willing to give me another chance. I hold out my hand to her and as she takes it, I pull her gently into my lap. I can't help putting both of my arms around her and taking a deep breath, smelling her sweet scent. Neither one of us says a word, only sitting quietly together as I contemplate her words.

She is saying yes. This is where she belongs. With me, in my arms. For once, I am at a loss for words. Maybe that's better than me scaring her with all my feelings.

All I can do is whisper in her ear over and over, "Yes, yes, yes. Please don't ever keep me from you again. I can't take it. All I can see is darkness when you are not part of my life. It breaks me, baby."

On the way home from her, I throw in a CD by Disclosure and listen to a song called "Latch: You Enchant Me, Even When You're Not Around." The chorus speaks to me.

Now I've got you in my space
I won't let go of you (never)
Got you shackled in my embrace
I'm latching on to you (never)

CHAPTER 7

The Perfect Picnic at the Winery

After I hold her for as long as I wanted, I tell her we need to go on the perfect picnic. I want this day to be particularly perfect for her. We drive up the interstate heading for New Kent Winery, listening to Hoobastank's song "The Reason." It's a beautiful winery with several excellent wines, including a White Norton and a White Merlot that I really enjoy. I take her to the lovely wooden tasting room and pay for two tastings at the counter.

They direct us to the bar where a woman waits with wine glasses and the tasting sheet listing all the wines we are about to sample. I find we both enjoy similar tastes in wine. We like slightly sweet white, blush, or red wines more than the dry, peppery deep reds filled with tannic acids. Sweet preferred over dry. Dessert wines are very special but only for sipping. These ice wines are produced late in the season after a frost has covered the vines. I definitely can tell the difference between wines aged in stainless steel as opposed to French oak barrels. I purchase three chilled bottles, and we go out to get the picnic supplies.

Looking around the surrounding land, I spot the perfect place for a picnic. I take her hand and lead her to the trees so we are isolated from the parking lot and other people who could potentially interrupt us. We spread the picnic blanket out far away from the tasting room, surrounded by the trees, and open a bottle of the Norton.

Becca likes wine, so I am happy to give it to her. I have two bottles with me, one the White Norton and the other the White Merlot, in case one is not enough to relax her. I also bought one bottle called the Vidal Blanc, but I left it in the car when I went to get the picnic basket. Lunch is chicken salad croissants and a garden salad with ranch dressing for us both. Decadent chocolate brownies with icing are saved for dessert. It's all delicious with the wine.

Becca spends the whole lunch asking me question after question. Silly questions, like what I eat for breakfast, what's my middle name (Gable, after my mom's favorite actor Clark Gable), and if I had pets growing up. I know it's because she wants to know me, really know me. I'll tell her anything she wants to know. I'll tell her everything.

I hope the cards and the romantic letter I sent her during the Week from Hell helped her know me better. I hope I am no longer a stranger to her.

In her own way, she is sharing more and more with me. I find out more tidbits of information about her life and favorite things. I discover she deems golden retrievers as the absolute perfect dog. She tells me about Charley, the male retriever who could read her mind and understand English. He had a severe seizure in Charleston, and Becca was with him when the vet administered the shot to take him out of his misery. She says it was obvious Charley was no longer the dog she loved. The seizure was simply too severe for him to recover. Evidently Tripp wasn't there at the time, hiding in the parking lot, not strong enough to watch Charley be put down. But Becca said she wasn't going to let the dog she loved die without her petting him lovingly. It was hard for her to watch as well, but it shows how much her dog meant to her. He was her "baby."

I learn about Chelsey, the sweet reddish retriever who would climb into bed with Becca during the night and lay her head on the pillow like a person spooning her as she slept. Then, she mentions Sunny, the blonde happy retriever who followed Chelsey around, always staying close to her. She had to give away both of these sweet loving dogs to a good home with children when Tripp left her. She was forced to leave the expensive four-bedroom house she could not afford by herself on her teacher salary and find a smaller, more affordable place to rent. The lease she signed for this rented townhouse forbade large dogs. She has photos of them in her living room. It is obvious they are still deeply entrenched in her heart. I ask her why she doesn't get another dog. She shrugs, saying it would be too hard for her now.

We sit together on the blanket, sharing the wine and talking. We have finished one bottle, and I have opened the second. They were both chilled when I purchased them, so they were very good. I decide to take a chance on how she is feeling with me. She seems comfortable and pleasantly relaxed with me. I think she's feeling the effects of the first bottle of wine. Not drunk, but slightly buzzed perhaps. I know I am buzzing away over here. Not with the wine, but drunk with her. I can certainly drive us home, no problem.

I scoot my ass over to her and pull her into my arms. She lets me kiss her tenderly, sweetly, innocently, with closed lips pressed together. I endure this torture for a long while, but I need to get into that mouth. I try to figure out how I can get my tongue inside her warm lips. Reaching over for my full wine glass, I take a gulp and hold it in my mouth, without swallowing. I bend Becca back over my arm and lean over for a kiss. She gasps slightly, giving me the access I need, or else I was going to have to swallow.

I let the wine flow into her and feel her swallow as I fill her mouth first with the delicious wine and then with my wine-flavored tongue. I explore as deeply as I can, moaning in the back of my throat as I feel her surrender her mouth to me completely. Her tongue makes its presence known, stroking mine and thrusting into my mouth. She pulls away a millimeter, but she licks my lips before leaving me aching without her.

God, what a kiss that was. I want more.

The sensation of letting the wine pour from me into her is just exactly what I want to do. I want to pour my liquid pleasure into her, feeling her squeeze it out of me just like the muscles of her throat allowed her to swallow the wine I gave her. I can't wait to have that special moment with her. Her, swallowing me inside her mouth, inside of her sweet secret womanly warmth.

We clean up our picnic items, and Becca sits back with her legs in front of her. She motions for me to lie down. Next thing I know, I'm lying with my head on her lap, and she's stroking my hair softly.

It feels so good, like she's cherishing me.

I look up and her breasts are right above my eyes.

What a great view this is.

I can't help myself. I nuzzle her breasts first with my face and slowly but repeatedly stroke her with my fingers. Over and over, passing over her nipples with gentle touches. I take a deep breath.

Maybe, maybe.

I won't push her too fast. She hasn't pushed me away. I reach slowly up, slide her straps down her shoulders, and pull her dress so that I can get to her right breast. She doesn't pull away from me.

Excellent.

Strapless bra found. I pull her bra down just far enough so that it pushes her up; her nipple is exposed to me.

Yeah, it's hard for me. Like a little tight dusky pink rosebud.

I look into her eyes and make sure she's still with me. She seems okay with what I've done so far. I don't want her to become self-conscious and pull away from me. She's leaning back slightly with a slight smile on her face, so I decide to take the next step, since she hasn't flinched or said no. She has to know what I want to do to her breasts.

I lean up and hungrily take her nipple into my mouth, stroking it over and over with my tongue. I groan against her, my other hand cupping her left mound, exposing it and massaging greedily with my whole hand. I roll her hard nipple against the middle of my palm over and over. Her breast fills my whole hand and it feels like heaven. I try to give both of them equal attention. I continue loving her until I'm about to come in my jeans if I don't stop soon.

I kiss both of her nipples one last time and gently put her clothes back into place. She seems to be speechless except for a low disappointed moan. Thank goodness we are far enough from the tasting room and secluded by the trees thick enough to keep from giving someone quite a show. It's private.

When I lay my head back down onto her lap, I can feel the heat radiating from between her legs. I bet she is warm and damp just for me. She has on a dress. The only thing stopping me from discovering her secrets are silk panties.

It's all I can do not to run my fingers up her thigh and under her dress to find out for sure. I could unzip, rip through that thin strip of silk, and be in her before she knows it. My dick twitches in response, but I don't want our first time to be a quickie out in public, in the woods on a picnic blanket. I plan on needing comfort and privacy for what I want to do. I need to get a grip. She's too important to me now.

We've been on a three-hour picnic in the woods. I take a deep breath, knowing the perfect picnic must end. I pull her up, kiss her again, and grab the blanket and other items before hiking back to my car.

I am simply incapable of leaving her alone. I'm going to follow her rules. But she did say yes and that she wanted me. She even said she was falling for me. She can't get away again.

Gavin Rossdale's song "Love Remains the Same" percolates in my head as I drive us home. Becca is next to me on the passenger seat, with her eyes closed. Riding in cars relaxes her, I see. I don't think she is asleep; she's listening to the music.

A thousand times I've seen you standing
Gravity like a lunar landing
Make me run 'til I find you
I shut the world away from here

CHAPTER 8

I Am Trying to Be Civil Here

I begin my slow (hopefully, not too slow) but steady seduction of Ms. Rebecca Lee Connelly. If she wants to know me first, then she's going to know everything. I take her out on dates as if we're young again. Innocent activities, spending time together. Since I know she loves history so much, I let her take me to all the historical attractions in the area. We tour Jamestown one day, going to both the festival park as well as out to the original island. Becca has been there so many times already she is my personal tour guide, knowledgeable in all the historical details.

We next wander up and down Duke of Gloucester Street going into the Governor's Palace, Bruton Parish Church, the Raleigh Tavern, and the Capitol Building. We go into a small jewelry store that seems to specialize in silver pieces. I see small Williamsburg-themed silver charms and think that I will come back and get Becca a charm bracelet as a remembrance of our visit. I hope she would like that, wearing a bracelet I gave her instead of her ex-husband. I like that it is silver, not gold like that other bracelet. It looks nothing like it, nothing to remind her of him.

I decide to get it the next day and give it to her. She is delighted with the bracelet and lets me help her put it on her wrist. Little silver colonial charms jingle sweetly when she moves.

It's the first piece of jewelry she wore that came from me. I hope it will always remind her of our day together touring the historic colonial capital city.

Yorktown Battlefield is next, the site of the ending battle of the American Revolution. The British Army under Charles Cornwallis found itself unable to escape the siege by the French forces under Rochambeau and the Americans under George Washington. The British fleet could not enter the York River to save them due to the French fleet's naval blockade by Admiral De Grasse sailing in Chesapeake Bay. The British warships were not able to enter the York River and rescue their army trapped between the river and the American and French siege lines. We take in the museum with George Washington's actual battlefield tent before driving the road circling the battlefield. There are numerous signs to stop and read, explaining what happened there in October 1781.

I can see she is enjoying this, showing me all these places. I've never gone before, so it's fun and educational for me too. We walk around Redoubts 9 and 10, the sight of fierce fighting between the British and the combined American and French forces. Surrender Field is actually the place where General Charles Cornwallis sent a lower-ranked officer to surrender to General Rochambeau, preferring to surrender to the French he respected as worthy adversaries on the field of battle. Rochambeau refused the surrender sword, indicating it should go to General George Washington, the American commander in chief.

Washington refused to accept it from someone other than his equal on the battlefield. He let the lower-ranked British officer surrender Cornwallis's sword to his lower General Lee Benjamin Lincoln as well. It was truly a world turned upside down for the British. The British drummers played the popular song at the time called "The World Turned Upside Down." This song was played during the time when the British Army walked in defeat in front of the victorious American and French soldiers. They had to lay down their arms in surrender to these combined forces.

Virginia is for Lovers. I am beginning to think Williamsburg and Virginia simply are one big historical battlefield, either the Revolutionary War or the War Between the States. She shows me actual earthworks left over from Union General George McClellan during the Peninsula Campaign of 1862. The Union forces stationed at Fort Monroe in Hampton were over 120,000 troops strong. The peninsula was defended by a mere twelve thousand Confederate soldiers. But McClellan was fooled into thinking the rebel forces were much stronger when Southern General John Bankhead Magruder marched his troops over and over in a circle to lead the Yankee spies into thinking they had never-ending troops. A battle was fought at Dam No. 1 in Newport News City Park. The Union troops advanced to Williamsburg and fought a battle there in May of 1862. It succeeded in only delaying their march to Richmond. Lee was able to defend the capital and stop McClellan in his tracks. The war then continued to 1865 when it could have ended in 1862 if McClellan had had the balls to keep going.

I'm learning a lot about Virginia. Not only is Virginia for lovers, as the old saying goes, but it is also for us to enjoy and explore. It is filled with history, beautiful landscapes from the beach to the mountains, museums, national and state parks, battlefields, and other adventures. Virginia is the mother of presidents, the first of the English colonies to be settled at Jamestown in 1607, and survived as a leader among the thirteen original colonies.

Her native sons made the American Revolution a reality, which led to the formation of the United States of America. Founding fathers include George Washington, Thomas Jefferson. Patrick Henry, James Madison, and James Monroe. These men forged a new nation from English colonies who dared to take on the mightiest of countries, Great Britain. Truly an amazing feat since they lost more than they won. But they won the final battle, and that is what counted. The French helped, but the U.S. has paid them back with American blood spilled on the beaches of Normandy to free the French from German occupation during World War II.

We're the lovers now. I hope. Real lovers, but not consummated lovers. Not yet. Soon, please. I have an idea about what I want to enjoy and explore as well.

We spend one Saturday touring the Mariners' Museum in Newport News. Besides all the beautiful figureheads from various ships and million-dollar lighthouse lens, they have a current interactive display on the battle between the *Monitor* and the *Merrimac* during the Civil War. This naval battle was fought in Hampton Roads harbor, the first ever between two ironclads. It was the beginning of the end for wooden sailing ships as battleships.

Becca quickly corrects me about the name. It turns out the battle was actually between the two ironclads USS *Monitor* and CSS *Virginia*. The *Merrimac* was the old wooden sailing ship used as the foundation hull for the *Virginia* before they applied the iron to it. The museum actually has the round turret from the *Monitor,* raised several years ago from the floor of the Atlantic Ocean off Cape Hatteras where it sank during a storm. I enjoy the interactive exhibits, again amazed by Becca's knowledge. I learn something from her all the time.

One weekend, she lets me drive her all the way up to Gettysburg, Pennsylvania. She really grew up touring Civil War battlefields on all her family vacations. I can tell this is a special place to her. Her ancestors fought for the Confederacy. They have lived in Tidewater for centuries.

We listen to my new Goo Goo Dolls Greatest Hits CD. I have come to realize music is just as important to her as it is to me. We share very similar tastes in songs and performers. I can tell the melodies get inside her and the lyrics speak to her as much as they do me. I feel as though words and music can say it for me if she would only pay attention and really listen. I know many of the lyrics to my favorite songs. I may not sing them out loud, but the words run around in my head constantly. Today we listen to Johnny Rzeznik and the Goo Goo Dolls sing "Iris," "Come to Me," "Home," "Stay With You," "Eyes Wide Open," "Think About Me," "What Do You Need?," "Two Days in February," "You Never Know," and "Let Love In." It's a great selection of songs, some of my very favorite ones.

I can't help but sing these words softly as I drive us north to Gettysburg.
You're the only one I ever believed in
The answer that could never be found
The moment you decided to let love in
Now I'm banging on the door of an angel . . .

I see her listening and she comments she hasn't heard this song by them before, but she likes it.

Yes, let my love in.

We cross the border into Maryland, pass signs for Antietam Battlefield, and head toward Pennsylvania. When she was in college, she wanted to drive to New York City with some friends. She had never been that far north at the time. She tells me her dad said there was no point going any further north than Gettysburg, Pennsylvania, because General Robert E. Lee didn't go past that town in 1863. She says her grandfather's name was Jefferson Davis Connelly, so her family is truly Southern, having fought for the losing side. I think from what she says, they lost their plantations and everything when the war ended. She was truly Scarlett O'Hara, the Southern belle in *Gone with the Wind*. Becca tells me it is her favorite movie of all time.

The scene after Rhett tells Scarlett, "Frankly, my dear, I don't give a damn."

Scarlett becomes frantic after he leaves, wondering how she can get him back.

"Oh, I can't think about this now. I'll go crazy if I do. I'll think about it tomorrow . . ."

"After all, tomorrow is another day."

Yep, that's me. Another day, another study in patience. It's bound to get better if I just hang in there.

Gettysburg is known as the turning point of the Civil War and was fought over a three-day period starting July 1 and ending on July 3, the day before the Fourth of July in 1863. Confederate general Robert E. Lee's Army of Northern Virginia pitted against newly appointed Union General George Meade. Neither general was particularly ready for the battle, which started without warning as the two sides ran into each other in this small town located at a junction of several roads.

She says Confederate general J. E. B. Stuart received a lot of blame after the battle for not providing Lee with accurate scouting reports of Union army movements. Lee had been caught by surprise by the strength of the Union army close at hand. And of course, Stonewall Jackson had been killed the previous May having accidentally been shot by his own men after the Battle of Chancellorsville in Virginia.

So Lee was without his eyes J. E. B. Stuart and his right arm Stonewall Jackson at this crucial battle. The South never again attempted to penetrate the North after the defeat here, and the war lingered on until it finally ended on April 9, 1865, when Lee surrendered to Union General Ulysses S. Grant in the McLean House at Appomattox Courthouse, Virginia. Becca says Wilmer McLean used to live in Manassas, Virginia, and moved away after the battles fought there. It is ironic the war came to his house again and ended in his front parlor. Becca says she will take me there if I want to see the room where the surrender by Lee to Grant was signed. So much of our nation's history occurred right in Virginia. I had not realized it until actually visiting the real historical places.

We go to the battlefield's visitor's center, tour the museum, and listen to the National Park Service guides' lectures. I buy the battlefield tour CD so that we can follow the signs while listening to a description of what occurred at each spot.

The battlefield actually stretches twenty-five square miles around the City of Gettysburg since many significant events in the three-day battle occurred at different locations. We slowly drive around, listening to the CD and stopping at places as directed. Little Round Top and Devil's Den seem to be the places in which she is most interested. We walk around it slowly, absorbing the horrible carnage that took place among these rocks and trees. Men were killed among these trees trying to take Little Round Top and among the boulders of Devil's Den.

There are black-and-white photos displayed there, so we can compare the past with what is now in front of our eyes. There is an eerie picture of a Confederate sharpshooter lying among the boulders, slumped in death. The rocks are recognizable as I realize we are looking at the same place and standing where the photographer must have stood as he took the photo.

We walk the battlefield at the site of Pickett's Charge, which ended the South's chance for a victory. She points out the opposing positions of Seminary Ridge and Cemetery Hill and says the battle began that day with a two-hour cannon barrage as the Confederates tried to weaken the strong Union defenses lined up in a fishhook shape across the wide field separating the opposing armies.

Becca tells me that the Major General George Pickett division massacred that final day was made up of largely Virginia boys. They were walking directly into murderous gun and cannon fire. Over twelve thousand five hundred men. It was soon apparent it had been a terrible decision. It came at a terrible cost for the South, causing them to lose this battle and ultimately the whole war two years later.

The Yankee soldiers taunted the Confederates by yelling "Fredericksburg, Fredericksburg" in their faces. The Southern troops had a fortified position behind a stone wall on Mary's Heights, and many blue-coated soldiers died trying to take that hill. But it was hopeless for them, and it cost General Robert E. Lee a significant victory. The Union soldiers at Gettysburg felt this battle was in retaliation for what had happened to them in December 1862 at the Battle of Fredericksburg. This time the Union troops had the protection of a stone wall.

General Lee apologized to the few troops who managed to return from the charge alive. Pickett never forgave him for the loss of his valiant Virginia division.

When asked years later why his infantry assault failed to win the battle of Gettysburg, Pickett simply replied, "I always thought the Yankees had something to do something with it."

It was very educational and enjoyable, but I am not sure how I feel about visiting all the Civil War battlefields in Virginia. I've already spent a good part of my life, trying to stay alive on active, dangerous battlefields. Since she tells me she has been to every Virginia battlefield there was, I think maybe I can escape those day trips. However, I really enjoyed the day, taking pleasure in how much she is enjoying it. She can reel off the facts of the battle because she has memorized it all. I guess being a teacher makes her very good at remembering facts. I like the way she explains things clearly and logically. I see her teaching me gently about Virginia. I hope it is because she wants me to feel at home in her beloved birth state. She was always a Virginian no matter what other states she might have lived in for a while. It is simply home to her.

She is a history nut.

Having spent all of the day on the battlefield, we didn't have time to visit General Dwight D. Eisenhower's home in Gettysburg. She says maybe we could stop at Antietam Battlefield in Sharpsburg, Maryland, when we come back up this way to see it. It is not that far away from Gettysburg.

Antietam seems to be another one of her favorite battlefields. She knows that battle by heart. She knows the commanding officers on both sides, Union General George McClellan and Confederate General

Robert E. Lee, with General Stonewall Jackson by his side. She tells me little interesting historical details that make the battle fascinating.

She explains the battle in the cornfield at dawn, Bloody Lane and Burnside's Bridge, the main scenes of the horrific carnage that occurred on that day in September 1862. I am shocked and amazed by the depth of her knowledge. She tells me she once drove up by herself to go to a Civil War reenactment of the battle one summer years ago. It was the 140th anniversary of the battle.

There were thousands of reenactors pretending to be Confederate and Union troops to the absolute last detail. They lived in tents and cooked their food over an open campfire. Authentic uniforms and supplies were everywhere to complete the illusion of being back in 1862. She noticed two men dressed up as Lee and McClellan and pretending to give orders. She saw artillery units with cannons that make a loud noise and a lot of smoke. Calvary units on horseback with sabers and pistols drawn and sutlers' tents filled with people selling Civil War goods, uniforms, and hoopskirt dresses. Thousands of people attended it, watching the pretend battle unfold as if it were the real thing.

Who knew she knew so much about a war that happened over a hundred and fifty years ago?

Becca falls asleep in the car as I drive us home that night.

Richard Marx's love song "Right Here Waiting" keeps me company as she sleeps. I can relate to every lyric.

I will be right here waiting for you
No matter how my heart breaks
I will be right here
Waiting for you.

I take her on day trips around the state. We visit the small charming town of Lexington. There we tour Stonewall Jackson's house before Becca takes me to a small museum on the campus of the Virginia Military Institute. They actually have Jackson's horse, Little Sorrel, stuffed in a glass museum case. We also visit Lee Chapel on Washington and Lee's campus. There is a stunning white marble statue of Robert E. Lee lying down as if asleep on the battlefield. We see where General Lee is buried and tour the museum there. We even find his horse Traveler's grave as we leave, and I toss some pennies on his marker.

I feel sorry for Little Sorrel ending up stuffed in a glass case for eternity while Traveler has a decent burial place.

We tour the grounds at Virginia Military Institute, or VMI. There is a museum dedicated to George C. Marshall since he attended the college. I had no idea Stonewall had been a professor before the war. Becca said his students would mock him since he was a boring teacher who simply read the lessons out loud to his class. He was a figure of derision to these young men. Little did they know what war lay in their future, and this same boring professor would become a god to them. They worshiped him once he showed how well he could command. He was ice cold in battle, his blue eyes blazing. He earned his famous nickname at the First Battle of Manassas, or Bull Run as the Yankees called it.

This July 1861 battle was the first time actual armies from the North and South fought although they were hardly ready for it. Picnickers from Washington DC came down to watch the excitement as if it were a fun thing to do. The tide of the battle changed when Jackson's brigade refused to give way to a Union charge.

Confederate General Bee shouted, "There's Jackson standing like a stone wall. Rally behind the Virginians!" Bee was then shot to death, but his words immortalized both the man and his Stonewall Brigade. The Yankees turned and ran back to DC in utter chaos. The road was clogged with panic-stricken picnic-goers and unseasoned Yankee soldiers. The rebels were too busy celebrating their victory to take advantage of it. They could have ended the war right then if they had gone on to Washington, the North's capital.

In front of the impressive stone barracks on VMI's campus, there is a statue of Jackson there, posed for all eternity overlooking his Stonewall Brigade. I see lemons all around it. She explains Stonewall liked to suck on lemons. He was a bit of a flake when it came to his health. We find his grave and monument in the old cemetery off the main street in Lexington. Family members' tombstones surround him, and his grave is decorated by a small Confederate flag.

He died by confused friendly fire in May 1863 at Chancellorsville. His arm was amputated in an effort to save his life, but he died of pneumonia a bit south of Fredericksburg. His wife was with him as his last commanding words were of his men's welfare. "Let us cross over the river and rest beneath the shade of the trees."

Becca says she has seen the small building and bed next to the train tracks at Guinea Station where he died on a Sunday evening, the statue marking the spot where he was shot by a spooked regiment of North

Carolina soldiers, and the small marker showing where Jackson's arm is buried. He died before age forty, leaving a wife and daughter behind. The South never recovered from his loss as a commander. It ultimately led to their defeat.

Although we both are very grateful the South lost, it was an interesting time of history to study. I am not sure what I would have done if I had been placed in the position many of the men had to make. Lee was offered the chance to command Northern armies, but he could not raise his hand against his native Virginia when she seceded from the Union. He paid the price though. His home at Arlington became a national cemetery with soldiers buried practically in his wife's rose garden. Becca says she has been to Arlington Cemetery to see the Tomb of the Unknowns guarded by respectful Marines and President John F. Kennedy's eternal flame, but she never actually got into Lee's home. I got to see this once as well and really enjoyed the changing of the guard at the marble tomb of unknown heroes.

Lunch is good in a cute little restaurant in town. Pepperoni pizza and sodas.

Again, a fascinating day. I didn't realize there was so much to see in Virginia. Becca showed me the things she is interested in and loves.

We drive home to Williamsburg listening to Jordin Sparks's songs "Battlefield" and "One Step at a Time." I like the second one especially.

We visit Richmond, which was once the capital of the Confederacy. I take her to the Museum of the Confederacy and see Lee's actual dress gray uniform and Calvery General J. E. B. Stuart's plumed hat. We tour the White House of the Confederacy where Jefferson Davis lved as president. Then the main visitor's center at the Richmond Battlefield where we see Tredegar Iron Works, the only real industry that helped the South produce war materials. It is now a museum. Afterwards we wander the sidewalk next to the James and throw rocks into the narrow rock-filled river. It is hard to believe this is the same river that is so wide down where the James River Bridge crosses it from Newport News to Suffolk.

I like Pat Benatar's "Love is a Battlefield" and "Hit Me with Your Best Shot." I can't seem to get these songs out of my head now.

I take her out for breakfasts, I take her out for lunches, and I take her out for dinners. We visit all her favorite restaurants and then start on ones to which she's never been. LeYaca turns out to be an incredibly romantic restaurant for dinner. We have an excellent elegant dinner together, laughing easily with one another. She enjoys her dessert of lemon chess pie so much it is hard to watch her eat it. I manage to slip one spoonful of my cherry pie past her lips. It is the one intimate act she allows me to have with her in a restaurant. I get so carried away I consider taking her to the backseat of my car in the parking lot that night before I reluctantly drive her home to her own bed and not mine.

Having her. Finally inside her. In public. In the dark backseat of my black BMW.

In a dark deserted parking lot. At night.

Temptation.

Umm. Maybe not such a good idea.

Not yet, anyway.

I stop, because I am all about the romance now and being the most patient man in the world. She lets me hold her hand; I kiss her hello and good-night. I get to suck her breast occasionally, but below the navel is still absolutely off limits. The ultimate no-go zone, hands off. I am feeling the need to take this a bit to the next level. My Marine buddies would be shocked by my patience. We've been on so many innocent dates I've absolutely lost count.

Patience is important.

CHAPTER 9

Racing Horses and Racing Hearts

    One evening we drive up the interstate to Colonial Downs Racetrack in New Kent. Becca loves horses, and I have never been to a horse race. She tells me how to get there and where to park. It is surprisingly inexpensive to get into the large colonial-style building and racetrack behind it. She explains how to read the program and the system of betting. We walk down to the stables where the thoroughbreds are being prepared and mounted by their jockeys before each race.

Becca exclaims at the muscular beauty of the large racehorses. One of the handlers actually brings a large brown stallion over to the fence where we are watching. He allows her to stroke the stallion's soft hair–covered face and nostrils. It is easy to see she is fascinated by the strength and power of these horses.

We watch as the tiny jockeys get boosted by a foot, swinging their legs easily over and mounting the small leather saddle on top of the racehorse's back. They settle into position by pulling up their knees and slipping their feet into high stirrups. They are now ready to ride the powerful thoroughbred stallions and win the horse race.

Umm. I am about to die, watching Becca watching the stallions. I try to calm down my racing heart and feel grateful my khaki shorts are loose so that my hard-on isn't obvious to her or anyone near us. I didn't know horse racing was so damn erotic a sport. Becca can mount me or hold on to the pommel of my saddle anytime she desires. She can be my jockey, riding me until we race to the finish line to win together. I have just the perfect saddle for her to try out. I know it will fit her perfectly. Knees raised into stirrups, ass high as she rides just like the real jockeys. They have to hold on tight to the reins so they don't fall off.

Oh God. Calm down, Stevens.

I try to keep my endgame in sight. Focus and concentration needed here, Stevens. Let her enjoy herself at the racetrack.

Between the two of us, we manage to place bets on the nine races held on grass and dirt racetracks. We start by walking down to the finish line as each race is run. We win some and lose some. After a while, we take the escalators to the upper level. The grandstands are excellent, and I enjoy watching her have a good time.

We eat mustard-coated hot dogs, and I have a beer, and Becca has a Dr. Pepper on this warm summer night. We're both tired and ahead by about twenty dollars when the last race concludes late in the night. The drive back to Williamsburg is a quiet one, both of us a bit lost in our own thoughts. Earl Kluge's jazz instrumental CD *Heartstrings* provides a calmness to me. She doesn't fall asleep on me since it is a fairly short distance. I reluctantly leave her at her door with a sweet, gentle kiss good-night.

I can be her strong stallion if she will only let me. I want to cross that finish line with her riding me, knees up and bouncing. A winning ride for us both. Bet on it. When will she give in to me?

The next night, we're sitting snuggled on her couch watching a movie called *A Good Year* on DVD. It stars Russell Crowe and is a love story about a British stockbroker who inherits his uncle's beautiful winery in France.

Wine and love. What's not to like?

The movie ends when the stockbroker makes the correct decision and chooses love with a feisty French woman at the French winery instead of wealth in cold London. Becca is soft and warm and feels amazing in my arms as we watch. I let my fingers start to roam a little. She has gotten used to me touching her. I don't let go when the credits roll, reaching over for the remote to turn it off. I turn back and continue to caress the woman in my arms, sighing a bit with frustration but determined not to rush her.

After a while, I can feel her taking deeper and deeper breaths, moaning slightly as she exhales. I reach up to her chin, tilt her head back, and quickly cover her mouth with my lips. I soon can't help thrusting my tongue slowly into the sweet recesses of her mouth. I feel my body heat up, and suddenly it's like both of us are moving in slow motion. Before I know it, she's under me, and her legs are wrapping themselves around my hips.

I settle into the softness of her body, trying to get closer and closer to her as we kiss. I grab her hips, digging my fingers into her ass hard enough to leave bruises if I am not careful. Becca's arms are wrapped around me, her fingers in my hair before scraping her nails down my back. I'm about to lose my mind, thinking I'm never going to be able to stop but knowing that I need to maintain control.

We are moving and dry-humping each other frantically through our jeans. My cock is thrusting at the apex of her thighs as hard as I can. She is holding on and moaning and heating up under me. I think we are both about to come in our jeans. As much as I want that pleasure, I need to calm both of us down before neither one of us is able to stop.

Our first time needs to be special; it needs to be romantic. Women need that, and I am going to make sure she gets it even if it kills me.

But what if she wants to now? What if she says yes to me right now? I don't think I have the strength to say no to her.

I wrench my mouth off hers and raise my head to stare deeply into her eyes.

Is she still with me? Is she going to stop me again? I'm not sure I can stop if she waits much longer. I'm just too excited, and I want and need her so much; my insides are all tied up in knots with desire for this woman and only her.

I lean over and put my lips next to the soft folds of her ear, making sure I am not too heavy on her. My heart is about to leap out of my chest; it is beating too fast and strong to stop now. I breathe out the words, "I love you, I love you, baby, don't you know? Oh God, I want you so much."

Please, please, please, don't stop me, don't stop me, I need you, I want you, let me love you, I want to love you now, love me back, please, please. I don't know what else to think but please. The words run over and over in my mind, practically shouting at me, and her. Can't she hear it? Does she hear it?

I keep it in, not wanting to overwhelm her and make the same mistake which caused me to have to endure the Week from Hell. I won't last if I have to do that again. It will break me. I'll have to admit defeat. Absolute, soul-shattering surrender. And I hate that. Oh God, please, no, not that. My heart aches at the thought that she will never want me and love me as much as I do her.

Haven't I been patient enough? I've tried my best. I have nothing left within me to give. I am breaking under the strain as it is.

I gaze at her, feeling her softness underneath me. I could lose my self-control if I am not careful.

How is she feeling? What is she thinking?

I try to look for signs that tell me she wants me as much as I do her. I'm afraid I might just project my feelings to her, mistakenly seeing what I want so desperately to see in her eyes. I am having trouble breathing normally. I realize I must look ridiculous with my mouth open and panting slightly. My heart is pounding out of my chest. She must feel it.

My God, I just hope I am not drooling or something. That doesn't sound attractive or sexy at all.

I lick my dry lips, thankful there is no sign of drool. My whole mouth is suddenly dry now.

My God, I'm a damn mess when I want to look my most handsome.

She doesn't seem to be trying to get away from me. She's not panting like me, with her mouth open. I guess I don't affect her as much as she seems to effortlessly affect me. I pull back to look deeply into olive green orbs framed by dark lashes. She has her soft arms around my neck, running her fingers through the hair on the back of my head, and I think she is watching me with love in her eyes.

I pray that it is love I see there.

"Becca, Becca, are you saying yes? Are you saying yes to me? Do you know me well enough now? Do you feel like you know me enough to let me love you? I won't hurt you. I could never hurt you. You can trust me with your heart. I swear. Please tell me you agree."

"Yes, Michael, yes, soon, but not tonight. I'm sorry, but not now. Soon, I promise. I promise. I'll let you make love to me. I trust you now. I want to make love with you. Soon, darling. Just not tonight. Please, I'm not quite ready, but I promise soon."

Oh God, oh God. When, when, when? When can I finally have you? I try to calm down and become the definition of patience. I take deep, deep breaths, trying to control my beating heart. Amazing self-control. My Marine buddies would be shocked by my restraint. I know they would never have been able to hang in there as long as I have. I am not a quitter. Persistence is my middle name.

She is worth it all. The end is in sight now; I can see that damn light shining at the end of the tunnel of my future life with Becca. She is the light I need in my life. Otherwise the future is simply dark and lonely.

She lets me hold her until I finally have the strength to leave her alone and go home, alone again.

She promised. She said it; she actually said it. I know I heard her say it.

I have a lot to get done the next morning, and so does she. I call her, but there is no answer. I leave a message. Two hours later, I get a message from her saying she had to drive down to Portsmouth for a bit of an emergency. Mackenzie hurt her knee and had to go to Urgent Care. Her daughter can't take her because she is at work, and there is no one else. Becca drives down and takes care of her, staying at Urgent Care, picking up medicine, and getting her settled back at home. She then drives an hour back to Williamsburg. I resign myself to the fact I will not be seeing her today. I text her to let me know when she is back home safely.

It is after nine in the evening when she calls to tell me she is home. Her sweet sexy voice is in my ear, my head, and in my heart. I close my eyes and imagine her sitting there with the phone pressed to her ear, listening to my deep masculine voice. She answers with a soft huskiness in her feminine tones. Her voice alone is making me weak. We talk about our plans for the rest of the evening. Bed seems to be about it.

"What do you have on now?"

"What? I have on a pair of sweat pants and old T-shirt. Why do you care?"

"Is the elastic at the top of your sweat pants loose, honey?"

"Yes, these are a bit baggy on me."

"Becca, please, baby, slip your hand down into your pants for me."

"What?"

Come on, baby. Phone sex? Am I allowed to hear you come for me?

"You heard me. Touch yourself. Imagine that it is me touching you. Do it now."

She is gasping, hesitating, wondering, but then softly says yes.

Oh God.

I hear her say, "You too."

Well all right then. You don't have to ask twice.

"Tell me, baby, are you touching yourself? How does it feel?"

"It feels good."

"That's right, honey. It feels good. It is going to feel even better soon, I promise. Pretend it is me touching you. I want to so much. Let me imagine it being me feeling you."

"Okay."

I can't take it. My own hard dick makes its appearance as I unzip quickly, grab on tightly, and start to jerk off listening to her breathing and moaning on the phone.

"Oh, baby, does it feel as good to you as it does to me? Tell me, tell me now. I need to know. I love you. I want to be the man pleasuring you so badly. This is all I can do for now. Listen to my voice. I'll help you. You help me and we'll do this together, okay?"

She gasps. "Okay."

It gets to the point where none of us could talk anymore, only gasp for breath, moan, groan, and yell as we pleasure ourselves to each other's voices together. I hear her come, and I scream for her. I hope my groan didn't hurt her ears.

Oh God. Please let the next time not be long-distance phone sex. I need up-close-and-personal service now.

We stay on the phone a bit longer as we both come down from this stunning surprise encounter.

Now that Becca has said yes to really letting me into her life, I start thinking about what to do next. I'm not going to make it much longer, and I'm hoping she feels the same way. I will decide when and where this is so going to happen. We're both adults, and we know how this works. She's decided she wants an exclusive loving relationship with me, so that's what I'm going to make happen. I am a mature man ready for a mature love with the woman of my dreams.

I finally found her. Yes, we have both been unable to satisfy our deepest yearnings for a connection with another human being, but I am ready, and I hope she is too. I want the whole loving experience for once in my life. For even the rest of my life, hopefully.

I think long and hard about the perfect romantic time and place to make this happen for us both. Setting is important. Every detail must make her comfortable with me and with what we do together. I want it to be a perfect night of our perfect first time loving each other physically, emotionally, and intimately.

I want our first night as real lovers to be very loving. I plan on a night so damn romantic she will be unable to resist me any longer. I have no problems with an exclusive relationship. There is no other woman for me, and I better damn well be her lover exclusively. Only me. Forever. I am hers, and she belongs to me.

Since the weekend is coming, I decide we need a real grown-up romantic date for our first time together sexually. After all, it is a very special occasion that I am desperately anticipating every night in my erotic, pornographic dreams and while I make myself come to relieve some of this sexual frustration gripping me by the balls.

I make reservations at the Williamsburg Inn for dinner Friday night. I think I can make it until then. I optimistically make a hotel reservation at the inn at the same time, hoping that we'll use it if things go according to my plans. The Williamsburg Inn is undoubtedly the most romantic hotel in the city. It is filled with colonial charm and elegance. The inn is a real five-star resort, written up in magazines and everything, famous for gourmet food, wine, hotel rooms, and colonial style.

I make sure I forget nothing. I realize I have been listening to Robert Plant's version of "Addicted to Love."

You can't sleep, you can't eat
There's no doubt, you're in deep
Your throat is tight, you can't breathe
Another kiss is all you need.

I call her on Wednesday and invite her out for dinner on Friday. I don't tell her where we're going, but I do say she needs to wear an evening gown. I plan on pulling out my tux for a night of dinner and dancing and, hopefully, exploring each other's bodies. She seems really surprised at my request she wear a long gown. I can get dressed up since this is a special occasion after all. I want her to feel beautiful that night, the night when we finally make love to one another.

Becca begs me to tell her where we're going, but I want to see her excitement when I surprise her. I even briefly consider a limo, but maybe that's too much. I'll drive us; my car is nice enough. I may be a somewhat distracted driver that night, but it's not very far from her home, and I think I can get both of us there safely.

The thought flickers in my consciousness that I have built up this moment so much in my mind, yearning for it nightly, that I may lose control of myself when it is really happening. I don't want to be a disappointment to her and have the evening end before we can get started. I vow that I will not let that happen. I don't care how many damn states I have to count in my head.

I want the evening, our first time together, to be perfect for her. I want her to be happy and secure in the knowledge that she made the right decision. I am the right man for her, and we belong together. I am certain of that, as certain as I am of my own name.

Wednesday and Thursday drag by, probably because I am so focused on Friday night. I can hardly wait. Becca and I talk on the phone, but I deliberately don't see her. I'm saving it all up for her on Friday. I tell her I'll pick her up at seven for dinner, so she needs to be ready by then. My tux looks good on me, I know. It's carefully tailored to my muscles, and I can move.

That night I pull up to Becca's condominium, anxiously hoping everything is going to work out the way I want. I even have a bouquet of wild flowers for her. When she opens the door, my mouth flies open instantly and unconsciously. I don't even say hello or kiss her yet.

I stare at the incredible woman before me. Becca is dressed in a strapless silver gown that hugs her curves perfectly. I'm glad I'm as tall as I am because I catch a glimpse of killer heels as I look at her from head to toe. She now comes up almost to my eyes. She laughs and smiles when I motion for her to turn in a circle so that I can admire every view, every angle. I tell her she is beautiful, hardly able to get the words past my tight throat.

My God, I wonder what she has on underneath that dress. I can't wait for tonight.

I lean in and kiss her sweet mouth quickly before we leave. She smiles at me gently, and I smile back, hoping I am not wolfishly grinning at her with lust.

Before we leave, I run back to the car to retrieve a potted flower I bought for her just for this night. It is a white orchid shaded with light and dark pink spots leading to its center bud. There are ten blossoms on the potted plant. The erotic shape of the orchid is how I hope to see her secret blooms tonight. It ends up decorating her mantle over the fireplace. It will be a reminder of this night with me. She exclaims at the uniquely shaped flowers and tells me she has never owned one before.

Not sure I agree with you, honey.
Patience, Marine.
I can't breathe.

The song Faith Hill made famous flashes suddenly in my consciousness.

"*Breathe*" is the name of her song.

CHAPTER 10

The Williamsburg Inn: I'm Going In

I'm going in in the inn. In Becca's life, in her heart and soul, inside her completely and totally. Permanently. Part of her. In so deep I am never, ever leaving. In. Where I long to be.

It's going to happen tonight.

The Williamsburg Inn is a five-star hotel with a highly rated elegant restaurant. Its colonial beauty is timeless tonight. The lights shining on the façade and columns make it look romantic. We arrive in time for our reservations and are seated near the dance floor. The dining room is large yet lovely. Candles glow on the tables. For a big room, it has an intimate atmosphere.

Becca is very happy about being at the inn, saying that she's always wanted to come here but has never been before. I am so proud to be with her tonight because she looks absolutely breathtaking. I knew she already was, but this is beyond. After seating her next to me, I just gaze at her across the table. I want to keep her close to me.

"I need to tell you how incredible you look tonight, Ms. Connelly. Every man here tonight wants to be with you, but turns out I'm the lucky one."

"Mr. Stevens, I must say you look good enough to eat in that tux. I'll do my best to keep the women who want you tonight at bay."

"Did you say something about eating? I'll have to remind you of that later, Ms. Connelly. But for right now, the only thing we have to eat is on this menu. Order anything you'd like. I know what I want. Unfortunately, I'll have the steak to eat first."

"So is that what you want to eat tonight? You're going to order the steak? How do you like it prepared, Michael?"

"I like my steak medium rare. It must be warm and tender on the inside and still slightly pink. So juicy I could cut it with a fork. I've always had my steaks prepared that way. It's my favorite way to eat steak. What do you think you are going to order for your meal? See anything you like?"

Do you like what you see when you look at me? Look at me.

"Yes, Mr. Stevens, I find that I see quite a lot of things that I definitely like. I plan on enjoying them tonight with you. I can't wait. I know it's going to be good."

"Have you decided what you want to eat tonight, Ms. Connelly? Tell me so I can make sure you get what you want. I need to be able to tell the waiter when he comes over here. Give me a clue how to keep you happy."

"Oh, Michael, I am already quite happy, just happy to be here with you. I think I will have the pink wild salmon. After living in California near the Pacific Northwest, I have developed quite a taste for it."

I'll show her what she can have a taste for now if she only let me. She can develop a taste for me and only me. I am confused by her seemingly innocent words. *I just can't help reading into them what I want to hear. It is catching me off guard, wondering if I am just imagining things.*

Becca tells me funny stories about once going salmon fishing in Alaska on a short trip north with Tripp. He rented a boat and took her out in Prince William Sound salmon and halibut fishing. She had a bad sore throat at the time and brought some Robitussin with her. She started chugging it straight out of the bottle to help her throat. No food in her stomach, so she got drunk on cough syrup. She laughs about staggering up the dock after getting back to the marina with the silver salmon she had caught. Evidently she sat down and couldn't get back up. Tripp had to practically carry her to their hotel room.

I laugh at that, but I don't like my mental image of her in his arms being carried into a hotel. Nope, don't like that at all.

She says she likes to eat salmon, prepared on the grill basted in butter. *Okay.*

Her words definitely can be interpreted in two ways, simply innocent on the surface but actually deeply sexual if I delve deeper beneath the surface. Damn, even I am doing it now. Delving deeper, oh my gosh. Umm. Everything she says is damn suggestive to me. Am I letting my imagination get the better of me? Reading things into her innocent words that I desperately want to hear?

Next, I hear another fishing story from the same Alaska trip. This time they went fishing for halibut alone. The halibut is a flounder that can grow to hundreds of pounds in weight. She caught a fifty-pounder and struggled to get it up to the surface. Tripp had to beat it to death with a baseball bat provided on the boat for such an occasion. The large fish could have hurt her flopping strongly in the bottom of the boat if they had brought it on board alive.

Yeah, I wish the damn fish had knocked him overboard.

They had the fish frozen and sent home to California. She says her freezer was full of it for months.

It is one of her favorite white-meat fish dinner to eat. Halibut Olympia, smothered in mayonnaise and onions.

"Have you ever eaten any halibut before?" she asks me.

"No, I haven't had the pleasure yet. Can you bake it for me?"

"I promise I will. It's an easy dish to prepare although it tastes very complicated. It is delicious. Tender, white, flaky fish in a mouth-watering sauce."

Okay. There is no Halibut Olympia on tonight's menu though.

I try to think quickly so I can keep up with our conversation. I don't want to be left behind by her clever thinking. I can be fairly quick on my feet as well. I have been known to be fast in the past. Fast thinking, fast hands, fast decisions, fast in everything, except for when I make love.

Then I can be slow, as slow as I need to be. It's not something I can really rush anyway. I want to savor the experience, not a "wham, bam, thank you Ma'am" situation. There's a time and place for both though.

Umm, my mind wanders. I suddenly realize I need to speak again. She is glancing at me beneath her lashes, waiting for me to respond to her.

"You can have whatever you want tonight. Just tell me, and I'll make sure you get it. I want to be certain you get whatever you have a taste for this evening."

"Thank you, Michael. I know you will. You take such good care of me, always making sure I am satisfied."

"It has become my life's goal to keep you satisfied, Becca, in all things and in all ways."

"I look forward to you achieving that goal. Perhaps even tonight. I might actually surprise you. I find I think the same thing about you. I think my pink salmon will leave me feeling satisfied, but only briefly. Some dessert might be especially good after dinner. I like something sweet after the main course. Chocolate is always a favorite of mine. Do you like chocolate too, Michael?"

So quick-thinking, so clever. I'm struggling here, barely controlling my thoughts. Suddenly, I love the idea of a sinful chocolate dessert. I need dessert tonight. The perfect finishing touch.

Wait, is she really just talking about the dessert, as in the real thing? Does she have a clue how I am interpreting her quiet words? Sexually, that is. I want her for dessert and I want to be her dessert.

Umm. A rich, satisfying, smooth, sweet dessert. My Becca.

"Yes, I enjoy a good chocolate dessert. I will look to see what is offered here. I'll order it for us if you like."

"Yes, I'd like that very much. Thank you. I'll look forward to enjoying that chocolate dessert a little later. Anticipation is the key to having dessert. Having to wait until after we finish eating always makes the dessert seem sweeter and more satisfying."

Well, that's taking the words right out of my mouth.

"Michael, are you having dessert too? I don't want to be the only one having it. Please join me. You can order whatever you like. I actually like to share. I'll give you a small taste of mine if you give me a little of yours, too."

It is so hot in this restaurant tonight. I am having trouble breathing; it is so hot. I try to take a deep breath. I'm starting to sweat under my tux. Oh no.

Damn! Does she know what she is saying to me? Gosh, she's quick, I'll give her that. I'm at a loss here, so turned on by her words, hoping she means what she is saying, underneath all her polite words.

"Yes, honey, I will have some dessert with you. You don't have to eat it alone. Don't worry. I will join you in that pleasure."

I struggle for what I can talk about next, hoping maybe I can find some normal conversation, some neutral ground long enough to give me time to calm my racing heart down. I have to keep up with her cleverness somehow. The mental image of me making love to her is all I can focus on.

She gazes at me intently before nodding her head slowly, letting me know she's pleased we are both planning on dessert tonight. I can't help myself, so I lean over closer to her lips.

"Ms. Connelly, if you keep looking at me like that, I find I simply have to kiss you." I do, swiftly, making sure I don't linger on her mouth too long. My tongue stays back.

I have to practically tear my mouth off her as it is. So sweet. I could make a meal out of her alone. Later.

I can see a slight blush across her cheeks. It's lovely to see. I just stare at her, afraid my mouth is open. Looking up abruptly, I'm startled by the waiter looming over me. I didn't even realize he was there.

We take our time but eventually place our orders for wine, entrees, and of course, dessert. I quietly make sure I only order one decadent-sounding chocolate crème brulee, one just for me, because I plan on sharing with her. I love breaking through the hot crispy sugar top to find the smooth creamy dessert inside.

Hell, now I'm doing it to myself, getting turned on by my own sexually suggestive words flickering through my mind.

I don't think she notices we will only get one dessert after dinner.

We'll share the dessert.

Feeding my sweet Becca is something I've been dreaming about for many nights. I don't care that we'll be in a public restaurant. If other diners want to watch me spoon chocolate crème brulee into her sweet, sexy mouth, then so be it. I know I'll be enjoying it, seeing her mouth open for me before I slide the hard spoon filled with sweet dessert inside her mouth.

Umm.

The Williamsburg Inn really knows how to do things right with elegance and sophistication. My medium-rare steak is perfection, and Becca tells me her pink salmon is mouth-watering. The wine complements our meals exquisitely. I keep Becca's glass filled frequently, hoping she will continue to be relaxed but not tipsy.

In the middle of our dinner, the small orchestra comes out and tunes up. They begin to play beautiful background music, soothing and lovely. I ask my beautiful girlfriend for a dance, and she accepts me, giggling. We dance slowly together to a hauntingly romantic piano piece. I recognize it as "River Flows in You." I have always loved this stunning sweet melody. I sweep her even closer into my arms as we move effortlessly across the dance floor.

Seems Ms. Connelly has taken dance lessons at some point. It's just one more thing for me to learn about her.

I love having her wrapped in my arms. I press her closer so I can feel the whole length of her against me, every sweet curve of her body. She takes the opportunity to kiss my cheek and quickly on my lips as we're dancing and then buries her face in the crook of my neck.

Her smooth cheek pressed to my raspy cheek. I can smell her sweet, unique scent. It fills my head.

Sliding my hand down her back and quickly running it over her curves, I can't detect any panties, so now that's all I can think about. When the music ends, I reluctantly let her go, and we can return to our dinner. Then again, the sooner we finish, the sooner I can have my dessert.

Both desserts tonight. Chocolate crème brulee and Ms. Connelly. The first dessert won't take that long, but I'm hoping the second one takes me the whole damn night.

The waiters come and clear our plates away, quickly bringing the crème brulee and setting it in front of me with one silver spoon. I look quickly at Becca, and I see she is looking a bit put-out and disappointed. That slight *v* forms between her brows. Hopefully she won't be disappointed for long. Looking into her eyes, I take the spoonful of the sinful dessert and slowly put it into my mouth, licking my lips and making a soft moan of pleasure.

"This is soooo good."

Becca doesn't say anything, but she pouts just a little, a lady-like pout, looking around the room, and I can tell she's wondering if she should call over the waiter to ask why her dessert is late.

That pout should be illegal.

"Sweetheart, look at me. I'm here to take care of you. Anything you want, you only need to ask me to make your dreams come true. Now close your eyes and open your lips. Trust me. I know you can do it," I whisper to her.

Taking a spoonful of the crème brulee, I slowly put it up to her mouth, letting the spoon touch her lower lip.

"Open a little wider for me, please."

Yeah, I know. I hope I get to say that again tonight.

I slide the spoonful of creamy sweetness into her mouth and watch her lips close around it. She licks her lips and makes a humming noise at the back of her throat. I watch enthralled as she licks her lips, even getting that little bit in the corner of her mouth I was just about to pounce on with my eager tongue.

I don't know if I'm going to be able to do this so she can finish the whole dessert. She looks too damn hot. It feels like forever, but between the two of us, we manage to finish the whole crème brulee.

We both can't stop giggling when it is done. I smile at her, and she smiles back at me.

One dessert down, one more to go.

By this time, I am starting to feel a little desperate.

Make that a lot desperate.

I rein myself in a bit.

Think control, Stevens. Control is essential tonight.

I think of Janet Jackson singing "Control" on her breakthrough album *Rhythm Nation*. She was proudly declaring her independence from her parents.

Are we ready?

I am.

'Cause it's all about control (control)

And I've got lots of it.

CHAPTER 11

I Love Making Love with Her

"Come. I have a surprise for you tonight, baby. Trust me."
 I take her hand and gracefully pull her away from our table. I have already given my credit card information to the desk earlier when I made the reservations, so everything will be charged to our room. I'm so glad I don't have to stop and deal with the check because I am in a hurry. I know exactly where I'm going. We walk down a long hallway covered in a luxurious carpet and vases of cut flowers. Stopping in front of a door, I

look at Becca intently. She seems a little confused. Taking a deep breath, I make sure I am giving her the choice for tonight's planned activities.

My plan.

I need to be certain she is with me completely. Her decision to participate.

"Honey, I am sure you can guess why I have brought you to this door. It is up to you what happens next. If you don't want to do this, tell me now. I would never force you to do something you don't want to do. All you have to say is no, and we'll leave, no questions asked. Do you want this, Becca? Do you want me as much as I want you? You know I want you to stay, so that we can be together tonight. Decide what you want us to do. But if you come in there with me, I'm not letting you go until tomorrow."

Or ever.

"I won't be able to stop later. So tell me now."

She looks back at me for a long moment and then whispers the words I want to hear, "You are such a gentleman to give me the choice. And I choose you. I choose us together. Take me in the damn room. Take me now, Marine."

Becca's words startle me into action. Fumbling with fitting the card key in the damn slot, I can't seem to get the door open fast enough for me. Or Becca.

I need to do better getting things into slots.

We burst through the door into a beautiful colonial bedroom with a canopy four-poster bed. Lit candles dot the room. I shut the door and try to take a moment to calm down, but suddenly Becca is pressed up against me, and I forget all about that.

"Oh baby, you're sure, really sure, right? Tell me; tell me you're positive you want this to happen with us tonight."

"Yes. I'm sure, Michael. Please. It's been so long for me, though. I need you to understand that and be patient with me. But I am sure I want us to make love together. I need you."

The words I have been longing to hear. Don't worry, honey. I'll take good care of you. I won't hurt you. Trust me. I'll make sure of it. Only pleasure for us both. Soon. I vow.

I gently lead her to the floral canopied bed and sit her down, standing in front of her. Cupping her face and neck in my right hand, I kiss her open mouth, swooping suddenly on her with my open lips and running my tongue up and down next to hers.

She tastes like chocolate crème brulee. So sweet.
Oh God, help me last.
My father told me a gentleman always makes sure the woman comes first. In every way. So that's the plan. Whether I am able to carry it out or not is another story. But I swear I'm going to do my best.

I lift my lips from her open mouth, slightly stunned by the passion arching between us.

"Ms. Connelly, I admit I've been a bit preoccupied tonight, during our dinner and dessert. I keep wondering what you have on under this lovely silk dress. It has been worrying me all night long. I know I should be able to figure this out, but I find I can't seem to put my finger on it. It simply eludes me. I don't think you have on a bra, because I could feel your nipples against me when we danced. But when I ran my hand over your ass, I couldn't feel any indication of panties. Tell me, Rebecca. Where are your panties tonight? Are you wearing any panties tonight? Tell me. Or I'm going to have to check and find out for sure."

"You can check, but you won't find any on me. My panties are at home, Mr. Stevens. They're at home."

What?! She doesn't have any silk panties on? No underwear to get in my way.

Oh God. Help me. I am shocked by Ms. Connelly. Maybe she's thought about me, too. Is that why she came out of her house tonight pantiless?

Things are definitely looking up. I mean, why else would she have done that if she didn't want me to find out about it sooner or later?

"I see. So you did it on . . . purpose? Just to drive me crazy? You do know we are no longer going to be just boyfriend and girlfriend anymore. We're about to be lovers, Becca. We're both adults, you know what I mean, what I want to do with you now. Tell me you understand and agree. I need to be absolutely certain. I can't stand the thought of scaring you away from me again. Or I am going to take you home. It will kill me, but we will leave right now if you say so."

I need to be sure she won't run from me again like she did when I overwhelmed her with my desire for her. If she does panic and back away, I am truly broken.

I know I have given her enough time to get to know me. So many dates, so much talking. I have been the epitome of a patient man. So I wait, wondering what else I can possibly do to convince her we belong together. I am running out of ideas. Are there any more hoops I need to jump through before I can have her?

I have many delicious plans for tonight. She can't change her mind at the last minute. Please, no.

As I look into her eyes, they seem to suddenly darken. "Yes, Michael. I want this. I want you. Please, don't make me wait much longer."

Absolutely, my love. I can't wait any longer either. Let's get naked now. I need to see you, really see all of your loveliness.

"It'll be my pleasure. Stand up, and let's get you out of this gown."

Becca stands up and turns around for me to unzip her dress. Her shoulders are smooth and gleam in the candlelight. I slide the zipper down slowly, letting the gown fall from my hands and pool around her feet. I hold her hand as I help her step out from her silver gown. She's naked except for sheer soft black thigh-high stockings trimmed with lace at the tops and five-inch black heels. Her breasts are full and round. Looking at her, I can see that her pubic area is waxed smooth.

Who knew that? What a sexy surprise. Ms. Connelly is full of surprises. I have never had the privilege before. A new experience for me. Oh my God. I can't wait to feel that soft smoothness with my mouth. How does she taste? Like sweet honey, I bet.

"Keep the stockings and heels on, Becca, please." I can barely get the words past my lips.

My eyes greedily run over her, from head to toe. She is a goddess, like Venus, to me. Her eyes will not meet mine. I realize she is shy and hesitant, standing there in front of me almost completely nude. I remember it has been many years since she has let a man see her this way. She is out of practice with feeling this exposed and naked. I put my hand under her chin and lift it, but her eyes still remain down.

"Becca, you are a beautiful woman. Never be shy with me. I need desperately to see you like this, all of you, everywhere. You literally take my breath away."

Her lashes sweep up, and I gaze into her green eyes until she nods.

Now I can't get my tux off fast enough. Becca comes over to me, replacing my clumsy hands with hers. She gently undoes my tie before helping me out of the jacket. I pull my shirt out of my pants and offer my cuff-linked sleeves for her to undo. When she's finished, I practically rip my shirt off, exposing my torso to her for the first time. She runs her fingers up and down my bare chest, looking as though she likes what she sees. She caresses the muscles in my upper arms as I hold her. She starts to kiss me softly all over my neck, my chest, and my abs. Her lips are moist, soft, smooth, and warm as she kisses, sucks, and licks her way around.

My muscles give me definition, and I can feel her hands tracing each contour of my abdominal muscles. She pushes me onto the bed slowly and bends over to take off my shoes and socks.

What a beautiful sight that is.
Oh God. She's bending over.

The next thing I know, she's kneeling in front of me, fumbling at my belt and zipper. I'm so hard right now I'm afraid that's all it's going to take. I've never been this hard and thick. When she pulls my pants down for me to slide out of, my cock bursts out, standing at attention and saluting her. Like a good Marine, it is snapping up briskly into perfect position.

I hope I don't scare her. I'm a big boy, and it's been a long time for her. I'll be as gentle as I can. I can't help how big I am, not that I would change it if I could, that is. It is what it is. I hope she can handle it, so to speak.

Now that we're both naked (except for those killer stockings and heels, of course), I lay her gently on the bed. I stretch out next to her, reaching for her mouth. Men tend to forget the power of a kiss. I think I'm pretty good at it, and I take my time, stroking her mouth with my tongue and licking her lips until she moans.

All I can think is she is beautiful. James Blunt's song "You're Beautiful" says it all for me.

You're beautiful, it's true
I saw your face in a crowded place
And I don't know what to do
'Cause I'll never be without you.

Now that I have her where I want her, I can be an amazingly patient lover. I gently stroke my fingers over her cheeks, her lips, and down her throat. I whisper how beautiful and sexy she is to me. I tenderly caress her breasts, stomach, navel, and then spend a great deal of time just tickling her back until she is completely relaxed and used to my touch all over her body. I touch everywhere except for the soft bud of her female rose. Her soft petals are pink and moist-looking. I hope she will open and bloom for me, letting me inside her.

I continue to touch her intimately, trying to maintain control. My mind is always on her and yet wanders at the same time.

Red roses, the symbol of a man's love for a woman. Romance.

A pure white lovely rose comes to mind, with beautiful snowy petals. No, she is not cold like ice.

And Becca is not the red rose, either.

She is the peace rose, her favorite flower raised lovingly by her daddy in her childhood backyard. She told me once it grew so large next to her bedroom window it reached the roof of her house, the royal queen of all the roses in her father's garden. The soft yellow-and-pink blossoms framed by dark green leaves were right there outside her window when she opened her eyes in the warm summer months. She said the roses were never cut and taken indoors; instead, they were allowed to bloom and decorate the massive rose bush itself naturally.

It is the soft yellow color of dawn's first ray of light. It is the dusky pink of a sunrise, the blush of a woman's cheek. She brings warmth and light to me, and I crave it with every breath I take. I need that warmth and peace in my life forever. I see now I have never felt truly at peace, truly safe in my life. I feel that now with her.

When we first met, Becca was the tight bud of a new rose. Her stem was covered with sharp thorns as protection. I scared the fragile tight bud when I overwhelmed her with my intense and sudden passion. I see now I needed to give the bud time to unfurl its petals.

I am thankful now for the Week from Hell. It made me realize what a life without her would be like: empty, cold, pointless, alone, and uncertain. Because of it, I found the patience to quietly clip off each sharp protective thorn one by one. I think I have just about gotten rid of the sharpest thorns now. Her bloom is not completely opened yet, but it is unfurling halfway now.

I am looking forward to see the ultimate stunning beauty of a fully opened blossom, its petals soft yellow and blushing, open to the sun and me, glistening with early morning drops of dew. She will bloom under my love, I swear.

She lies in my arms, giggling occasionally as something I do tickles her. I whisper, "Are you okay, honey? Are you still with me?"

Becca murmurs yes, yes, yes, over and over in my ear as I love her. I gently bite her bottom lip before burying my tongue deep in her warm mouth.

I want her to want me to do that to her all over. Her tongue tangles up with mine as she tastes and explores my mouth as well. I take deep breaths, trying to stay in the moment. My hands continue to roam all over her soft body, touching and teasing, but never quite getting there. Becca starts to moan, and her hips lift up slightly before she starts to move just a little. Her hips begin to twist in a circular motion. Giving part of my attention to her breasts, my free hand is able to glide down her smooth stomach, reaching her exposed yet hidden treasure.

My mantra is, "Always prepare the pussy. Caution before entering."

Since I am a bit big, I need to know she is ready for me before I go any further.

I slowly insert one long finger inside of her, rotating it around and around, judging her tightness. Her thighs spread a bit wider for me.

God, she's really tight.

I can feel her slick, wet walls weeping moisture for me. I try to stretch her a bit by inserting two fingers this time. I move my fingers around, deeper and deeper.

While I'm there, I might as well take a run at her G-spot. I find it on her front wall, stroking and pressing against it rhythmically. Becca moans even louder, and her hips begin to really move. I hold her as still as I can as I slide three fingers in her and stretch a bit more. I need to make sure I don't hurt her. The last thing I want to do is hurt her or anything like that.

I take my fingers out and spread the moisture all over the outside of her and then dive in for her hidden clitoris. It's hard, and I run my fingers over it in a circle, over and over and over again. I can do this all night if that's what it takes. I have fast hands. My middle finger is slightly deeper in her moist cleft, but basically my fingers move in a circular motion on her. Her hips are matching my movements, twisting and rising under my hand.

I lean over and suck her right extended nipple bud between my lips, sucking hard, then licking it, sucking hard and then licking. My fingers never stop massaging her damp folds. I can only hear her panting breaths getting faster and faster.

Sometimes she whispers to me, "Just like that, just like that, don't stop, please, don't stop."

Hell knows I'm not about to stop now.

I have her where I want her, watching this beautiful woman enjoy the sexual pleasure I am giving her. I am totally focused on her, monitoring her movements and sounds. I want to watch and feel her reach the ultimate peak of fulfillment under my hands. I don't want to use my mouth on her yet. I plan on saving that for later, after she really gets used to me.

My fingers speed up, sometimes dipping into her deeply before pulling out. She's so tight it's taking my breath away. Becca spreads her thighs even wider apart for me, giving me total access to all of her. Her knees are slightly bent as her legs move restlessly. Her body starts to stiffen slightly, and I can see a rosy blush spread across her breasts.

I think she's getting close to coming for me.

I notice her legs straighten completely out, still moving her hips and her breathing become more and more staccato. I keep my fingers moving on her, sometimes gently, sometimes harder. As I massage her moist folds, I dip my middle finger into her, knuckle-deep, and mirror the movements of my cock that will soon be doing the same thing to her. I hear shallow rapid breaths now coming from her.

Soon, please. I don't know how much longer my hard cock can wait for pleasure.

I want, desperately want, to watch her come. I want to feel her come undone under my fingers. I look up at her. Becca's eyes are closed, her mouth is slightly open as she pants, and I've never seen a more sensual woman. She's enjoying everything I am doing to her, feeling the sensations inside her body.

Her head tilts back, straining her long neck, and I hear her groan. "I'm so close, oh my God, Michael, Michael, so close for you, so open," she whispers my name and moans softly over and over.

"Don't worry, baby. I'm here. I'll get you there. Feel me touching you. I'm loving you. My fingers are inside of you, and you feel so warm and wet for me. Come for me, baby. Let me feel you come on my fingers. Just let it . . . happen. For me. Give in to it. Surrender to me," I whisper to her over and over, words of love and my desire for her.

I begin to notice a change come over her gradually but like a wave breaking forcefully. Her breathing becomes softer, and then it seems she is almost holding her breath. Her hips are now barely moving under my fingers. Her eyes are closed in concentration. She groans over and over with every shallow breath. I can tell it is about to happen to her. Total sexual surrender to me. I possess this woman. She is mine. Absolute possession of my sweet Becca.

With a final flick of my fingers, she falls apart in my arms. I watch her hips buck up violently as her orgasm sweeps through her. She is melting beneath my hand. She trembles under me, moaning, and suddenly, she screams my name. "Michael! Ohhhhhh! Michael! Michael! Michael! That's it, feel it with me."

And that is the sexiest sound I have ever heard. Becca, screaming my name, only mine. She screams for me. I make her feel like that. Me. Jesus, I wonder if the people next door could hear her. Hopefully, in a five-star hotel, the walls are plenty thick.

Yeah, that orgasm was all for me and all because of me.

That was the first orgasm that I gave to Becca. Maybe I should start counting them now. I've lost track of kisses by now. Keep track of all climaxes on a calendar, a journal, or something. I'm going to be the only man to ever see and hear her lose control like that.

Only me, from now on. She's mine.

I stop moving my fingers gently and cup her warm, steaming wet pussy in the palm of my hand. I try to soothe her as she comes down from her orgasm.

What a perfect first time. My only complaint is that I didn't get to stare into her green eyes when she came for me. If I'm lucky, maybe later.

I lie next to her patiently, letting her calm down a bit. But then my hands start to wander again. There is a beautiful sexy woman lying close to me, and I can smell the scent of her arousal all around me. It is a definite turn-on for me. I know I'm not going to be able to hold on much longer, so now, finally, it's my turn.

I can't breathe, feeling as though I've just run my usual six miles at a full-on sprint. I'm losing my mind and all control. All I can see is her. She fills my whole field of vision. There is no one else more important in my world than she is to me. I can touch her, hear her, smell her, and taste her. She is finally letting me know everything there is to know about her.

There is one more thing I need to make sure of first.

"Honey, do you want me to wear a condom tonight? I have shown you all my medical checks. I would never, ever hurt you. Tell me what to do. I want you to be totally comfortable. I will do whatever you want, just tell me, please."

She breathes softly, "I know you now. I trust you. I want to feel all of you inside me. Nothing to separate us. It's okay. I trust you. You won't hurt me."

Oh yes.

I start to kiss up her legs, taking my time and stroking the insides of her thighs above the stockings. When I get to her slit, I kiss it quickly but force myself to keep crawling up her body until I'm lying on top of her. I nudge her legs wide apart with my thighs. I think she's finally soft and wet enough to be able to take all of me inside her. My cock is lying hard between us, definitely more than ready for the challenge. I start by rubbing the top of my penis in her warm, silky sweetness, swirling it around before I insert just the very tip into her.

Oh fuck, even that much feels so good.

I pull back, feeling her tightness pull at me a little. This time, when I thrust forward, I go a little deeper. The walls of her are all around me, kissing and stroking me. It's so damn good. I pull out, but not all the way, before I push into her again, this time going deep almost all the way. I stay there for a moment, letting her get accustomed to the feeling. She murmurs my name.

I know this game I'm playing, but it's getting harder and harder to follow the rules. This time, I can't help but to thrust all the way in, balls deep inside of her. It's as though I can feel her tightness expanding to take all of me inside. She grips my ass as she wraps her legs around me, pulling me in deeper as if that is even possible.

I can see her stocking-covered legs and high heels wrapped around me out of the corners of my eyes. It's so hot and erotic. She's my every dream come true, all in one big fantasy.

I hold still for a minute, but then I whisper to her I'm going to move now. I whisper to her to tell me if I hurt her in any way. Not sure I could stop now, but I don't want to hurt her. I try, I really try, but the more I move, the more I have to move. I can't help but speed up until finally I'm pounding my dick into her.

I bury my face into her hair next to her ear. She moans and continues to dig her fingers into my back and my ass. I think she wants even more, so I do my best to give it to her. I start to moan and whisper in her ear how much I want and need her. Of course, as usual, I can't keep my feelings all bottled up inside me. It all rushes out of me, whispering to her, my lips kissing her ear as I breathe the words.

"Baby, do you want me? Because it's all for you. Every inch of my aching cock belongs to you. Do you feel me inside you? Take it; take all of me because I'm here for you. You belong to me, and I belong to you. Never forget it. I'll never let you go. Come for me again. This time I want to feel you come around me. Tight, squeeze me tighter. Oh baby, I'm not going to last much longer. You feel too good inside. I'm going to give it to you, all of me. I want you to love me as much as I love you. Oh God, let it go. Feel it, baby."

I knew I wasn't going to be able to be quiet. Everything I'm thinking and feeling bursts out of me. Becca is moving frantically underneath me, breathing hard and whispering how much she wants me. I suddenly feel her stop moving as she gasps, but inside her pussy is milking me dry.

I feel her orgasm number two coming on. Undulating pulses are all around me as Becca screams and groans again before suddenly jerking and thrashing upward under me. I hang on.

And that does it for me. I'm lost in it.

I feel my orgasm start in my legs and travel up and up through my whole body. I groan out her name almost incoherently, telling her I love her as the strongest orgasm I've ever had rips through me. It makes everything else pale in comparison. Jerking off alone is little more than a sneeze compared to this feeling. I pump out copious amounts of semen into Becca, feeling as though I can't get close enough to her. Collapsing on top of her, I let her breasts pillow me as I gasp out her name and struggle to breathe. My cock is still inside of her as we both try to calm down. Finally I find enough strength and will to slowly slide out of her. Even then, I'm still semi-hard.

How could that be happening? What is the world is wrong with me? Can I get enough of this woman?

Becca looks at me stunned. "Oh my God, Michael, oh my God. You're going to kill me. It's been so long, so long for me. I've never, I've never. . ." She has no more words as she snuggles against me and puts her head on my shoulder when I wrap my arms around her.

I hold her tight.

"You are an amazing lover, Michael. Wow."

I smile at her, "I think you've got that backwards, baby. You're so beautiful to me, so amazing. What an incredibly lucky man I am to have finally found you."

"I think I'm the lucky one," Becca murmurs softly, so softly I'm not sure if I heard it right.

I hold her in my arms as we relax together under the covers. I'm enjoying the feel of her body close to me. Soft murmurs as we adjust to the new relationship that now exists between us. I think the passion between us has stunned us both. Finally, we get up and head for the spacious bathroom. There is a beautiful big tub and plenty of bubble bath. I feel sure two people can fit into that tub. I look at Becca and she giggles at me, reading my mind.

Well, damn. Might as well.

I light the candle next to the tub, and it fills the room with a soft glow after I turn off the overhead light. I fill the tub with warm water and add just enough of the soap to make some bubbles. I turn to see Becca peeling her stockings slowly down her long legs. I like how they stay up by themselves although I admit I *love* the look of a garter belt. It tends to focus a man's eyes to all the right places.

What a sight to behold as she takes them carefully off. She had already taken off the heels, but I will hold that memory with me for a long time. The stockings and high heels made her legs look a mile long. And they were all wrapped around me.

I know I will dream about those legs around me for a long time to come.

Becca hesitates, but then she quietly tells me, "Michael, it's never been like this for me before. I didn't know I could want you so much. You make me feel wanted and beautiful to you. I don't think I've ever felt like this so deeply. Is it always like this for you?"

I take a deep breath, "No, baby. This is definitely special. We're made for each other. I think I'm just as overwhelmed as you are about what has happened between us."

"God, if it is like this for everyone, how would people ever get anything done?" I look at her in surprise before we both start to laugh.

The bath is soothing for both of us. We stay together holding each other in the warm soapy water until our fingers wrinkle. I wrap her in a soft white bath towel and carry her back to the floral-covered canopy bed. By this time it's past midnight, and I can tell Becca is just about asleep. I've worn her out. I lay her down gently, and then I pull her into my arms with her back to my chest. My arms are wrapped around her as she drifts off to sleep, relaxed and content.

We have entered a new phase in our relationship. I have finally turned the page to find the sweet romance. I am so looking forward to reading Becca like an open book, everything ultimately revealed. I want to see this story through to its conclusion. I close my eyes, the song "Turning Page" by a group called Sleeping at Last going through my head softly and offering me hope.

I lay awake for hours, watching her sleep. Her face is soft and relaxed. Her lips slightly parted as she breathes. She moves very rarely but is always touching me in her sleep. This is the first time I have seen her asleep, truly vulnerable to me. She must trust me to allow me this intimacy. She does not snore or talk in her sleep, but sometimes she breathes deeply before settling down in deep sleep. Her face is pressed into the pillow, and she sleeps with one leg raised and bent at the knee on her side and stomach. Sometimes she faces in my direction, sometimes she turns to face away. But she's always near me, touching me somewhere.

It is all I can do to let her sleep. I want to wake her up with my caresses and slip my tongue past those parted lips. I don't give in to the temptation though. It is enough to get to sleep with her after sharing ourselves. I know having her once is not going to be enough for me. It didn't slake my hunger for her at all. It simply increased my need to have her in every way possible. It will never be enough for me.

What an incredible night. It was better than I could have ever hoped for. The reality is surpassing the dream. I can be romantic when I try. I tried my best. I am a perfectionist after all. It was worth the entire torturing wait. I can love her now. I am firmly in her life. She has let down her guard enough to let me into her heart. I picture snapping several sharp thorns off her slender stem.

Forever. We sleep together.

Maroon 5's "She Will Be Loved" is playing in my dreams tonight when I fall asleep.

CHAPTER 12

Sweet, Sexy Seductions

I slowly wake to a new dawn, feeling so content and satisfied. I look over at the face of the sexy angel sleeping next to me. I have my hand curved protectively over her left breast, feeling a hint of her nipple. I guess I slept like that. As I gaze at her, green sleepy eyes slide open. She lays there staring at me. I stare back, hoping she isn't having any regrets.

"Good morning, baby. How are you feeling this morning?" I whisper. I feel my cock start to twitch and grow.

It's the morning, so there it is. I can't help it. Sometimes I have an out-of-control cock.

Becca scoots over to lay a bit closer to me. As she stretches out touching me, it becomes obvious she notices my morning erection. She lays there for a moment before asking me how I am feeling.

"Good morning to you too, Mr. Stevens. How are you today?" She glances down at my hand, which is still cupping her breast, not letting go when she moved.

I answer that I am feeling quite up today.

"Feeling me up already, Michael?"

I think it's pretty clear how I'm feeling, but we did have a late night last night, and it's still very early in the morning. I'm trying very hard to be good and not wear her out. After all, we're a real couple now. We can make love whenever we both want.

"Can't seem to stop myself. My hands end up on you all by themselves. I have no control over it. You feel so good." I start to caress her gently, wondering if she is up for this.

We did stay up late last night. I seem to be already up for it. Obviously. Up and wide awake.

Becca takes a deep breath. She appears to be considering something. The wheels in her mind are definitely turning. I don't know what's going through that head of hers, but I aim to find out. "Becca, is there something wrong, baby?"

Whatever it is, please tell me. I'll try to fix it.

She turns and looks at me. "I didn't get enough to eat last night."

I'm dumbfounded. We had a delicious meal, I thought. I mean, we had dessert and everything.

What does she mean? Maybe we'd better get up and go to breakfast. I know it must be good here. I don't want her to be hungry for food, only for me.

I just looked at her, not knowing what to really say other than I am glad she has a good appetite.

I am about to suggest we get dressed and go to breakfast.

"Come here to me," Becca murmurs softly. Before I can react, she turns in my arms and starts to kiss her way down my chest. I swallow quickly, not knowing what to do other than lay back and enjoy. I put my hands behind my head and watch. I know this position shows off my chest and muscled arms. I hope she pays attention to that.

I want her to know I'm her strong man, and she's my soft woman. I am very conscious of the differences between us. I feel masculine next to her sweet femininity. I'm not really used to women taking control, but I'll give it a try for her. Her lips are soft and moist on me. Sometimes she licks and sucks gently and sometimes she kisses, but she keeps slowly working her way down my body. She gives both of my nipples equal attention before kissing down my rippled stomach.

Oh yeah, this is good.

My dick is getting harder and harder, but she ignores that until she gets to my happy trail below my belly button. She swirls her tongue in my navel and then begins to lick her way down south. I can see where this is heading. My cock does too, already stiffening and almost swaying in the breeze. I can't help a small grin as I lay back to watch.

What a wonderful way to wake up. Please, shit, give me some stamina.

Think control, Stevens. What can I think about to help me last? The alphabet? Too short. I guess it is back to the fifty states for me.

Becca's mouth finally reaches the tip of my dick. She takes it slowly into her mouth, tightening her lips around me. Suddenly I can feel her warm, moist tongue licking the underside of the head of my cock.

That feels simply amazing. How did she know that?

She starts to take more and more of me into her mouth, sucking softly and licking up and down my length. She does this over and over, slowly increasing the strength of her caresses. I hiss the breath into my mouth between my teeth as she finds a particularly good place to caress. And all the while I'm watching her head as her mouth moves on me. I reach down and put my hands in her hair. I move her head gently in time with her caresses. I can't help moving my hips, trying not to thrust too harshly into her welcoming mouth.

"Oh baby, oh, just like that, don't stop, just like that." I am barely breathing out the words. I can't stop whispering to her as she loves me.

My hips can't stop either, and neither does Becca. She tightly suctions her mouth around me and gradually lets me slide out of her mouth for a minute.

Oh no! Don't leave me, don't stop now.

She blows softly up and down my length, cooling me off but really making me even hotter for her. Becca grabs the base of my cock and begins to move her hand up and down me, squeezing me at the same time as she's taking my cock back into her mouth. Her lips tighten around me.

I start to worry a little about her teeth. They are close, too close to me. Don't bite me, please, baby.

She moves her hands down to my balls and gently squeezes, causing me to cry out. Her hand moves back to my cock, grabbing tightly this time and pumping up and down with her mouth moving just like her hand. I can feel my balls start to squeeze upward, and I know I'm about to come in her mouth if she keeps this up. I try to grunt it out, letting her know that if she doesn't want me to come in her mouth, she needs to get the hell out the way now.

This time, I can't talk, I can't even think. She keeps on sliding her mouth up and down my thick cock all the way to the back of her throat. I didn't think anything could be better than last night, but this is shaping up to be one hell of a blow job. Many minutes, hours go by as she loves me.

The abso-fucking-lutely ace of all blow jobs ever.

My chest comes up off the pillow as my body bows in pleasure. My head slams back on the pillow beneath me. I feel it coming up inside of me.

Oh my God, oh my God, don't stop, don't stop, please don't stop now, baby, baby, don't stop now. Just, just like that.

Suddenly, my throbbing cock twitches on its own and seems to erupt into Becca's mouth. She takes all of it as I spurt everything I have into her, pulsing over and over and over again. I feel myself give her all of my heart and soul. This is not just a physical act to me. It's not just sex. I hope she feels how much I am giving her of myself.

I give all of me to her, nothing held back. I can't give her any more of me. My hoarse groans of extreme pleasure come up tearing out of my mouth as I yell practically at the top of my lungs, "Fuuuccckk! Becca, baby! *Fuck!*" through my stunning orgasm. I think I almost pass out from the feeling. I am panting with every ounce of strength I have left.

Oh fuck, fuck. No.

I begin to become aware that I screamed it out loud unconsciously. *Oh no!*

The whole hotel probably heard me, not just the people next door. She surprised me so much I lost my head. I try hard not to use obscenities in front of a woman, especially one as special to me as her although I may slip at times. I've been around Marines so long, surrounded by tough guys who talk like that all day, and I can cuss with the best of them. Sometimes no other word than "fuck" will do in the situation.

I know my thoughts are sometimes a bit crass, but I try to keep them to myself. I feel terrible, yelling that out in front of her. I can only hope she somehow understands I lost all control. She did that to me. Spent, I collapse back onto the pillows, unable to even move anymore. I see Becca licking her lips as she slides up my body.

She leans in and gently whispers in my ear, "You taste good. And you feel like steel encased in silk in my mouth."

I've died and gone to heaven. I know it.

When I have regained my strength and can focus again, we decide to get dressed and go down for breakfast. I am still feeling a bit shaky, not quite believing what she did to me. I let Becca shower first, knowing she will take longer than I will. I admit I'm a little nervous of being attacked again if I were to join her in the shower.

I mean, I know I'm a fast reloader, but I need a little time here. We'll have to save shower sex for another time. I am starting to doubt my ability to handle this woman. She is obviously enjoying handling me.

She is pleasantly surprised to see that I had packed some clothes for us to wear this morning. Nothing quite like going down to breakfast in a gown and tux. Granted the clothes aren't what we would normally wear, but the T-shirts and jeans at least make us appear respectable. I've done a good job guessing Becca's size because the jeans I picked up for her fit—maybe a little tight, but I like that.

Of course, I know Becca has no underwear on because I thought she'd have some panties on her under her gown, so I didn't get her any. I didn't bother with a bra, liking that idea. Her ass in the tight jeans looks especially great to me since I know she is pantiless. My mind keeps returning to that fact. Her unrestrained breasts bounce slightly as she walks.

I can't keep my eyes off her as we head toward the dining room to eat.

I hope others don't notice her braless state even though it is blatantly obvious to me. Who knew her gown was going to be strapless and that she wouldn't wear a bra as well as panties?

The hostess leads us to a table looking out over the luxurious garden. I have my hand on the small of her back as we make our way through the tables. I pull her chair out for her and then quickly slide it under her as she sits down gracefully. I take my own seat across from her swiftly.

No underwear at all under that silver gown last night. So no underwear under the jeans and top this morning either.

She continues to shock me just a bit although I can't help feeling delighted. I like seeing this sexy, playful side of her. We have a delightful breakfast before heading out to look around the property. Checkout is by one o'clock, so we still have plenty of time.

We spend part of the morning exploring the hotel. There are shops and even a clothing store. The Golden Horseshoe Golf Course is right next door, so we walk down to watch the golfers teeing off on the first hole. It is interesting to talk to some of the people we meet as we stroll around the grounds.

Most of them are tourists from out of town staying at the inn. We find there is a day spa at the hotel. Becca says she wishes she had time to take advantage of all the inn's spa could offer. I think maybe we'll come back sometime so she can do it: all the facials, massages, and manicures she wants.

Speaking of taking advantage, I realize that there was one last thing I hadn't done that I had originally planned. I only hope I still have the strength left after last night and this morning.

As we get back into our room, I immediately stand in front of Becca and pull her T-shirt over her head. I quickly dispense with her jeans as well. She stands beautifully naked in front of me, looking at me and wondering what is going to happen next.

I swiftly drop to my knees in front of her, grab her ass, and place my mouth directly over her sweetness. I want her to spread her legs wider for me, but she immediately steps back and puts her hands as a shield over her mound.

I immediately realize she is saying no and can't help protesting. "No, Becca, don't hide yourself from me. Never from me. I love you, I want you. I want to know you as intimately as I can. I want you to know me that way also. There is nothing you should hide from me, no reason to feel self-conscious or embarrassed in front of me. You are a breathtakingly stunning woman, perfect for me."

I make sure she is looking at me before I continue. "I know it has been a long time since you have felt this vulnerable and exposed in front of a man. But here I am, just as exposed and vulnerable to you. I lay everything I am out in front of you, hoping you will know me and let me in your heart. There is nothing else more important to me. I love you with every breath I take. Now that we have been together like this, it is even better than I imagined. I am stunned by how I feel, about the emotions you bring out in me simply with a look or a touch. I can't get enough of you. Let me live my life trying."

I look up at her, pleading with my eyes. I want to give her this more than anything. Becca gave me such an amazing gift this morning. I want to do the same for her. I reach out again and pull her hands away. I bend upward so my mouth can fit over her pussy, and I grab her ass and begin to lick her folds with my tongue. She is struggling against me slightly, twisting and turning as if she wants to get away. I find her clit and give it all of my attention, but not too intensely.

I love that she's waxed and that the folds around her are smooth and bare. I can see everything she has. I love what a woman looks like in all her secret places, like a soft flower, its petals protecting the sensitive core. I want to know this part of her body better than she does herself. She can't really hold still very well and keeps moaning and turning in my hands. I thrust my tongue in and out of her, tasting her sweetness. Before I can really get started, Becca pulls away from me again, twisting out of my grip. I look up at her, startled.

"What do you need, Becca? I'm here. I'll give you anything you need. Tell me."

"I can't, I can't do that. I need you to be inside me. Now."

"You got it then, babe."

Becca pushes me back on the bed, making sure my head is on the pillow. She reaches down and simply unzips my jeans, pulling me out. Of course, I am hard. I always seem to be hard for her. She throws her leg over me and centers herself on my cock. Before I can think straight, she quickly lowers herself down on me moaning as I completely fill her. I'm still fully dressed while she is totally exposed to me, a beautiful feminine figure.

So damn hot.

She grabs my shoulders, leaning over my chest, and starts to move quickly up and down, pressing hard on me. I put my hands on her ass and try to match her rhythm. She keeps moving and moving up and down on me, riding me and rocking back and forth.

Then suddenly she leans back on my slightly upraised knees and puts her hand between her legs. I see her fingers moving over and over in a circular motion down between her thighs. She starts moaning loudly, and her fingers fly even faster. I can't believe what I'm seeing in front of my own eyes. She is pleasuring herself on me, undulating her hips and grinding her pussy down on to me.

It is so intimate and erotic that I am spellbound, watching her and holding my breath. I am being allowed to see how she makes herself come.

She thrusts her full breasts out and starts to knead them, pulling on her nipples with one hand while the other continues to work her clit. I love she is sharing this with me. I love knowing this about her. My cock fills completely inside of her, skin stroking skin, as I feel the back of her because I'm in her so deep. Becca starts to stiffen her legs tightly around me, and her breathing changes speed.

I'm getting close to climaxing just watching her, listening to her.

"Open your eyes for me, baby. I love you, I love you. I want to see your eyes when you come with me inside you. Look at me," I beg her, hoping that she's close, too.

I don't want to come before her. I need to let her go first. I start to think of state capitals, trying to shut my mind off what's happening to me and right in front of me.

Richmond, Raleigh, Columbus . . .

Finally, I feel the beginnings of Becca's orgasm stirring deep down inside around my dick as it is cradled by her pussy.

Thank fuck.

Her trembling before the strength of her orgasm sets me off. Both of us stare into each other's eyes as sharp waves of pleasure hit us at the same time. I knew I wanted to see her eyes while she comes. Her eyes lose focus as she rides it out, staring into my eyes as well. They say the eyes are the windows to the soul, and I want to see deeply into her.

She screams suddenly, "Michael, oh Michael, I love you, I love you!" I know my eyes are burning into hers as I feel everything happening to my body.

Gray fire lancing into soft, olive green.

And I groan her name as I pump myself into her, telling her how much I love her, too. My eyes almost close involuntarily as I come spurting all I have to give inside of her, my gift to my woman from a man who is enjoying possessing her. I watch her eyes turn dark with passion deep in those green depths. I see the surprise and wonder as it sweeps into her gaze on me.

"I love you, I love you, I love you. Love me please, baby." I breathe the words passionately to her.

I mean it with everything inside me. She is everything to me. She said she loves me. Oh God. Thank you. She has said she loves me. I need to write it on my calendar at home so that I never forget this day.

I sink back onto the pillows with Becca on top of me, still joined. Her face is flushed and sweaty, and her hair is all over the place. Bedroom eyes and bedroom hair make her look seductive and sexually satisfied for me.

She's so sexy. But I still can't get over the fact we came together. In all the times I've ever had sex, I know that has never happened to me. I knew it could, but I never could seem to make it happen. Only with Becca. Only her.

My only regret is I didn't get to taste her come in my mouth. I won't forget she didn't get it that way. I love giving oral sex, so I'm definitely going to try it again sometime soon. I know I can do it. Maybe if she's lying down, that would help her lose control better. She seemed a little shocked by it. Perhaps it's something she's not used to doing. I remember it has been a long time since she has had a sexual relationship. I now feel certain Tripp never did that for her if she is so shy about it. I'll try anything. Because someday I'm going to taste her pleasure.

I'd say this was the best date ever. This is going to be damn near impossible to top.

I love the song by Snow Patrol called "Open Your Eyes."
Every minute from this minute now
We can do what we like anywhere
I want so much to open your eyes
'Cause I need you to look into mine.

CHAPTER 13

Family Matters

We go home after our amazing night and morning and spend Saturday watching old movies and cuddling on the couch. I love how relaxed Becca is being with me. I learn more and more about her by just spending time with her. I love watching her fix us a little lunch and how she sits close to me. I can't keep my hands off her, and suddenly I find she's touching me, too. Just little innocent touches, but touches nonetheless. When I think about last night, I get a little breathless, as if this is all some kind of dream that's going to go away if I'm not careful.

I must not fuck up again. I remember that Week from Hell and plan on not ever going back THERE *again.*

Late in the afternoon, I leave Becca's to run a few errands. I don't want to crowd her or overwhelm her, so I try to give her some time and space. I ask her if it is okay for me to come back tonight. I certainly don't want to assume that just because we shared the most amazing sex of our lives, it doesn't mean I don't have to ask permission first. I'm hoping to get into her bedroom this time. I don't want her to think I think it's a done deal after last night. She shyly tells me she would love for me to come back.

That sounds good to me. I am definitely coming back to her.

Besides, I have to make a phone call for a plan I have up my sleeve for Sunday. Since Becca has agreed to let me into her life, I need to meet her family. They need to know who I am since I'm not going anywhere if I can help it. I've looked up her sister's phone number in Portsmouth and call her to introduce myself to her once I am home. Their names are Roger and Sara Sheldon.

From her sister's reaction to me telling her who I am, I can plainly see Becca was telling me the truth about there not being a significant man in her life for quite some time. Her sister Sara seems a bit shocked. It dawns on me that she hasn't been told about me. That concerns me because I would have thought Becca would at least tell her sister that she's dating someone now. Sara has no idea who is this strange man talking to her.

Umm. What the fuck?

I tell her more about who I am and invite her and her husband Roger up to Williamsburg for lunch on Sunday at the Williamsburg Winery. They have a delightful restaurant called the Gabriel Archer Tavern, which has outdoor seating on a patio beneath a beautiful wisteria-covered trellis. I've heard Becca say this is one of their favorite things to do, so I'm hoping it would be okay. I don't care what I have to do, just so long as her sister and husband meet me and know I'm now a part of Becca's life.

Permanently, if I have my way, but I keep that to myself.

Thankfully, they ultimately agree to come up, after quite a bit of almost pleading on my part, and meet us at one o'clock at the winery for a little lunch together. I want to meet them, and I want them to get to know me.

I debate whether I should tell Becca my plan for tomorrow or just surprise her. Maybe I'll tell her tonight. I don't want her to be mad at me for going behind her back. I don't want to be a secret in her life, so it's important for me to win the approval of her family.

I know my sister Anne will love her and accept her, only being happy that I've finally settled down somewhere safe and close.

But I know Becca is very close to her family, so naturally I'm determined to make the best damn first impression that I can. I definitely feel they are very protective of her, watching over her during these years she's been alone.

And I need to get past her sister first before I take on her older brother.

I return to Becca's in the early evening, kissing her hello in the foyer. I never want to lose sight of kissing her hello and good-bye. I think it's an important reminder that we are lovers, not just friends. I admit I have lost track of our kiss count. That is a very good thing in my mind.

Hopefully, I'll be allowed to give her so many orgasms that I lose track of those as well. I think again of keeping an orgasm calendar. Sounds good to me. I want to know how many I can give her. Triple digits? Now that's a goal to strive for.

We go upstairs and settle in for an evening of relaxing and sitting close together on the couch to watch mindless television. I brush kisses across Becca's neck and temple every so often, letting her know I'm here with her. When it starts to get late, I can tell she's beginning to get tired.

Well, then, the sooner I make love to her, the sooner she can sleep. Seems simple to me. Besides, I have a plan.

Finally she reaches up and puts her arm around my neck, pulling my mouth down to hers for a sweet kiss. That doesn't last for too long because suddenly I can't seem to get enough of her. I stand up, sweeping her up into my arms. She protests a bit, but thank goodness she's giggling.

My arms are strong enough to carry her anywhere. I make my way down the hall until finally I make it to her bedroom. There was a time when I thought she'd never let me in here.

I'm so fucking glad I'm actually here.

I lay her down on her bed and stand up straight looking down at her lying there and looking so damn tempting.

Oh, what to do? There are so many possibilities.

I lean over her, starting to slowly undress her. Part of me feels as though I'm unwrapping my birthday presents, one present at a time. She is slowly revealed to me in all of her beauty. Becca is already starting to pant as she reaches for my clothes as well. It doesn't take her long to get me undressed.

I run my hands all up and down her soft, smooth body, murmuring to her how lovely she is. Unbelievably, she starts whispering in my ear all the things I need her to say to me. She tells me shyly how sexy I am to her, and how good I make her feel when I'm inside her. And that she is falling in love with me as well.

That's the greatest thing I've heard in a long time. I realize if I don't step things up a bit, this is going to be over before I want it to be.

I run my fingers slowly down her, stopping only when I slip two fingers inside to check how she's doing.

It's only the gentlemanly thing to do, I think.

Finding how warm and slick she is already lets me know she wants me, too. I think I'm in the mood for something a bit more energetic tonight, so I really need her to be wet for me. I stand her up next to the bed, but tell her to bend over and hold on to whatever she can.

I think she better really hold on because I think I may get a little rough and get carried away. I don't want to hurt her, though.

Looking at her bending over for me, I run my hands lovingly over her sweet full ass, telling her how good she looks to me. I can see everything I need to. My cock is so ready to be inside of her. I move to stand behind her and stroke my hands up and down her back. Positioning myself, I ram my dick deep inside of her suddenly, thrusting in and upward, hoping she can take me like this. I feel her pussy clench involuntarily around me as I start to move, I mean, really move.

I grab the sides of her ass and piston myself over and over inside of her, muttering to her to hold on tight. Her internal muscles keep doing delightful clenching things around me. It's like she's grabbing on to me. Her tight pussy is caressing me not only on the way in, but on the way out as well. Unbelievably, I hear her tell me to move deeper and harder.

My God, I'm giving you every aching inch I've got. I'm doing my best for you.

My head starts to fall back as my stomach muscles keep me moving in and out of her. My balls start to tighten up, and I know I'm about to shoot my load inside of her. I'm trying hard to last, so when I feel her start to tremble around me, it's almost too good to bear.

Thank fuck, she comes deeply groaning, clenching me and shuddering around me. I thrust into her five more times before I can't hold on anymore. I grab her as close as I can get her and push myself in as deeply as I can. I feel the warm stream pulse out of me over and over as I throw my head back and moan deeply, shouting her name through gritted teeth.

Oh shit! I think my eyes have rolled back into my head.

We fall together across the bed, gasping for breath and trying to slow our heartbeats. Long quiet moments pass as we calm down together in each other's arms. Before we get into bed, I go into the bathroom and get a warm, wet washcloth. We are both a bit of a mess. I tenderly clean Becca up between her legs since I'm the reason she's dripping me all down her thighs.

Actually I find I like that, I like that a lot. Shit, there seems to be a lot of it. I'm feeling quite proud of myself.

We climb into bed and pull the bedcovers up over us. She snuggles tightly to me, putting her head on my shoulders as we both still try to calm down. I reach over and put out the light, shrouding us in darkness. Becca sweetly kisses me good-night before passing out next to me. It's so comforting to hear and see her breathing softly in her sleep next to me, her lips slightly open as she breathes. She must trust me now, considering how easily she falls to sleep with me. It takes me a little longer to fall asleep, but after that great orgasm, it becomes automatic to relax.

My last thoughts are of olive green eyes, and I am a lucky man.

When we wake up the next morning, I'm draped all over Becca. My arms are around her, and my thigh is nestled up between her legs so high I can feel her moist heat. I can't even get enough of her while I'm asleep, it seems. As she slowly wakes up next to me, I remember I have a surprise for her. Somehow I forgot out about it last night. I guess I was a bit distracted and overtaken by subsequent events.

When she's fully awake, I decide to tell her. I try to keep my mind on the conversation, but my hands are tending to wander just a bit. I kiss her good morning before I start.

"Becca, honey, I called your sister yesterday. She and Roger are coming up today so I can meet them. I thought we'd have lunch with them at the winery."

"What? What do you mean you called my sister? You called her without discussing it with me first?"

Uh oh, she sounds a little pissed at me. Damn it.

"Please don't be mad at me. She didn't even seem to know I exist. When were you going to tell them about me? I want them to know me since I'm not planning on going anywhere. It's time for me to know your family and your friends as well, for that matter. It's all part of me being included in your life. You said yes, you know."

I'm feeling slightly hurt here.

"We've only really just met, Michael. I know we've been dating for a while now but, it's too soon for you to meet them. We're still getting to know each other."

"You don't want me to know your family? Or for them to know me?"

"Michael, I guess I haven't mentioned you to Sara because I wanted to make sure we really are a couple before I told her. But, since you seemed to have already arranged it, I guess... it'll be okay. It's just I haven't introduced anyone to them for a very long time. I haven't dated since before I married, you know."

"Honey, I don't think we could be any more of a couple than if we tried. We are definitely now a real couple. I think it's obvious to anyone who even looks at us we're lovers. I can't keep my eyes or hands off you for any length of time. I want to meet the people who love you and who you love. I want to them to know me. Don't be nervous. They're going to love me. I can be very charming when I want to be."

My fingers slide softly up and down her back and then lower to draw circles on her ass.

Yes, I really am your very own Prince Charming. Get used to it. I'm serious and here to stay now.

"Yes, Mr. Stevens, you most certainly can be. I'm sure your charms and fast thinking gets you many things."

"Is that so, Ms. Connelly? And who have I charmed lately?" I caress her full breasts lovingly.

I wonder briefly if she'll let me make love to them. I've got to somehow make that happen.

"I'm afraid it's just me that you've bewitched with your considerable charms, Mr. Stevens. It better be only me. I never had a chance once I looked into your eyes. When you came to my rescue, well, it was already a done deal."

"I'm incredibly pleased to hear that. Perhaps I can charm you to take a shower with me now? I'm feeling the need to clean you thoroughly."

Shit, I want to run my soapy hands all over her.

"Are you saying I'm dirty, Michael? Do I smell or something?"

She looks horrified.

"Most definitely, Ms. Connelly. You smell like a sweet, aroused woman, the most wonderful scent in the world to a man like me. I think I've created an insatiable maniac."

At least I hope so.

"Come and let me get you clean again."

Umm. Ms. Connelly. I'm thinking "Mrs. Stevens" sounds a hell of a lot better. She's mine. I suddenly want everyone to know it as well.

Something to think about . . . for certain. Mr. and Mrs. Michael G. Stevens.

I know I can't imagine the rest of my life anymore without this woman by my side. I don't want to live my life alone. I hope she feels the same way, too. We're good together.

I get her up and out of the bed, pulling her to the shower before she can think. I think it's most definitely time to try a little shower sex. The warm water washes down on both of us as I pull her into my arms. I lather up my hands and start to wash all up and down her legs. I work my way up to her hips and glide soapy hands all over her as much as I can reach.

I even wash her hair for her, using her sweet-smelling shampoo and conditioner before rinsing all the soapsuds away. I want to take care of my woman. Becca's hands have been busy cleaning me, too, but I'm completely focused on her. Looking into her eyes, I reach around, putting my hands under her ass and lifting her to me. Naturally, my cock is ready for this action. Her legs automatically wrap around my waist as I slowly ease into her, holding still once I get inside.

Her back is against the cold, wet tiles in the shower. Maybe someday I'll take her with her legs up on my shoulders.

Yeah, that sounds good.

Completely exposed to me.

Helpless.

"Michael, please! Please, move!"

"No, baby. I'm making love to you. Let me love you. I'm going to go slow. I need it . . . slow. Just enjoy me in you."

Using my hands, I move her back and forth on me, as slowly as I can go. No matter how much she begs and moves, I'm giving this to her slow. I want it to last forever. She starts trying to thrust her hips, but I clamp down on her movements. I want her to just absorb all the pleasure inside of her. She whimpers, making my whole body heat up, but I don't give in. I'm sliding slowly, almost barely moving.

I start to notice Becca has practically stopped breathing. Her long legs are all around my waist as I brace her up against the cool shower wall. The warm water continues to wash over us. I love how she looks all wet and barely breathing for me. This is so erotic, and it's rapidly becoming too good to last.

Maintaining my slow slide in and out of her is getting harder and harder to do. But I grit my teeth and hang on. Becca suddenly moans from deep inside her as a powerful wave of pleasure pulses over and over through her. Her arms are around my neck as she holds on to me and shudders with the feeling.

I love watching her come. It's the most intense thing in the world, knowing I am the man who makes her feel that way. Three hard thrusts up and into her and suddenly I'm joining her, groaning out her name incoherently. For once, she took my voice and breath away. We stumble out of the shower, grab towels, and fall back into bed for a well-deserved late-morning nap.

When we both wake up again, I look at the clock and realize we've got things to do. Becca's sister Sara and brother-in-law Roger will be here at one. I need to get home, change into fresh clothes, and groom myself so I can make a good first impression. I leave Becca to her own preparations, kissing her quickly and telling her I'll be back at twelve-thirty. I want to make sure we're first at the tavern instead of them waiting on us.

When I get back, she is dressed in a lightweight pink summer floral dress with sandals. As I kiss her, I sweep my hands up her dress, checking to be sure she has panties on this time.

Thank goodness.

They're blue silk and lacy and pretty. But at least now I know they're there. I could not make it through lunch if I was torturing myself thinking of a pantiless woman next to me. She laughs at me, telling me I'm nuts.

Yeah, I'm nuts about her. My nuts are nuts for her, too.

I'll show her my nuts. I actually have nuts. I happen to be quite attached to them. They belong to her as well now. She can have my nuts whenever she wants.

We arrive at the outdoor tavern with plenty of time, getting a table on the patio outside under the wisteria-covered trellis. I go ahead and order a bottle of the Governor's White. It's a Riesling, and Becca tells me it is the wine they usually order. While we wait, I glance over the menu, thinking everything looks good. I notice she seems to be a little nervous, so I take hold of her hand and pull it over to me, kissing her knuckles softly. She takes a deep breath, slowly letting it out before smiling at me.

That's my girl. It's going to be fine. I promise. Let me meet your family.

When Sara and Roger arrive, I stand and hold Sara's chair out for her before shaking Roger's hand. We ask about the drive up from Portsmouth and basically make small talk as we all make up our minds about lunch. Sara turns to me after ordering. I plan on having a turkey-and-brie sandwich while Becca ordered shrimp and grits.

She likes grits?

Eww.

"Michael, you certainly surprised me when you called. I didn't know Becca was seeing anyone. How long have you been dating?"

"Since we met around the middle of June. I saw her across a restaurant and eventually got up the nerve to introduce myself. I've been lucky enough to be able to get to know Becca now. I am new to the area. I retired from the Marines and chose to settle here. My sister and her family live nearby in Richmond. Becca has done a great job of showing me around. She is an excellent tour guide and makes everything so much fun. I've enjoyed spending time with her and thankful every day she said yes when I asked her out the first time."

Becca speaks up. "Michael, you know it has been just as fun for me too. I have enjoyed sharing my favorite places with you."

"I know, baby, thank you."

Sara continues. "You said you were in the Marines. What did you do?"

"I retired as a Colonel with thirty years' active duty. After many tours in Iraq and Afghanistan, I was ready for a change in my life. I could tell I had advanced my career about as far as it was ever going to go. It is time to settle down. I've moved around so much in my life that a stable home appeals to me. I bought a house in the Two Rivers neighborhood off Route 5, about six miles north of Becca's place."

I know exactly how far it is from my house to hers.

"Well, I hope you like Williamsburg as much as we all do."

"Yes, I am finding I like it very much. Becca is a large reason for that."

Even though there is a difference in their ages, it is apparent that Becca and Sara are simply sisters, laughing with each other easily. I make a point of telling them about myself, my career in the Marines, and the places I've lived. Turns out Roger had been a Marine as well when he was younger. We regard each other with the kind of respect fellow Marines have for one another. I can see this has scored big points for me as far as he is concerned.

Our meals arrive. My sandwich is just what I wanted. I watch Becca try the shrimp and grits. The shrimp are in a red sauce with peppers and onions on top of the grits. She loves them, saying they are just as good as the ones she could get in Charleston.

"Here, Michael, eat my grits."

What did she say?

"No, thank you, honey. I am happy with my turkey."

My own turkey sandwich.

"You don't like grits? What's the matter? Didn't your mom fix grits for you when you were small? You grew up in Mississippi."

"She made me eat cream of wheat."

Creamy hot cereal in the winter.

"Are you sure you were born in the South? Cream of wheat sounds like a Midwestern or Northern thing to me."

"Honey, remember? I told you I was born in Jackson."

In Mississippi, it's the capital city of the state.

"Well, won't you give them a try?"

"I don't like gritty things in my mouth. I prefer smooth textured foods to eat."

Definitely smooth.

"Michael, these are unique, unlike anything you have ever tried. Okay?"

"I don't know. I can't understand the appeal of grits. Are you sure all Southerners enjoy grits?"

I don't believe it.

"Oh yes. I am a true Southern girl. I enjoy eating my grits."

"Then I hope you enjoy them, baby."

Enjoy me.

"I plan to enjoy. They are delicious and different from any grits I have ever tried before."

I'll give you something unique and delicious to enjoy later on.

I can't believe we are having this conversation in front of Roger and Sara. They are silent, just listening and watching us. I guess they are used to Becca's quick thinking. Finally, Becca grins at me and gives it up. She finishes her grits in record time.

I gradually start to try to get to know them and find out that Roger is some kind of genius when it comes to physics and astronomy. He tells me about all of his expensive telescopes and his astronomy group. I think it would be interesting to go out sometime with him and look up at the stars. He seems to know the names of all of them.

Becca says, "Roger loves Albert Einstein."

I laugh when he sticks his tongue out at her, mimicking the famous photo of Einstein doing the same thing. Becca giggles at him.

I make sure they know I've settled in Williamsburg now. Every so often, I catch Sara staring at me curiously with her mouth slightly open.

Please don't drool at me, but I hope you like what you see.

My eyes stay on Becca as much as possible because she's just so damn cute. I know she really has no idea how beautiful she is to me.

Yeah, I'm definitely planning on staying here now I've got Becca in my life.

Lunch is casual and gets easier as we all relax and get used to being together. Maybe the second bottle of wine I ordered had something to do with it. Sara definitely starts laughing and smiling a whole lot more. We are the fun table on the outdoor patio.

I start to wonder if she's getting a little tipsy. From what I've heard, they all enjoy wineries quite frequently. It's become a favorite day trip of theirs, driving all over the state and finding little out-of-the-way wineries. I hope I'll get to come along sometime.

After our meals are finished and we are still working on the second bottle, Becca quietly excuses herself to go to the restroom. I'm sitting there alone with her family. I can see they are going to seize this chance to talk to me without her being there to hear.

Sara looks at me and says, "Michael, you need to know something before this goes any further. Becca is . . . fragile. Her emotions are delicate. She was hurt very badly when her marriage failed. She was young, and she's not really over the pain from that time. She had married Tripp so fast we couldn't believe it. But what could I do? She seemed so happy and really enjoyed living in California and South Carolina, even though she was a long way from us."

"I had no idea there was a problem until they moved back to Virginia soon after our mama died. There were little clues, looking back. We left for a trip to France and when we got back, she called us suddenly to tell us

Tripp had left her. She was incoherent and sobbing. It was a very difficult time. She couldn't eat or sleep and seemed to want to stay in her bed all day. It was the only place she felt safe."

"She was in a daze all the time, struggling to make sense of the new reality of her life. One moment she thinks she is happily married, and the next thing she knows she is alone and abandoned by the one man she had trusted with her heart and life. We've had to deal with times over the years when she got really down, still blaming herself for not being a good enough wife to him. I don't understand. I know once she surprised him with a weekend at the Greenbrier Resort in White Springs, West Virginia. She arranged for him to play the championship course there as well. I know she loved him because she missed him when he was away on his ship especially while they were stationed in South Carolina."

I see her look at me as she pauses and considers whether to go on or not.

"She has always just wanted to be loved, really loved by a man. She believed in the fairy-tale, happily-ever-after ending, like Cinderella and Prince Charming, I think. It sounds unrealistic to me, but not to her. Even after everything she has been through, I think she doesn't want to believe real love is a romantic fantasy perpetuated by media, greeting card companies, florists, novels, and movies. No wonder those loves are so perfect. They are written that way for us to read or watch the actors portray as they memorize their lines and pretend to feel real emotion. The men are always perfect and the women gorgeous. No problems; each knows exactly what to say and how to act."

"But I know she is disappointed in herself. Both Jason and I have master's degrees and she doesn't. Being with only one income made it impossible for her to further her education. I know she is a bit competitive with us. She wants to feel like she belongs with us, even though we are so much older than her. My son is only four years younger than her since Becca was an unplanned surprise for my parents. I married young and started my own family soon after."

"Like our Mama and Daddy, both Jason and I have been married to the same person since we were young. We have raised children. Becca did not have that special privilege to experience motherhood and a family to take care of. I know she wonders what it would have been like to carry and bear a child of her own. She will be alone in her old age, with no children by her side. She feels like the failure of the family because of all of this. I think the future scares her a bit, but not as much as it did when Tripp first left."

"She's been alone since that time and I worry, but she just never seems to let anyone get close to her other than her friends. You seem to be the first man she has let into her life. I am surprised."

"So we need to know that you're not going to hurt her. I know it's still relatively early in your relationship, so please leave now if you feel less for her than she does for you. We would rather deal with a small hurt now than what could happen if she falls in love with you and you leave her. She can't take it and I don't want to see her fall apart all over again. The thing is she really believes in happily ever after, even though she has not found it. She says she doesn't, but I know deep down she doesn't want to give up the hope of finding it for herself. She is closed tightly to any possibilities because of her fear of being heartbroken and left again by someone she trusts."

Damn, she doesn't pull any punches.

"Sara, I swear to you I will never hurt her. She doesn't know it yet, but I know how I feel. I plan on being the man who will love her until the day I die. I want Becca to fall in love with me because I already love her. I don't want to scare her away, so I'm trying to let her see we belong together in her own time. I want nothing more than to take care of her for the rest of my life. I don't plan on leaving her. Ever. I hope you now have no doubts about my position. I'm laying it all on the line to you."

They both look at each other before looking back at me. "But, Michael. You've only known her for a very short time. You can't possibly be so sure yet. It sounds like to me you've both gotten a bit carried away quickly. Attraction can be like that. But real love takes time, understanding, and commitment."

"Sara, I'll give Becca all the time she needs. As far as I concerned, she can have the rest of my life just so long as she lets me be with her. I'm not going anywhere. She's let me into her life now. From what I can tell, she doesn't do that lightly. I think she is beginning to trust me. I want to share my life with her. I'm not a womanizer who will change my mind. I want to settle down with her and build a life together. She can trust in me and believe me when I tell her I love her. I'll take care of her."

"Well, okay, I guess. It's just that she was so hurt by her ex-husband. He up and deserted her, no warning, leaving her with nothing but huge bills and a house she could not afford on her own. She was so traumatized

I thought we'd have to put her in the hospital. She had trusted him, and he betrayed her. It has taken a while for her to get her feet under her again and able to take care of herself. We never want to see her broken like that again."

"Believe me, Sara, I know. That's how we met. Becca was meeting Tripp to give him back some bracelet he wanted for his daughter. I happened to be there and didn't like the way he was looking at her. I know it sounds unbelievable, but I knew right away she needed me. Let's say I stepped in and made him leave."

Master of the understatement. Yeah, that was fun. I enjoyed the hell out of it.

Look what I got because of it.

Maybe I should send him a fucking thank-you note for being such an asshole.

Sara's eyes widen slightly as she takes in this new information. She is now looking at me as if she likes what she sees. Becca comes back to the table quietly, and I reach over to take her hand in mine. I feel as though I have to touch her, and I want them to see me do it. That she lets me touch her.

We finish our wine and walk out to the parking lot to say our goodbyes. To my surprise, Sarah gives me a quick hug as well as they leave. Roger and I shake hands.

I'm feeling pretty good about this now. I knew I could charm them, but I admit that was a little rough.

Sister down, brother to go.

I hope he likes me.

Now, I have to meet the girlfriends.

I drive her home, the old Daryl Hall and John Oates classic "Sara Smile" in my head.

Becca looks at me when we get home. She smirks before saying, "You'd better watch out, Stevens. You called my sister; now I'm calling yours. I want to meet her. Make it happen."

She does and I do. We drive up to Richmond the very next day and spend it cooking out with my sister Anne and her husband in their backyard. They even have a built-in pool there. I made sure we brought our suits with us so we could make use of it. When Becca takes off her T-shirt and unbuttons her shorts, my mouth flies open at the sight of her in her navy blue two-piece swimsuit. Her breasts are held up by thin straps tied around her neck and the bottoms are small enough I can see the curve of her ass below it. My penis fills quickly and pushes at my swim shorts.

I am very conscious of my sister and nephew nearby. I know I can't fool my brother-in-law Bill. I am sure he knows exactly what is happening to me. I dive into the deep end of the pool quickly to hide my hard-on and to try to cool off a bit.

My ten-year-old nephew Jeff is running around making a bit of a nuisance of himself and splashing everyone, but we all have a good time. I briefly wonder what it would be like to have Becca in the swimming pool. Her bathing suit can be easily removed with a few knots to untie. I imagine untying the knot behind her neck and pushing my face into her full cleavage.

Get a grip, Michael. There are women and children here.

Bill does a great job grilling the hamburgers and hot dogs for our cookout. We eat outside in our wet suits and wet hair. I am treated to the sight of Becca eating her hot dog, covered in mustard. She ends up with mustard in the corner of her mouth. I can't help cleaning her up with a sweet kiss and lick. I like mustard. She smiles at me afterwards and continues to bite the end of the hot dog right in front of me.

Fuck.

I watch as she devours two hot dogs hungrily. I don't even remember eating my own hamburgers.

God, I can't keep my hands to myself or my thoughts under control. Get a grip, Stevens. We're with my family, for goodness' sakes. There are children present.

Anne seems to like Becca immediately. I knew she would because she can tell how happy I am for the first time. And Bill is already hooked. I warn him to back off just a bit from Becca, but he is married to my sister happily, so I have to cut him a break. He can look but not lust.

I wasn't the least bit nervous about her meeting my family.

CHAPTER 14

Just Getting to Deeply Know Her

After dropping Becca off at her place, I drive home myself, needing a little time and distance as well. We've made plans for her to come over my house tomorrow, so I know I'll get to see her. I can relax a little, knowing I have that to look forward to the next day. Even though we have been dating for a while now, I haven't pushed her to come over yet.

My house is so empty it is just easier to spend time in her house because she actually has furniture for us to sit on. I want her to absolutely like my house so maybe someday she'll live here with me. I don't push her at all, knowing she would never move in with me before marriage. She really is that type of girl.

I'm fine with that, knowing my ultimate goal with her is marriage. For the rest of our lives.

Other than the brick colonial house itself, there's really not much to see. It is on a beautiful piece of land, however, with a gorgeous view of the river. Living in the corps for so long and moving around a lot, I didn't collect many things because it was much easier to be light and more mobile. I don't have any souvenirs of my times in Iraq and Afghanistan because the last thing I need is to be reminded of those places.

So, I don't have much stuff. I have an old couch in the great room with my small TV. I do have a bed, of course, but not much more in my bedroom. I do, however, have a state-of-the-art grill with a very nice backyard patio. I think I could grill out, and Becca and I could eat outside. I know she likes salmon, so pink salmon steaks I can do. I begin to make plans so it can happen.

After talking to Becca's sister in particular, I know I need to do some serious soul-searching. I begin by thinking about my life before I met her. I guess I had been fairly content with things, but getting out the Marines was and still is a huge step for me. I really loved everything about it: the constant work, the military routine, even living in tents and picking sand out of my mouth *and other places* when I was in the desert. Being a colonel and giving orders defined who I was as a man. Even when it was dangerous—and believe me, there were countless times it was—I still liked being in control. Men looked up to me for guidance, and I felt their respect. I was a good Marine.

But part of my life ended when I decided to retire. Thirty years was enough to give. This is a big adjustment for me. No job, new city, new house, new life, no friends in town. After investing and saving, I don't have any money problems at all. My inheritance from my parents and grandparents makes it possible for me to not worry about working. Maybe I'll do something when I get bored, but right now I'm enjoying the stress-free life after working so hard for thirty years.

Becca thinks I'm intense. She should have had my job for thirty years. Talk about intense. No wonder I don't waste my time. I need control and I am decisive. It is how I survived those tours. I have been doing that my whole adult life. The corps was good to me, so I can have pretty much anything I want within reason. I really could have lived anywhere because I had no real emotional ties to any place.

My sister Anne and her family took me in for a short while when I first got out, before I purchased the house. She is so glad I am finally somewhere out of harm's way. I guess I never really appreciated the fact she was always there, worrying about me when I was far away, especially during my many tours in Iraq and Afghanistan. I needed someone to worry about me because there is no way in hell those two places are really safe.

So it made sense to me to buy a place fairly near her. I didn't want to be too close to her because after all, I'm a grown man. Williamsburg seems to call to me. Its beauty and charm make it a special place.

Thank God it does, or I would never have met my Becca.

I don't know why I really ended up that night at the Bistro. I just thought I'd spend some time there getting a drink. I still can remember exactly how she looked that night because after all, it was a short time ago. It seems as though I've known her my whole life. Since I've met her, I've been swept up in my desire for her. I know, on one level, it is overwhelming to me, too. My sexual attraction to her has been complete and all-consuming.

I can't live without her. I don't want to ever be without her again. My whole future is dependent on her. I need her.

I hope to God her sister isn't right that this whole thing is a short-lived attraction that will burn itself out. I mean, I've fucked her, but I still can't get enough of her. I've fucked her now six times, but every time I think about it, I realize it actually was making love with Becca. All her six orgasms belong to me.

I feel love for her, not simply lust.

It certainly isn't meaningless to me; in fact, I've never had such a good time. I know there are many more ways for me to have her, and I have a really good imagination. But I don't think I'm the kind of man who will use a woman and really hurt her deep down. I mean maybe some of those one-night stands were a bit like that, but those women knew what the score was, so I wasn't hurting their souls. They were using me just as much. They really meant nothing to me, other than a real pussy to get off in. I know that sounds harsh, but it's true.

I never dreamed about them or wanted to hold them so much that I ache. And it's not like there were *that* many. I am a man, so there were women, but I was busy being a Marine, for fuck's sake. That took up practically 99 percent of my time.

Lord knows there were no women during those long tours in Iraq and Afghanistan. I wasn't about to take any chances there. Sure, it was difficult, but I was so busy it helped keep my mind off it. The Marines I was with were the same way. We all took care of our basic needs as quietly and privately as we could even though it was often impossible.

But at least it took the edge off and helped us all concentrate on our jobs as Marines. We were there to do a job, not fool around. It was simply too dangerous to not have my mind and focus on the job at hand. My life depended on it as well as the lives of the Marines around me. We took care of each other, trying to survive together.

Watch my back, Jack, and I'll watch yours.

Iraq and Afghanistan are very dangerous places.

It's the only way I made it. I didn't want to die there like some of my buddies had.

So now I know I need to be very careful with Becca's emotions. I picked up on that the first night we met. Tripp must have done a real number on her self-esteem and confidence. He really is such a dick, and I wish I had been able to knock him senseless that night. It would have been a pleasure. I can definitely beat the shit out of someone if I want. The Marines teach you creative, useful things.

I have trained quite a lot in the martial arts and can handle myself in a fight. I know all kinds of ways to subdue an attacker. I enjoy the training so much; I know I am going to need to find a class here in Williamsburg.

Thoughts of my fist hitting that smug bastard's face flicker briefly through my consciousness. I actually hope I get the chance to hit him someday, but I don't want him to come back and bother Becca again.

Stay away, asshole. He needs to go back to wife number three and forget about my woman. Go back to where ever he is living now.

I don't think Becca believes he lives in Williamsburg, but she hasn't wanted to keep up with his movements over the years. I hope he doesn't live in Virginia anymore, but since he drove to the Bistro, I think he must not live far away. It bothers me, knowing he could be closer to her than she thinks. She doesn't belong to him anymore. He already has a wife, so I don't know what he thinks he can really offer her.

A quickie with the first wife. Find out if it's still the same or something like that. Just go away, Tripp. Go be the third wife's asshole husband. That's who you are now. Live with it.

The only good thing he ever did was leave her for me. Thank goodness he left her when they were in Williamsburg close to her family. I would hate to think of her lost and alone if he had deserted her when they lived in California or South Carolina. At least she was on familiar ground and had friends and family near to help her through it. I only hope I can someday get Becca to accept she would never have been really happy with him. It's all about him and what his needs are.

When he left her, it actually was a blessing in disguise. She didn't know it. She deserves so much more than a self-centered jerk as a life partner. I'm glad she didn't waste the best years of her life being married to the asshole. But I have to admit, I am worried she seems honestly to have been alone all the years since.

Where are all the men around here? Are they blind or something? Don't get me wrong: part of me is glad she's been alone because the thought of her with anyone else is agonizing.

But I hate she seemed to be so unhappy since I never want her to be unhappy. It's not easy to be alone, especially for a woman. I guess she didn't let anyone get seriously close to her. Never allowed it or even remotely considered it. Guys would have had to jump on the hood of her car to make her notice them. I get the feeling she was at home, school, drugstore, grocery store, bank, and post office and didn't try to socialize beyond her friends at school for many of these years. I am glad she has a good group of lady friends, a few married.

I think she simply always said no as protection and never let herself get into a situation in which she felt uncomfortable. God, that's really something and says a lot about how she feels inside. I've got to fix that for her. She needs to know I want her for my everything, and she is that for me. I plan on being her everything as well.

So is my love for real? Is it the real deep-down irreversible love she needs? I know I have the passion and desire for her. All anyone has to do is see me with her to know. I'm fucking obvious. I swear other people must be able to see the connection between us since it burns so strongly to me. Sara said real love requires time, understanding, and commitment.

I know I can give her the time, just as long as she continues to let me be a part of her life. I don't think I could stand it again if she kicked me out of her life like she did that *awful week*. I can be a lot more patient than I've shown her so far, especially now that I've actually had her. I have to admit that waiting to have her the first time just about destroyed me. I really, really wanted her and couldn't seem to think about anything else.

It has been an all-consuming fire inside of me. Couldn't stop. I was a walking hard-on, for pity's sake.

For the understanding part, I think I have a pretty good handle on how she feels and why she feels the way that she does. So that's taken care of. If she lets me love her the way that I know I can, her self-esteem and confidence are bound to improve. I'll make sure of it, by telling her every day she's beautiful, and I love her with all my heart and soul. I'll make her sure of my love, so she never has to worry again about being deserted and abandoned by someone she thought she could trust with her heart.

As far as the commitment goes, I definitely do not have issues with that. I committed to thirty years in the service. I can absolutely commit to spending the rest of my life with the woman of my dreams. That's fucking easy. It's what I've been waiting for my whole life.

I'm feeling better now I've given our situation some thought. I decide to send her a quick text for fun.

> **Becca: Thinking of you always. If you need me . . . for ANYTHING . . . give me a call or text. Michael**

It's now getting to be early evening and the sun is almost down, so I head off to the Fresh Market to prepare for tomorrow's cookout at my house for a change. I love this grocery store. It is actually a beautiful grocery store with everything I could possibly want and more.

What can I get to go with salmon steaks? Should I get a salad or baked potatoes? Both?

As I'm walking to the store, trying to decide what to do, I am suddenly delighted to receive a text from her:

> **ANYTHING?? Wow, that opens up a wealth of possibilities, Mr. Stevens. I might have to take advantage of this opportunity since I don't receive offers like this every day. Ms. Connelly**

So . . . it appears she wants to play a little. Okay, I'll bite.

> Yes, Ms. Connelly. When I say ANYTHING, I mean ANYTHING. Take advantage of my offer all you want.

I lose my ability to concentrate on shopping for food, wandering aimlessly up and down the aisles, willing her to text me back. It seems to take forever before I finally hear the welcome little buzz letting me know I have a text.

> Michael, I am very glad to learn that you mean what you say. Becca

I quickly text back:

> Becca, you're going to learn to trust me. We're lovers, remember? Your ONLY lover, Michael

I don't hear anything back from her, driving me crazy. I manage to finish the shopping by picking up potatoes and fixings for a salad to go with the salmon. I grab a bottle of the Williamsburg Winery's Governor White before I pay.

I drive home, waiting for that damn buzz. It just doesn't come. I get home and put everything away, making sure that I am completely ready to have her come and see the house for the first time. Suddenly I hear my phone buzzing across the room, and I practically leap across the sofa to get to it.

> My ONLY lover Michael: So, if I wanted to be loved tonight, you're available? Your ONLY lover, Becca.

Wow. So bold . . . Maybe, just maybe. If you ask me nicely.

> Yes, I'm available to you whenever you need loving. Do you want me to come over now? (Love THAT signature, baby)

Please say yes.

> Ok.

I think that's nice enough for me.

That's all it takes, baby. I'll be there as soon as I can. M.

I try very hard not to break any land speed records driving from my house to her house. After all, I need to actually get to her in one piece, or she won't be getting any loving from me tonight. If the other drivers on the road had any idea of where my mind was, they would have given me plenty of room since I am most definitely a distracted driver right now.

Stupid 35 mph speed limit.

Try to focus on the damn road, Marine. You're driving a car, for crying out loud.

Oh shit, I'm not a Marine anymore, am I?

Fuck it, once a Marine, always a Marine.

Arriving at her house, I stride up to her door and ring the doorbell, trying not to ring it over and over until she gets there.

Loving coming up, delivered to your door. My package is boxed and wrapped up right now, but it can be quickly unwrapped with a little help.

When she finally opens the door, I just stand there looking at her. She's smiling and blushing at me. Finally, she moves to the side so I can come in the door.

"I'm under the impression you need some loving tonight, Ms. Connelly. I'm here at your service. Since I was actually in the service, I think I can handle any request you may have. I'm experienced and quite capable. I am also dependable and want to be responsible for you. Just tell me what you want and I'll see what I can do."

She giggles before wrapping her arms around my neck and pulling my mouth to hers. I keep kissing her as I lift her up into my arms. It's not the easiest thing to climb steps, hold a warm woman, and keep my lips on hers all at the same time, but I manage it rather competently, if I do say so myself. When I get to the top of the stairs, I don't stop in the great room at all, but I head straight down the hall to her bed. I gently lay her down in the middle of her bed and stand looking down at her.

"I'm so glad you let me know you wanted to see me tonight, baby. Tell me what you want me to do to you."

She looks at me under her lashes. "Take all of your clothes off for me, Michael."

"I will if you will, Rebecca." She agrees breathlessly.

We accomplish this task rapidly and competently. Clothes are flying everywhere it doesn't matter at all.

"Okay . . . now what, Ms. Connelly?" I start to have trouble breathing. I swallow, trying to calm down. It's obvious to everyone in the room how ready, willing, and up I am for this little adventure.

"Lay down on the bed on your back, face up."

"Again, I will if you will."

I do as she commands. I'm used to taking orders and following them perfectly. I admit I love awakening this side of her, the bolder, sexual side of her. I am glad she feels comfortable enough with me we can explore it together.

I could have told you.

It's obvious to me Tripp didn't know what the hell he had in front of him. He had no idea of how to handle a woman like her, the special treasure he once had in his grasp. He didn't awaken her deep desires.

Thank God, now I have that pleasure. It's for me to see. Only me, from now on.

"Tell me what to do next, baby. What do you want me to do to you?" I whisper gently and tenderly, as I finally have her naked and on the bed with me.

I'm already sweating slightly, feeling hot and bothered. I haven't even touched her yet.

And believe it or not, she really does. In fact, this time, she whispers constantly to me, directing me and showing me what she wants and needs. It's mind-blowing to me. I think I'm a good lover because I've always tried to anticipate what my partner needs, but then sometimes I do a lot of guessing, fumbling around, and hoping I'm right.

This time, I don't have to guess at all because she tells me right away what to do. I follow her every whispered order, and since I can follow orders quite well, I soon find out it really works for her. I've never had a woman take control quite like this. All I can say is I hope she does it again and again because I love pleasuring her. And of course, I'm having the time of my life. Becca makes sure I'm taken care of like I take care of her.

Seven.

Making love with her is such a surprising sensual and erotic adventure. I never know what's going to happen next. She shocks me at every turn, teaching me the sweet intricacies of knowing another person intimately. And considering the fact I'm a grown man, it is saying a lot.

When we're both so tired we can barely lift our heads, Becca tells me she wants me to hold her. We're both a bit covered in sweat, but her sweet natural scent still fills my head. I pull her into my arms, never wanting to let her go. I tickle her back with long strokes of my fingers as she goes to sleep wrapped up in my arms next to me.

I know I've never felt a love like this before. It has to; it just has to be real. R*eal love. Just like in the damn movies and books.*

Who knew?

CHAPTER 15

My House is Our Home

The next morning, after our very interesting express-delivered loving, we piddle the time away together in Becca's place. I realize we're starting to move and adjust around each other in comfort and ease, two lovers completely calm and satisfied with each other. Nothing really seems to be awkward at all anymore.

I now have been awarded a small space in the bathroom cabinet for my shampoo, toothbrush, and deodorant. As much as I love the smell of Becca's shampoo and conditioner, I prefer to smell a little bit more masculine. We take care of breakfast and showers and dressing easily although again I can't really keep my hands off her for any significant length of time. She lets me touch her whenever I want, never pulling away. I wonder if this is what it's like for married couples. We spend a lazy morning enjoying each other's company. It's very relaxing and gives me a glimpse of what our future could hopefully bring.

Please, baby. It's my plan.

But after a while, we both realize we've got things to get done and errands to run: the bank, the post office, the grocery store, the drug store . . . you name it. I leave, giving both of us the time to take care of our own stuff. Becca promises to be at my house at six o'clock. I've given her *extremely* detailed directions, so there is no room for error when she comes over tonight.

We've basically spent all our time at her house since it has furniture and is more comfortable. I have just the bare minimum. To say I'm looking forward to having Becca finally at my house is an understatement. Part of me hopes she loves the house, and part of me hopes she'll see how much I need a woman in my life after viewing my sparse living arrangements.

I've never really given much thought to interior decorating before since most of my living spaces over the years have been barracks, military housing, or, God forbid, a tent. Since I was alone, it didn't matter to me what where I lived looked like. I couldn't really decorate it even if I wanted to. My space didn't actually belong to me. I hope Becca will have ideas of how my/our home should look. I may not know what to do, but I do know how. I can wield a paintbrush and hammer with the best of them. Anything you need fixed and I can usually figure it out.

All I need is someone telling me what to do about the decorating. After Becca's performance last night, I know she has no problem telling *me* what to do. I'm putty in her hands. I'll do anything she wants. If she wants my whole house to be purple, then hell, that's what I'm going to do. I hope she doesn't, but I sincerely pray she wants to help me turn my big empty house into a home of which we can be proud.

I may not be any good at interior decorating, but I am damn good at landscaping. I enjoy working in the yard since I've never really had one before. I've already made significant improvements to my yard even in the short time I've been living there. I have had mulch delivered to my house recently. There it sits, all piled up in my driveway, waiting for me to get my ass into gear. I've been so caught up in Becca I've let it slide.

Perhaps I need an afternoon of some mindless physical labor to keep me straight. I spend the whole afternoon working in the yard and generating quite a sweat. It's pretty hot and humid out here. Working in the yard requires digging in the dirt and sweating. I don't mind getting dirty and sweaty. Not to toot my own horn, so to speak, but I have a natural talent for this.

Only Becca can toot my horn now. Not interested in tooting my own horn anymore if I can help it.

Spreading mulch around all the flower beds and trees is not as easy task as it appears since my front yard and backyard are pretty big and seem to be getting bigger by the minute. I ended up covered in the stuff and have to take my T-shirt off to keep cool. I briefly wonder what Becca would think seeing me like this. I've always been fresh and groomed around her. By the time I finish, I am so fucking sweaty, dirty, and exhausted I strip in the garage before going into the shower. Believe me, that cool water felt great. I hope she likes the results of all my hard work when she sees it tonight. I stand in the shower for a long time, making sure I wash carefully.

I really don't want to smell like mulch tonight.

After debating what to wear tonight, I realize I really don't have much longer to wait for her before she gets here. I hope she's on time. I fire up the grill so it will be preheated and ready for the salmon. I already have the salad fixings all tossed together and baked potatoes baking. So I feel ready. And then suddenly, she's here.

In my house.

I kiss her swiftly and take her on the grand tour. I proudly show her everything, even all the closets, garage, and storage areas. We wander from empty room to empty room. It really is a beautiful two-story brick colonial-style house with an attached garage in a gorgeous family neighborhood. It needs a little tender loving care.

I can do that—correction, we can do that.

I only have a little furniture in the great room and my bedroom, of course. She seems to like the kitchen a lot and raves over the outdoor deck and patio. I show her my bedroom. I have *no* problems having her in there with me.

Becca seems to like the size of the master bedroom and, of course, the adjoining bathroom with its big glass shower and huge tub. That was one of the main reasons I bought the damn house. While we are in the bedroom, I hope she notices the size of my big bed. So far she seems to like my house as much as I do even though it is *big* and *empty*. Maybe she'll even want to live here with me. After I finish showing her the house, I take her hand as we walk outside. I want her to see all my hard work in the yard.

I show her the mulch.

Look at all of it.

She seems amazed I was able to get all that work done in one afternoon.

I'm strong, baby. See what I did? Do you think my yard is pretty? I want you to like it a lot.

She comments on the backyard, pointing out some of her favorite flowers and bushes. She seems to like azaleas and nandinas a lot, so I make sure to remember. The grill is definitely ready by now. It doesn't take long to cook the salmon, and we eat outside watching the sunset over the river from my patio. Becca tells me how delicious everything is. She cleans her plate, so I guess I did okay. We spend time sitting outside and enjoying the breeze as it slowly gets dark.

I've opened a second bottle of wine, and she seems to be enjoying herself. I know I don't have to worry about her driving home tipsy or drunk because she's not driving anywhere near her home tonight if I can help it. I'm going to make sure. The boom box I have outside with us is playing a great duet between Jason Aldean and Kelly Clarkson called "Don't You Want to Stay (for a Little While)?"

Don't you want to stay for a little while?
Don't you want to hold each other tight?
Don't you wanna fall asleep with me tonight?
—We can make forever feel this way.

"Becca, what do you think of the house? Do you really like it?"

I want it to be your home, too.

"Of course, Michael. It's beautiful. I can see why you decided to buy it. I have always loved this neighborhood, and you have a lovely location here with a view of the James. I am enjoying watching the sunset over the water tonight."

"I'm glad you like it too. I know it is empty now, but I have plans. I want it to be my home for the rest of my life. I saw that big master bedroom with adjoining big shower and big tub, and I knew I had to have it. When I see something I want, I don't fool around. I make sure it belongs to me as soon as I can. Like you, for example. I knew I wanted you the moment I first saw you walk into the bistro that night."

She was exquisite that night. I rescued her.

"Oh Michael, I remember. You suddenly appeared, and the next thing I knew you had your arm around me and were pretending to be my boyfriend. I still don't know why I didn't scream and push you away. I was so shocked, and then I slowly caught on to what you were trying to do for me. You even kissed me when Tripp came back and you made sure he left again. I'll never forget our first kiss."

"I knew it the moment I kissed you I wanted to know you."

"Michael, I have to admit you were very intense, very quickly. It was a lot for me to handle."

"Oh, baby, don't you know by now you can handle me anytime. I like it when you handle me. I am putty in your hands."

I'll do anything to make sure you are happy.

"Michael, you are nothing like putty. Putty is soft and pliable. There is nothing soft about you, you know."

"Yeah, I know. It's a problem where you are concerned. I like to keep in shape, though. My muscles definitely helped me all those years on active duty. I exercise all of my muscles, going to the gym and running like a crazy person through the neighborhood."

"You are gorgeous, honey, and in perfect shape. I am intimidated by you sometimes. You're so big and strong."

Big and strong all over. Let me show you.

"I like your shape too, you know. Let me show you my big bedroom, big shower, and big tub. I'm big and strong and like big things. But you never have to worry. You know I'd never hurt you."

"Honey, what am I going to do with you? Do you think about making out all the time?"

I've told you before. Anything. Yes, I seem to have a one-track mind when it comes to you. I'm trying to make up for all the lonely years.

"With you, I do, only you."

"I am relieved to hear that, Mr. Stevens. I admit I liked the look of your bedroom and bath."

"Let me make sure you experience the full Stevens effect. That master bedroom and bath are one of the main reasons I bought the house in the first place."

"Maybe later, I'll think about it. Right now I am enjoying the evening out here, drinking wine with you."

"Would you like me to pour you some more? We need to finish the bottle. You know how I feel about wasting anything. Here, give me your wine glass."

I just look at her expectantly, eyebrow raised and wine bottle in hand. She is hesitating.

"Between the two of us, we should be able to drink it all. Come on, honey. Hand it over."

Have some more, baby. Relax. I'll take care of you. You're safe with me.

"Are you trying to get me tipsy, Mr. Stevens? Don't pour me too much."

"No worries, baby. The last thing I want is for you to pass out drunk after throwing up. I need you conscious for what I have in mind."

Awake

She gives in and lets me pour her another glass.

Good, baby, drink up. I plan on drinking you later.

"What exactly are you talking about now? I might have to go home."

"I don't think so. Route 5 is dark and twisty. You had just enough wine to relax you, and I'm not about to let you take a chance with your life. Stay here with me."

"I'll see. I don't know yet. Let me think about it."

What do you have to think about? I'm here, you're here . . .

"Baby, my house is empty and my bed is empty. Stay, please."

Stay with me. I want to make love with you in my bed for a change.

"Convince me, Michael. Why should I stay the night in your big bed with you?"

"Because I love you, Becca. I can't sleep without you anymore. Let me show you how much I love you. It almost frightens me, the depth of my feelings for you. I can't imagine ever being without you again. You have no clue because I don't have the words. Nothing seems enough to make you understand. I'm left with 'I love you,' three small words. I only hope they are enough."

"I . . . you say the most romantic things, honey. I love you, too. With every beat of my heart, I am yours."

"Then let me remind you to whom you belong. Are you finished with your wine? It's getting a bit chilly out here now the stars are out. I need to keep you warm, and I know how to keep you very warm, Ms. Connelly. I happen to be quite hot. I can share a little bit of my warmth to keep you comfortable and satisfied."

Don't you want to stay . . . for a little while?
All night is a little while.

"Oh, darling, you've finally convinced me to stay."

"Ms. Connelly, as I have told you before, it will be my pleasure. And yours. Give me your hand, my love. You've made me an offer I can't find the strength to refuse."

I can't help myself. I sweep her up into my arms and urgently carry her through the French doors, through the vaulted great room, and into the master bedroom. I lay her gently on my bed. I may not have much furniture, but I do have the greatest, most comfortable king-sized bed. That is one thing I would never scrimp on.

My big bed is empty no longer. I can hardly believe it. She makes me work for it and makes me laugh with her slightly wicked sense of humor, dry sarcastic comments, keen observations, and tempting sexual innuendos. Ms. Connelly has been a delightful challenge right from the start. But I like a challenge. Thank goodness she is finally here. I can be very persuasive and don't give up easily.

As I slowly undress Becca, I realize all I really want to do is hold her in my arms and fall asleep with her in my bed. It's been a hard, busy day, and I am admittedly tired. This is a bit different for me since it's been almost impossible to get my fill of her, and we've been making out like bunny rabbits every chance I get. I think Becca feels the same way. It's enough for us to be together.

I get naked as fast as I can and join her under my crisp, clean sheets. I love she sleeps nude like I do, enjoying the feel of all her soft, warm skin pressed up against me. She sighs contentedly, putting her head on my shoulder and her hand on my heart. I relax with her close to me and feel the effects of the two bottles of white wine. Sleepy pillow talk whispers and kisses. I close my eyes, content with the universe, and drift away into unconsciousness.

It's a bit of a different story when I wake up suddenly in the morning.

After all her suggestive teasing last night, I think I've been dreaming erotic dreams of Becca all night long, and I have a morning erection of gigantic proportions. I can tell this situation isn't going to go away on its own. She is still sound asleep next to me. I have to do something to take care of all this sexual energy. I don't want to sneak into the bathroom and make myself come.

What if she caught me? I lie there, breathing deeply and trying to figure out what to do. I mean, after all, I have an alluring woman in my bed. Surely I can think of something.

All I can see is the sheet sticking up in front of me like a small tent. Becca stirs next to me, whispering my name, but seeming to not really wake up yet. I want to make love to her, but for the first time ever, the thought crosses my mind, I need to go first this time.

Me first, not her.

If I don't, I'm afraid all this sexual energy will cause me to pound her into next week. After I come once, I'll be able to calmly give her what she needs. An idea pops into my head and stays there, tantalizing me with all its possibilities. I guess it's worth a try. I know I want to, and I hope Becca will want to as well.

Moving slowly, I gently crawl out of bed and head to the bathroom. I am simply following my dick there. I have some Shea butter in the medicine cabinet. I really like how it feels and smells. Taking the cream, I slather it all over my cock. Already this is feeling better and better, taking a little of the edge off my ache. I make sure I'm about as slippery as I can be.

On my way back, I stop and put into the Bose speaker system a Sara Evans CD. I like her voice quite a lot. Padding silently to the bed, I slip back under the covers but leave both of us naked to below our waists. Becca is lying on her back, her beautiful rounded tits right in front of me.

Perfect.

I begin to slowly cover the space between her soft mounds with the Shea butter, gently spreading it around. I concentrate on putting the cream in the valley of her breasts and not on the sides next to her arms. I don't want it to be slippery there.

As I move my fingers around, sleepy olive green eyes slowly open, staring at me.

"What a different way to wake up. Mr. Stevens, what are you doing?" she quietly asks me, gazing at me under her lashes.

"Oh, just a little prep work. Nothing for you to worry about, Ms. Connelly," I whisper back slowly, keeping my voice gentle and low.

"Really, Michael? What exactly are you prepping me for? I have no idea."

I can tell by the look in her eyes that I am not fooling her at all. She knows exactly what I am up to. What I am up for. I'm so damn obvious. I can't hide my feelings from her.

I lean over and whisper into her ear, "I want to make love to your breasts. Sit up for me, honey."

Her eyes widen, but she does as I tell her. Okay then. She sits up, leaning her back against the headboard. I crawl up on my knees, slowly making my way to her until I am straddling her hips facing her. I look into her eyes, making sure she is still with me. She nods at me gently, looking back at me curiously.

I tell her to take her hands and hold the sides of her breasts, bringing them together and creating a deep, deep cleavage. Rising up on my knees, I bring my dick level with her breasts. I start to push into the valley between her two full breasts . . .

Oh, wow, this feels . . . different. Her round breasts are so soft, they feel like pillows all around me as I stroke up and down, in and out. I can tell this isn't going to take me long at all. I might not break my record, but it may be close.

I buck up and down, sliding between her tits faster and faster. She pushes them together for me, providing the slippery friction I need to come. I know my eyes are screwed shut in concentration, and for once, I am unable to verbalize my feelings.

Next thing I know I feel her gently caressing my balls with one hand as her other hand tries to keep her tits pressed together for me. I am surrounded by softness and without any real warning; I feel Becca's warm tongue lick me as I peak out of the top of her cleavage during a thrust.

Oh God!

I come hard, shooting everything I have all over her chest. I shudder with the after effects, collapsing back down onto her lap. Becca buries her face into the curve of my neck. I hold her tight, not caring we're both covered in Shea butter and my ejaculate. I hope she enjoyed watching me loving her. I know it was a selfish thing to do, coming first without taking care of her needs. I take a deep breath and let it out slowly, before turning to her. Now that I've come, I'm calm enough to give her my full attention.

And I know exactly what I want to do.

A little unfinished business, as far as I am concerned.

"I'll be right back, honey. Don't go anywhere for me."

First things first.

I get up to get a towel to clean up both of us. I really don't want to end up with messy sheets for what I have in mind. Throwing the towel on the floor next to the bed, I don't waste any time, grabbing Becca by the legs and hauling her swiftly back down into a lying position.

Before she can say anything, I get between her thighs, pull them open widely, and shove my broad shoulders under her legs until they are up around my ears. Becca squeaks and twists, realizing my intentions, and tries to cover between her legs with her hands. I push them aside, wanting to somehow keep them out of my way.

Should I tie them down? I've never done that to a woman. It's never really crossed my mind before. Images flicker through my mind: Becca tied down and unable to get away from me. Suddenly, it's strangely appealing. And damn tempting. I'll have to give it some thought.

Don't have time right now; I've got a squirming woman on my hands.

"Michael, Michael, no, no, it's too . . . too much . . . too much for me! I can't, I can't let you do that."

I look down at her, "What, baby? You can't let me? It's not too much . . . what? You think it's too intimate? Too intimate for me or you? Don't you know I want to know everything there is about you? Nothing we can say or do is too intimate for me. Remember . . . I said I'll give you *anything* you want. Let me love you this way. I love you. I want to taste you. I want you to come against my lips and in my mouth. I need to feel you like that. Please, baby. I'm begging you."

"Oh my God, I just don't know . . . I really don't . . . I've never done . . . I'm embarrassed."

"It'll be okay, honey. I promise. Don't be embarrassed. Not with me. Never with me. I love you. I want you. Nothing about you can be too much for me. I want to do this with you. Trust me. Let yourself feel how I can make you feel. Just relax and let me."

I stare deeply into her wide eyes until I see her grant me permission. I grab a pillow and scoot it under her butt so it is raised for me. Not giving her a chance to slip away from me, I lower my head slowly toward her folds. She is so beautiful to me, so open for me. I groan out loud as my lips finally touch her. I can smell the musky scent of an aroused woman right in front of me.

There is no way in hell I'm stopping now. I lick her moist slit, thrusting my tongue into her, overwhelmed by the sweet yet salty taste in my mouth. I put my hands under her and grab her ass to make sure she's in position for me. I'm not letting her slide away this time. My hands hold her thighs apart, giving me access to her secret woman place. I kiss and lick and stroke her smooth, soft folds over and over again, loving the musky way she tastes and smells. I am beyond thrilled that she is granting me this pleasure.

Even while I am pleasuring her orally, I can't be quiet. In between licks and kisses, I whisper words of love and encouragement, my lips touching her smooth soft folds as I speak.

"Oh, baby, you taste so good, so good, like honey, like honey on my lips, I want all of it, give it to me, let it gush out of you into my mouth, I need you, I want you, open for me, let me feel you get hot under my lips, come for me, come for, come for me, feel it, feel it, let it happen, let it out, you can do it, I can't wait much longer, you taste too damn good to stop now."

I lick, I kiss, I nuzzle, I taste, and I thrust my tongue over and over and over. I can do this as long as she needs or at least until I fall over the edge.

Becca is moving slowly now, moaning, gasping, and thrashing her head back and forth on the pillow. I find her clit hidden among the wet folds and suck softly. Becca's breath hisses between her teeth and her hips buck up, but I hold her tightly, keeping my mouth moving over her sweetness.

Sara Evans sings "Gotta Have U" as I make love to Becca.

I love knowing her intimately, no secrets between us, nothing hidden from me. I need to know everything there is to know about her. I want to know this part of her better than she does herself. The sight, the feel, the taste, the sound, and the scent of her are branded on my brain forever. I'll die remembering this moment.

She starts to whisper, "Michael, Michael, I can't take much more. Oh my God, oh my God, I'm so close, so close for you, honey. I love you so much. Never, never leave me, my love."

I whisper against her, "Just like that baby, feel it. Let it come. I want you so much. Come for me, Becca."

My open mouth and tongue swoops down on her again as I thrust two fingers into her swiftly, pushing and pushing deep inside. She screams, "Oh, Michael! Ohhhhh!"

Her voice washes over me, making me heat up as I continue to run my rough tongue up and down her smooth folds and keep my fingers inside feeling how wet and hot she is for me. I want it to last much longer, but my cock is as hard as a rock, and Becca is already almost there.

Suddenly she grabs my hair and screams out, "Yesssss! Oh yes! That's it! That's it! Oh Michael!"

As she thrashes upward under my mouth and I try to hold her, I realize my mouth is completely full of moisture. It seems to be welling up out of her, not quite gushing, but almost. I give her time to come down from her pleasure, kissing her intimately over and over as she calms. Lifting my mouth gently and slowly from her, I look up at her panting beneath me.

That was incredible. I never knew before now that a woman could do that for me. Where the hell have I been all these years? I learn something new from this woman every damn day.

"Michael, Michael, I love you, I love you." She can barely breathe the words.

I'll do anything, anything to see and hear THAT again.

"Come to me, come inside me now. I am empty without you. Fill me up," she demands.

YESSS!

Now I need to take care of my damn business fairly urgently. Sliding myself up her, I slam my throbbing cock inside those incredibly moist folds. She's still quivering, feeling the end of her climax. It takes me all of about twenty thrusts before I lose my steel control and my mind. Groaning out her name almost incoherently, I feel waves of incredible pleasure rocket through my body, and I spurt rhythmically over and over into her warmth. My open mouth is pressed to hers, and I know she can taste her own arousal on my lips.

I surface slowly to reality and then become aware of Sara Evans singing her hit song, "I Could Not Ask for More."

I slide against her slick, sweaty body and lay my head next to her, murmuring over and over how beautiful she is, how much I love her. When both of us are able to breathe again, I roll over to her side, not really wanting to leave her. I pull her into my arms, feeling quite satisfied.

I knew I could do it.

Becca whispers to me gently, "You taste better."

No, baby. Not possible. Nope.

CHAPTER 16

I've Got a Fucking Life Now

As the days slowly go by, Becca and I settle into what I think is a great relationship, a loving exclusive relationship. I can be calm now, secure in the knowledge she won't withhold herself from me. Naturally, I continue to take full advantage of any rising opportunities that present themselves in front of me. I think she is enjoying my amorous attentions to her as much as I am hers to me.

I am a happy, happy man.

I actually now have my own drawer in her house so I can keep a change of clothes there when needed the next morning. I learn more and more about her friends and activities. She seems to have different groups of ladies she considers friends: high school friends, college friends, work friends, church friends, neighborhood friends, and her Philanthropic Educational Organization (PEO) friends.

I find out she belongs to this PEO group that seems to be basically a philanthropic educational sorority for women of all ages. They do little things to raise money for scholarships to help young women from the United States, Canada, and from around the world get college educations. Not only do they meet once a month, but a small, select group of them also get together for canasta frequently and have lunches out, trying some of the many excellent restaurants found in Williamsburg.

I start to attend Williamsburg United Methodist Church on Jamestown Road with her and enjoy holding her hand quietly during the Sunday morning service. People speak to her often as we make our way to some seats, and she introduces me to several. I've never really been an overtly religious guy, thinking of myself as more spiritual. But I know there were times when I should have really been hurt more than I actually was. Maybe there was some power looking out for me.

And looking at Becca makes me in awe of the wonder of nature or whatever higher power there is. There must have been a master plan considering how the universe works and how man and woman fit together so wonderfully.

The beauty of the physical world fills me with such wonder sometimes. The way the universe works and all the amazing, unique varieties of life and landscapes. That's why I love to travel as much as I do. I feel myself relax, knowing I am where I want to be. I enjoy hearing Becca sing the hymns softly beside me and take comfort in her peacefulness. I can see she really does have a full life. Being here with her helps me feel at home and more comfortable in my surrounding community.

Slowly, I am starting to feel more and more at home in Williamsburg. I start hanging out at the Two Rivers golf course, making friends with the guys there. Next thing I know I have a regular golf date with three really nice guys twice a week at Two Rivers Country Club. I am not that great of a golfer although I enjoy trying. Maybe if I play more, I can start to see an improvement in my game. I know Becca once told me she likes golf, but I can see it is really more watching the professional tournaments when they are on television.

Umm.

She says she has played a little a long time ago.

Maybe we could try it together sometime, if I can convince her.

A lot of the pleasure of golf actually is about being outside on a beautiful golf course, enjoying nature and spending time with others while I play. The golf makes it even more fun, pitting myself against the golf course. I don't take it seriously other than the fact I don't want to embarrass myself in front of the other guys. They are all nice family guys who have lived in Williamsburg for years. It appears as though they hang out at the clubhouse all day, every day.

It's great to start to have regular guy friendships instead of the mainly working relationships I had with guys in the Marines. I have a few close Marine buddies I want to keep in touch with now that I am no longer active duty. We call each other some, but we mainly e-mail. Maybe I can get Keith to drive up here and play a round of golf or two with me.

In the meantime, I'm enjoying getting to know these neighborhood guys, and we really get to know each other after meeting week after week for a round. Their friendly, funny, teasing banter around the golf course makes for a fun day. Getting to know them and having friends here make me feel part of Williamsburg.

My love for Becca grows and is reborn every day. She is fascinating, and I can't believe the way her mind works sometimes. She's such a *girl* even though I know she's a full-grown independent woman. There are times when she is completely illogical according to my way of thinking. I don't want to laugh at her, but sometimes it is so funny. Lord knows she gets really pissed if I laugh.

She also gets a little mad with me when I point out any fallacy in her thinking. I've found out she could be stubborn at times, but then so am I. Our arguments so far have not been serious ones because I refuse to let us have a disagreement get out of control. I respect her and want us each to have equal say in our relationship. She has been independent for quite some time, so I have to allow her to have her opinions.

I can't order her around like I did my Marines.

I make the mistake of chuckling at her one afternoon after she says something I think is completely illogical. She can tell by my expression I find her statement crazy. I don't even know what I found so funny about it because I should have let it pass by.

"I've been thinking of contacting a real estate agent so I can put my condo up for sale. I have outgrown it now. I need more storage, a bigger closet, and I don't really like the stairs I have to climb to get to the main living areas. I want to start looking around for somewhere else, perhaps something with a garage as well."

I am dumbfounded. Where did she get this idea? I am not sure what to say to stop this. If things go according to plan, she will be moving into my house, where there is plenty of storage, bigger closets, more bedrooms, spacious bathrooms and me.

I make the mistake of chuckling out loud. "I don't know, honey. The steps are not that bad."

"Are you laughing at me? I am serious and have given this some thought."

"I'll help you. It's not a big problem."

"It is while carrying in groceries and heavy suitcases when I travel. Yvette, Lauren's mom, doesn't come over because her bad knees won't let her climb my stairs. I want for my friends to be able to visit me."

I actually like the downstairs foyer. It provides somewhat of a natural barrier to someone rushing into her house willy-nilly.

"I think you should think about this carefully. The real estate market is always better in the late spring and summer when people are desperate to get settled before a new school year starts. It is now late August. You have missed the best time to sell. Why don't you wait until then? One more year?"

Wait for me to propose, for us to get married, so we can share my house together. I'm thinking by Christmas. She should be able to come to the same conclusion I have already reached so soon.

We belong together—emotionally, sexually, physically, intellectually, legally together. I won't settle for less than the whole package with her. I need to give her time, but not too much time. I won't survive.

"I've decided already, Michael. I want to start looking for some place new."

I make the mistake of chuckling at her again. She can tell by the look in my eyes I think this is a crazy idea.

She gets really mad with me, feeling hurt I think she is stupid or something. It escalates into a big deal in her mind, and I try desperately to defuse the situation. But she is having nothing of me. Becca points out that as a gentleman, I should have kept my thoughts to myself and not made her feel bad.

There is nothing I can say. She is pissed at me. And she is getting more and more pissed by the second.

"Michael, don't laugh at me. I'm not stupid. You just don't agree with me. We don't always think the same way, you know. I need you to listen, not always be so damn logical."

"Well, it's just that . . . don't you see . . . you're not making any sense, honey. Think it through and I know you will realize it too."

Be reasonable, please. You can't move now and then so soon move in with me.

"I'm glad you find me so amusing, Mr. Stevens. Go, go home now. I can't talk to you anymore. I'm so mad at you, but I don't want to say anything I will regret later on. It is best if you leave me alone. Go home."

"Baby, I know you can be a bit impulsive sometimes, leaping into situations without thinking through all the possible ramifications. I want to keep you from doing it again. I don't want you to make a stu— . . . a foolish mistake."

Oh, almost said "stupid." "Foolish" is not much better. Either way I am insulting her intelligence. At least that is the way she is taking it. I don't think she is stupid or a fool. Right now, I'm the one who is being stupid and foolish, trying to reason with an unreasonable woman.

"I'm a grown woman. I am not a fool. Yes, I have made impulsive decisions I have regretted and have been fooled before. But I have tried to learn from those mistakes. They made me the woman I am now. I learned what I can and cannot do. I don't need you to protect me from my own decisions. I have been on my own for many years now and survived it without your help."

"Now, honey, that is so not going to happen. I am here to protect you. I want to and I need to protect you. Get used to it because it is not within me to stop now."

Remember me? I am the one who rescued you. It's my job to look after you and protect you. You are not stopping me from my duty as your lover and future husband. I don't care how mad you get at me.

"I'm done with this conversation now. It's over. I think it will be best if you don't stay tonight. Go home. I need some time to calm down a bit before I see you again. Obviously we both do."

I realize she has just kicked me out of her bed tonight. I didn't need time to calm down before, but now, since she is refusing to let me sleep with her, I am damn well not calm.

"Fuck, Becca?! Are you telling me to leave you alone tonight? I can't leave you when you are so mad with me. I've got to fix it. I can't stand it. Look, I'm sorry."

"Don't you dare cuss at me, Marine. I won't have you talk to me like that. Besides, you are only apologizing because I am asking you to leave. You don't really mean it. I have had enough now. My decisions are my decisions alone. It's my life. This is my house, and I will sell it and move somewhere else if I want to do so. You are not in charge of me. I don't have to do what you tell me. I am an independent grown woman."

"Yes, I know exactly how grown up you are. I am keenly aware of the fact that you are most definitely a woman. Come here and let me show you the differences between us. I know exactly where they are."

I make a move to take her in my arms.

I need to touch her.

"I am not giving in to your incredible sexpertise, Mr. Stevens. Back off. Don't you touch me now. I mean it. Go home and sleep in your lonely bed tonight. Perhaps then you will think first before you try to give me orders."

Sexpertise? Is that a real word? Sex expertise. Sex expert. I am liking the sound of this word. I am incredible.

She is staring in my eyes, as if daring me to issue her an order.

Now I can't touch her? Damn, damn, damn. Touching her is the only thing that calms me down. She said she wanted me to calm down. Well, let me touch you then.

"Ordering you is the last thing I want to do with you, honey. I want you willing to please me, not commanded to do so."

I am not ordering her around. I know how to give orders, and believe me, Marines used to jump when I gave an order. They obeyed quickly and competently, only asking how high they needed to jump to please me.

"Then let me make my own decisions, Michael. I can do it. Trust me."

I do trust you. I just know this is a bad decision. We are going to be married in a few months if I get my way. It is the plan, the only plan in the world, as far as I am concerned. Cooperate, cooperate, baby. I need you to cooperate. I need several more months to make you comfortable with me enough to say yes when I propose marriage to you.

"Honey, don't you know I am thinking only of you? Does my opinion mean nothing to you? I thought we were now part of each other's lives. I never decide anything important without talking it over with you first. I want you to grant me that same privilege. I need to protect you and feel as though I have some say in our future together. Our lives must be intertwined in order for us to move forward. Please don't shut me out. I can't stand the thought. It is too much for me to handle."

Don't break my heart.

"I understand, but I am done with this now. Yes, I care deeply about your opinions. I want to consider your thoughts and feelings in everything I do. But when Tripp left me, I had to learn to live on my own. I was scared to death to have to make such important decisions as where to move, how to purchase a home I could afford, and how to feel safe in my living environment. I had to buy a car on my own as well and learn to deal with repairs to the house and car. I went through a car wreck and had insurance companies to contact. I learned I could handle things on my own. I don't want to be caught unprepared as I was before. It is important to me to feel independent as well as to know I can depend on you."

You can always depend on me. I am extremely dependable.

Shit, shit, shit. Nothing left to do but give in. Fall back, Marine, regroup and then redeploy. I have learned to do this over and over and over again. Better to give in some during this battle than lose the whole goddamn war.

"Okay, Ms. Connelly, I surrender. Since you are forcing me to leave, I will go home to my lonely bed and survive the night without you. But you had better damn well miss me in your lonely bed as much as I am going to long for you beside me in mine."

Deep, deep longing on my part. I hate to sleep alone now. I can't.

"Yes, I feel it will be a long night for both of us, but I need some time to calm down. I am sorry I am so mad at you, but I am. Obviously, I don't enjoy arguing with you. I'll see you. I think I will be able to talk to you when I have had time to forgive you. Good night."

She ends up practically throwing a very reluctant me out of her house, and I drive home, wondering what the hell happened. It was all so sudden and unexpected. Her mood swings can sometimes be hard to predict. She is a woman, and I must remember to understand we simply do not think the same way at times.

My bed is big and empty and lonely. I stare at the ceiling for the majority of the night, trying to think how to fix this mess. Finally I just get up to surf the Internet on my laptop. I end up watching Gwen Stefani's music video called "4 in the Morning." The lyrics are me right now. I watch beautiful Gwen with luscious pink lipstick–covered mouth roll around on her bed on white sheets, singing about a love she is afraid is slipping away from her. I click *Play* on it over and over until my eyes are red from staring at it. It is a long, long night of worry and panic.

One night in Purgatory again. So far, that is.

The next day, she won't answer the phone, return messages, or answer a text from me. Slight panic ensues on my part, fearing a return to the Week from Hell. I have to stop this before it really gets out of control. She is normally a very reasonable, understanding woman. I know she is in there somewhere.

I don't want to drive over to her home because she is making it very apparent she is not ready to deal with me at all. I make it one more night. The next day, I have to do something. I need to see her. So I end up doing the only thing a man can think to do in this situation. I end up with a dozen long-stemmed red roses. Thorns removed. I head to her house and ring the doorbell.

I wait. I ring.

Her car is there; she must be home.

I wait. I ring.

I wait. I ring.

Is she going to really leave me out here alone with the damn roses?

I wait and then ring the doorbell again.

I knock on the door. I am wondering if I should toss a pebble on her upstairs window. I think about getting out my phone and calling her. Where is she? Did she go for a walk around the neighborhood or get picked up in a friend's car?

Finally, finally she answers the door and lets me in. I almost drop to my knees to apologize profusely. The words, "I'm sorry, I'm sorry" are about to burst forth. But she takes the flowers, kisses, and hugs me before she leads me upstairs. I guess the flowers said it for me. All seems to be forgiven.

No Week from Hell for me. Just a Night, Day, and Another Night from Hell. I almost didn't survive it.

We spend a lot of time together, as much as she'll let me. She's never really made me go more than two days without seeing her. We stay at her house since I basically still have no furniture. I love hanging out with her, doing whatever she wants. Of course, I love making love to her.

I find I absolutely hate sleeping alone now. For someone who has basically slept alone the majority of his life, this is big. I love waking up with her. We make sure we make love most days either at night before we go to sleep or in the morning. Sometimes I'll wake her up even in the middle of the night, or occasionally an afternoon love in the light of day. I am thrilled when she wakes me up for loving or attacks me first all over the house.

I don't get to have her every day, but it's more than enough to keep me satisfied and no longer frustrated. I'm an extremely happy guy.

I find out she hates to shop, which is surprising in a woman. This is shocking to me because first of all, she has a lot of clothes and shoes, and second, I want to give her things.

So where did all that stuff come from if she doesn't like shopping?

I've tried to buy her jewelry since I really want to see her wear something I've given her. So far, I've given her a charm bracelet, some earrings, and two necklaces. I pick out classic diamond pieces so that she'll be able to wear them the rest of our lives. There is definitely one diamond in particular I want to see her wearing, the one which says she belongs to me and no other. But I am still making sure I don't rush her too much. She could run on me. I can't have that happen. She did once already. I will do everything I can to avoid that situation again.

There's nothing right now keeping us together other than our love and desire for one another. I know that's a lot, but I find I really want her to be mine legally as well. I worry if something should happen to her, I would have no legal say in her care. God forbid that should happen, but she needs someone to be there for her.

I've made arrangements to change my will, so she'll be taken care of if something should happen to me. I know it's only been a while since we started to date, but I am sure in my decision. If I am gone, I want her to be taken care of no matter what. It gives me a little peace of mind.

By now, we've been dating during the summer for a little over two months. I decide it's time for me to meet her best girlfriend Mackenzie. I'm a little surprised we haven't met yet. I want Becca to want to show me off to her friends, for Pete's sake. From what I can tell, these two women have been through everything together. Mackenzie is divorced as well, and I feel sure they must have been a comfort for each other during those times. They're always on the phone with each other every night and texting constantly during the day at all hours. I know she knows about me by now. Judging from how women talk, she probably knows more about me than I'm comfortable thinking about. I can only hope Becca keeps our most private moments private. I trust her.

One afternoon after I notice her receive yet another text from Mackenzie (she has her own ringtone that I can recognize now), I broach the subject cautiously.

"Baby, do you want to invite her up here to have lunch with us sometime? I'd like to meet her. What do you think?"

"Michael, Mackenzie doesn't drive up the Interstate 64 anymore. I have to drive down to Portsmouth to see her."

What? Well, okay then.

"We can drive down there and meet her somewhere. Do you have a special place in mind we could go?"

She thinks for a moment. "She likes Outback Steakhouse."

Good.

Medium-rare sirloin and a baked potato for me.

I'm liking this woman already.

"Okay. What day would you like to go? What about this Saturday? Call her and set it up."

Becca looks at me. "Michael, you don't have to do this."

"What are you talking about? I want to meet her. She is obviously a big part of your life. I want your friends and family to know me, as I will know them. Let's do it."

She calls Mackenzie, and I overhear them making the necessary plan. We'll drive down and meet her at twelve-thirty for lunch. Saturday comes and we make our way to Portsmouth. It's actually a pretty little city next to the Elizabeth River and across the water from Norfolk. Becca grew up here, so she shows me her old neighborhood and the house in which she grew up. We get to the restaurant early and sit down with menus and wait.

When Mackenzie arrives, I stand up, introduce myself, and help her into her chair. She is a tall woman, and cute. I can immediately see they really are best friends. We place our orders. The conversation flows easily, and I'm glad to see I'm included. I like watching Becca interact with her best friend, relaxed and happy.

Our lunches arrive, and we work our way through the salad and bread first. My medium-rare steak finally shows, and I contently enjoy myself. The food is excellent. I think I'm making a good impression because Mackenzie talks to me frequently. She is watching me as much as I'm watching Becca. We have a nice, long lunch, not rushing because the conversation is so good.

I like her. She has a dry, slightly sarcastic sense of humor I find funny, and I can tell she loves Becca, too.

My Marine buddy Keith pops in my head. He's a tall, good-looking guy who still holds himself like a Marine. I know him to be a stand-up guy who is dependable and responsible. That's why we hit it off and became friends. I called him during the Week from Hell, but he really didn't understand about Becca then.

We drove down one day so he could meet Becca in person. I think one look at her was all it took for him for him to understand she was totally worth all the pain she put me through when she withheld herself from me for that week. The uncertain waiting was hell, not knowing if she was going to give me another chance.

After meeting him, Becca mentioned her friend Mackenzie was single. Now that I've met her, I think I'll ask Becca to ask Mackenzie if she would accept a phone call from him.

I've even driven down to meet him at the shooting range on Virginia Beach Boulevard. I have a 10 mm handgun, and Keith owns a 9 mm. I enjoy challenging him to see which one of us ends up with the best target score. I end up with a tight grouping in the chest area while he misses a few shots at the head. I like shooting and improving my skills with a gun. Having been around them often as a Marine at war makes me treat all firearms with the respect they deserve as a killing weapon.

Becca surprises me when she says she has shot a .22-caliber rifle, a .357 Magnum, and a black-powder rifle as well. I ask her if she has guns in her house, but she says she doesn't. It was Tripp who used to take her to an outdoor firing range when they were married.

Bastard. But I am glad she has had some experience with firearms and knows whether or not a safety is engaged on a handgun.

Mackenzie seems to be around the right age for Keith, although I am not that good at judging ages. I wonder if maybe they might like each other. I've never been a matchmaker before. But I think it might be possible for me to make sure the two of them meet each other at some point. We could double date if they start to go out too. It might be fun, and I know I want Becca to get to know Keith better. I rein my thoughts in, trying not to get ahead of myself. I tend to jump the gun sometimes. After all, they have to actually meet each other first.

I make a note to remember to ask Becca what she thinks of the matchmaking idea. She could feel Mackenzie out first to see if she would be interested in meeting one of my Marine buddies and would want me to give Keith her number. I'll give him a call as well.

Who knows, it might work out. Now that I'm happy, I want others to be as well.

When it is finally time for us to say good-bye, we walk out into the parking lot to go to our cars. I tell Mackenzie how nice it was to finally meet her. She smiles at me and gives me a quick hug.

As she pulls away, she looks up at me and quietly murmurs, "Thank you for making her so happy."

Yeah, I can be charming.
One girlfriend on my side now.
I knew I could do it.

We get in our cars, and I watch to make sure Mackenzie's car starts and she drives away safely home. I turn to Becca.

"How did I do, Ms. Connelly? Did I pass the girlfriend test? Do you think Mackenzie liked me?"

"I do, Mr. Stevens, I do think she liked you very much. But not as much as I like you."

"I'm very glad to hear that. I want you to like me."

"Let me show you how much I like you, Michael."

Okay. What's going on here? We're sitting in a parking lot at a restaurant in the middle of a sunny afternoon. There are cars all around us. However, I don't see any people walking to get in their cars.

I am sitting in the driver's seat, and Becca moves as close as she can get. I feel her fingers find my zipper and pull it down slowly. I rise up a bit to give her access to me as she reaches in and finds me. I harden instantly at the touch of her hand on me. She pauses a moment and then removes her hand, leaving me exposed and wanting. I see her reach into her purse and pull out a small bottle of hand cream. She pours some on her right hand before running her now slick palm up and down my dick. Her hand grips me tightly, pulling me up and then sliding back down.

She is giving me an incredible hand job in public.

I struggle to maintain my composure. If anyone saw us, they would only see us sitting close together. She keeps up the pressure, gradually increasing the strength and speed of her caresses. I lean my head back on the headrest with my eyes closed. It is all I can do to concentrate on all these feelings and emotions.

The feel of her hand sliding up and down me, how hard she is gripping and caressing my cock, is extraordinary. I try hard to hold still in my seat, but find I am thrusting my hips upward without thinking. I swallow the groans welling up in my throat. Becca is so close, breathing encouraging sexual words in my ear. She tells me to come for her.

I begin to feel it coming over me, the inevitable building of immense sexual pleasure. I am about to come all over the place. Unbelievably, I feel her warm mouth swoop down on me, licking, sucking, and deeply taking me between her lips. That's all it took. I throw my head back even further, grunting out, "I love you!" as I lose all control in her mouth.

She swallows and licks me clean slowly and completely before raising her head from me. I look at her in complete amazement and unable to verbalize a coherent sentence. She looks quite pleased with herself.

Such a bold move on her part.

"Oh, honey, that was so good, so surprising. What did I do to deserve such attention from you?"

"Don't you know I pay very close attention to you, sweetheart?"

The thought crosses my mind. I had wondered if once I had her, my desire would gradually go away, having satisfied that sexual curiosity. But my desire seems to have grown even more if that is possible. Once we started to have sex, it has become absolutely impossible for either of us to stop. We can't stop wanting each other desperately, it seems. So desperate, she makes love to me in my car, in public, in a parking lot, in the middle of a hot, bright summer day. The genie has been let out of the bottle for us both. He's refusing to go back in now.

I drive her home across the bridge tunnel and up the peninsula. It takes us an hour to get home and for me to get her in her bed, naked. I exact my revenge on her for the very public sexy attack I endured in my car today. I have her in private. I spend a good forty-five minutes simply kissing her all over her body. Everywhere and I mean everywhere.

Slow tender kisses; moist licking kisses; deep, tongue-penetrating kisses; softly sucking kisses; slightly painful biting kisses; open-mouth, teeth-clashing kisses; worshiping kisses; sexy kisses; passionate-attack kisses. She loses all control when I enter her roughly, pounding my love into her intimately. I soon follow her lead as I let my climax overwhelm me.

She is my one and only love.

CHAPTER 17

Career Crisis Coming On

Late August has now arrived. And then I realize it is time for her to go back to work.

Shit.

For someone who is not a morning person and who seems to love to sleep late, all of a sudden she has to be up at five-thirty. She's out the door no later than six forty-five.

I hate this.

She stays gone the whole day, not getting home until sometimes after six or even seven at night.

And the students haven't even shown up yet. I know once school really starts, she'll have meetings, papers to grade, report cards, lesson plans, high-pressure tests, etc., etc., etc., to prepare for at night. She won't have any time for me. She's told me she doesn't enjoy teaching as she once did. It sounds like an incredibly high-stress job to me, and I know about high-stress jobs.

She tells me she really used to enjoy it when she first started out. She says the kids were different then—happier, cooperative, and fun to be around. She loved them, and they loved her. She even became so close to a girl named Lauren she once taught they became friends when she grew up. Becca says she loved Lauren right from the start, almost like a daughter, even though she isn't actually old enough to be her mother. Lauren came to Becca's wedding and became a teacher as well. She even asked Becca to be her daughter's godmother. They keep in touch with each other every so often since Lauren lives with her husband Samuel and daughter Mason in Portsmouth.

It wasn't until the last five years or so the neighborhood around her school seemed to change. It became filled with gangs and broken families who have lost control of their children. Often the police show up at her school, and there is always a security guard there in case some crazy person decides to shoot up the school or a kid goes really crazy. Lockdowns. Her pay isn't that great, the kids are frequently serious behavior problems, and the administration is useless.

She tells me she is often caught between angry kids, angry parents, and angry principals while all she's trying to do is her job. She frequently doesn't have the time to even eat lunch or go to the bathroom because it is only twenty-five minutes, and she has to watch the kids get their lunch and be seated, check e-mail, and get ready for the afternoon lessons. No lunch or bathroom breaks often. That's no kind of job to have. I could take care of her easily. She really doesn't need to work.

Besides, then we could travel whenever we want to. I think briefly of a driving trip back to Jackson, Mississippi, and wonder if she would like to see where I was born. But there really is not much there, no family anymore. My parents are buried there since they moved back after Dad retired from the army. I want to show her the world. We could spend a month or more exploring England or maybe France, two of the most beautiful countries I've ever seen.

Wait, no, Switzerland is the most stunning. Those snow-covered rocky Alpine mountains and crystal-clear lakes and milky blue glacier rivers are unforgettable. I'd like to take her there. That's what I want to do. But when I feel her out about quitting her job, she seems shocked.

"Michael, I can't quit my job. I have to support myself. I have a mortgage, car loan, and other bills to pay, you know."

"No, you don't. Not really. Not anymore."

She doesn't know I received several million in my inheritance from my parents and grandparents.

"What are you saying, Michael? That'll you'll take care of me? We've only been seeing each other for a few months. I can't depend on you financially."

"I'm saying you don't have to work if you don't enjoy it anymore."

Fuck, I can tell I'm on the losing side of this argument right now.

"What else can I do? You're not going to take care of me, Michael. I take care of myself. I have now for quite some time. I'm not going to be dependent on you by quitting my job. What if something happens? What if we break up? I'd be left without a job, a way to make money. I won't be caught unable to take care of myself again."

Well, that's definitely not going to happen. We're not breaking up. No way in hell. Over my dead body. Goddamn it, if you'd only marry me . . . then would you let me take care of you? Let me. I'll make your life fun.

"But I want to take care of you, baby."

I don't think she's going to give in. She's not budging on this. Stubborn woman.

"This isn't up for debate, Michael. Let it go."

Okay, that didn't go so well. But if I see this job stress her out and exhaust her, I'm going to have to step in. Twelve or more hours a day working is ridiculous. I guarantee I'm way more stubborn than she'll ever be. I'll give her until Christmas. That's when I plan on proposing. And it's going to be as fucking romantic as I can make it. I am ready to be her husband and for her to be my wife. Mrs. Stevens. I want my life to really start already. With her.

My worst nightmare comes true when Becca starts teaching in the fall. She is so busy during the day by the time she gets home and starts on even more work; she's exhausted and falls asleep as soon as she gets into bed. Before I know it, she's out the door in the early morning and gone again, repeating the same thing day after day during the school week. Sometimes she even comes home in tears after having had a particularly stressful day.

From what I can tell, she's trapped alone in a room with disrespectful little hellions for seven hours a day, let alone all the work she does before and after school. She has no time on her own during the day, meetings scheduled during the resource times when the students go to gym, art, music, and the library.

That is why she has to work before school, after school, at home during the evening, and weekends. I notice she tries to take a break only on Saturday, but then she has to catch up on laundry, cleaning, groceries, and errands. Sundays are spent typing lesson plans and preparing for class.

I know not all the kids are bad, but there are enough who make it hard to teach sometimes. There are so many more students with learning problems or health issues needing to be addressed. Some students are dealing with abuse at home or homeliness. She has IEP meetings all the time, trying to get them the help they need. School psychologists, counselors, social workers, etc.

There never seems to be enough hours in the day for her to finish everything she has to do. She is responsible for spelling, grammar, writing, reading, math, science, social studies, health, handwriting, library research skills, and computer technology. When the students go to lunch, she has to stay with them until they all have lunch and are seated eating. There were times when she was called back to the cafeteria because of behavior issues. Even though she is supposed to have a twenty-five-minute duty-free lunch, it just isn't possible.

The students used to come to her basically ready for fifth grade with all the prerequisite skills, but that is no longer true. Even something as simple as cursive handwriting. Becca said she simply had to give up fighting that battle. She had to go back and start with many of the basics, lessons they should have already learned in previous grades. That put her behind, and it wasn't something she could rush. But she had to, leaving some students behind, simply trying to cover everything before high-pressure tests at the end of the quarter.

The student scores were examined extensively, and of course, it was hard to see some students were not as successful as she had hoped. But how could they have been when she had to throw lesson after lesson at them, just hoping some of them got it? She says the school system piles on more and more responsibilities and never takes anything off her plate. She tells me she tries so hard to do as she is told. But there is so much that it becomes an impossible task. I see that it is wearing down her confidence in herself as a competent teacher.

She says her end-of-the-year test scores have basically been good, and I know she is proud of that. But she is seeing a difference since she is not being allowed to teach the way she is comfortable with, the way she knows works for her and her students. The school system is micromanaging the classroom teachers, keeping them to strict schedules and a strict curriculum. I understand why they did it, but I can see Becca liked her freedom as a teacher when she could plan her day and spend as much time on a subject as she needed to until she felt confident they understood. The schedule would make her stop suddenly no matter what because it was time to move on to something else. She hated leaving the students hanging and still confused about the lesson. She would rather have extended the time a bit until they got it. But she couldn't.

Becca says she used to have time to talk to the students in the morning before they really start into the lessons. She enjoyed the stories of their lives and shared with them her stories. It made them love each other and know one another as a classroom family. Now she barely knows about their lives, and they don't feel close to her.

Becca loves to read, and she tells me she used to read to the class after they came back in after recess and lunch. It was just a little downtime before getting back into the academic lessons. Reading to them was her favorite time of the day, and the students really looked forward to it as much as she did. They could just relax, enjoy the story, and not feel any pressure to learn.

But the tight schedule took that time away from her as well. She really loved reading out loud to them and sharing her favorite books. The kids loved it too and would often try to check the book out from the school library so they could read along with her. She tells me a mom once called her to say for the very first time that her son asked for a book for his birthday instead of a video game. She was so proud of that. She fostered in the students a love of reading. But that is not allowed any longer.

I can see Becca is exhausted by it all already and feeling defeated.

The school year is a marathon from start to finish. She has to deal with professional development, guidance lessons, graduate courses, faculty meetings, bulletin boards, display cases, writing tests, quizzes, classwork, homework, learning centers, substitute teacher plans, something called 504 plans, planning assembly presentations, keeping parent contact logs up-to-date, cutting out and making teaching materials, developing math and reading games, dealing with special-education students and their assistants in the classroom, science experiments, and materials.

There are SOLs in every academic area; pacing guides; interactive notebooks in science and social studies; graphic organizers; streaming videos for lessons; DVDs; word processing; PowerPoints; writing workshop lessons to teach writing skills; revising and editing student papers for their final copies; teacher training; summative units for evaluation; hall duty; lunch duty; field-day games; curriculum development conferences; endless lesson plans; developing tests; grading papers; computer skills; averaging grades; observations; parent-teacher conferences during the day, after school, and in the evening; school board meetings; PTA meetings at night; phone calls or e-mails to uncooperative parents; and daily school-related e-mails to constantly check so that she is kept informed.

Meetings with the principal and assistant principal, keeping track of student medications with the nurse, teacher evaluations, interim reports four times a year, report cards four times a year, honor roll ceremonies after each grading period, handing out healthy vegetable and fruit snacks, paying for student lunches when they have no money, monitoring their behavior at the lunch line and table, restroom and water breaks twice a day for the class, recess, and dismissal procedures to make sure all her students get on the right bus and home safely.

The list of responsibilities grows and grows. Keeping student educational records organized and up-to-date, posting grades online, keeping websites up-to-date with assignments, sex education lessons twice a year with the nurse, career day, DARE lessons with a local police officer, grade-level meetings, social committee duties, child study forms and meetings to write IEPs for struggling students, meeting with school psychologists and social workers, school-improvement discussions, snow makeup days, classroom management procedures, quarterly tests, math and reading cards, and end-of-year exams.

She has to keep track of the behavior-modification program, attendance reports, absence notes, sorting graded papers for student folders and checking for parent signatures, guidance lessons, collecting money for fees, lunch orders sent on time to the cafeteria each morning, child abuse awareness, blood-borne disease training, field trips, parent luncheon, and the end-of-the-year promotion activities and ceremony.

And of course, making sure the students actually learn what she is teaching them by constantly monitoring their knowledge and academic performance so she can adjust instruction to fill any need. Since she is in a new grade for her this year, she has to learn a whole new curriculum and set of SOLs, the absolute guide of essential knowledge and skills for the fourth grade.

This is besides the fact that she spends a great deal of her own money buying school supplies for her class: things like pencils, pens, notebooks, scissors, tape, crayons, glue, paper, card stock, poster boards, and magic markers. During the holidays, she tells me she makes homemade treats to the students as well as a gift for each of them at the Christmas party. She buys construction paper so she can make things she calls math, science, social studies, writing, and reading centers and games.

It's ridiculous how many things for which she is responsible. It's overwhelming, and I am stunned by it all. I had no idea. I try to be supportive and take care of her as much as I can. I can see she can't do this the rest of her life.

After she agrees to marry me, I'll end this nightmare for her. I will. I can be very persuasive.

Career crisis calmly solved by my charming competency and caring concern.

For my future wife.
Rebecca.
Teachers do it with class.

CHAPTER 18

Falling More in Love in the Fall

The only time she is able to relax some is on the weekends. I try to make them as fun as I can. I almost have to force her to take a break from her work. While the weather is still warm in September, we drive down to the Outer Banks in North Carolina to spend the day. The water is too chilly to get in now, but we both enjoy just sitting on the beach and listening to the waves. We people-watch, but mainly I Becca-watch. She looks so cute in her bathing suit top, shorts, baseball cap, and sunglasses. Of course, I apply and reapply and reapply her sunscreen as much as I can. I can't have her if she has a sunburn.

We eat lunch outside at a cute restaurant in Duck called Roadside Inn. It serves great salads, shrimp and grits, and bread pudding with Jack Daniels whiskey sauce. I remember Becca also ordered shrimp and grits at the Winery when I first met Sara and Roger. They seem to be a favorite of hers. I watch her take a bite and close her eyes as she enjoys it. These shrimp are nestled in a brown gravy on top of the bed of grits. I can see her about to bust. Her eyes are sparkling with amusement, and I know what is about to happen. I eat and wait for it to happen. I don't have to wait long. She is like a well-oiled Southern comedian.

I may have to cover her in oil someday.

"Here, Michael, eat my grits."

"Becca, you know I told you before I don't care for grits. I am not sure I even like shrimpy things either."

I am not a shrimp guy.

Anywhere.

"But these grits are not gritty, I promise. The shrimp are tender. You will like it."

Not as tender as you, my love.

"Thank you, but no."

"I don't really understand. You are from Mississippi. Southerners eat grits. It is found all over the South."

"My mom was from Iowa. She liked Cream of Wheat instead."

"I guess that explains a lot. Cream of Wheat is nothing but tasteless mush, Michael."

Mush? Now oatmeal is mush, not cream of wheat.

"It's what we ate in the winter for breakfast."

"Mama fixed Daddy bacon and scrambled eggs every morning. I remember waking up to the smell of frying bacon when I was a little girl. Sometimes she would dip the hardened grits into an egg batter and fry it in an iron skillet. Daddy liked it but I actually wouldn't try it then."

Bacon is a basic food group. I would have liked her daddy.

"I bet you were a cute little girl."

"No, I wanted to be like Jason, so had my hair cut short and with side bangs similar to him for a while. Probably it was when I was in the fifth and sixth grades. After that, I grew my hair long and straight. I was tall and gangly as a teenager but filled out in college."

You wanted to look like a boy? No way in hell you could be mistaken for that now.

"Look how you turned out, my love. I love your long legs, especially when they are wrapped around me."

I wish you could spread them for me now, but . . .

I reach for the butter and spread it on my soft roll, smiling to myself as she looks at me wondering what is so funny.

Yeah, I know. Not really so soft. The bread yes, me no.

"Shhh. There are children at the next table."

"I'm sorry. I forget where I am sometimes. If I keep watching you enjoy those grits though, I am going to have to take you somewhere so I can take you. Do you know where I can take you to take you?"

Take me now please.

"You can take me home later, Stevens. Home it will have to be. Show some true grit. You can hang in there, I know it."

"I am full of grit. I was the grittiest Marine there ever was in Iraq. Maybe that is why I don't like grits. It reminds me of all the gritty sand I had all over me when I was there. It got everywhere. Really hard to get off."

"Oh really, Marine? Everywhere? How hard was it to get off? Did you get it off in the shower? You'll have to show me later."

I am about to giggle, I know it.

"I will. Count on it."

"I will too. Count on me to find all your gritty places. Now let me eat my grits in peace, please. Enjoy your rabbit food salad."

We talk about maybe renting one of the beach houses for a week next summer so we don't have to drive down and back to Williamsburg in one day. I like she is seeing a longtime future with me. I put in a Beach Boys greatest hits CD for the ride home and we sing "Good Vibrations," "Wouldn't It Be Nice," and "God Only Knows" together.

On Saturdays during the fall, we go to several football games at William and Mary's cute little brick Zable Stadium on campus. Go Tribe! Becca knows as much about football as I do. She likes to sit in the end zone stands under the scoreboard instead of the fifty-yard-line seats. From everything she says, she really understands the plays, penalties, and scoring.

She follows the NFL's Washington Redskins and Peyton Manning with Denver for some reason and actually was one of the volunteer trainers for the Tribe football team when she was a student here. She says all she really did was tie the players' shoelaces and squirt water in their mouths during timeouts. She tells me the locker room at the stadium was where she saw her first real live naked man in all his full frontal glory.

Evidently she saw quite a few of them all at once.

Umm.

Many Sundays are spent watching professional NFL football games on television while Becca grades thick stacks of student classwork, homework, and tests so she won't get behind in her work. It usually takes her all day to get it all done and then has to type lesson plans for the following week. I think she works too damn hard. She really only can relax a bit on Saturdays, for goodness' sakes.

She does seem to manage keeping an eye on the football games, though, and makes comments about the plays. She gets excited if the Redskins or Denver Broncos win, which isn't as often as she would like. She knows so much about the professional NFL players, coaches, and stadiums.

When I ask her about it, she just says she watched games with her dad and brother when she was growing up. Since there was only one television with three channels, there wasn't any choice in the matter. I think she watches SportsCenter because she knows past and present players. Maybe I'll take her to an actual Redskins game. She says she has never been to a professional game, only high school and college. And her dad once took her to an exhibition game in Norfolk between the Redskins and the Steelers when she was little.

How do I get tickets for a Redskins game? Internet, I guess.

When the fall leaves change colors, we drive to the Blue Ridge Mountains, stopping at wineries and quaint restaurants for lunch. We even take her sister and brother-in-law with us on a winery outing. We end up going to Trump Winery near Thomas Jefferson's Monticello in Charlottesville. The tasting room and restaurant are delightful and set back in the trees. We eat outside on the side patio under an umbrella table. Lunch is delicious, and Becca suggests I try the Cru wine. She says it is unlike anything I have ever tasted. It is truly unique, a cross between a sweet white wine and hard liquor. I buy a bottle for us to take home and enjoy. Roger and Sara seem to have a good time with us. Since I'm still around after five months, I think I passed their test.

One Sunday night not long after that, we're watching the football game between the Broncos and the Cowboys in her great room when the doorbell suddenly rings. Becca goes downstairs to see who it is. I can't really hear anything because the game is on, but suddenly I think I hear Becca say, "No, you can't come in."

Now, I'm wondering what the hell is going on downstairs in the foyer? Who is it?

I sprint across the room, going down the steps so fast that I'm practically falling down them. Not my most graceful entrance, but at least I'm downstairs and standing next to her. When I look out the open front door, I cannot believe my eyes. Her ex-husband Tripp is standing there on the porch.

Fuck! What the hell? I stare at him, completely at a loss.

Tripp holds his hand up, shooting me a look of disgust. He's looking at me like he can't believe I'm standing right there in front of him. I know he wishes I wasn't.

He says harshly, "I need to speak to you, Becca. If you don't let me come in and talk to you, you'll be hearing from my lawyer."

What?

"You are not coming in this house under any circumstances, do you hear me?" I say to him just as harshly.

He turns to Becca and stares at her. "Is that what you want?"

Becca doesn't blink. "I told you that you can't come in. What does your lawyer have to say to me?"

Tripp has a smug smirk on his face as he says, "Becca, we're still married. Legally. Our divorce was handled improperly, and it was never completely finalized. Legal procedures were not followed correctly after that, and our lawyers didn't notice fifteen years ago. I assume there was a mix-up at the courthouse. The fact is we are actually still married according to the law, nullifying my marriages since then. You're legally my wife. I just found out myself."

All the breath leaves my body.

Oh no. Oh no. Fuck. Shit. Goddamn it.

Becca whispers, shocked, "But . . . but I signed the papers. I saw your signature."

I step in front of her protectively. "She's with me now. She'll never be your wife again."

Tripp smirks slightly and stares at her. "But you are my wife, Becca. Maybe you could give me another chance. When I saw you again . . . I've changed. You loved me once, you can do it again. I want you back."

He seems to care less that I'm standing right there glaring at him.

"You're . . . already married, aren't you? Haven't you been married three times? Divorced twice, once to me and then to your second wife," Becca murmurs.

"I don't want to be married to my third wife. Not anymore. This whole legal mix-up came to light when I tried to divorce her after seeing you last summer. My third marriage is now nullified. It was during this third divorce proceeding I found out about our marriage being official."

"Tripp, I'm with Michael now. I love him and he makes me happy, happier than I ever was with you. I once thought I'd give anything for you to come back to me, but it simply isn't true any longer. It hasn't been true for years now. I was young then and foolish, caught up in the idea of love. It is obvious to me you didn't ever love me. You wouldn't have left the way you did if you had. I don't want you back, and I certainly never want to be your wife again. No matter what, we're not getting back together. Please leave me alone."

Tripp glares at me before turning back to look at her, saying, "You don't really mean that. We are legally married. I know you once wanted us to get back together again after I left you. We can make it happen now."

I have had enough. More than enough. He doesn't seem to actually get that I'm standing right there glaring at him. Does he see me? I sure as hell see him. I'm right here next to her and not going anywhere. Becca is mine, not his anymore. I make my presence blatantly clear.

I grit through my teeth. "My attorney will be contacting you to take of this whether you want it or not. She will absolutely be through with you . . . legally. I'll make sure of it. Becca's not yours. She's belongs with me!"

Before I can stop myself, I launch myself toward him, my fist connecting first to his mouth and swiftly then to his jaw.

I've wanted to do that for a while now. It feels fucking great.

He staggers back and falls down the steps on the concrete. Blood is dripping from a cut on his lip as he stands and sneers at us. I'm a little surprised he hasn't tried to hit me back.

190

Yeah, go ahead and try it, asshole. I hope you do. Give me a chance to really beat the shit out of you.

"I guess it doesn't matter then. She was actually a disappointment in bed." After that parting shot, he stalks off toward his car.

I'm not about to tell him what I know for sure. It only took the right man, and that right man is me. Never was him. Never will be him.

I gather her into my arms as she suddenly bursts into tears. "Don't worry, baby. I'll take care of this. It's a matter of some legal paperwork. I'll call my attorney tomorrow, and it will all be over soon. I promise."

"Oh Michael, are you all right? Did you hurt your hand? I can't believe you hit him. What he said, what he said about me . . . I'll never be free of him, will I? He's already caused me so much pain. I don't think I can take anymore."

"Why won't he leave me alone? He's the one who left me, not the other way around. So why does he all of a sudden want me back after all these years? I haven't seen him since we did taxes together one last time after what I thought was our divorce. That was the last time. I don't have any idea where he has been living since he left. It was only when he called out of the blue to tell me he wanted Granny Ruth's bracelet for his daughter I even learned about his three children and second and third wives."

"Becca, don't worry about me. My hand feels great. He deserved to be hit. He acted like I wasn't even there. I am convinced he is delusional, thinking he can get back with you. I will call my attorney and set up a meeting. There's nothing he can really do if you just stand firm and not give in. He can't make you stay married to him if you don't want to be. It will all be over, and he will be gone from our lives. I promise."

The only man you're going to be married to is me, baby.

"Michael, thank you so much. He is scaring me. I never thought I'd be scared of him, but now I am. He's not the same man I once loved and married. He seems so different. It's like I don't know him anymore. It has been so long, so I guess that's true. I don't know what I would do without you now. You make me feel so much better, so safe and secure. I know you'll take care of it. Because I can't stand the thought I am still legally married to him. I have to get out of this nightmare somehow."

"He is just trying to control you all over again, Becca. Since he is divorcing wife number three, he's alone and looking for something. Evidently he's a serial monogamist. He can't have you, so now that is all he wants."

"Since I saw him again, I have been doing some serious thinking. Tripp grew up as an army brat, moving around his whole life every few years. He is used to reinventing himself over and over, leaving behind friends and making new ones quickly. He has disposable lives. He can throw away any life and start over almost as a brand-new person. I grew up in the same house, living there with my parents until I was grown. I should have realized we didn't want the same things or have the same values. I wanted a loving, stable marriage I could depend upon forever. I wanted to feel secure and loved and cared for like my parents' marriage."

"I should not have been surprised when he left me, starting all over again somewhere else, because that is what he had done his whole life. He could be whoever he wanted to be, meeting new people and living in new places with a new life. He did it again with wife number two and now wife number three. From what little I can tell, it appears he hangs around for a bit before leaving again. Those poor women, unfortunately expecting him to commit to them for the rest of their lives, like I once did. His second wife gave him three children and that didn't keep him from leaving either. He is just incapable of a long-lasting exclusive loving relationship. I shouldn't have been shocked when our marriage failed. It was doomed from the start, only I didn't know it yet."

She pauses a bit before continuing. "I thought I was happy at first. I was young and naïve. So stupidly swept away and in love with the idea of being in love and loved in return. He brought me red roses all of the time. It was the first time I had ever been so far from Virginia and my family. I only had him to depend on to make me feel safe. He did. We had a great time in California, and I am thankful I was able to experience it."

She pauses as if remembering. "Things began to fall apart a bit in Charleston even though I refused to really see. I was unable to think about it since my mama was dying of cancer the last spring we lived there. She died in May, and we moved to Williamsburg two months later."

"Cracks began to form when I found out Tripp was accused of sexually harassing a younger female officer who served under him on his ship in Charleston. Yes, obviously he wanted a younger woman under him at his service. I mean, after all she had to obey his orders since he was the Executive Officer on board. He wouldn't tell me much about it, and I had no way of finding out what really happened between them. I know she pressed charges, and he received a letter of reprimand. Next thing I knew he was passed over for promotion and basically kicked out of the service and unemployed."

"He got a part-time job in town, but the pay was very low, and we began to struggle to make ends meet on my small teacher salary. I bought him suits and shirts and ties to help him interview, and we set up a meeting with a headhunter to help him get his resumes out. He finally got a job in Maryland. I found out about the job at his sister's wedding rehearsal dinner when he told everyone at our table something about which I knew nothing. And I was his wife; he should have told me first he had accepted the job."

"Before I knew it, he moved up to Maryland the next week and rented a small high-rise apartment. He had no intention of me and our two dogs following him during the summer after I finished out the school year. It all happened in a matter of around six weeks from start to finish. He let me see the apartment once, but I found a framed photo he had taken of me stuffed in a drawer instead of out where he could see it. Our marriage ended a week and a half later when he came home on the weekend long enough to tell me his life was in Maryland and mine was in Williamsburg. At least he faced me in person instead of calling on the phone. I should have seen it coming."

"Now I see that marriage as the biggest mistake of my life. I never should have married him. We didn't know each other and got married quickly, very quickly. I was young and caught up in the attention because I had never had it before. I hope you understand a little better now why I felt like I needed to know you well before we got seriously involved. I don't want to make the same mistake and leap into anything too soon. I'd rather be alone. I know I can do that."

Becca pauses before continuing. "I will not be fooled again like I was when I was young and lovestruck. It causes me too much self-doubt and heartbreak. I can hardly believe this is the same man I once thought I loved. He seems so different, like a completely different person than the one in my memories. So now what do I do to make him leave me alone? I just can't, I just can't see him again. I am afraid I'll have to see him in court or some lawyer's office to try and end this mistake of a marriage."

"Don't worry, baby. I'll call my attorney now and see what I can do."

I don't remind her I was an army brat too. I don't want her to think I can't commit. To me, just the fact I haven't ever really had a stable home makes it the one thing I wish for the most. I have no need to move around constantly. I'm glad to see she finally understands she would never have been happy with Tripp if he had stayed. I know it hurt her at the time, but it was for the best in the long run. I am only mad he still has some kind of insane legal claim on her. I will take care of this and make it all go away.

And I do immediately. I talk to Jake Haskell, my attorney in Richmond. He gets the ball rolling on their divorce as quickly as he can. I admit the whole legal process took a while, us meeting with him, my attorney, and his attorney.

I find out I can't handle it all for her. She is going to have to be present during the proceedings. Becca is calm and brave during our meetings with him, not giving an inch. Tripp really doesn't want to let go of her, so I know he didn't mean what he said. Or maybe he just gets off having some kind of control over her. I guess he is shocked when he sees she's grown into the beautiful woman she is now and not the girl he married. Even though I am there, he saw a chance and tried to take it. I'm glad it's finally over when she is legally free of him. But somehow I can't quite relax. I won't forget about him.

With that drama now behind us, I can concentrate on appreciating my Becca. Once she calms down about it and realizes it is completely over with Tripp, she seems like a different woman. I hope she's starting to realize she is so much better off without him.

He's truly a delusional asshole.

Friday evening I decide to take her out to dinner at the Trellis since we've never been there at night. When I pick her up that evening, she has on a beautiful dark green dress that brings out the color of her eyes. I can't take my eyes off her. I manage to get her to the restaurant without wrecking the car. We're seated in the back corner of the Trellis.

Back corner in the dim candlelit restaurant. No other tables too close. Very few other patrons eating dinner.

I realize I like how our table is a bit . . . isolated.

Dinner, of course, is delicious, and the wine complements everything. Looking over at my beautiful date for the evening, I make a decision. I am already sitting close to her so that I can put my arm around her when I want.

I lean over and breathe into her ear, "Go take your panties off for me, honey, please. Go now."

Her eyes widen, but believe it or not, she gets up and goes to the restroom.

I'm a little shocked. I wasn't sure she'd really do it, but damn. So bold and daring. I really had no idea. Who knew she would agree to this naughty game?

My cock springs to attention, but I tell him not yet. This isn't his turn now.

I don't think she has really thought this through completely from start to finish, but I am determined to give it a go. I know I can do this without anyone knowing if she just cooperates a little for me. After all, I don't want her to be embarrassed.

Umm.

When she comes back and sits next to me, I whisper to her in her ear, "Are your panties in your purse now, Ms. Connelly?" She nods, looking at me. Her eyes are a bit wide, wondering what is going to happen next.

"What color are they? I want to see. Give them to me."

"Black lace."

I hold out my hand. She frowns a bit, but reaches for her purse and hands them to me quickly. I hold them concealed in my fist up to my nose and breathe her aroused scent in deeply before putting them into my pants pocket. They are slightly damp. I know now she is aroused already for me. Looking in her eyes, I know she knows I know.

Good.

Staring into her eyes, I slowly but surely run my hand up her dress under the table.

Fuck! She has on a fucking garter belt under that dress. God, I wish I could see what color it is.

I glance down as my fingers slide her dress up just enough for me to see the tops of her stockings and the garter clips. It is black.

Oh God. I like black lingerie.

I push her thighs gently a little apart for me. When my fingers reach her, I slip two of them quickly inside of her, making her jerk.

I rest my lips on her ear, "Be quiet. Don't move at all. Let me. Keep still for me, baby. Hold still."

The only thing moving on both of us are my fingers caressing the inside of her sweet opening. I make sure the other people in the restaurant can't see what I'm doing to her in public. I surely don't want them to see Becca coming. That's for me. It looks as though we're close together.

I am surprised she is letting me do this to her, but I'm not stopping now. With one hand in her, I use the other to eat my meal. I could do this all night. I even give her a sip of her wine, watching her eyes struggle to hold it all in. I kiss her temple softly, breathing into her ear how beautiful she is to me.

And all the while, my fingers stroke her, teasing around her clitoris repeatedly. I can't believe this, but there's no way in hell I'm not going to finish her off. I think briefly of leaving her frustrated and then ending things at home or even in the car if we can't make it that far. She's starting to get wetter and wetter, her body rigid, but she's not moving, or even breathing, and she's not making a sound.

I lean over and whisper to her softly, "I love you so much. Come for me baby. Feel it. Let it come."

The choice of what to do next is taken out of my hands, so to speak. I watch in awe the changes sweep over her quietly, but intensely.

Her hips thrust forward as instantly I feel her jerk and clench all around my fingers. I suddenly feel her inside walls pulsing around my fingers and milking them. Her head falls back and she closes her eyes, clenching her teeth. She still manages not to make a sound or move much the whole time her insides are convulsing. I think she is holding her breath.

I'm amazed.

I slip my fingers gently from her after she finishes. My hand is drenched, and I wonder how big of a mess we've made together. She has on a dark colored dress thankfully. And a coat.

She seems stunned. I look into her eyes, before casually running my finger under my nose, as if I have an itch. I smear her moisture there, wanting to keep her scent in my head.

The most wonderful scent in the world to me.

Her eyes widen as comprehension dawns. I know she knows I know what I am deliberately doing. I almost lick my whole finger before stopping myself. We are still in public after all. I don't want to shock her too much. I love the way she tastes and can't get enough of her. I know I can be a bit much to handle sometimes. But she can handle me all she wants. I want to be handled by her, every part of me. She said I was intense.

Yeah, I know. I definitely can be. Hopefully, she is starting to appreciate my intensity now we are together. I know I don't scare her anymore. She trusts me.

"Would you like some dessert, Ms. Connelly? Before we leave? You can have a piece of *Death by Chocolate* if you so desire."

She releases the breath she's been holding slowly. "No, I think I just had dessert, Mr. Stevens. It was so good. I really enjoyed it. But now I can think of one other thing I desire tonight. No more dessert for me, but I know you have a bit of a sweet tooth. Let's go home so I can feed you something sweet."

"Good choice. I'm so glad your dessert was good for you. So let's get you home so I can have my own dessert. I didn't get any tonight. I need to see that garter belt, Rebecca. I think you need to let me eat the dessert we will have soon at home. Let's go home. Now."

I motion to the waiter to bring the bill so we can leave the restaurant and go for the evening.

I'm so turned on by then. I just hope I can drive us home safely. Route 5 can be a bit long and twisty, especially in the dark. I focus on the road, trying very hard not to visualize my love in her garter belt. I can't wait to get her home and have my own piece of dessert. All mine and mine alone. It's such a sweet dessert of which I can't seem to get enough. My woman loves me, shocks me, surprises me, and beguiles me with her many facets, from her innocence, passion for life, her intelligence, and love for me.

We make it in the front door before I have her pressed up against the wall in the foyer. I make sure she has on the black garter belt, black silk stockings, black stilettos, and no panties or bra. She bends over giving me the sight of her full ass cheeks waiting for me. I squat down and run my hands up each of her legs all the way up to her ass. There I spend a great deal of time tickling her with my fingers and biting her softly. She starts begging me to fuck her.

That's what I was waiting for. She bends all the way over and grabs her ankles. It is simply too erotic to stand, and I unzip quickly to enter her from behind. I have on my clothes, only my cock is naked and pounding into her. I grab her waist and rock against her until she is screaming for me to fuck her even harder.

I do my best until we both get so hot; we are sweating and sliding against each other. I begin to despair it isn't going to happen for her, when we are both taken by surprise by her overwhelming intense orgasm. I follow right behind her and we collapse mindlessly on the wooden floor. It takes us a half an hour before I can find the strength to get up and take my wife to bed for the night.

I think about how completely happy I am now. It's too good to be true and I fear too good to last. Please, God, give me this happiness. Let me spend the rest of my life making sure my love is happy too. I am so lucky and thankful I went to the Second Street Bistro for a drink that hot summer night.

CHAPTER

19

Thankful Celebrations

In November, I decide to start painting the interior of my house. There is no need to hire professionals when I am perfectly capable of doing it myself. Becca and I go to the hardware store to pick out colors. I'll slowly work my way through the house one room at a time. Everything is white right now. I'm starting with the great room.

In my own sneaky way, I make sure that any paint colors picked by us together will go with her stuff as well. I think it's only practical since I plan on her stuff becoming part of our stuff. She has a lot more than me in that department, but since my house is so much bigger than her condo, I know we'll have to fill in more. I love to buy furniture. I don't want to push my luck about her moving in with me yet although I would love that. She is a bit old-fashioned that way. I know she doesn't want her family to see her living with a man when she is not married to him despite the fact that she is a grown woman in her forties.

We end up picking out a soft taupe color for the great room. I think this will go well with Becca's big navy blue couch and love seat. Painting gives me something to do while she is at work, and I find I really enjoy it. It's easier to paint while my rooms are still basically empty. I finish up the great room late Thursday night and really like how it turned out. I hope I'm not jumping the gun, but if she accepts me when I propose, I'm hoping I can get her moved in sooner rather than later.

Friday morning finds me cleaning everything up from my own little painting party. A celebration of the first painted room in my house is in order. Trying to think of something fun and different, I head to the store for some chocolate syrup. Maybe a little cliché, but there's a reason it is so popular. It must work.

I've never really played with food before, so I hope we both like it.
I text Becca when I know she has her free lunch period.

Ms. C: Do you like chocolate? Mr. S x

It takes a while, but I finally hear back from her.

Mr. S: I'm a woman. Of course, I like chocolate. Ms. C xx

I have to wait three long hours to her to read my next text, knowing she's in class and has no time. Finally the school day is over, and I know by now she should be back in her room working. She usually stays late doing lesson plans, but I need her to come on home as soon as possible. I send it to her.

B. I have a chocolate dessert waiting for you here at my house. You really should eat it before it's all gone. M xox

M. What kind of chocolate dessert is it? I'm not sure I'll like it. Is it A LOT? B xxx

> Ms. Connelly: I KNOW this is your favorite kind of dessert. Hot fudge. I promise. You won't be disappointed. And yes, your portion will be very BIG. Mr. Stevens XOXOXOX
>
> M. I just don't know. I'm not feeling very hungry right now. B

Shit! Does that mean she's not in the mood for me? Maybe she's had a stressful day. I know how to relieve that stress. AND *where's* MY KISS? *How come I never seem to get a hug?*

> B. If you come home, I think your appetite will return when you see how delicious this particular dessert really is. M XXXXXXXXOOOOOOOOO
>
> Michael: I am on my way to your house. I'm so hungry. Feed me your sweet dessert. Will try not to wreck the car while driving and drooling. Becca XXXX
>
> B. Come to me in my bed. Mx

Okay, I have about a half an hour before she gets here. I put a sign on the front door, telling her to come into my bedroom to get her dessert. I wait for her on my bed, stripped naked. I have the chocolate syrup next to the bed. My cock is, of course, cooperating nicely. When I hear her come into the house, she calls out for me.

I yell back, "I've got your dessert ready in here." I only hope I don't look stupid. I drizzle the syrup all over my saluting cock, letting it drip down my length, lean back, and put my hands behind my head. When Becca comes in the room, she stops and stares.

Just don't laugh, please.

"So, we're skipping dinner tonight and only having dessert. Is that your plan, Mr. Stevens?"

"Yes, please."

Please?! I'm sticking with this plan. Actually feeling quite sticky, here.

"That is quite a lot of hot fudge you have there, Michael. I'm not sure I'll be able to finish such a large portion, but I am going to try. It definitely looks hot and delicious to me."

Try for me, baby.

"I know chocolate is one of your favorite things, so . . . here it is, all yours, just for you. I saved it for you. I hope you enjoy it. Only trying to keep you happy, honey. You know what they say, 'happy woman, happy life.' You know I'd do just about anything to please you. It makes me happy to see you happy."

Hint, hint, hint. Pay attention to what I am suggesting. You're a smart girl. Figure it out.

"Michael, yes, it is true I like chocolate. You know I do. I can't resist it. I almost crave it. I love it. I don't know. It is just soooo much chocolate, all at once. It might be a little too sweet for me to handle. But I do have a sweet tooth. I love a good dessert. It's the perfect way to end a meal."

I am all the dessert you need. I'm sinfully sweet. Satisfying.

I watch her closely. Her eyes are starting to have a mischievous sparkle in them. She knows exactly how her words can be interpreted by me. She is so damn quick-thinking and clever. I try to keep up with her. Everything she utters is so damn suggestive. She has mastered the art of the double entendre, sexual puns, and innuendos.

I can see she is fighting a smile, barely winning the battle of not breaking out into a full laugh now. I continue to sit there patiently, naked with a chocolate-covered erection. My ability to concentrate on the quick-witted conversation is seriously compromised. I try again.

"I think you can handle it, baby, I really, really do. I know it's sweet, but I don't think it is too sweet for you. Just give it a try. For me? If it ends up being too much, well, then just don't eat it all. It's okay if you don't. I promise. Don't worry about it at all. Just give it your best shot, and we'll see how you do."

She purses her lips and pauses as if considering.

What in the hell does she need to consider first?

"I don't think I'll be able to finish it."

Honey, don't you see me dripping with chocolate syrup? Kind of obvious here. Clean me up. Lick it all off me, for heaven's sake. It's drying. Help!

"Becca, you haven't eaten anything since lunch time. I know you barely have time to eat a decent lunch at school. You're bound to be a bit hungry, right? I don't think we'll eat dinner until much later tonight. Let's have a little dessert first, just to take the edge off your hunger."

Drying. On me. Please don't let it start to itch. Doesn't she see what is happening to me? Help me now. Come on.

"Yes, I guess so. It's just a lot to try and finish."

She doesn't really seem to be staring at me, fascinated by my penis dripping with chocolate. I start to see the corners of her lips curl slightly. I am afraid she is fighting a giggle. I'll die if she starts to actually laugh at me now. I must look damn silly, though, I know.

It's suddenly funny to me as well. The lengths I will go to in order to have my love astonishes me. Yeah, I know I'm funny. I hope I tickle my love's fancy to death. I like to tickle her.

"Honey, you're good at finishing things. I know you can do it. You always eat everything I give you. Nothing goes to waste. Ever."

"Maybe if I could have a smaller piece of chocolate."

God, the way her mind works drives me nuts. Here I am. My hard dick and nuts are covered in chocolate, for Pete's sake. It's drying up. ON ME. Not so sure about this plan anymore. I prefer liquid chocolate syrup, not a hard chocolate candy shell. Is this going to cause shrinkage?

Oh no. Not that. I am panicking a little.

"It doesn't work that way, sweetheart. This particular portion size is the only size it comes in. Sorry, but there's nothing I can do about it. It is what it is."

Don't argue. It's not going to change.

"But it's so much chocolate. So thick and smooth and sweet. Not sure I can do it. Though, you know I hate wasting something so good, so very good to eat and enjoy. It's almost a crime to let a good thing like that go to waste. I always clean my plate and never turn down a good dessert."

"Then, don't waste it, my love. Don't. I promise you I won't let you let anything go to waste. I love you so much. Come here. Your dessert is waiting for you. Not sure it can wait much longer, so come closer, please, baby. It's all for you and you alone. Please, hurry."

I'm desperate, rapidly losing the battle of control. My God, she hasn't even touched me yet.

Finally she puts me out of my misery. She didn't laugh at me although she giggled some. After all, me covered in syrup was a bit amusing.

And it wasn't too much for her to handle at all. I knew it all along. My love enjoys her chocolate. A lot. I am so thankful.

I had a very good time being . . . dessert.

Over the week, I continue to paint my way through the house slowly but surely. I don't have many rooms left to go, and I think I can finish before Christmas. Thanksgiving is almost here, and I'm getting a bit nervous. Becca's older brother Jason and his wife Elizabeth are coming to stay for the holidays. We haven't met before because they live six hours away. I feel sure they've heard a lot about me by now. I help Becca shop for the turkey and all the fixings.

Okay, time to charm the older brother as well.

Her brother Jason and Elizabeth arrive on Wednesday, but I'm not invited over until noon on Thanksgiving. I have to watch the Macy's Thanksgiving Parade all alone. When I arrive at her place bringing wine, we all make it through all the introductions smoothly.

I end up in the great room watching the NFL pregame show with her brother while Becca's in the kitchen. The whole house smells great, so mouth-wateringly great, the roasting turkey making its presence known. I can see she's gotten out the china and crystal as well. I keep my eyes on Becca as much as I can. I offer to help, but her eyes tell me to stay the hell out of her kitchen. I step away quickly.

Jason and I talk comfortably about sports and travel. Elizabeth tells me about some of the European trips they've been on with Becca. From what I can tell, the two of them have been in every European country there is. I tell them about myself, my background, my military career, and my retirement here.

It dawns on me Jason being a man knows exactly what I do with his sister, but calm down when I think, *Goddamn it, we're adults, she may be still his little sister, but she's my woman.*

I know he knows I have sex with her. Well, he doesn't know great we are together. He doesn't need to know the intimate, incredibly erotic details, just that I love her. She loves me too. I know he must notice our love for one another.

Finally, Sara and Roger arrive. And then we're all seated around the lovely table, having a great meal and amusing conversation. I can tell her family really loves her by the way they all tease each other gently. I think we've started to relax. I know what I'm thankful for this year. I have never felt such gratitude.

Thank you, God, for bringing this wonderful, loving woman to me. She's given me a life, a life I desperately want.

After pecan or pumpkin pie with whipped cream, we end up watching the Detroit–Dallas game finish up. The Lions are losing, as usual. Becca comes and sits close to me so that I can put my arm around her. She settles back and gets comfortable. She makes comments about the game, letting me know she knows the Lions and Cowboys. We spend a pleasant evening watching football and chatting. Her sister and her husband leave before it gets too late.

Finally, I realize that it's probably time for me to go home as well. Even at our age, Becca would still feel funny having her family know she's sleeping with a man without being married to him. Old-fashioned I know, so that's why I'm going to miss sleeping with her tonight. I've got to be without her while her family is staying in her house. It's going to be a long weekend since they don't plan on leaving until Sunday. This will be the longest time we've gone without sex since the Week from Hell when we first met.

It may get ugly before Sunday.

They all walk me out to the parking lot, saying our good-byes. Jason shakes my hand and leans toward me as Becca and Elizabeth talk over to the side. "Don't hurt her, Michael."

I look him in the eye as I quietly reply, "I've already ordered the ring. I'm just waiting for her to be ready, Jason."

A fucking big diamond ring just for her. It screams "Hands Off" to all other men.

And with those few words I tell him that I'm seriously in love with her and will be there for the long haul. His eyes widen a bit, but he doesn't say anything else. Kissing Becca quickly good-bye, I get in my car and drive home, feeling pretty good about my chances of winning her family's approval.

As I pull out of the parking lot, I notice a late-model silver Mercedes sitting on the side of the lot facing Becca's front door. It strikes me as strange this car is not parked in one of the reserved spaces around Becca's condo complex. It sits there in the dark and I can tell someone is sitting in the driver's seat, but can't see since the windows are dark. Have I seen that car there before? I can already recognize the neighbors' cars, and this is not one of them. It's like someone is waiting there and watching. I leave to drive home, wondering about it. Maybe it's nothing.

Okay, Okay, Okay . . . Sunday.

Becca invites me to spend Friday with them. We drive down to Norfolk and spend the day touring the zoo there. I hadn't realized what a great place this is. We walk around, amazed by all the animals. The tiger walks very close up the glass where we're watching him, so we get to see him up close and personal. The giraffes are right in front of us, eating their hay from tall poles. I enjoy watching the male and female lion lying close together contentedly. We have lunch there as well.

All in all, it was a good day with her family at the Virginia Zoo.

I get to hold Becca's hand while we spend the day together, and I try to get in little touches and kisses as casually as I can. I kiss her hair, her temple, her hand, that sweet spot under her ear, and even the curve of her neck and shoulder. Being so close and yet so far is agonizing. I just keep repeating "Sunday" in my head.

On Saturday, we all drive down together to Portsmouth, where Becca grew up. We meet Sara and Roger at the Commodore downtown. It's a beautiful art deco theatre that has stood the test of time. We go to the movies there, but instead of individual seats, I am surprised to see small tables with dim lamps. Turns out we can order wine, beer, and food before the movie. They bring it to the table for us.

Of course, I get Becca and me a carafe of Riesling wine to share during the movie. This is kind of cool, drinking wine during a movie. I scoot my chair as close as I can to her as we watch the movie. Thank goodness there is no sex scene in this movie because the last thing I want is for her family to notice me with a hard-on. I hold her hand during the movie, stroking my thumb back and forth over her knuckles.

If this is all I get, I'm going to make the most of it.

Occasionally I lift her hand to my mouth to kiss the back of it. On one such kiss, I quickly suck her little finger into my mouth, caressing it with my tongue, before sliding it out between my lips. Becca looks at me with wide eyes before turning back to the movie. Maybe it's hopeful thinking on my part, but I think I see just a hint of desperation in her eyes.

I start to fantasize about taking her up to the dark balcony up above us and giving her a quickie. No, wait, we're with her family. I have to sit here and be a gentleman. Focus, Marine.

Hoping everyone else's attention is on the movie, I wait before bringing her hand back up to my mouth. As swiftly as I can, this time I pull her whole thumb into my mouth, sucking hard before releasing it as well. As I lower her hand back down, I notice Becca shift in her seat.

Maybe I'm getting to her. I hope she's starting to get wet for me, a little hot and bothered. I want her to be frustrated, so I just hold her hand quietly during the rest of the movie. If she is as frustrated as I am, tomorrow should be great after her family leaves.

When we return to Williamsburg, I go back to my big empty house to wait until tomorrow. I putter around a bit, jumping from one thing to another, not finishing anything at all. It's a long evening. When it is finally time to go to sleep, I climb into my big, lonely, lonely, empty bed, wishing Becca was here with me.

It's been since Tuesday night before her family arrived since we've made love. Today is Day 4 without Becca. I still have to make it until tomorrow. Sunday can't come fast enough for me. This is almost as bad as the Week from Hell although I take comfort in the fact at least this time I'm sure of her love for me. And of course, I dream of her soft arms, breasts, legs, and moist warmth wrapped around me. I wake up suddenly, practically coming in my sleep.

Fuck! I'm not fourteen years old anymore.

Glancing at my clock as I try to calm down, I see it is early Sunday morning. *Thank God.*

Sunday.

I wait all morning as patiently as I can for Becca to call and tell me her company has left. At twelve o'clock, I get a text from her:

They've gone.

Short and sweet.

I grab my car keys and head out the door. It takes me ten minutes to get there. I didn't get a speeding ticket although I certainly deserved one.

When I get to her house, it's everything I can do not to pound on her door and yell for her to open the goddamn thing. I can hear her as she turns the deadbolt from inside and the door slowly opens. I rush in, and the air whooshes out of me as I finally see her. Judging from what I see before me, I think she's missed me, too. She's standing in front of me in simply a bra and panties.

Wait, nothing simple about this particular bra and panties.

They're sheer and pink and fucking sexy. The panties are a thong, a small bit of lacy silk covering her smooth folds but leaving her ass beautifully uncovered. And the bra can barely contain those full tits, cupping them up and together. I can see her nipples hard and pouting, eagerly waiting for my mouth.

"Did you miss me, baby?"

"Yes, yes, so much."

I love that she wears sexy things for me. I'll buy her all she wants, just as long as I get to see her wear them for me.

Next thing I know we've wrapped our arms around each other, my mouth swooping down to her open lips. I place my right hand on the curve of her cheek and jaw, holding her mouth in place as I kiss her. I sweep her back pinning her against the closet door in her small foyer. I swiftly pull down the panties, lifting one of her legs to free it and then leaving the thong to pool around her other ankle.

God, I hope she's ready for me, unable to take the time to really check first. I quickly unzip, pulling my cock out and guiding it into her. I pull both of her hands up over her head, gripping her wrists as I start to move up and in her.

"Baby, I've missed you so much. I love you. Do you love me, too? Say it for me. Tell me you love me. Tell me you want only me. I need to hear you say it for me, honey. Say my name."

I love hearing her whisper it for me.

"Oh Michael . . . Michael . . . Michael. I love you so much. I've missed you. Fuck me, hard please. Fuck me hard."

What did she just say to me? I think Ms. Connelly is getting a little carried away here.

And that does it for me. I can't get close enough to her, can't seem to get all of me into her. She's matching me thrust for thrust as I keep her trapped up against the door. I keep one hand holding both her wrists above her head, while my right hand pulls the sheer cup of her pink bra down under her breast, exposing her pouting pink nipple for my eager palm.

I love pink things. It is my favorite color at the moment.

I keep my open mouth on her lips, gently licking inside her mouth as I thrust into her. My palm massages her full breast endlessly. She is trying to lift one leg around me to get me even closer inside her.

Suddenly it's not enough. I can tell this isn't working for her today. I know women can have trouble reaching orgasm frequently. It has happened to me before. No matter what I did, it wasn't going to happen.

Becca has been very responsive to me so far. I don't want her to get frustrated and give up on it. I am not a quitter. I can think of something to fix this, I know. I pull out of her so suddenly she gasps. Twisting her in my arms, I lay her against the carpeted stairs. I pull one of her legs up the air, holding her ankle with my hand. I push forcefully into her, hoping this angle will give us both what we need.

A different angle results in a different feeling.

Oh, yeah, this feels good. I hope it feels as good to her as it does to me.

I think this is working now. Needless to say, it doesn't take that long before we're both moaning and groaning out through our release. I wish it had taken a little longer, but obviously, neither one of us could wait anymore. We didn't even make it up the stairs, for Pete's sake.

It's now a very good day. I am so grateful this year. It was an excellent Thanksgiving.

Thankfully, I can breathe again.

CHAPTER 20

Grand Illuminations

Becca goes back to school after Thanksgiving. We're now back enduring the grinding routine of endless school days as she works herself to death. I can see the stress starting to get to her. It appears as though there are high-pressure tests coming up, grades to average, interim reports to fill out, parent-teacher conferences, and holiday assemblies and parties to plan.

I am stunned by the amount of shit she has to fill out on each damn student report. It takes her two days to finish all of them, working each night until late. I swear to myself after we're married, I'm putting a stop to this shit. I know I can't make it through another school year, watching her do this to her. These weeks before Christmas should be fun, not like this. Her whole life should be fun. I try to make the weekends as enjoyable as I can.

The first weekend in December we attend the Grand Illumination in Colonial Williamsburg. It's an annual event, with fireworks, the Fife and Drum Corps, and colonial entertainment. We spend Sunday evening strolling up and down Duke of Gloucester or D.O.G. Street. Becca enjoys all the natural holiday decorations on the houses, taking pictures of many of them.

As the cold evening progresses, we get hot cider and gingerbread cookies from the Raleigh Tavern bakery. We watch the Colonial Williamsburg Fife and Drum Corps march down Duke of Gloucester Street to a colonial drum beat. Becca says one of her friend's sons is a member. They add to the holiday atmosphere. Becca suddenly points out one of the drummers on the back line and I see a teenage boy with a snare drum. He is marching with everyone else in perfect unison and staring straight ahead in his red and white uniform. She says he is Jeremiah Daniels, the son of Dave Daniels who used to teach fourth grade with her in Newport News but then took a teaching job with a school system much closer to their home. I can tell Becca likes his father and him. The boy looks like a clean-cut young man around 15 or 16. But I know what boys that age are thinking about in their heads.

Yep. I was a teenage boy myself once.

Girls and sex.

When it gets late enough, I go back to the car and get our folding chairs and a thick, soft blanket. We set things up in front of the Governor's Palace to await the fireworks at nine-thirty. It's starting to get cold now, so I cover us both with one warm blanket. The Palace Green is starting to get crowded with chairs and blankets. I hold Becca's hand under the blanket.

Umm, this has possibilities. I need to keep her warm.

I get out the thermos of hot chocolate, and we share the same cup, snuggling under the blanket to keep warm on the cold December night. Suddenly, we're joined by a couple Becca has been good friends with for many years, Kevin and Suzanne. They set up their chairs next to us to enjoy the evening holiday festivities. Talking to Kevin, I find out he's ex-Army, a Lieutenant Colonel when he retired from active duty. He and Suzanne were stationed in Germany and all over the country.

Damn, I'm impressed. Lieutenant Colonel.

We get to talking easily and immediately comfortable around each other. He has a quick sense of humor and is really funny telling me about his experiences in foreign countries. It's clear they both love Germany, after being stationed there. Kevin obviously has enjoyed Europe quite a bit and tells me they travel there frequently. He's been doing some military-related consulting work occasionally ever since retiring from the army. I ask him about that, wondering if I might do that if I really get bored.

I quickly find out he also spent quite a bit of time in Iraq, as well as Kosovo and Ukraine. We have a lot to talk about. I am interested in his impressions of Baghdad since we've both been there. We weren't in the city as the same time, though.

They tell me about how they all became friends. Suzanne and Becca met when they taught together and spent a lot of time going for long walks around Colonial Williamsburg and the campus while Kevin was out of the country. It turns out they once took Becca with them on two trips to Europe, one to Vienna and the other to Germany for a little under two weeks. It was her first times to visit Europe at all. I guess they must be really *good* friends to have taken care of her like that.

The more I talk to them, the more I think I'd like to really know them. I think Kevin and I have a lot in common and could definitely be friends. I can tell Becca loves them, and they are a very big part of her life.

Becca warns me to not drink all the wine Kevin and Suzanne have with them as we wait for the fireworks. They all laugh about the time Kevin got Becca drunk by sneakily refilling her wine glass and telling her they had to finish all the open bottles after a party. I think she had to spend the night with them at their house. Becca still seems a bit embarrassed although she laughs about how it happened. I'm just glad she didn't try to drive home. They refused to let her.

When the fireworks begin, I hold Becca's hand in mine as we watch open-mouthed at the holiday display in front of us. The fireworks with the Governor's Palace in the background make a stunning holiday picture. We snuggle together under the soft blanket, me doing my best to keep my hot woman warm on this cold December night. It's a nice way to begin the Christmas season. I want to make this holiday season one Becca will never forget.

I don't even mind my toes are so cold they're going to be frostbitten, turn black, and fall off.

When we get home, I treat Becca to a very personal Grand Illumination.

Fireworks eventually ensue, lighting up our night with brilliant colors, blinding flashes, and lasting into the early hours of the morning.

The only thing stopping us is the fact she has to go to work the next morning. I think I allow her about two hours of sleep. I feel guilty, but hope she thinks it was worth it. She is so not a morning person. I feel a bit sorry for her class today.

Becca is really busy during December, trying to teach as well as shop for Christmas presents. We decide to go out for dinner and drinks at Second Street Bistro, the restaurant where we first met. When we arrive, I make the hostess actually seat us at the same table we were at when I pretended to be her boyfriend.

We order an appetizer, look over the menu, and make our choices. Becca orders wine, and I have a Michelob. As we talk and wait for the appetizer to arrive first, I glance around the room, remembering the night when I first saw her. To my astonishment, I see a blond-headed woman in a black dress seated with two other ladies across the room. Our eyes meet, and I recognize and remember her even though it has been years since we were friends.

Well, we were a little more than just friends. Friends with sexual benefits.

Her name is Deborah Wilson, and we knew each other when I was stationed at Camp Lejeune Marine Base in Jacksonville, North Carolina, eight years ago. We had a brief sexual affair with each other since she was living there at the time. I met her at the Officers' Club one evening while she was obviously looking for someone with whom to hook up. I obliged her. It turned out to be a little more than a one-night stand. It lasted about three months and ended when I left for Afghanistan.

I didn't love her, and I didn't think she was in love with me. It was just a sexual relationship to me. I made no effort to keep in touch with her even though she wrote me a couple of times when I left. After a while, I never heard from her again. I certainly did not think our paths would ever cross. That is, until tonight, when I see her looking at me with recognition as well.

What is she doing here? She is the last person I want to see while here with Becca.
What do I do? Do I ignore her?
Do I go over and say hello? What if she comes over here?

I am debating all of this is my head, when I see her get up from her seat and come walking toward me. There is nothing I can do to stop her. I stand up to greet her as a gentleman. Becca turns, and I know she is wondering what I am doing and who this woman is to me. Deborah speaks first.

"Oh, my goodness, Michael Stevens! It is you, isn't it? I wasn't sure at first, but when you looked at me, I knew it was you. It is so good to see you again! What has it been? Six years or more? How are you? I'm glad to see you made it back to the States safely. Have you moved here to Williamsburg? Are you still in the Marines?"

"Hello, Deborah. It's great to see you, too. Let me introduce you to my girlfriend, Becca Connelly. Becca, honey, this is Deborah Wilson. We knew each other back when I was stationed in North Carolina. We haven't seen each other for about eight years now."

I watch as Becca shakes Deborah's hand, murmuring that it is a pleasure to meet her. I can see the questions going through her mind by the expression in her eyes. I feel very uncomfortable, standing there with a woman I had a sexual relationship with once and the love of my life. I try to be normal, but I don't sit down or offer her a seat to join us. I want her to leave as soon as possible.

"Yes, Deborah, I'm in Williamsburg. I am no longer in the Marines. Where do you live? I guess not in Jacksonville?"

Please don't say you live here as well.

"I live in Richmond. The company I work for transferred me here in June. It is so good to see you again. Nice to see a familiar face. I was so worried about you when you left Camp Lejeune for Afghanistan. I wrote you, but wasn't sure you got my letters since I never heard from you. I'm so glad to see you are okay."

Shit. Now Becca knows she worried about me and wrote me letters.
Shit. Obviously, we were more than acquaintances.

I look at Becca and see her glancing back and forth between Deborah and myself, frowning slightly as she wonders about our relationship.

I need to stop this. Deborah needs to go back to her friends and leave me the hell alone. I am not interested in her anymore. I ignore her comment about not responding to her letters.

A Real Love At Last

Fucking in the past. Past fucking, never loving. I never said "I love you" to any of those women. They were a temporary sexual fascination only. Just a blur of women, don't really remember their names or faces. I paid attention to only sexually necessary female body parts.

When it was over, we both moved on. Click delete, click delete.

No innocent girl-women who were hoping for a fairy-tale husband to love them. I didn't lead anyone on deliberately. I didn't want to break anyone's heart. I thought I made it very clear I was only interested in a brief period of fucking only.

Are these women going to show back up and bite me in the ass?

Becca suddenly joins the conversation, to my horror. "How long did you and Michael know each other?"

It was nothing, baby, nothing but sex.

Oh, shit. I did not love her. She used me as much as I used her. I was glad when it was over.

She was getting a little too clingy for me at the time.

Fuck!

Deborah smiles, "Michael and I knew each other quite well in Jacksonville. I missed him a great deal when he was transferred away. I have often wondered about him and wished we could reconnect with one another. I enjoyed our friendship very much and hope I can again."

Reconnect as what? Friends? Lovers? Goddamn it. Is she flirting with me in front of Becca?

She knows Becca is my girlfriend, not my wife.

In her mind, I am still available.

In my mind, I damn well am not available to her.

"Yes, I can see how you could have missed him. Michael is a very special man. I have enjoyed getting to know him as well. We have spent a great deal of time together since we first started dating. I know I am a lucky woman to have Michael love me and be such a big, important part of my life. I love him and don't know what I would do without him."

Hey, is Becca staking her claim on me, to an obvious former lover? She is not a stupid woman at all, not easily fooled. I know she can tell Deborah and I had a sexual relationship at one time. Deborah is making it very obvious that she would even entertain the idea of resuming that same relationship with me.

Becca is trying to put her in her place, letting her know I love her and she loves me. There is no room for any other woman in my life.

I like the idea of a jealous Becca. It makes me feel loved and wanted.

Well, damn. She can be just as jealous of me as I am of her. It's nice to know the thought of me with another woman is bothering her.

I am still standing there, hoping this former fuck buddy will turn and go back to her friends. I think Becca has made it clear I am off limits. Deborah looks a little shaken but politely makes her good-byes and walks back over to her table. I hate that she is even there, so close. I wonder if we should just leave and go home. I am about to suggest it when the appetizers arrive. I sit back down quickly.

I swear to myself if she tries to contact me again I will go thermonuclear on her ass. I am no longer available to her sexually or otherwise. She won't know what hit her if she messes up my fragile relationship with Becca. I won't be the Southern gentleman she remembers.

Becca is very quiet and contemplative as she eats the twice-baked potatoes covered in cheese, green onions, and sour cream. I am scared to say anything, hoping it will fade away. I can see the questions she has about my relationship with Deborah in her eyes. She looks like she wants to say something to me but stops herself several times. Finally, she just comes out with it.

"You fucked her, didn't you, Michael?"

I can't lie to her.

"Yes, I fucked her for three months eight years ago. I was briefly stationed at Camp Lejeune before being deployed to Afghanistan for my third tour."

"Did you love her?"

Are you kidding me?

"No, I have only loved you."

"Did she love you?"

She was simply using me to get fucked.

"I didn't think so at the time. I thought I was clear on the relationship I wanted. It was just sex, no attachments. She seemed okay with it, but now I think about it, she was more involved right before I left. I didn't contact her again. She did write me a couple of letters, but I did not bother to read them. I tore them up, threw them away, and didn't write back. It was over as far as I was concerned. I have completely forgotten about her."

"She is living in Richmond now. Even though I am right here, she made it very plain she would like to see you again. She wants to fuck you again, Michael. Are you going to contact her? Keep in touch with her?"

"No. The thought never crossed my mind. I want you, no one else."

She sighs deeply, looking me intently, before she softly says, "You better damn well never fuck her again. I'll leave you. Don't think I will give you a second chance, Marine. You're mine. If you can't live with that, then leave now. No other woman for you anymore for the rest of your life. Only me. Michael, do you understand? Only me from now on."

"Yes, ma'am. I am very happy to cooperate. The same thing applies to you as well. Only me. I am your only lover. No other man will ever touch you again. I'll kill him if he does."

"You are not going to have to kill any other man, my love. I guarantee it. I love you, Michael. I will never want anyone else."

"Good. You have no reason to be jealous of her. It was a long time ago, and I barely remember her. I have always been looking for you."

"Thank goodness we found each other."

"I totally agree, baby. This restaurant is very special to me. I desired you from the start. Your walk when you came in just about put me on the floor. I couldn't stop watching you. I ended up hiding my hard-on under the table. It was that fast for me. I knew I had to get close to you somehow. I can't believe how it has all happened. It was an impulsive decision to help you one night and now look where we are together."

I pray to God no other women from my past ever show up again.

Our meals arrive. I want to eat as fast as I can, so I can get her home, naked, in her bed, in my arms, and me inside her. I hardly taste my food. I am in such a hurry to get her alone I refuse to order us dessert. I want my woman for dessert tonight. I watch her closely, trying to see if she is thinking the same things I am.

She talks during dinner, telling me funny stories about her students and the other teachers at school. We discuss possible Christmas presents for my sister, brother-in-law, and nephew. Turns out Becca and Anne call each other a lot. They have become close friends. We decide to invite them down sometime for dinner at a restaurant, maybe even one of the taverns in Colonial Williamsburg. She suggests King's Arms Tavern for dinner or Chowing's for drinks and colonial entertainments called Gambols. I know we will drive up to their house in Richmond for Christmas after Becca's family leaves.

I drive us home in the dark. As far as I can tell, I am spending the night with her. It's only a little after nine when we get there. Becca invites me up and turns on the television.

Umm. It's still early.

I suggest one of her movies on DVD. She has many romantic movies since she loves a good love story. We cuddle on the sofa, me holding her against my chest with her legs stretched out in front of her. We watch a movie called *Fever Pitch* with Drew Barrymore and Jimmy Fallon.

I have never seen it before, but it is a cute, funny movie about the love story between a rabid Boston Red Sox fan and his girlfriend in Boston. Jimmy Fallon as an actor and Drew Barrymore as the actress. I find myself laughing out loud at parts of it. I enjoy having her lean against me, and I am able to let my hands wander a bit. Not too much, but enough to remind her whose arms she is in. When the movie is over with a happy ending, it is late and bedtime. I am so comfortable on her large sofa. I get up to turn off the DVD player and television.

Becca watches me closely. Instead of taking her back to her bed, I decide to stay where I am. The navy blue sofa is long enough for my frame. I walk over to her, looking down at her body stretched out for me. She spreads her legs apart without me doing a thing.

Okay. I think I have just been issued an invitation I can't refuse.

I unzip my zipper and pull my erection out for her. She doesn't say anything, just watches me as she leans up and pulls off her panties under her skirt. I motion with my hand, and she lifts the skirt up until it is bunched around her waist. She is nude from the waist down. She leans back on the end pillows and spreads her thighs even wider apart than before. I can see everything, just waiting for me.

"Come closer, Michael. Let me convince you I am the only woman you will ever need to fuck."

I take my time, making her wait and building the anticipation. It's all I can do not to stoke my own erection in front of her before I enter her.

"Baby, I don't fuck you. Fucking is for amateurs. I pour my heart and soul into you every time we make love to one another. Don't you feel it, too? Are you giving me your heart and soul as well?"

"Michael, I give you all of me. There is nothing more I can give you. You already have me. Come here to me. Let me have you tonight."

"With pleasure, baby, with pleasure."

I lower myself down onto her body, entering swiftly in one move. I have all my clothes on; the only part of me exposed is my long, thick cock moving in and out of her. I feel her tightness expanding for me, allowing me access to her warm, wet entrance. Becca's thighs are on each side of my thrusting hips, high and wide open for me. I rise up slightly to get a deeper angle of penetration as she strokes her fingers across my chest, on my shoulders, and my face.

She reaches around me and grabs hold of my ass roughly, pulling me in even deeper. Neither one of us can be quiet, moaning incoherently, gasping for breath, whispering directions and words of love and want. It seems to last forever to me. I have amazing control and stamina tonight, and Becca is with me all the way. She is absolutely the sexiest woman I have ever had the pleasure of being with in this intimate way. I am pushing our groins together, rocking and grinding hard.

I lower my mouth down to hers, kissing her deeply. I begin to feel the faint stirrings of pleasure in her and start my own climax because of it. I am lost in her. I keep my mouth open on hers, thrusting my tongue deeply inside, mirroring the thrusting movements of my penis in her. She moans, gasps repeatedly, thrusts upward in extreme pleasure, and cries out against my lips, but I don't stop kissing her. I come inside her suddenly and violently in my desire for her, giving her all of me, groaning loudly, but muffled against her lips as well. I feel the last of my throbbing spurts into her. I kissed her all the way through it.

When I can tear my lips from hers, I bury my head into her neck and try to get my breath as she wraps her legs tightly around me. I feel our heartbeats start to slow as we calm ourselves down. We murmur soft words of love to each other, and I fall asleep on the navy blue sofa, still on top and inside her. I feel sure now she understands she has no need to be jealous of any fucking in my past. I drift off, holding her close to me. We sleep on the sofa all night, entwined in each other and deeply in love.

Leona Lewis's song "Bleeding Love" has me written all over it.

But I don't care what they say
I'm in love with you
They try to pull me away
But they don't know the truth
Yes, I keep, keep bleeding love all over the place.

CHAPTER 21

My Marriage Proposal

    I want this joy for the rest of my life. I want to marry her. Please, God, please. Let her say yes to me. Just. Say. Yes.

    Snow Patrol is now my favorite band. I listen to their song "Just Say Yes" in my car.

    During the next two weeks in December, I make my preparations for proposing to Becca. I want it to be so romantic it's the only proposal she'll ever remember, *not that other one* she received from the fucking asshole ex.

    I decide we should go back to the Williamsburg Inn, this time for a whole weekend. Going back to the scene of the first place we ever made love seems romantic to me. I even make sure we have the same room as last time. I call for dinner reservations, spa reservations for her, and a golf tee time reservation for me. This is all happening the last weekend before Christmas since her family is coming back to stay with her over the holiday. Becca will finish up school that Friday, so she'll be able to relax. It will be the last weekend we have together alone, so I can propose to her then.

    Like I told her brother Jason at Thanksgiving, I've picked out the engagement ring, and it should be ready just in time. I think it's a stunning gold ring, with a big, gorgeous, high-quality five-carat center round diamond surrounded on each side with gradually smaller and smaller diamonds. I want it to be big enough anyone can see it from a bit of a distance and know she's already taken. It's engraved with our initials inside the thick gold band.

    The closer it gets to that Friday, the more nervous I start to feel. I don't think she'll say no to me. After all, we've been dating since June. That's long enough for both of us to know. We're adults, and I sure as hell am not getting any younger. I want to start our official life together as soon as possible. I've finished all the painting in my house and want to move her stuff and her into my home as soon as I can. It will be our home when she's here, living with me.

    Our home. Together.

    When she gets home from school late Friday afternoon, I call her, and I can hear in her voice she's tired but is starting to relax now she knows she has two weeks off ahead of her. She doesn't have to go back until after the new year. In fact, I hope she resigns and never goes back. I tell her I have a surprise for her tonight, and she needs to change into a cocktail dress with heels and pack an overnight bag. She's surprised, but she says she will.

    I tell her I'll pick her up at seven. Now I need to get ready and make myself as irresistible as I can manage. The black tux comes out again, and I pack a small bag with clothes for tomorrow. Since we're so close, I figure we can run home and get whatever more clothes we need for the whole weekend if necessary.

I text her before I leave the house:

> Ms. Connelly, can't wait to see how sexy you look tonight. Mr. Stevens XO (Your LOVER)
>
> Mr. S. I'm trying my best here. Ms. C xx (Your LOVER)
>
> I'm picking you up tonight for dinner, dancing, and making love, Rebecca. Are you ready for me, honey? M XOXO
>
> Absolutely ready for ANYTHING WITH YOU, Michael. B XXXX

Hell, still no hug. But four big kisses.

I'm COMING. NOW.

When I finally arrive to pick her up, I notice that same strange silver Mercedes parked in the same location in her lot. I remember it from Thanksgiving. I can still tell there is someone inside watching but can't see clearly in the dark. Whoever is inside the vehicle has a direct view of the condo. It starts to bother me strangely. I don't have any real reason to go up and confront the person inside the Mercedes.

I mean, after all, they're just sitting in their car in the parking lot. It's creepy to me, sitting there in the dark, watching. I think about going up and knocking on the window, thinking of what to say. I don't, though. But still I am uneasy, wondering why it is there. It's as if I can feel someone watching me as I go up and knock on her front door. Eyes somehow focused on me.

Behind my back.

Becca quickly opens the door for me. I kiss her swiftly and then find myself strangely tongue-tied. I usually don't have much trouble talking. She looks scrumptious in a blue silk short cocktail dress and five-inch heels. Her long, smooth legs look exposed to me. Not sure I want other guys to see quite so much of her charms. Those legs are meant to be wrapped around me.

Taking several deep breaths, I lead her out to my car, tucking her in safely in the front seat before putting her overnight bag into the trunk.

She still doesn't know where we're going. When I pull up in front of the inn, I look at it, pleased with how classy and festive it looks in all of its holiday finery.

"Becca, I thought we'd spend the whole weekend here this time. Let's go and enjoy ourselves so you can relax. It's the start of your Christmas break. I want you merry."

Marry me. I am asking you tonight.

"Yes, Mr. Stevens. I'd like that very much."

We check in. Taking her to the room, I think she recognizes it. Opening the door for her, I suddenly reach down and lift her up into my arms and take her over the threshold.

Just practicing a little.

"Do you remember this room, Becca? I have very erotic memories of this room and bed and shower and bathtub. I think it was you with me."

Yeah, the scene of the crime, as it were.

"Yes, Michael. It was me. Don't you ever forget it. This is where we first made love together. Right there on that bed. And then the bed again. Again and again."

Shit. I'd better get her to dinner fast before I lose sight of my plan.

"Come with me, my darling. Let's go eat dinner. You are going to need your strength for later. Eat something. Food for now."

Trying to stay calm and enjoy every moment, I place my hand on her lower back as I lead her into the elegant dining area. Once again we are treated to first-class dining and dancing. The spacious colonial-style room is lit with candles, and I enjoy seeing Becca obviously enjoying herself.

I try to wait patiently because I want her to love every moment of the evening. It's not like the time is dragging by even though all I can think about is getting her back to the room and hearing her say yes to me. Dancing with her is the best part since she's close to me in my arms. Dessert with coffee just finishes the night off perfectly.

Well, not quite perfectly. Not yet anyway.

"Are you finished, Rebecca? Ready to go, my love?"

"Yes, Michael. Let's go back to our room now." She smiles at my endearment to her.

Okay. This is the moment I've been waiting for since June. I hope I don't fuck anything up. If she says no, I think I'll have a damn stroke. I could die right in front of her.

When we get back to the room, I see the staff has lit the fireplace and candles as I requested.

Good.

Romantic fireplace. Check.

Candlelight. Check.

Big fucking diamond engagement ring in my pocket. Check.

Huge canopied bed. Check.

Hot, desirable woman. Double check.

Me. Double check, check.

The room is bathed in the soft glow of candles and flickering flames. I sweep several pillows from the bed and place them on the thick carpet in front of the fireplace. I stand in front of Becca and slowly, but lovingly, unzip her dress and help her out of it. She has on a pale pink bustier with garter belts and a matching silk thong.

Yeah, pink. So feminine.

I almost lose my mind before stepping back and getting out of my tux as fast as I possibly can. Damn cuff links slow me down, but she helps me when I get caught in my shirtsleeves. When I'm finally undressed next to her, obviously wanting her, I lay her gently down on the floor with her head on the pillows.

Leaning over her, I gaze at the endlessly fascinating woman halfway beneath me. The firelight touches her face and hair, making her glow. Her darkening eyes are on my mouth. Taking a deep breath, I present my proposal to her softly.

I need to get this right. This is the moment of truth. I've waited a lifetime for her.

"Becca, I'm asking you to marry me now. I love you with all my heart and soul, and I want you to be my wife always. For the rest of our lives. I want to be your husband more than the air I breathe. Say yes to me. Say yes, so I can spend my life loving you. Please say yes, baby. I have never felt this way before ever in my life. I wanted desperately to have such a love but couldn't find it until I found you. You are my love, the woman of my dreams. You bring joy, love, and happiness to me. I feel content and complete when we are together. I am incapable of staying away from you, I don't have the strength, and I never want to be far from you."

My throat tightens up suddenly with all the emotion I am expressing. I find I am having trouble talking and breathing. I try to take a deep breath, before I finish telling her everything in my heart and my wish for a future spent with her. I am suddenly aware of moisture in my eyes.

Oh no. Don't fucking cry, Stevens.

"I need you more than anything or anyone. I know I belong to you, and you belong to me. Forever, I promise. I can't imagine the darkness and misery of a life without you. You're the one I want, the woman I need as my wife and life partner. I'll do anything you want, be anyone you need, beg you if necessary, if only you'll say yes to a future with me. Let me be your husband and love you as long as I live."

As I watch her, her beautiful green eyes suddenly fill up with moisture. A single tear traces down into her hair. Holding my breath, I reach up and wipe it away with my thumb.

Don't cry, honey. I will cry too, don't cry. Please.

She stares at me for a long moment until finally, I heard the words I've been waiting for. Her sudden smile lights up the dark room. I smile back, relishing her every word.

"Yes, Michael. I'll marry you. Yes, yes, a thousand times, yes. I love you with all my heart and soul as well. Let's spend the rest of our lives together. You mean more to me than any man I've ever known. I trust you with my love, my heart, and my life forever. You make me feel happy, beautiful, safe, and totally loved. I want to be your wife, loving you until the day I die. I promise you."

And those words make me the happiest ex-Marine in the whole fucking world.

"Thank you, baby. I want to marry you now, right after I make love to you."

She said yes. I can breathe again. I take a deep, steadying breath before letting it out slowly as I feel relief flood my whole body.

She laughs softly. "We can't get married tonight, Michael. You'll have to wait a little bit."

"If we could, I would. Don't make me wait long, please. I've already waited my whole life for you. If you won't marry me tonight, then I'll give you until Valentine's Day. That will be our wedding day, so I know you'll never forget the day I make you mine. Officially. Legally. Mine. Now let me make love to you, Ms. Soon-to-Be Mrs. Stevens. I've been fantasizing about it all night."

I gently slip her thong down her long legs and off but leave on the bustier garter and stockings. *Hot.* And I make love to her tenderly over and over again in front of that blazing fireplace all night long. I only let her rest a while before I'm gently waking her up again with my mouth, my hands, and my dick.

This is how you seal the deal. I'll die remembering this evening the rest of my life.

Becca wakes up slowly the next morning, stretching and humming happily in my arms. We're still on the damn floor. Thank goodness the carpet is as soft and thick as it is. I can't believe we never made it to the bed. I guess I'll save that for tonight. The woman lying next to me suddenly squeaks, realizing she has a big hunking diamond on her left ring finger. When I put it on her finger last night while she slept, I kissed it, hoping it never leaves her finger again.

I even take a picture of her with my phone, so I can have a photo of my fiancée wearing my ring. I put it there on her left ring finger. Now it's going to stay there.

Saturday passes by in a blur of happy activities. Breakfast in the main dining room, spa treatments for Becca, and a round of golf for me on the Gold Course at the Golden Horseshoe Golf Course. I let her have the whole afternoon to herself getting pampered while I make a mess of the damn championship course. I find it's a little too daunting for my golf skills, but I have a good time hacking away. I try not to be too embarrassed in front of the guys with whom I'm playing.

It really doesn't matter to me . . . nothing is going to spoil my happiness on this weekend.

After I get back to the room, Becca is already there, having been massaged, bluffed, and polished to death. We're both a bit exhausted after last night, so we stretch out on the bed and nap the rest of the afternoon away. We end up with room service for dinner because I don't want to be out in public. I prefer private time with her. We have a quiet evening together, the two of us, talking and laughing. I make love to my fiancée before falling asleep under the canopy bed.

I can only hope she is as happy as me. I pray this weekend is the romantic proposal of her dreams.

She said yes.

Snow Patrol sings a song used in the romantic comedy set in Ireland called Leap Year. "Just Say Yes."

Just say yes, just say there's nothing holding you back
It's not a test, or a trick of the mind
Only love.

CHAPTER 22

Marry, Marry Christmas to Me

We get home on Sunday, realizing we have a ton of stuff to do before Christmas. Jason and Elizabeth are due in on Tuesday and will stay through Thursday since the holiday falls on Wednesday this year. They definitely seem to think they come to stay with her on the holidays. I think it became a tradition when Becca's marriage failed. They obviously didn't want her to spend the holidays alone. Of course, Williamsburg is a Christmas wonderland, so it is the perfect place to be.

We put up the tree; decorate it with white lights, an angel and ornaments; finish Christmas shopping; and wrap the presents. Becca washes and changes the sheets on the guest bed and basically cleans up around the place. We go to the grocery store since we've got to feed them as well. It takes us to Monday night before Becca says she feels ready for company.

It suddenly starts to dawn on me I might *not* be able to sleep with Becca Christmas Eve night and Christmas Day. Her family is there again, staying in the guest room right next to her bedroom. She didn't let me sleep with her when they were here at Thanksgiving. Maybe when they see my diamond engagement ring on her finger, she'll feel comfortable enough about it to let me stay with her in front of them.

They have to know we're lovers, for goodness' sake. I mean, I'll try not to make love to her since we both tend to be a bit loud, and I know the walls between her bedroom and the guest room are bound to be thin. I can be happy as long as I get to touch her all night long, instead of going home by myself to my big empty house and my big empty bed.

Jason and Elizabeth arrive during the middle of the afternoon on Christmas Eve. They seem to have accepted the fact that I'm there, and I know she called to tell them we are getting married. I made sure Becca told Jason to bring his golf clubs with him. I know he is an avid golfer. That afternoon, we head out to Two Rivers Country Club for a round. I want to get to know him better and for him to feel comfortable with me since I am going to marry his sister now.

We talk casually as we make our way around the course next to the James River. Jason is a gifted golfer, and Becca has told me he plays a lot on his own country club course now that he has retired. In fact, golfing seems easy for him while I still hack my way around the golf course. He has a smooth natural swing and often makes pars and birdies.

I struggle to keep up but can't since I am a bogey-or-worse golfer. But he never makes me feel embarrassed by my golf skills. We lightly tease each other around the course. Jason has a funny, wry sense of humor. Gradually he starts to open up a bit when we stop after the ninth hole to take a break, get a drink, and let some of the foursomes behind us play through.

"Jason, how often do you come to visit Williamsburg? Just on the holidays?"

"Well, we definitely drive here for Thanksgiving and Christmas. Elizabeth loves the natural door decorations in Colonial Williamsburg. We get to see Becca as well as Sara's family. Becca usually comes to stay with us for a while during the summer. She seems to enjoy seeing some of the sights around Bristol. We drive to Blowing Rock, North Carolina, frequently for lunch and ice cream. We go to baseball games with the local rookie team, attend the Appalachian Highlands Festival in Abingdon, go to nearby wineries, movies, and museums. She watches all my videos of our vacations and seems to enjoy it as well as learn a lot from them. Once we drove into Kentucky to see Daniel Boone's Fort Boonesborough and visited the Kentucky Horse Farm. Becca loved seeing Secretariat's and Seattle Slew's Triple Crown trophies and jockeys' uniforms."

"Yes, I can definitely tell she likes to travel, see historical places, and have new experiences. Once we are married, I hope to show her the world."

"She has already seen a lot of the United States. I think she only has a few states left. A bit competitive with me. I've taken her with us to New England when our daughter Kelsie worked in Connecticut. It's no trouble just to let her ride along and she is a good traveler. We've visited New York City, Boston, Lexington, Concord, Martha's Vineyard, Nantucket, and Salem. Elizabeth and she once drove up to see Kelsie by themselves and stopped in Philadelphia, Valley Forge, and Fort McHenry in Baltimore on the way back to Virginia."

"When Kelsie started her new job at the Detroit Zoo, she went with us to visit. We saw the sites in Detroit, drove up the coast of Michigan visiting lighthouses, and ended up staying at the Grand Hotel on Mackinaw Island. Becca had seen it in a movie she loved called *Somewhere in Time*. It seemed she had a crush on Christopher Reeve after seeing it. They even had some of the costumes, props, and other items used in the movie. Next thing I know, we're walking the island and finding locations used for some of the scenes in the movie. She seemed to like finding those."

"You're very good to her, Jason. Thank you."

"Well, it was so hard for her when Tripp left. Looking back, they married very quickly. Next thing we knew he was asking Mama if he could marry her and I gave her away in the wedding. They moved to

California for three years and we flew to visit once. It was the first time I had really spent time with him. They seemed happy. While we were there, we took a brief trip north to Alaska. We enjoyed seeing Anchorage, an old copper mining ghost town called Kennecott, and taking a boat tour out to Columbia glacier and a salmon bake."

"When Tripp was transferred to Charleston, we visited them there as well. It was hard to see her very much since for most of her marriage, they lived in other states. I thought Tripp loved her. When Mama died, Becca was alone in Charleston since he was out to sea working on his ship. He actually had a helicopter airlift him off so he could get to an airport and fly to be with her. He was late for the funeral, but he made the effort to support her. I thought it was proof he loved her. That was only two years before he left."

"It was a shock to me when I found out he deserted her. It happened to her on her last day of school before summer break. Actually, Sara, Roger, Elizabeth, and I were on a two-week trip to Europe when he left. We all had no idea what was going on with her at home. She was totally alone without family to help her cope."

"When we got back, we called to tell her about our vacation. It was then she told us Tripp wanted a divorce. Her voice was so soft and broken, I could barely hear her on the phone. I think being left like that scared her to death and she was deeply frightened she wouldn't be able to make it on her own. She only had her teaching salary and you know how underpaid teachers are for what they do. She obviously couldn't stay in their home because she couldn't manage the mortgage all on her own."

"I was working and couldn't go, but Elizabeth was on her summer break. She went down to help her find a place she could afford on her teaching salary. She told me Becca wouldn't eat, couldn't sleep even though she wanted to stay curled up in bed, had obviously lost weight, and didn't want to talk about Tripp at all. It was as though she couldn't face the sudden change in reality and if she didn't talk about it, it wouldn't be true."

"Elizabeth took her to a lawyer since by then she had received a letter from Tripp's lawyer listing everything in the house he wanted. It was like he had the house memorized. He had walked out on her, and a little over two weeks later, she is being contacted by a lawyer with all these demands. He wanted practically all of the furniture, leaving her with not much at all. Most of that furniture was bought with Becca's inheritance after Mama died. He never came back to see her again at all, although I think Becca had to see him one last time so they could do taxes together after the divorce was final."

"A month later, she moved out of their four-bedroom, two-story house into a small townhouse nearby. She had to give her two golden retrievers away, and I know that broke her heart when she couldn't keep them with her since she was renting. She eventually managed to buy her own condo and settle down a bit, teaching year after year after year. No men that I ever heard about, not the whole time. At least she had her teaching job in Newport News. Elizabeth was a teacher as well, high school though. Over the years, I could tell my wife wasn't exactly enjoying her job very much, so she retired as soon as she could and started being a travel agent from home. Then I began to notice Becca saying some of the same things about teaching I had heard from Elizabeth. Teaching is a much, much harder job than it seems on the surface."

"Jason, believe me, I have struggled this fall, seeing how much she works. I am able to take care of her completely financially. She will never have to worry about money again. Somehow I am going to talk her into resigning. Now that we are engaged, I hope I can persuade her to listen to me. I want her to marry me, move into my house, travel with me, and enjoy her life. She makes me happy and I want her to be happy as well."

"Yeah, I can tell you make her happy. That is quite a ring you placed on her finger, Michael."

"My way of telling every other man to back the hell off."

We finished the eighteen-hole round, and I enjoyed talking to him quite a lot. He is very funny at times, and I tried to keep up with him by telling him some the crazy things that happened to me when I served. He beats me quite badly, but it was a fun afternoon round of golf. No harm, no foul, no blood or currency exchanged. I hope he is comfortable with the fact I am marrying his younger sister as soon as I can and I will be a permanent member of his family. I'm not leaving her like the asshole ex-husband.

Turns out we're driving down to her sister's house for Christmas Eve dinner. I head home to shower and change before returning to Becca's in the early evening for the drive to Portsmouth. When we arrive at Sara's, I get to meet her nephews and their families as well. Everyone seems happy to see my diamond on Becca's finger, and the women all ooh and ahh appropriately.

They damn well should. That diamond cost a small fortune, but I don't care. I think Becca is very proud to show it off, and I am happy. A lucky man.

Dinner at Sara's house is a bit chaotic, but we're all in the holiday spirit. I like watching Becca interact with her family, and I hope they like me. I keep her as close to me as I can all evening long.

The evening finally comes to a close, because I know it's late and Santa's coming. We drive back to Williamsburg in the dark, Becca and me in the dark back seat of her brother's SUV. I wonder if I'll be exiled tonight. I can't stand the suspense much longer. It's Christmas Eve night.

Santa's coming to town, loaded with presents for all good girls and good boys.

Leaning over, I breathe quietly in her ear. "Do I get to stay with you tonight?"

I can see she's startled. I guess she hasn't thought far enough ahead yet. I can see her thinking.

"I'm your fiancé now, Ms. Connelly. That gives me certain rights, you know. I plan on exercising all of those rights. You're wearing my ring. They're married, we're going to be married. It's not like it's a big secret. People in love and engaged or married sleep together."

She whispers back, "I don't know. I've never done this before, not since I was married. I guess it will be okay."

"Well, I've never done it either, so we'll help each other, okay? We're in our forties, for Pete's sake. Don't you think they know we sleep together?"

"Okay. All right. You can stay."

Yes.

"Thank you, baby. I couldn't stand the thought of not being with you on Christmas, especially our first one together."

When we get back to her house, I can see Jason and Elizabeth are a little startled that I don't really seem to be leaving. It's getting later and later. Finally, Becca simply announces she's going to bed. I get up and follow her to her bedroom, quietly closing her door behind me.

And that's that, as far as I concerned. They now know I'm there, and I'm sure as hell *not* leaving. The next morning we wake up early because, after all, it's Christmas. I wish I could have woken Becca up with my amorous attentions but tell myself to be patient. She seems excited to get up.

Her brother is already up in the great room and watching SportsCenter on TV. Seems he is an early, early riser. Becca gets started on coffee for us, as I sit down and talk to Jason. Elizabeth gradually appears. By the late morning, we have all had breakfast, showered, and dressed. It's time to open presents under the tree. I am looking forward to seeing Becca's reaction to my present. We open presents one at a time under the tree. I don't need a present because Becca already gave me what I wanted for Christmas.

She said yes. YES.

Suddenly I find that Becca has given me a gift certificate to pick up a brand-new big HD flatscreen television at Best Buy. From what it says, it is state-of-the-art new. It's big. Being a guy, I like big. Becca's television is still an older model, and mine is smaller than hers. I have been wanting to get one and know exactly where to put it in my great room. We'll be able to enjoy it when she moves in with me. SOON.

Merry Christmas to me.

Now it's my turn. I give Becca a big envelope. She looks at me curiously. She slowly opens it and pulls out the piece of paper, reading it quickly. I have given her a trip to Switzerland starting on Sunday, February 15, the day after Valentine's Day. I watch as her eyes go a bit wide. I can see the wheels turning in her head, frowning slightly as she tries to figure out how she can take time off during the school year. But then she takes a deep breath and thanks me with a quick kiss.

Hasn't she figured out yet that this is a HONEYMOON? *I'm not the least bit worried. She is going to resign at the end of the semester in late January. That's my plan. We have a lot to do. She has to move in with me. I am thinking we'll rent out her condo, maybe to some graduate students at the law school. We don't have time for her to work anymore. Her job is getting in the way of both of our happiness. She's mine, and I take care of what is mine. It's that simple.*

Becca shows the trip to her sister-in-law and brother. They seemed thrilled since they've already traveled extensively in Switzerland. They know what a beautiful country it is and keep telling her how much she is going to love it. Becca is still a little shocked. She keeps thanking me, but hey, it's my job to make her dreams come true.

It's now late morning. We've finished with all the presents. Jason and Elizabeth say they're going to go down to the historic area and look at the holiday decorations. We've already been, so I tell them to go without us. After they leave, it occurs to me we have a little time to ourselves.

Alone.

Okay, Mrs. Stevens-to-be, come here.

I don't waste a moment of our time. As soon as I'm sure their SUV is out of the parking lot, I pull Becca down the hall with me, a man on an erotic mission. She seems as eager for me as we get right down to business. It's Christmas Day.

A little special Christmas joy for us both coming right up.

I don't exactly know how long we have before they get back; an hour, maybe.

We both undress quickly, clothes, and underwear tossed carelessly on the floor, and before I know it, we're on her bed with the door closed, spooning. I have my arms around her, burying my face in her sweet, soft hair. My chest is pressed against her back, and I love the feel of her round ass touching my lower abs. Slowly, but surely, I make my way inside, coming into her from the back. I rock against her rhythmically, feeling how tight and slippery her sweetness is for me.

My fingers reach around in front of her to tease and touch her intimately. I move my fingers against her just like I've watched her do it when she makes herself come. She's breathing hard and moving against me, just like I am for her. It doesn't take long before I can't take anymore and neither can she. Inside her is my happy place. I think I almost see stars behind my closed eyelids as I lose control inside of her and feeling her climax at the same time all around me. She whispers my name over and over again as we both calm down from it. My arms are bands of steel holding her against me.

"Merry Christmas, fiancée. I love you."

"Merry Christmas to you as well, my love."

What a Christmas this is. Marry, marry Christmas to me. She is going to marry me for sure. I feel merry with delight at the thought.

CHAPTER 23

A New Year, a New Life

After her brother and sister-in-law leave, we have a few normal days to relax before New Year's Eve. This will be our first one together. Turns out Williamsburg has a great tradition going on that night. It's called First Night. I find out her friend Courtney and her husband Chris are coming to stay with her so they can attend First Night together. It seems to be a tradition with them. We just got rid of one set of guests, and now there are more people arriving? Becca has more company; every time I turn around, someone is coming to her house and *staying*. This must be Becca's Bed and Breakfast Inn.

On the 31st, we head down to Merchants' Square. Becca tells me we have to purchase a button at the Wythe Candy Store to wear tonight. It gets us into all of the events that evening. So we do, purchasing buttons for us and Courtney and Chris, my treat. I'm ready to go, looking forward to it. Courtney and Chris arrive in the late afternoon.

This is the first time I've met her. She was Becca's bridesmaid in *her first damn wedding*, and they roomed together in college. I hope she likes me. Becca shows Courtney her engagement ring, and the two of them talk excitedly about it and weddings. They obviously love each other. It doesn't seem to matter how long it's been since they've seen each other. It's like they pick right up where they left off.

That's a special friendship. It has stood the test of time.

"Thank you so much for letting us come and go to First Night with you this year. It has become a tradition with us, and it wouldn't be New Year's Eve without spending it in Williamsburg."

"Of course, we love having you here. I am looking forward to it as well. I've never been, so I have no idea what's going to happen tonight," I answer easily.

"You're going to love it. It is fun and the perfect way to start a new year. Michael, Becca's been telling me a little about you since you started dating. I am glad to finally get to meet you in person." Courtney looks at me shrewdly.

"I'm glad to meet you, too. I'm always happy to get to know her friends."

"Tell me again how the two of you met."

I pause, remembering that night, considering how much I should say. I wonder what Becca has already told her about me.

"We met at the Second Street Bistro. I was there having a drink, and Becca came in to meet her ex-husband. Things happened, and I came over to introduce myself. That's how it started."

"So she was there with Tripp? I'm surprised. She hasn't seen him since the divorce. He treated her so badly. Such a jerk."

I remember Courtney was her bridesmaid when she married the bastard.

"Yes. I ended up joining them when I noticed Tripp was making a nuisance of himself, in my opinion."

"I see."

I wonder briefly what Courtney had thought of Tripp as Becca's husband but don't ask anything. I guess I really don't want to know. I know he's an asshole. She has to know he is as well, considering he abandoned her friend.

She looks at me before saying, "I'm glad you introduced yourself. I can see how happy you both are. You've given her a gorgeous ring, you know. When will you be married?"

Please don't ask me how I proposed. That's private.

"We haven't decided yet. We'll let you know so you both can come."

Valentine's Day.

We leave the house a little before seven New Year's Eve. I drive the four of us in my car. I park the car on campus luckily near the football stadium and head out to the campus center first. The events are scattered all over campus and the downtown area of Williamsburg. We obtain a map and a schedule of the different entertainments. It is surprisingly fun walking around the campus at night and attending so many varied events. We can choose from classical music, rock, country music, comedians, and Celtic musicians. We attend as many events as we can. The time passes quickly, and before I know it, it's time to head for the football stadium for the fireworks after midnight.

We sit in the stadium and watch the people. Instead of a ball dropping like in Times Square, Williamsburg has a huge pineapple, the symbol for hospitality. The whole crowd counts down the last seconds until midnight. When it is finally the start of a new year, I sweep Becca into my arms, bend her over my arm like a Hollywood kiss, and plant one on her deeply. I'm so thankful I have this woman to kiss at midnight.

I dare Chris to beat that kiss with Courtney.

The fireworks are really outstanding, surprising me since this really is such a small town. It is easy to see that everyone is having a great time, us included. Such a nice way to ring in the new year instead of getting shit-faced drunk. I've done that before, so I speak from experience. I am looking forward to this year because she's part of my future.

After it is all over, we make our way safely home, avoiding all drunk drivers, and when everyone is settled, I make sure the front door is locked and lights out in the great room. Chris and Courtney go to the guest room. I don't care about what they think. I'm as quiet as I can be, but I am going to ring in this New Year right.

Making love to my girl. I want to start the year with a bang, my own unique brand of fireworks lighting up the night.

Knowing we need to be quiet, I sit on the bed in just my boxer shorts waiting for my fiancée to join me. When she comes over near the bed, I sweep my eyes up and down her from head to toe, whispering, "Strip for me, honey. Let me see all of you. Strip."

Her eyes widen, but she doesn't say a word. She begins to slowly and seductively remove each article of clothing until she is down to her bra and panties. Red silk lace tonight. We still say nothing to each other. I pause to kiss her mouth until we are both out of breath with desire. I move to sit on the edge of the bed and pull her close enough so that she is standing in front of me between my thighs. I reach up and leisurely lift one bra strap before letting it slide off her shoulder and down her arm. I repeat this procedure for the other strap.

Umm, not a front closure, I see. I always prefer front clasps.

I motion with my finger for her to turn around. She does so I can unhook the back of her bra. She spins back to face me, and I am treated by her full breasts there for the taking. But I resist. I still have work left to do. I pull her close to me, inhaling the scent of an aroused woman. It almost brings me to my knees, knowing how much I love pleasuring Becca orally. She still hasn't touched me yet. She is being very obedient tonight, the first time we make love in the new year.

I need to get my boxers and her panties out of the way quietly. I am getting so aroused, I am feeling restricted. I take her in my arms gently as I stand up close to her. She is holding her breath and smiling. Her eyes are drawn to the tent of boxer shorts in front of her. I can tell she is itching to touch me. I nod, letting her know she needs to remove my shorts. She shocks me when she proceeds to pull my shorts down using her teeth. It gets a bit tricky, but she perseveres. Still we are silent, only communicating with hand signals and glances.

I am losing control; now I am naked and ready. I take her hand and gently place her on the bed on her knees facing away from me. I am treated to the beautiful view of her smooth back, the subtle curved shape of her waist, and her full, lush hips. I can kiss the sweet spot on the nap of her neck and curve of the shoulder.

I stroke her back, tickling her with my fingers until she leans against me with her head falling back in sweet surrender. I cup her chin in my hands, pull her hair back, and swoop down on her open lips, drowning in her completely. Another scorching kiss to begin the new year. I drink deeply as she does the same to me.

Still quiet.

Perhaps I really am capable of being the strong, silent type.

I am on my knees behind her, almost thrusting my aching length against her ass. My hands can roam freely all up and down her front, from her seductive breasts to the moist petals further south. Knowing I can't last much longer and Becca is breathing quite hard by now, I gently push her chest down on the bed so that she is propped up on her elbows. She is gloriously right there in front of me, covered only by the fragile barrier of her sexy red silk panties.

Umm. I like those, but they are in the way now.

Perhaps I can just push them slightly to the side. Or simply rip the damn things off her with my strong fingers. I can always buy her more. But somehow I like the look of her hips covered in sexy, red panties. I gently move them to the side between her legs and ease my way inside of her until I am buried in to the hilt. Becca is moving her hips as she feels me fill her and thrusting against me.

Neither one of us is in control, yet I want so much for this to last and last and last for us both. I refuse to give in to her demands, gripping her full hips to slow her movements down. I must take charge of our lovemaking if I am to maintain it. We continue to be unnaturally quiet during our lovemaking, a first for us. The only sound is our breathing, quietly becoming faster and faster.

I move in and out of her slowly and lovingly, making her wait for it. Only steady sliding motions. Gradually I speed up, over and over until I have to close my eyes, the sight in front of me too erotic to bear. I am lost in her, lost in the fantasy of my very own tempting fiancée. She is grinding herself against me frantically when I begin to feel the familiar warm rippling sensation of Becca climaxing all around me.

I breathe as softly as I can. "Come for me, come for me, come for me, come for me."

It is like a chant I can't stop.

I stop moving and bury myself deep inside her so I can enjoy her pleasure. She is shuddering beneath me, struggling to breathe and be quiet during her orgasm. I am still on my knees tightly pressed against her from behind. Feeling her lose control does it for me, and forcefully I shoot hot streams of me into her welcoming softness.

She can feel me trembling and twitching inside of her as I come. I am gasping for breath, keeping my deep involuntary groans of extreme fulfillment locked inside my head. I give her everything I've got until we both collapse down onto the bed, me lying completely on top of her. We both managed to stay quiet.

Who knew that would make it so special?

I whisper, "Happy New Year, Ms. Connelly. I love you."

I can't wait to call her Mrs. Stevens in forty-five days.

She whispers back, "Happy New Year, Mr. Stevens. I love you, too."

Happy New Year to us. An excellent way to start our new life.

The next morning, Courtney and Chris return to Roanoke after breakfast. Becca fixes us coffee, tea for Courtney, Spanish omelets, and toast with blackberry jam. They don't say anything, so I guess we were quiet enough last night. I really liked them. Courtney was a lot of fun, and I only hope she liked me. She seemed happy enough about our wedding plans. Chris was a low-key kind of guy who seemed thrilled when Becca made sure he had his morning coffee before they left for the four-hour drive home.

I realize I only have a couple of days left before Becca has to start back to school. We spend New Year's Day watching the Rose Bowl Parade and college football games all day. During the course of the day, I gradually start to introduce her to the idea of moving all of her furniture and stuff to my house by the end of the month. I can see her thinking about it and considering what to do, but after a long moment, I see her slight nod in agreement.

Good, she's starting to think ahead.

I tell her I will make all the arrangements while she's at work. She doesn't have to worry about a thing. She has too much to do teaching. I will take care of it all, the move and the wedding. It is about to become a very busy two months.

I can't wait.

Next, I gently lead her to the idea of our wedding day being on Saturday, February 14. Valentine's Day.

A bit cliché, but what the hell. It's romantic, and I know we'll never forget our anniversary. Valentine's Day is a day for lovers.

I am more than willing to do anything she wants, but we really don't have much time, because *she is* going to marry me on Valentine's Day. I don't need a big wedding, and I don't think she really wants one again either. All I need is her. I'll take her to the courthouse if I have to and just get it done. But I can see she wants our wedding to be romantic even though it will just be immediate family and friends. I want her to have whatever she wants.

Romance.

CHAPTER

24

I Learn My Lessons Willingly

Before she returns to teaching in the new year, I sit her down to have a serious talk about her job teaching fourth grade. I tell her I am appalled by her responsibilities and admire her work ethic deeply. The school system seems to expect their teachers to spend their own money on the things she needs to teach and to make it so the students can learn and are happy.

I am incredulous.

I have watched her do this job since late August. I won't be able to make it until June, let alone another school year after we are married. I can't stand watching her work herself to death and deal with the stress overloading her every day. She argues a bit, telling me she has to work. She is not willing to give up her ability to care financially for herself. So I have to deal with the fact she doesn't trust me completely to care for her.

Financially dependent on me.

I lay it all out for her. I get out bank statements, financial records, my will, my investments, the whole financial portfolio for her to see and understand. Not only has she saved and invested quite competently despite a teacher's pitiful salary, but I also put just about everything I could away in savings while serving my country.

Being me, I didn't need much at all. My living arrangements, clothes, and even my food was taken care of by the Marines. I had no family to spend it on, no need for fancy expensive cars at that stage in my life. So I am a wealthy man. I thought she could tell from my car and home, but she never asked me about it. I tell her about my inheritance not only from both sides of my grandparents but also from my own parents. I have more than enough to take care of us for the rest of our lives and never work another day again.

I speak gently but logically. "Please, honey, look. Look at the numbers. I have money. More than enough for us. I will always be here for you. I could never leave you. If something happens to me, you will not be left penniless and unable to survive. You won't have to move out of our home with nothing like what happened to you with Tripp. If God forbid you want to ever divorce me, I promise you I will give it all to you. My life would be so empty without you if you left me; I would die anyway. I don't need anything but you."

Her eyes fill with tears as she considers what I am offering her. I am giving her the freedom to enjoy life with me. No more stress, no more work, no more problems and worries. I am giving her my love and a new life with me.

"Michael, are you sure this is the right decision? I don't want to be impulsive and not think through the consequences of giving up my career. It is all I had left to help me survive on my own. My job saved me. It gave me a little financial security, a feeling of purpose and accomplishment, and my friends and colleagues. It used to give me satisfaction and joy, but I have lost all of that now. It is a chore, a burden that never lets up, or lets me rest. I am always behind, always unable to feel as though I am doing a good job."

"I used to feel I was a good teacher, but I don't anymore. I am mentally and emotionally and physically exhausted by it. I know most people think teaching is playing with kids all day, having weekends and holidays off with a good long summer break. But it is not that. It is a damn marathon of work. If only they would let me teach the way I know how and the students were cooperative the way they used to be, I could still do it. But I have over twenty years now. I won't make it to thirty so I can retire if it keeps on like this. I am not sure what to do. I don't want to be an old lady with no retirement income to survive on financially."

"I'm here now. Depend on me. Trust me. You can trust me with your life, not just your heart. You don't need to work anymore, baby. Just let it go. Let me take you away from all that stress. Please, I need to do that for you. I need it desperately. It breaks me to see you so exhausted all of the time. I want your life to begin and end with me. I can make you happy. It makes me incredibly happy to do that for you. Let me. I'm part of your life, you know. You've said it twice, when you let me in as your lover and now as you agreed to be my wife. I am in and I am never coming out. Depend on it, Rebecca. Depend on me. It's okay. I'll help you. I'll help you write your resignation letter and go with you when you submit it. Let's do it soon so you can leave at the end of the semester this month."

"What will I do with all that time? I have always worked, except for summers off."

I reassure her. "Baby, it won't take you long to adjust. I am still adjusting myself to some degree but it is just so much fun. You'll see. You will wonder where you even found the time to go to work. There is so much we can do together once you are no longer tied down to a school day and a school year. I want to show you the world. You have to move in with me and we have a wedding to plan. Time is running out. I can't wait much longer to call you my wife, the only Mrs. Stevens I am ever going to have."

I can see she is finally convinced by the loving and hopeful look in her eyes.

She simply nods to me after making one of the most important decisions in her life. In some ways, I know it is just as important to her as it was to decide for us to get married. That decision was easy for us both, but this one was difficult for her to comprehend. I have convinced her to take the leap of faith with me. She will now be able to enjoy a new fun-filled life with me instead of one with work and worries.

She leaps, and I catch her securely in my arms and in my heart.

True to my word, after Becca gets back to work, I go with her to the administration building. She hands in her formal resignation. She has to teach two more weeks to finish out the semester. The new teacher will come in her last week and gradually take over. Over the course of those weeks, Becca stays really late every day, making sure everything is organized when she hands over the reins.

She has quarterly assessments and report cards to complete before the next teacher can be in control. When she comes home after her last day, I watch her take a breath and physically relax for the first time in months. The sheer relief it is over shines in her eyes. I haven't seen her this relaxed since last summer before school started up again.

That night I help my fiancée celebrate the end of her teaching career. I let her boss me around like she did her class, using her teacher voice and giving me orders. I follow all directions obediently like a good little boy. I know if she had been my teacher, I would have never been able to concentrate on any academic lessons. Becca continues to teach me new things, just like a good teacher would. She is patient, kind, competent, and very good at giving instructions. She has spent her adult life being a teacher for years, seven hours a day.

"Now then, Mr. Stevens, pay close attention. I am going to teach you something new and exciting tonight. Are you ready to learn?"

"Yes, ma'am."

What do you want me to learn tonight?

"I need you to do exactly as I say. If you have any questions, please raise your hand to let me know. Do not speak unless I call on you. I will not have disobedient students interrupting my instruction during class. Do you understand?"

"Yes, ma'am. I will raise my hand if I have a question. Understood, Ms. Connelly."

I have the feeling I will be raising more than my hand.

"Come here. I want to you to be naked. Unbutton your shirt, please. Slowly."

Naked student coming right up, so to speak.

I do.

"Take it off now and throw it on the chair."

I do.

Okay. Muscular torso revealed. I know she likes my shoulders, chest, and ab muscles.

"Now slip your shoes off so that you are barefoot, please."

I do as she instructs.

"I'm going to unbuckle your belt. Let me. Hold still."

She does.

Pants down drooping down on my hips, exposing navel and beginnings of happy trail. Cock still covered, unfortunately.

"I am unzipping your zipper next. Is that okay with you, Mr. Stevens?"

"Of course, teacher. Unzip me."

Absolutely unzip my pants. I am waiting for more teacher instructions.

She does. My pants are open and the bulge of my erection is exposed under my boxers. It is blatantly obvious this lesson is going to end successfully.

Becca slips my pants down my legs, and I kick them away from my ankles. She is still fully clothed. Her soft hand reaches through the front slit in my underwear, and she starts to caress me.

I stand there at attention giving her all the access she wants to me. Her hands vary the rhythm and strength of her grip as she pumps her hand up and down my erect dick. I close my eyes and enjoy. The next thing I know she has dropped to her knees and hungrily swooped her mouth to me as deep as she could.

I let her make love to me with her mouth for about as long as I can stand. When I am about to let go with everything I've got, she surprises me when she suddenly stands in front of me, leaving my cock bereft of attention.

Everything abruptly stops. Oh no.

"Lay down on the bed please. Face up. Put your head on the pillow and place the other pillow under your hips. Do so now."

I comply quickly with her instructions. I am waiting for more teacher commands. I start to ask her a quick question. I get out a strangled word before she stops me immediately.

"Mr. Stevens, I am the teacher in control of this classroom. You are my student. Obey me. You do as I say. I will not reward disobedient boys. You did not raise your hand before speaking to me. I do not tolerate interruptions well. Do you have a question you wish to ask me now? Have I been unclear in your lesson so far? I want you to learn this lesson very, very much."

My hand might not be raised but my cock is. Isn't that more important? Doesn't she notice my raised situation? Pay attention to me, teacher. I am your willing student.

"Yes, Ms. Connelly. I will do my best to learn what you want me to learn. I am happy to take all tests to prove my ability. I am a smart student, smarter than you think. I will catch on quickly. You'll see how intelligent and capable I am."

"You need to master all my homework assignments. Perfectly with no mistakes at all. Check your work carefully before you give it to me. I want you to pass the final exam with flying colors. An A effort is needed. I will be satisfied with nothing else from you. If you do not make an A on the final test, I shall consider my instruction to be lacking. We will have to try again tomorrow to see if you can learn successfully. What is your question? I am happy to answer and clear up any misunderstandings on your part."

"Ms. Connelly, as your prize student, I am wondering if I am allowed to touch the teacher during the lesson? Is that allowed, please?"

I need to touch you with my cock at the very least.

"You will be allowed to touch me only when I say and only where I say. Is that clear?"

"Yes."

"Yes, what?"

"Yes, ma'am."

"Put your hands behind your head now, please."

I do. She stands next to the bed, looking at me naked and ready to learn anything she wants to teach me. She frowns slightly, her expression telling me she is wondering what to do with me next. Then she reaches under her full skirt and pulls her mint green lace panties down and drops them carelessly to the floor.

She climbs on the bed slowly and then straddles me but doesn't mount my cock yet. It is there right in front of her unguarded pussy I know is there but is still hidden under her bunched skirt. She reaches down like my erect cock is a pommel on her saddle and holds on to me. Her hands and hips begin to move up and down.

We are playing horse and rider now.

I spread my thighs apart, and she spreads her thighs apart as well. I picture her wet pussy there poised above the empty space below her. I am getting more and more excited wanting to fill that empty space below and inside her with my thick penis. We move like this for a while, but then she stops and stares at me. I am having a difficult time keeping my fingers locked behind my head. I want to see her. I want to strip away that dress covering all the secrets this incredible teacher is keeping from me.

"I think you may touch me now, Mr. Stevens. Listen carefully and follow my instructions to the letter. Take your right hand and put it under my dress on my warm pussy. It is empty and wet waiting for you. I want you to caress me with only your fingers. Do you understand?"

I can only nod.

Urgently.

"You may touch me now. Be gentle, please. I am feeling very aroused, but not ready for this lesson to end quite yet."

I try, try to follow her orders. I am a good student, and she is very clear about what she wants. I am used to following orders after all because that is what the military is all about. I massage her intimately, feeling the slick moisture well up against my circulating fingers. She leans her head back to enjoy my touch on her sexually.

I continue to fuck her with my fingers until she tells me to put my thumb inside her and move it around. I do so. She commands deeper and faster. I do. I think I find her G-spot on the front wall of her vagina and stroke it firmly with my thumb buried inside her as deep as I am able. She is blushing and moaning now. I can tell she is close. Her body has heated up all over, and we are sweating and sliding against one another. Her hands are still holding on to my just-about-to-explode erection. I am not lasting much longer. It is sexual overload, and I am about to fall over the cliff.

I raise my other hand. She sees it and whispers, asking me what I want.

"Ms. Connelly, this lesson is about to be over. Please let me enter you. I need to do that now. Give me permission, I beg you."

"Yes, Mr. Stevens. I think it is time. Help me."

My hands fly swiftly under her skirt, lifting her hip and impaling her forcefully on me. We are both about to lose it. She bends over me and kisses my open mouth, invading it deeply with her tongue. My hands are on her hips, raising and lowering her on me frantically. We barely last five minutes before this lesson is gloriously and loudly concluded, both teacher and student immensely satisfied by the mastery of the lesson. We collapse in sweaty silence, me completely naked in total surrender and Becca still covered by her blouse and skirt, pantyless again.

She was so right. Becca is a master teacher. I can tell she found the joy of teaching again in our bed with me. I am grateful I am her only student. She can teach me anything she wants, and I am her most willing student.

CHAPTER 25

Super Wedding Preparations

We spend our now workless days preparing for the move and making wedding arrangements. Even though it will be February, we decide to chance a quick outdoor wedding. It might be a bit cold, but it won't take long. Hopefully no ice or snow since the winters here are usually not bad.

Becca wants to get married on the bridge at Crim Dell on the campus of the College of William and Mary. It was once voted the most romantic place on any college campus by a magazine, no less. That sells it in my mind. I arrange for our minister, flowers, limo, music, and invitations.

I do everything I can to make sure Becca's wedding bouquet is made of the peace roses she requested. I am not going to fail to find them like I did during the Week from Hell. She is the beautiful, fragrant, furled rose that brings peace to my life. I plan on wearing my tux, so I really don't need anything, but I know Becca will want a new gown. Once she quits, she'll have time to find the perfect one.

We're only inviting twenty-two people, her brother and sister and their spouses, her nieces, her nephews and their wives, great-nephew and great-niece her friend Mackenzie, Keith, Kevin and Suzanne, and Courtney and her husband Chris and Lauren and her husband. My sister Anne and her husband Bill, and son Jeff will also be there. I decide I'll simply take everyone out for dinner at the Williamsburg Inn after the marriage ceremony. We don't need a rehearsal dinner or formal reception of any kind.

Since our wedding is going to be a small romantic affair, I decide to take care of the music myself. I talk to Keith about it, and he says he will be glad to help me, even taking care of making sure the music plays at the wedding ceremony and dinner at the inn. He has the equipment I need to transfer songs to a CD that can be played on a battery-operated CD player outdoors. I think about the song choices long and hard and ask Becca for some of her favorites. Between us, I think we come up with a romantic selection of music that fits our love story perfectly.

I drive down to Keith's place in Norfolk. He greets me at the door and invites me in. I know I can trust him after everything we went through together in Iraq. He's tough, a little rough around the edges, but he had my back many times. There were times when neither one of us would have made it if not for each other. He has met Becca now and congratulates me on sealing the deal with her.

"Damn, dude, you haven't wasting any time getting your hands on her, have you?"

"Yeah, I know. I knew it the minute I saw her. She was tough to get though. I almost went crazy for a while."

"I can see why. She's fucking hot. I can hardly stand to be with the two of you. The lust between you is fucking obvious. You are a lucky bastard to have found her."

"I love her. It's simple. I can't live without her."

"I'm jealous, I admit. Shit. Maybe someday. We'll see what happens with Mackenzie. She is making me work for it as well. I guess women who have been divorced tend to have their guard up a bit."

"You better fucking well treat her right. She's Becca's best friend. Don't make me regret wondering if you two would like to meet."

"Yeah, she will be with me at your wedding. Let's get this music shit taken care of now."

"All right. Thanks for helping me with it. I think I brought everything we need. I just don't have the electronics you have, and I don't know how to fucking do it."

"No problem, dude. It's easy."

We spend the afternoon burning a CD of Becca's and my favorite music, appropriate for the occasion of our wedding ceremony. Becca chose "Bella's Lullaby" from *Twilight*'s soundtrack; two beautiful soaring pieces of instrumental music from the recent *Pride and Prejudice* movie; "Collide" by Howie Day; "Just Say Yes" by Snow Patrol; an erotic song called "The Lightning Strike," also by Snow Patrol; the seductive slow version of "Crazy in Love," Sofia Karlberg's cover of Beyoncé's song on the *Fifty Shades of Grey* soundtrack; "Oh What a Night" by the Four Seasons; "Satellite Heart" from the *New Moon* movie soundtrack; and "I'm Kissing You" by Des'ree. She also adds two beautiful seductive instrumental pieces called "The Truth" and "The Solace," both by Automachine.

I add "Use Somebody" by Kings of Leon, "The Scientist" by Coldplay, "I Want to Hold Your Hand" by the Beatles, "Love Me Tender" by Elvis Presley, the piano melody "River Flows in You," a song I call "I Can Breathe" but is actually "Heart of Stone" by Iko from *Breaking Dawn Part Two*'s soundtrack, "Forever" by Haim, Savage Gardens's song "Truly, Madly, Deeply," The Verve's "Bittersweet Symphony," "Beautiful" by Mandalay, "The First Time Ever I Saw Your Face" by Roberta Flack, and "Fumbling Toward Ecstasy" and "Possession" by Sarah McLachlan. I wish I could add "Sex on Fire" by Kings of Leon, but I know that song is too explicit for a romantic wedding ceremony.

Appropriate to me, but not for the occasion.

Also, I make sure we have a separate CD with two special songs. I want Becca to come to marry me while "A Thousand Years" by Christina Perri plays softly in the background. And I have plans to have our first dance as a married couple to "Can't Take My Eyes Off of You" by Frankie Valli and the Four Seasons. Not only will Keith make sure the music plays before our ceremony, but he will also take care of the song for our dance at the reception dinner. I also plan on playing the CD on our wedding night since Becca will miss most of the music. I want us to make love as a married couple listening to the romantic music and words that say it all for us.

Becca is finally starting to comprehend she is not an overworked, stressed teacher anymore. For her whole life. She never has to do it again, all that stress and work. I know it will take her a while to adjust to the fact that she is no longer working, not having to get up at the crack of dawn anymore. Hopefully she will start to realize it's like being on summer break all the time. She didn't seem to have difficulty staying busy then. She has many friends and a full life. We have a lot to do together. Sometimes she is just happy to spend the day reading and hanging out. I want her attention, and now we have the time to be together.

Fine by me.

To celebrate the end of her teaching career, we go out to purchase our wedding rings. I want her to wear a gold band studded with diamonds that will go with her diamond engagement ring. Inside the band, I tell the jeweler to inscribe our initials, the date of our wedding, and the words "You're mine. I'm yours." We find what I want in the jewelry store on Richmond Road.

Then Becca takes me to a jewelry store in the historical area. She already has something in mind that she wants to give me as my wedding ring. Walking into James Craig Jewelers on the Duke of Gloucester Street near the Capitol, she shows me a gold ring called a Gimmel ring. It apparently is a historical design. It features two hands interlocked. In fact I can pull the hands slightly apart and then put them back together as though the hands are holding on to one another.

She looks at me hopefully, telling me it reminds her of how much I hold her hand. I really like it. I like that it will remind me of our love always. She sighs happily when I agree. We order it in gold to match her rings, with the same inscription that she'll have on hers. I have never worn a ring before. When I was a Marine on patrol, it was dangerous to wear anything that might catch on something and rip my finger off.

Looking at the ring, I know I can't fucking wait for her to put it on my finger. I'm never taking the damn thing off. Someone will have to cut off my finger. It says I belong to her.

Soon it's the end of January, and the Trevelyan moving van pulls into the parking lot at Becca's condominium. Next thing we know, we are overwhelmed by moving people and boxes. These guys are extremely efficient because soon it's a done deal. They've attacked her stuff like locusts. They drive to my house and start unpacking competently. The furniture goes into place where I say, and the boxes are stacked in their designated rooms. All I can think is Becca is now officially living with me. She no longer has a home to go to if she wants to get away from me.

She's with me in OUR home. All just part of my master plan.

The next day, while I'm drowning in boxes, Becca goes to meet her friend Mackenzie down in Portsmouth. Their mission is to find the wedding dress. My matchmaking plan actually came to fruition. Mackenzie and Keith have been seeing each other starting in the fall. I know from all the phone calls and texts flying back and forth after each and every date. They really seemed to have hit it off. I received a thank-you call from Keith, so he's pleased with the way things are progressing with Mackenzie. We still haven't gone out all of us together yet, but I feel sure it is just a matter of time before we do. After hours and hours and hours, Becca finally comes home not saying anything, but the smile on her face says it for me.

Mission accomplished, evidently. She has a wedding gown. Good. One step closer.

Now that the wedding plans are virtually all in place, we can relax a bit. The NFL playoffs have finished and the Super Bowl is on Sunday. I call Keith and Mackenzie to see if they want to come up here for a Super Bowl party. He agrees and promises to bring Mackenzie with him. They will arrive around four on Sunday afternoon. Becca goes to the Fresh Market and gets wings, chips, nachos, and beers.

The Denver Broncos are playing the Washington Redskins this year. Becca is in a pickle. She loves Peyton Manning but is a diehard Washington fan. She ends up going for the Redskins because she just can't root against them. It has been a very long time since they have made it to the Super Bowl. She wants them to win. I take the Broncos just to make it a fun competition. I drive her crazy taunting her about rooting for the losing team. She gives it back to me though.

Keith and Mackenzie arrive and we settle down to snack and watch the pregame on my new Christmas-present television. The picture is outstanding, and I thank my fiancée once again. She smiles happily, stuffing her mouth with wings. By six, the game finally begins. Keith and Mackenzie are also rooting for the Broncos, and I feel sorry for my lonely little Redskins supporter. She doesn't change her allegiance though. She is loyal through and through.

Becca knows so much about football. I watch and listen. She discusses the quarterbacks, the running backs, the wide receivers, the linebackers, the offensive and defensive linemen, the kickers, and the coaches like she knows what the hell she is talking about. I lose all my focus on the game.

Quarterbacks throwing passes deep into the endzone. Tackling. First downs, touchdowns, field goals kicked through the uprights straight through the middle, extra points, wide receivers diving and leaping to make impossible catches with their sure hands, protective offensive linemen, dominating linebackers, calling plays in the huddle.

I can't help it. Suddenly all I can think about is getting my fianceé alone and scoring a touchdown deep in her.

The game continues. The Broncos are ahead 24–20 at halftime. I go get a cold, cold beer for both Keith and me. Maybe a cold beer will help me cool down a bit. Keith watches me a little strangely.

Soon the halftime entertainment is over, and the Redskins kick off to start the third quarter. A Broncos receiver catches the ball and runs it all the way back across the goal line for a touchdown. Becca groans in frustration. My ears perk up at that sound. I have heard her sound like that many, many times and not because the Redskins are losing the football game. I like her sexually frustrated sometimes. It makes the end result much more satisfying.

Things are looking grim for the Redskins. Peyton Manning is amazing as he leads his team down the field at will. The fourth quarter is a disaster for Washington, and I see hope fade from her eyes. Keith and Mackenzie are rubbing it in a bit, but I don't tease her about her losing team. Although the Redskins rally a bit at the end of the game, it isn't enough. They lose to the Broncos by two touchdowns. She smiles a bit sadly but is a good sport about it. She says there is always next year. She likes Peyton, so she is not completely devastated by the loss. She can be happy for the Broncos as well.

Keith and Mackenzie leave around eleven for the late, long, dark drive home down Interstate 64. I clear up the dishes a bit because Becca is about dead on her feet.

I do my best to cheer up Becca that night before we fall asleep together. I score a touchdown easily. I run into her, and she blocks me senseless. I have to come up with a new play. I rush ten yards for a first down before she calls time out. She tosses several long passes my way since I am now a wide receiver. Her defensive line is tough though. I have to be quick to get past it and score. We tackle each other repeatedly before passing out wrapped in each other's arms. Super, super football night. The Super Bowl has nothing on us.

CHAPTER 26

You're Mine, I'm Yours

It seems like it is taking forever, but the day of our wedding arrives. Of course, I know we aren't supposed to see each other the day of the wedding, but I don't care. I can't sleep without her. I made sure last night we made love one more time as an engaged couple living in sin. The last time I do it with Ms. Connelly. Becca wants to spend the morning getting mani-pedis. She is also going to the spa again, I hope for a facial.

Please don't let her get a wax because I don't want her to be the least bit irritated. Judging from what I felt last night, I don't think she needs one, but what do I know about it other than how it feels to me.

I think she has an appointment to get her hair and makeup done before the ceremony. Mackenzie appears to be coming up to go with her. The ceremony is at two in the afternoon, and it is turning out to be a beautiful, crisp winter's day. It's perfect. Since she's busy, I stay out of her way, giving her the time and space to get ready for me. Before she leaves me on the morning of our wedding to go to all of her beauty appointments, I remind her about her responsibilities today.

"Ms. Connelly, I expect to see you at two o'clock this afternoon. I'll be the one waiting for you on that bridge you like so much. Meet me there. Wear a long dress. I think it should be white. You look lovely in white. Do that for me, please."

"I'm planning on it, Mr. Stevens. I know where the bridge is, and I won't be late."

"If you are, I am afraid I will have to come and hunt you down."

"Hunt away, Marine. I know you will find me."

Yes, I will find you.

"That's good. I like to hunt you. It's fun when I find you."

"What do you plan to do with me when you find me later?"

"Why, Rebecca? Don't you already know? I could have sworn we have already discussed this. You must not be listening close enough to what I tell you. You need to pay attention. It should not be a surprise. I plan on making you mine today."

"Michael, I've been yours, and you've been mine for quite some time now. I can't be any more yours. It's impossible."

"Oh, yes, you can. You can be mine legally. We haven't done that yet. I'm looking forward to it. Sounds like fun to me. I can't wait. The anticipation is killing me."

"So legally means a lot to you, does it?"

"Yes, Mrs. Soon-to-Be Stevens. It means the whole world to me. It means it will be damn hard for you to get away from me now."

"I happen to like it when things are damn hard for me."

Yes, I know, me hard and thrusting hard. Focus, Stevens.

"My God, Rebecca, you're going to give me a heart attack. Don't you know I'm trying so hard to make it until tonight? You're all I can think about already. I want the next time we make love to be when we are officially husband and wife."

If she keeps on teasing me, I may be forced to make love to Ms. Connelly one last time, hours before she becomes Mrs. Stevens. No, I need to get hold of myself, so to speak. I'm already breaking the custom of not seeing my bride on the wedding day. Better not tempt fate any further. No bad luck for me.

"I think we need to practice just in case. We don't want to mess up later on, you know. I've been feeling a little rusty in that department lately. I'm not sure I remember what to do. I need a little refresher course."

Perfect practice leads to perfect performance. Umm. I am definitely perfect for her as she is perfect for me. We fit together perfectly.

"Please, God, give me strength. You are very tempting, you know. I can definitely remind you what to do, if you so desire."

"I desire a lot of things, Michael, and they all seem to involve you. I plan on showing you a little later. Now I've got to go. I have beauty appointments this morning and don't want to be late. I need all the help I can get. I've got to make myself perfect for you."

"You're already perfect for me. You can't get any more perfect. But I'll let you go now before I forget all my good intentions. I plan on being so hot today you won't be able to take your eyes off me. You won't possibly say no because I am hot for you and only you."

"My God, honey, what am I am going to do with you?"

"You already know my answer to that question. I've told you and told you. I've even showed you repeatedly what you can do with me. I think you know what to do. Practice makes perfect."

"But Michael, I am a slow learner. I need to be told and shown over and over and over."

I can still show you a thing or too. I have a good imagination. Don't think you've seen all my slow moves yet. It will take me our lifetime to show you everything I've got just for you.

"I don't think you are slow at all, my love. I can think of a few times you have been amazingly quick. Really, really fast."

"Well, I don't know. Maybe you're right. I can be slow and I can be quick sometimes. It all depends on my mood, you know."

"I'll do my very best to get you in the mood today. I plan on being *hot*. That ought to get you into the right mood. It seems to have worked perfectly in the past."

"All right, Michael. See you on the bridge at Crim Dell. Two o'clock. I expect you to be extremely *hot* for me and in the mood to become my loving legal husband today. Forever, nothing less will be acceptable to me. Obviously, I'll be the one wearing white. Make sure you marry the right woman. I'll be very mad with you otherwise."

Me too.

"No worries on that score. I love white. White dresses, white panties, white bras, white garter belts, white stockings, white stiletto heels. I know white when I see it. I will definitely recognize you."

"I'll see what I can do, then. I plan on making all your dreams come true from this day forward, remember?"

"Becca, you are the dream come true. Don't you know that already? I've told you and told you. Pay attention. I don't think you really listen to me. You don't seem to remember much of what I tell you."

"Tell me again, my love. Tell me you love me desperately."

Desperately fits this conversation to a T.

"I know I'll be feeling pretty desperate late this afternoon. I love you. Is that what you want to hear?"

I LOVE YOU! MARRY ME TODAY!

"That and other things. I plan on hearing everything you think later in the evening. You do tend to just blurt it all out frequently. Make sure you tell me over and over again. Later."

"I can't keep anything from you. No hidden secrets on my end."

"I have a hidden secret from you, Michael. You'll have to wait to find out later."

"Oh no, I can't stand that. The suspense will kill me, and I won't be able to concentrate during our wedding vows. I want to hear you when you promise to love me forever. I need to make sure you say the right things."

"Forever, Michael. You'll just have to hunt for my secret. Don't worry, it will all be revealed sooner or later. I know you'll find my secret. You're smart. I know it will be easy for you to figure out. You've never had any problems in the past, at least so far."

"So where do I look? Where do I begin? I want to know all your secrets, Becca. I don't like it when you keep anything from me."

What is it?

"My secret will be where you want it to be. On me, Marine. On me. It will be there, I promise. Easy for you to find if you just look a little. You said you liked white, so I'm making sure you are satisfied."

"I know I'll be satisfied. It's all a matter of time now. Tonight. Promise me you'll marry me today."

"It's my plan. See you at two, Michael. Remember, hot, so hot it doesn't matter that it is a winter day. I don't want you to feel cold."

"Okay, baby. I'll be in my tux waiting impatiently on the bridge. It won't just be me there. Expect our friends and family to watch and see how hot we are together. Be sure it's me you are marrying. Kevin will also be in his tux. Don't make a mistake and marry him instead. I am the only man you are marrying today. In five hours, Ms. Connelly. Five hours. Hurry. This wedding can't happen soon enough for me."

I am not going to make it. She is so damn clever. A true master of the double sexual entendre. I'm wrapped. I try hard but can't keep up with her quick wit. She makes me laugh.

She tries to leave before I can grab her and make love to her the morning of the day we get married. All my good intentions suddenly nearly shot all to hell.

Tonight, then. Tonight. How many hours is that? I need to count it up.

"Okay, Mr. Stevens. Let me go now. I have things to do and places to go before I become your wife and you become my husband. I want to surprise you."

"Ms. Connelly, the sooner you go, the sooner I can get ready to be your groom. Get going, Ms. Connelly. That's the last time I am ever calling you that name again. You will be Mrs. Michael Gable Stevens for the rest of your life, starting today. I love you. Later, on the bridge. Be there."

"No worries, my love. Later. I'm the bride, remember? Nothing happens without me. See you on the bridge. Wait for me. I'll come and find you. Bye for now. See you at our wedding, Mr. Stevens. Be the groom, okay?"

"Okay. I promise. Get going. I need to make myself look like a groom now."

She kisses me one last time as a single woman. I kiss her back, letting her slip out of my arms reluctantly. She smiles gently at me as she leaves.

I spend the time getting ready for her as well, showering and grooming myself, so I look as good as I can for her on our wedding day. I dress carefully in my tux, thinking I look pretty handsome when I'm done. I like the way it fits me.

Damn, though, if she wanted hot, Becca should have seen me when I was in my dress Marine uniform. There's nothing quite like that uniform. It's damn special, and I always loved it. The other services don't even come close. Since I'm out now, I can't wear it, but maybe I'll get it out someday to show Becca how hot I can look in my dress blues.

I could take her to one of my retirement banquets. I could wear my dress uniform there with her in an evening gown. I'd like to show her off to my old Marine buddies. I keep in touch with some of them by phone or e-mail frequently, but they don't live anywhere near me now. Keith is the closest one to me since he is only an hour away in Norfolk. I would really like for my friends to see my woman and be as jealous of me as hell.

Yeah, that's now a plan.

I think to myself, "*Becca thinks I'm intense.*" She should have seen me on night patrols in Iraq and Afghanistan. Now those were two intense places. I was the walking and talking definition of *intense*. Always on high alert, twenty-four hours a day, never letting down my guard for a moment. I didn't want to die there, and I certainly didn't want to be responsible for other Marines' deaths. We had to keep each other alive. Watch one another's backs every day, every hour, and every minute.

It really does give me nightmares at times, even now that it has been a while. I remember everything, and it feels as though it happened just the other day. The nightmares are less and less frequent now. Sleeping with Becca keeps me calm and able to sleep the whole night through unless she wakes me up in the middle of the night wanting me. Talk about insistent. I give in quite easily though. I don't mind being awoken from a deep sleep to pleasure her.

Thank goodness that scary part of my life is all behind me, and I can look forward to the future with my love. It's really going to happen today, the start of it all.

The dream coming true; reality, not fiction. My new and improved life. Not that I hated being a Marine. It is just I am filled with love for Becca. She gives me everything I need to feel satisfied as a man.

When I'm done getting ready, I leave the house before Becca gets home. She's going to want to change into the wedding gown without me seeing her. She will look beautiful to me no matter what she has on as a wedding gown. Mackenzie will be here to help her get dressed. I know the limo will pick her up and bring her to me at Crim Dell on William and Mary's campus.

I go to the Lodge, the hotel where my sister Anne and brother-in-law Bill are staying. He's going to serve as my best man, so I give him Becca's ring, telling him he had better not fucking lose it. I watch which pocket the ring goes in.

Finally, it's time. We make our way to campus. The minister is already waiting for us on the top slope of the bridge. Our friends and family are gathered there as well. The bridge looks picturesque, a gentle wooden slope over a large pond of still water surrounded by trees. It's a lovely spot on a lovely campus even though it is the middle of winter. It's a crisp, clear day. I am not feeling cool at all. I'm warm, definitely warm. I hope Becca won't be chilled in her dress. I don't want anyone to see her nipples pouting through her wedding gown.

Pouting pink nipples belong to me. I know I will see them tonight. I am looking forward to reintroducing myself to two of my favorite parts of Becca's sexy body.

I wait patiently, feeling Mackenzie and Courtney's eyes on me. Courtney stands with Chris, while Keith has his arm around Mackenzie's waist—making his move at my wedding, I see.

Who knew I could be a matchmaker?

The only thing I knew about it at first were the texts flying back and forth, discussing dates and everything else. Poor Keith. I hope they are happy together. Maybe someday he will be as happy in his marriage as I know I will be in mine. I wonder if he knows his every move and word has been discussed and dissected in detail by Becca and Mackenzie. Becca had shown me some of the texts she received from Mackenzie after I arranged for Keith to give her a call and introduce himself:

> **Becca.** Some friend of Michael's named Keith gave me a call. Do you know anything about him? He wants to meet me. What do you think I should do? Mackenzie

> **Mackenzie.** I know Michael thinks the world of him. They served together so he must be a good guy. Becca

> **Becca.** I told him I would meet him for drinks at the Biergarten Restaurant downtown Portsmouth. Mackenzie

> **Mackenzie.** Good choice. You can eat outside and be in public. Becca

Becca. I thought so too. What should I wear? Mackenzie

I guess everything must have gone well because I soon saw this text:

Becca. OMG. He's HOT. ExMarine tough. Thank Michael for me. OMG!!! Mackenzie

I can now claim to be a successful matchmaker, just one more of my many talents. Keith even called me to thank me for initiating the introductions. They've been dating ever since. I see them both today at our wedding. He has his arm around her waist. The music is playing softly but loud enough for everyone to hear.

I love all of our songs. Our love songs.

I look over at my soon-to-be wife's two best friends. This is the first time the two best girlfriends have seen me in a tux, of course.

I hope they think I look damn hot. Hot for Becca, that is. From the way they keep staring at me, smiling, and whispering to each other, I think maybe I might be right. Everyone else seems happy to me. If only Becca would get here. I'm ready. Where is she? How much longer do I have to wait for her?

Someone must have told Keith Becca was ready. He goes to the CD player. The music changes to "A Thousand Years," and I start looking for her. I see her make her way out of the trees and toward the slope of the bridge. Suddenly it's like I have tunnel vision or something. Everything around Becca blurs slightly and all I can focus on is her. She's coming to me.

I can't breathe.

The words of this song are perfect. Our love will last for a thousand years.

I have died every day waiting for you.
Darling, don't be afraid I have loved you
For a thousand years.
I'll love you for a thousand more.

Her hair is up, so I can see the graceful lines of her neck. A short lacy veil is behind her. Her creamy white gown is a glossy silk with a bit of lace, undulating in front of her legs. It is off the shoulder, giving me a view of her full, lush cleavage. It hugs her in all the right places, making that hourglass figure overpower me. She is carrying a small bouquet of soft yellow roses tinged in pink. Peace roses. I feel such a peaceful emotion sweep over me. I am completely at peace in the knowledge that we are meant for one another as husband and wife forever. Life partners to share every challenge and joy life can offer us. She's smiling at me tenderly, and I stare at her loveliness as she comes to give herself to me.

Every dream of a woman I ever had when I was that lonely Marine in so many dangerous places and for so many years is suddenly coming true for me. She's here. With me.

She finally reaches my side, and I take her hand, kissing her knuckles one last time before she becomes my wife.

We stand together surrounded by our special loved ones. The minister starts talking, and I try, really try, to focus.

Come on, Stevens. Listen.

It's a miracle when I respond appropriately because I'm looking at Becca. My voice barely even sounds like me. I hear her recite her vows to me with her soft, husky voice. I think she's trying not to cry. If she starts, so will I. I catch on to the fact that it is time to exchange the rings. Bill hands it to me, and I don't think I can get it slipped on her finger fast enough.

Becca hands her bouquet to Courtney and gets my wedding ring. She looks intently at me while sliding the Gimmel ring on my left ring finger. She surprises me by lifting my finger to her mouth and giving the ring a quick soft kiss. I'm still not breathing until I hear the minister pronounce us husband and wife.

My wife. Her husband. Officially. Legally. Forever mine. Forever hers. I take a deep quiet breath as I turn to face her. I reach down and take her hand, bringing it up to my lips so I can kiss her knuckles. I whisper, "Mrs. Stevens."

My heartbeats are pounding in my ears, yet unbelievably one part of my brain signals something to me. I hear the hauntingly romantic ballad "I'm Kissing You" playing softly near us. Yes, that is the correct song for this particular moment in our lives. Everyone can hear it. I smile at my wife, and her answering smile tells me of her joy. The chorus of the song reaches my enthralled brain.

'Cause I'm kissing you, oh
I'm kissing you, oh.
Touch me deep, pure, and true
Gift to me forever.

I can kiss her now, in front of everyone. I sweep her close to me, laying her across my arm so that she is supported entirely by me. Before I kiss her, I breathe the words, "You're mine, I'm yours," into her ear.

Holding her tightly in my embrace, I swoop down on her startled open lips and make our kiss as passionate as I can, surrounded by our friends and family. I just manage not to French-kiss my wife in front of our guests. I am in no hurry to rush now. We are married, and I can kiss her as long as I like.

What a kiss. Memorable forever. Our first kiss as husband and wife.

Becca is rather flushed a sweet pink color when I finish, leaving no doubt in anyone's mind that *we love* each other. Passionately. Everyone gathers around for hugs and congratulations.

I don't feel cold at all even though it is winter. All I can feel is warm and happy.

As soon as we are all able, we go back to our cars and head toward the inn. Becca and I travel in the limo. Unfortunately, it is a very short ride, so I'm only able to get to second base, almost forgetting where we are. I manage to stop before getting too carried away. I just hope the driver didn't turn around. I don't want an audience. Being an experienced limo driver, he has probably already heard and seen everything. He must know to keep his eyes on the road and just drive. I am not happy about him seeing my new wife at all. She is mine and mine alone. I must try to behave myself better when we get back into the limo later to go home.

For our wedding night.

The inn has set up a special round table for us so that we can all sit together. As usual, the wait staff know what they're doing. Everyone seems to enjoy the elegant meal and wine. I motion to Keith to play the song we recorded for just this moment.

"Mrs. Stevens, I hope you are having a good time. May I have the honor of a dance with you? I feel the overwhelming need to hold you close in my arms. Dancing is the only option available to me at this time. Dance with me, baby." She nods shyly.

When the music starts, it is playing the song I requested, an old Frankie Valli and the Four Seasons song called "Can't Take My Eyes Off of You." We move to the small dance floor. I raise her left hand to my lips and softly kiss her knuckles as I slightly bow. She is staring at me and giggling slightly. I take her hand and lead it to my shoulder so she can touch me on the curve of my neck. My right hand settles on the curve of her waist, and I take her right hand in mine. We are now in the proper position to slow dance. I want to dance with my wife.

Leaning toward her with my lips buried in the soft hair at her ear, I softly murmur, singing softly the words to her as we dance our first dance together as a married couple. It's true, all the words I whisper in her ear. I really can't stop staring at my lovely new wife. She feels so right in my arms.

I love her. She is finally mine, my wife forever now.

The words are in my heart and soul as I gaze into her happy green eyes.

You're just too good to be true
Can't take my eyes off of you,
You'd be like heaven to touch.
I wanna hold you so much.

My lips breathe the words touching her ear, so this is a private moment between us as we dance. When the song finishes, she looks at me with love in her green eyes, reflecting back to me the love I know she sees in mine.

She whispers, "I love you so much, Michael. I feel the same way toward you. Thank you for the most romantic wedding a woman could ever want. I'll never forget this day, how handsome you looked on the bridge waiting for me to come to you. I can't wait to start our real lives together."

And I never forget even a single moment of this day.

When we return to the table, I gradually begin to talk to everyone, getting to talk more with Courtney and Mackenzie since they're Becca's best friends, and they don't know me that well. I want them to think their good friend will be safe in my care. They seem to, and I can see why they are all such close friends, laughing easily and teasing Becca about the coming honeymoon.

The waiters come out with our small beautiful wedding cake. I wanted hot fudge to somehow be included but couldn't figure out how. We ended up with a delicious almond-flavored pound cake, exquisitely decorated with butter cream frosting. I watch Becca, and she seems really happy as we cut the cake. I gently place a piece of our wedding cake into her mouth and she does the same to me. I almost lick her fingers before stopping myself. We toast with glasses of pink champagne.

I start to find myself trying to think of reasons why this dinner should end now. Dessert and coffee are over. I think we're done here. Becca's fingers keep tracing a circular pattern on my thigh. It's driving me crazy. We need to get out of here. We've got things to get done. I'm ready for the wedding night and the honeymoon to begin. Desperately, I search for an excuse to leave. Suddenly, I realize I really don't need one. I'm the damn groom—we leave when I say. I stand up, grab her hand, and haul her up. Unbelievably, our friends and family all seem to finally get the message. Hugs, kisses, congratulations, wishes for a safe flight and fun honeymoon, etc.

Taking our leave, I steer her toward the front doors where the limo still awaits us. The driver jumps quickly out to open the door for us. We're going home. I know we could have just stayed here at the inn for our actual wedding night, but somehow I want our first married time to be in our bed. Since it is several miles from the inn to our home, I'm able to make it to third base this time, but since the damn limo can't drive itself, I have saved the home run for home territory. Besides, I really don't want our first intimate time as newlyweds to end up being a quickie in the backseat of the limo. I am aiming for extremely erotic experiences that require privacy.

I have plans.

CHAPTER 27

Oh, What a Night!

When the driver pulls up to the house, he rushes to open our door. I am afraid he knows how desperate I am and wants me out of his limo, somewhat afraid of what I might do next. Becca and I spill out the limo door, and I immediately put my arm under her thighs and hoist her up. I carry her all the way to the door, over the threshold, through the great room, and down the hall to our bedroom.

She's giggling. I realize my smile is the smile of a wolf in gentleman's clothing.

I like the way she has fixed it up so far, incorporating both my things and hers together. I get the CD from our wedding, load it into the Bose sound system, and make sure it is playing softly in the background.

Our romantic, sexy, seductive love songs that say it all for us. Music to make love to.

I light several candles in our master suite, leaving the harsh artificial lamps off. Romantic music and romantic candlelight for our wedding night. I try to think of everything to make this perfect for us. A night for us to remember forever.

My wife, my wife.

"Mrs. Stevens, you take my breath away. I've never seen you look more lovely. I love you, baby. Thank you for marrying me today."

Frankie Valli and the Four Seasons' song, "Oh, What a Night!" (December 1963) plays on the bedroom's sound system.

"Thank you for marrying me too, Mr. Stevens. I have to admit I've always loved what you look like in that tux. Of course, then again, I love what you look like out of it even more. Show me. I can't quite remember. I need to be reminded."

"Good to hear. Let's see what you look like out of your white dress now. I'll show you mine if you show me yours. Stand up and turn around for me, honey."

Turns out the back of her dress has about a hundred tiny little buttons. No wonder she needed Mackenzie help to get her into the darn gown.

Damn it. I've got to slow down to get her out of it. Okay, I can do slow.

I make my way down her dress, one button at a time, revealing her smooth soft back. I discover a white strapless bra first. It starts to dawn on me that I am finding the hidden secret she spoke of earlier in the day.

What a delightful secret to uncover.

As I continue undoing buttons down her back, I slowly uncover a lacy white garter belt. Going even further, there appears to be a white thong. Not much coverage there. I like this hidden secret. And then I can see the tops of lacy white silk stockings. A vision in white. I finally am able to let the whole silky gown drop to her feet and pool around her five-inch stilettos. Since she really belongs to me now, I start to slowly pull the tiny thong down her beautiful thighs.

Nothing in my way. Not even that.

I soon discover this isn't working. I realize I have to take the garter belt off and unhook the stockings before this is going to happen. The silky white thong is under the garter belt, so I have to remove it first so I can get her naked. I do that as competently and rapidly as I can. Thank goodness these are the kind of stockings which stay up on their own. I reach up and unhook her strapless bra as well. Becca knows this is really the way I like her, the way she was our first time together. Naked, except for stockings and high heels.

My very own centerfold.

Damn.

How did I get so lucky?

Taking her hand, I lead her over to our bed and make sure she's comfortable on the pillows. Walking over to her mahogany dresser, I pull out a white scarf she has. I am still fully dressed in my tux. I walk back to her and sit down on the bed next to her. I show her the scarf and whisper to her, "Trust me?"

God, I love the way she looks waiting for me. Waiting for us to make love. Anticipation is always the key to a successful seduction. The waiting leads to intense wanting. Overwhelmingly erotic, sensual desire. The need to be one with her.

She replies, "With my life."

"That's good, Mrs. Stevens. I think you've actually seen enough now. Close your eyes for me."

I gently tie the white silk scarf across her eyes, making sure it's thick enough that she can't see anything through the thin material. And then I leave her alone. It's hard to leave her, but I head for the kitchen and the refrigerator. Since she seemed to like hot fudge so much, I decide to have a little whipped cream of my own. She's dressed in white after all. When I return, she's still lying there waiting for me but not so patiently.

"Michael, Michael, tell me what you are going to do. Please, darling."

"All in good time, my love. All in good time. Be patient and trust me. I hope you know you can trust me by now."

My voice is suddenly deeper and softer. Gentle. Soothing her.

"But . . . but I want you. I love you so much. Take me. Now."

"You've got me. I'm yours. I belong to you, body and soul. I most definitely am planning on taking you. After all, it's our wedding night. It's expected. By everybody. I expect to make love to my wife. I won't disappoint you tonight. It will be the night we remember forever. Don't worry. I've got it covered."

"Come closer to me, husband. I need to feel you, touch you. Why are you so far away from me, Michael?"

"I'm right here, baby. I know you can't see me, but I can see you. Your soft skin looks so creamy in the candlelight. You look like you are glowing. It gives me an idea."

"What idea have you come up with now? I am breathless with excitement here."

"A River Flows in You" is seductive music.

"Just take a deep breath and relax, my love. I'll take good care of you. It's just your skin looks so creamy pale it makes my mouth water. I just wonder how your creamy skin will taste to me. Your skin reminds me of the smooth petals of a rose, just waiting for me to unfurl them to find your secret center. Just like a sweet-smelling rose."

"Michael, you say the most erotic things sometimes. You know how I taste by now, Michael. Hurry, I want you. Love me. I need you."

"I love you too, my sweet. I just can't stop wondering how creamy you are if I lick you. I want you to lie still now. Don't be afraid. I want to make sure you are good and creamy for me. All over. I want to surprise you just a little. Trust me."

She is squirming slightly by now, listening carefully. Our wedding music continues to play in the background softly, making the mood seductive as I listen to the romantic melodies and words. The music and lyrics say it all to her.

I take off my jacket; undo my tie; have trouble with my cuff links; and slip off my shirt, socks, shoes, and my pants and underwear in one fell swoop. I sit carefully down next to her and then stretch out so I can touch her.

I take the cold whipped cream and shake it up. I can see Becca is listening to every sound, trying to figure out what is going on. I take the cold can, hold it to her right nipple, and apply a generous dollop of fluffy whipped cream. She startles in surprise.

"Satellite Heart" by Anya Marina is appropriate. She is the sun, and I revolve around her in orbit, a gravitational pull holding us together.

I can't tell yet, but I hope the coldness of the cream is making her nipples pucker. The left nipple gets the same treatment. I put some in her navel and then hold the can over her soft folds. Taking my time, I put a good amount on her silky sweet secret place. My very own creamy dessert. All for me and me alone. Her natural delicious taste all mixed up with the sweetness of the whipped cream.

Now then. I ate one piece of our wedding cake, but I think I have room for a little more sweet dessert. After all, I adore dessert. I don't think a meal is complete without it. I plan on making a meal out of my brand new wife.

My open mouth suddenly swoops down on the right nipple, taking all the whipped cream into my mouth as I lick it clean. I think the sudden change from cold whipped cream to hot wet mouth is exciting to her because she moans for me. I do the same thing to the left nipple as well, earning a little louder moan. I spend a little more time at the navel, slowly licking the cream up one lap of the tongue at a time. Becca is starting to move her hips. This is delicious. No way am I full yet.

"Becca, baby. Open your mouth for me."

"Rolling in the Deep" by Adele.

Her pink lips open at my command. I take the can of cold whipped cream and squirt a mound of cream into her mouth. Before she can close her mouth and swallow, I kiss her passionately, sharing the cream in her mouth with her. She moans and opens her mouth wider, allowing me all access with my tongue. I kiss her until all the cream is gone.

Her hips almost begin to twist with desire. I look down at the invitation waiting for me between her thighs.

More sweet cream for me.

Becca continues to move her hips in a circular motion, tempting me, but I see what is happening to the whipped cream I deposited there for me to enjoy.

Oh no! I don't want that whipped cream between her legs to go anywhere but where it already is. My last sweet taste of cream.

I grab her hips and hold her still tightly. She moans really loud this time and bucks her hips up, practically up to my mouth.

"Possession" by Sarah McLachlan.

Okay then, that works. I swoop down with open lips.

I start licking up the whipped cream between her legs, swirling my tongue around and sucking. I like having whipped cream like this.

I'll never take a hot fudge sundae with whipped cream for granted again. It's now my favorite.

Umm. Don't hot fudge sundaes usually include a cherry on top?

I can't think about that right now. I have to concentrate on the yearning, sexy woman in front of me.

When I've finished and all the whipped cream is gone, I decide this loving needs to be for both of us since it's our first time as husband and wife. I take my lips from her and slide up her body on top of her, letting my cock rest at the entrance to her. She might not be able to see me, but she can hear me and feel me. I whisper words of love as I slowly enter her.

All I can say is that I make love with my wife. We make love to each other, together. She whispers to me how much she loves me, how much she wants me, and how my intensity toward her makes her feel completely loved and desired. She says I make her happy.

The music seems to fill us with the melodies and words of love. I hear the seductive, sexy melodies and words of "Crazy in Love" and then the sensual song by Snow Patrol called "The Lightning Strike." So very erotic, building in intensity as the music reaches a peak. The music is in my head, and all I can concentrate on is the beautiful woman under me. I am moving in her in time with the music. I whisper to her over and over again, letting her feel my warm breath tickle her ear as I kiss it and circle my tongue inside.

"Becca, Becca, don't stop. Just like that. Oh God, oh God, I love you, I need you, I want you until I can't think of anything but how good you feel to me when I'm inside you, deep, deep inside you. It's all for me, all for you. Baby, love me. Love me. I need you to love me. Oh, baby, are you close for me? Does it feel good to you? I can't stop, I can't hold myself from you much longer. Come for me, come for me now. Oh God, please, please let me feel you come all around me."

The lightning strike, the lightning strike. I am struck by lightning.

I just can't get enough of my wife. I lose all control as I feel her lose control under me. It suddenly becomes too much for both of us to handle—the music, the love, the desire. We actually climax at almost the same time while clutching each other closely.

It's a good thing the neighbors are not close because we get rather loud in here, screaming each other's name. I gently untie the white scarf and remove it from her eyes. I see the love she feels for me shining there in those green depths.

Becca's love really did hit me like a bolt of lightning. A hot searing lightning strike. From the very start lasting until now on our wedding night. I hope it lasts forever.

The second time together is a hard, fast affair. She has to hold on to our wrought iron headboard tightly with her arms over her head. She is lying on her back with the pillow I placed under her butt. I take my time at first but eventually am entering her missionary-style. I grab both of her feet, bend her legs, and put her feet directly on my chest, shoulder-level. I tell her to keep her hands on the iron posts of the bed and not let go. I want to focus on her and not my own pleasure until later. Her roaming hands distract me a lot. We slow down together to make it last.

I hear the words and music to "The First Time Ever I Saw Your Face" play gently around us. The lyrics echo through me.

And the first time ever I lay with you
I felt your heart so close to mine
And I knew our joy would fill the earth
And last 'til the end of time, my love

Having her feet against my chest makes her vulnerable and wide open for me. She pushes her legs and feet against me offering some resistance, but I am just too on her. She is not really trying to kick me away from her. We rock against one another for a while until I simply have to thrust deeply in my wife's wet tight warmth. It is all for me, every squeeze, every secret caress from her whether voluntary or involuntary. The sensations drive me wild until I can't stop pounding my dick into her. She is giving it all back to me as well, urging me huskily to get even closer to her. I feel as though I am climbing into my wife's beautiful body and joining her in bliss. She is an angel from Heaven above to me.

Halo by Beyonce.

The pillow under her ass makes all the difference for both of us. It is simply too erotic, too intense, too mind-blowing a series of sexual sensations all at once. Becca is moaning and crying out for me to give it to her; she needs to come. She is still gripping the headboard above her head, not letting go for anything. My ass pumps, rapidly rocking against her and then thrusting deeply. The angle between us due to the raised pillow makes me feel I have never ever touched such a deep place inside of her.

It's too much for us both. I am not sure she is going to make it. Perhaps all this stimulation is more than she can take, but then thankfully I feel and hear it happen for her. I am so relieved to feel her come, knowing I have made sure she gets her pleasure before I let go of all my control. She is screaming for me to come with her.

It is always important to me to take care of her and never leave her hanging in frustration. There are times when sexual frustration can make it even more pleasurable when we both give in to it, but not tonight. Not now. This is our wedding night. I am already there, no need for denial to build my expectations any higher.

I realize I can't hold it back now. Reciting states, capitals, elements, and speeches won't help to keep it from coming. I surrender to it, letting the incredible waves of ecstasy sweep through me. I demand for Becca to feel me come inside her, hoping she can sense my joy in her. I am left gasping for breath, her feet still against my shoulders with me buried inside her depths.

What a wonderful place to be, my favorite place in the world. Her legs stay in place but then gradually slide even further apart, allowing me to lay directly on top of her body in complete surrender.

Her legs and arms wrap all the way around her as we both relax in complete sexual release.

"I love you, husband."

"I love you, wife."

I love everything about my wife. We doze sleepily but never lose complete consciousness. I whisper my love to her, and she does the same to me. It is exactly what I need and want to hear from her tonight of all nights.

We rest for an hour. The third time is for her and me to watch. I gently take her into our master bath and position her in front of the sinks with the large mirror behind them. I stand closely behind her, touching her smooth back and soft yet firm ass. I step even closer, getting into position to enter her from the back.

"Truly, Madly, Deeply" by Savage Garden now.

I whisper in her ear, "Baby, I want you to watch us. Watch us make love together. Look at how we fit so perfectly for one another. I love you. Keep your eyes open and watch. Watch us love."

My arms are around her as I push her thighs slightly apart, bending her over for me so I can gain entrance to all of her wet warmth. She moans as I slip inside, and I enjoy the intimate slide of skin against skin. I pull her back up straight against me, against my muscular chest and abdomen. My right hand goes to pleasure her between her legs while the left wraps around to grab a tit. I am completely holding her, in charge. My fingers move on her moist hairless folds, teasing, touching, stroking, sometimes hard, then gentle. She is panting and moving against me as she becomes lost in the sensations I am giving both of us.

We stare into each other's eyes, locked together in the mirror. Her arms are up, caressing my face, my mouth, and running her fingers through my hair. She slips a finger between my lips, and I suck on it hungrily before letting her slide it slowly from me. Her lifted arms make her breasts look so temptingly full and lush. My left hand enjoys squeezing her extended nipples gently and feeling it against the center of my sensitive palm. It is hard for me to keep from losing control and gripping her full breast too tightly.

"Beautiful" by Mandalay.

But I never want my sexual touch on her to cause even a moment's slight pain. It is so damn erotic seeing her lose control with my arms holding her and my dick enjoying every movement, every breath she breathes. The image of us locked so intimately together is suddenly burned into my consciousness forever.

I will never forget how we look making love to one another as husband and wife.

"Oh, Becca, baby. Look at you. Look at me. I'll die remembering this, us together like this. I can't hold on much longer. The sight of you like this is so damn erotic I can hardly believe it. Come for me. I want to watch and feel you at the same time. Let go, let it happen. I love you, Mrs. Stevens. I love you."

Her head suddenly falls back, and I bury my mouth in the curve of her neck, kissing and biting softly. I continue to whisper encouraging words in her ear. She is moaning and panting and moving frantically against me as I keep up the rhythm of both my cock and my fingers, rapidly thrumming her.

One of her hands comes down from my hair, and I watch her place her fingers over mine as I stroke her. Her fingers guide my movements, and I follow her lead exactly as I am being shown. It is as though we are both getting her off together.

I put my left hand under her chin to lift her mouth to mine. My right hand never lets up on her, never stops pleasuring her. I swoop down on her open mouth as she gasps. My tongue tangles up with hers as we taste each other's passion. I can never get enough of how she tastes all over her body. My eyes close briefly as I lose myself in my wife's loving kiss. I feel her change as she tears her mouth away from mine.

"Fumbling Toward Ecstasy" by Sarah McLachlan again.

Her breathing suddenly stops as she seems to hold her breath, only gasping occasionally. Her hips almost stop moving as I make love to her. She is getting close to having an orgasm.

Please, please. Come for me now. Come, baby, come.

Then I feel it and hear it and see it begin for her. For me. She screams for me as her climax sweeps through her overwhelmingly pleasurable. I feel her begin to collapse against me as she loses control and melts, but I have her tightly in my arms. I won't let her fall. I can't stop now. Her powerful assault on all my senses takes me down.

I glance quickly at the mirror, realizing we look like a soft porn movie. Umm. Maybe hard porn, actually.

All I can do is feel my own orgasm almost bring me to my knees as I thrust deeply into her to shoot hot streams of my cum deep inside my sexy wife. I don't know how either of us is still standing as we withstand it. I am completely drained of strength as I sink to the carpeted floor holding my incoherent and exhausted wife. I don't want to slip out of her, trying to stay as close to her as I can. I have to as I gather her into my lap and arms, kissing her face and mouth over and over tenderly.

In between sweet shared kisses, she whispers, "I love you, Michael Stevens. Thank you for loving me back. I am your wife in every way, and I need you as my husband, my love, my partner for the rest of my life. We're in this marriage, this life together now. Never leave me. I won't survive."

"You never have to worry about that, my love. I am the one who can't survive without you. I will love you until the day I die and even after that. Our love is so strong it must be eternal."

Eventually we find the strength to crawl back under the covers and fall asleep even though the music is playing softly still on repeat. But I wake up in the dark, filled with the scent and touch of a warm woman in my arms. I stroke my fingers up and down her back while she sleeps. I don't want to wake her, yet I do. I can tell when she slowly gains awareness. She is awake now, and I am definitely up too.

The soaring instrumental music of "Liz on Top of the World" from the Pride and Prejudice soundtrack plays as our accompaniment.

I have a good imagination, so I try to vary my sexual activities and positions, making certain she never gets bored, heaven forbid. Fair and equal. We are equal partners in this marriage after all. I let her rest a little in between events, but I never really let her sleep until we are done as far as I am concerned. She never complains and seems to love it as much as I do.

"Oh, Michael, Michael, Michael, I love you, I love you, I love you. Oh, my God, I never knew I could love anyone as much as I do you. Never, never leave me. I won't be able to take it. I need you so much. I'm yours, only yours. Thank God you're mine."

"And I, you, my love. And I, you. You are my whole world. Promise me you love me. I love to hear you tell me."

"I love you, Michael Stevens. I promise. With all my heart."

"I give you my promise, my wife, to love you for every minute of the rest of your life. Never doubt my love for you. My world begins and ends with you. I want your life to begin and end with me as well. Any experiences I had before the day we met are nothing to me. I wasn't truly alive until you. I never want to be parted from you. My life means nothing to me without you. My love for you is complete and eternal. I swear this to you on my sacred honor," I whisper in her ear as we both begin to pass out from sheer exhaustion.

"Bella's Lullaby," the piano piece from Twilight, will lull us to sleep.

I am stunned by the sheer sexual passion we are capable of producing in each other. It has been blindingly good from the very start, but we have now reached a whole new level of intimacy. I never knew I could find such joy with someone. It is amazing to me. She seems to feel the same way as me, and I am filled with such gratitude it is true. I will love this woman every day for the rest of our lives.

She is mine. Completely mine. As am I for her.

As we go to sleep at dawn, pleasantly tired and sated, all I can smell is sex. I take a deep calming breath and let it out slowly, falling to sleep wrapped around my brand new wife.

I hope she's just a little sore tomorrow, not much though, enough to remind her of where I've been. Only I get to touch her in her intimate places. I have been there now repeatedly. Overused just a bit. Although I know I can never get enough of her, I don't want to spoil our fun. After all, I need her ready for the honeymoon. I enjoyed the heck out of our wedding night. I am so lucky. We're legal. Officially.

Honeymoon coming right up. A romantic journey to romantic Switzerland. More white peaks and white mountains to conquer.

"Heart of Stone" by Iko ("I Can Breathe").

I can breathe

I can breathe water, water
I can breathe
I can breathe water, water
Both of our hearts are no longer made of unyielding stone.
We let each other in.
My heart and my wife's heart are made of real love from now on.
For the rest of our lives . . . and beyond.

CHAPTER 28

Romantic Honeymoon in Switzerland

I have a really hard time getting up the next morning even though it is noon before we wake up. It's even harder to get Becca awake. I think we wore both of us out. Thank goodness our flight isn't until the early evening, so we have time to sleep late. Our bags are basically packed, and all we have to do is get to the airport in time to check in and turn over our luggage. The flights leave from Newport News to Atlanta, then Amsterdam, finally arriving in Zurich, Switzerland. First class all the way because traveling in coach sucks. It's a long flight, and I want Becca to be able to sleep to avoid jet lag due to changes in time zones. But traveling is still somewhat exhausting.

When we finally arrive in Zurich the next day, we're both a bit wiped out. It takes both of us a while to adjust to the different time zone. We grab a cab to the Hotel Regina I've booked in downtown Zurich and check in with the reservation desk. Zurich is full of all the famously secure Swiss banks, so we walk the golden mile, supposedly the richest mile in the world considering what is held secretly in the vaults of all those banks. After resting a bit with a little lunch, we walk around the downtown area, but basically Zurich is just a big city. Of course, we get some Swiss hot chocolate before returning to the hotel. I make love to my wife before she goes to sleep, wanting to make sure we christen every European hotel in which we stay. She giggles a lot. Before and afterwards, thankfully not during.

I love that giggle. It tells me she is happy being my wife.

The next day, I rent a car so we can continue our tour. Thank goodness the Swiss drive on the right side of the road. We end up in Lucerne, a beautiful city that began in medieval times. We stay at the Hotel Europe and walk the sidewalk next to Lake Lucerne. We continue to the pedestrian downtown area where there is a wooden bridge and water tower spanning part of the water. There are swans everywhere. The wooden bridge is filled with paintings on the rafters above. They date back to the 1100s. Evidently, Lucerne had a real problem with the plague at one time because many of the pictures we see refer to the Black Death. We tour the cathedral and wander the streets, going into stores that sell the beautiful Swiss watches for which Switzerland is famous.

I want to show Becca the mountains, so we take a train up to the top of Mount Pilates. The view from the top is stunning. We get hot chocolate again because it's cold. I'm beginning to sense a pattern here. The ride down the mountain was even more fun, packed inside a cable car, hanging and swinging slightly, high above the mountain below. On the way down, we see an Alpine slide and walking trails.

Who in the world walks up this mountain? There must be crazy Swiss people here.

It's damn steep and rocky. Cows with large cowbells around their necks graze on some of the mountain meadows. We head back to our hotel for dinner.

That night I try, try, and try to have Becca in the shower. It seems the bathtubs are rounded at the bottom in Europe, and that curved smooth surface under our feet makes them slippery as hell. We're slip-sliding all over the place until I finally figure out to put a wet towel under our wet feet. The towel helps us gain some traction. We are in a shower tub together, hugging one another under the hot stream of water. I push her up against the shower wall, grab her hands, and intertwine our fingers. I raise them above her head as I slip between her spread thighs. One of her legs immediately wraps around my ass to give me greater access to her.

We move together intimately, slow . . . slow . . . slow . . . deep thrusts on my part. I am kissing her open mouth, and we are both panting. I raise my head and suddenly realize I can see us together in the shower in the large mirrored, covered wall. It isn't steamed up yet, and I can see the image of us making love.

I have seen this somewhere before. I realize shockingly that we look like a fucking porn movie. Feeling it all and seeing it all is fascinating and hot. I am getting so turned on by our own images of locked-together bodies. I feel Becca's raised leg leave me so that she is standing on two feet now. I am still inside her, feeling the gates close around me. It is now a tight, tight pussy. I almost have to stop thrusting and end up grinding against her as hard as I can. She catches me off guard when she comes loudly against the cold shower wall under the warm water of a Swiss shower.

Becca slides out of my arms in the slippery shower and drops to her knees in front of me. In the mirror behind us, I am treated to the sight of my wife taking my cock in her mouth. My mouth flies open as I gasp loudly. She likes me dripping with water from the shower and seems to be licking and drinking me with thirst.

When she starts sliding her mouth up and down my hard dick, the sight of her kneeling in front of me and her head moving is sensuality personified. We are definitely making our own private porn movie, better than anything I have ever seen. Seeing it and feeling such pleasure all at the same time. She is so gorgeous she makes women porn stars look ordinary in comparison.

I wonder briefly if she will ever let me take erotic pictures of her for my own personal and private magazine spread. No other photographer but me allowed. I like the idea of her naked except for ropes of gleaming pearls dangling all over her, in her mouth, around her neck, and between her tits, even roped tightly between and inside her moist slit. Rubbing large pearls there against her might be fun for her as well as me.

I wonder where I can buy large quantities of pearls before I am suddenly overcome by events in the shower. Becca's teeth have come out to play, not just her mouth, lips, and tongue. I have worried about her teeth before. It sends me right over the edge into sexual oblivion. My wife swallows rapidly every drop I give her and licks me dry in the shower. She is gifted in this area. I tell her so, and she smiles at me, a little proud of herself. I know I am proud of her too. I am the luckiest bastard in the world.

Now that I have accomplished my goal of shower sex, we need to get out before we wrinkle every part of our bodies. I quickly find getting out of the tub and combination shower enclosure is a bit tricky. The edge of the tub wall is high, higher than what we are used to in the States. When we step out, we have to step way, way down. It definitely is awkward. Both of us hold on to every towel bar we can find as we climb out. Not the most graceful I've ever been, but at least we don't fall and break something. That would surely ruin my plans for the perfect honeymoon.

After breakfast at the hotel the next morning, we head out south toward my favorite city of all, the ski resort town of Zermatt in the Swiss Alps. Along the way, we stop and tour Castle Chillon. It's a medieval stone castle built right next to and somewhat over a lake. It is filled with tapestries, suits of armor, and even has a dungeon. Lord Byron toured there once and wrote a famous poem about the place. He carved his name in the stone wall of the dungeon, and his poem was about a well-known prisoner once held there. Leaving the castle, we gradually work our way deeper and deeper into the Alps, stopping and visiting waterfalls actually flowing inside the mountain cliff face, and even see a group of five hang gliders floating over a mountain canyon.

We arrive in Zermatt, but I have to leave the car in the parking lot at the train station. The downtown area of the mountain town is pedestrian only. They do allow electrical golf carts so the businesses along the street can stock up. We check in to my favorite hotel, the Matterhorn Inn. It's an old-style European hotel that looks like an old wooden Swiss chalet.

When we check in, the desk clerk hands me a big old-fashioned key on a huge red tassel as opposed to the card key all the other hotels use. The incredibly small elevator is off the lobby. I push the button, and we enter an elevator about the size of a closet to go to the third floor where our room is found.

We are together is this small, small elevator as it clanks its way upward. I push Becca against the wall, swoop down with open mouth on her. At the same time, my fingers rapidly make their way to her panties between her legs. My thigh pushes them apart for me, and I feel Becca grant me the access I need to get to her. My strong fingers rip right through her fragile damp panties and delve knuckle-deep into her warmth. This sexual attack happens in a few short seconds.

The elevator arrives on our floor as I reluctantly remove my fingers from her sweetness. The doors open, and I drag her down the hall, searching for the correct room number.

I slide the key into its slot, burst through the door, pulling her inside and kicking the door shut with my foot. I push her against the door, reach down to pull out my aching cock, and slip it into the correct slot waiting just for me. It unlocks the door to my wife's secret desires. She jumps into my arms, and I catch her with my hands beneath her ass as we move frantically against one another, seeking and finding just the right amount of pressure, penetration, and friction.

She is ordering me, telling me what she wants, how she wants it, and where she wants it now. Being a good military man, I follow orders competently and without hesitation. We reach the absolute pinnacle of desire together, the door to our room receiving much pounding and sexual rhythms.

Since we are in a Swiss mountain ski town dominated by the hard stone peak of the Matterhorn, it seems appropriate to me we climbed our mountain of desire together. I mentally congratulate myself on planting my flag at the top of the mountain. Proof forever I had been there as the sole conqueror of that mountaintop that is my beloved wife now.

We stroll down the main pedestrian street, stopping in small shops to look around. Many of the shops sell ski clothes and equipment. Others contain the usual tourist items of sweatshirts, magnets, coffee cups, and key rings. When we reach the cathedral, we can see the rocky Matterhorn in front of us, in all its majestic glory. It has a distinctive forbidding shape and stands out from all the other Alps. I think Becca takes about a hundred pictures of it. It is covered in ice and snow, glowing in the late afternoon sunlight against a clear blue sky.

Next to the cathedral is a small graveyard filled with the graves of climbers who didn't make it off the Matterhorn alive. Most of them appear to have been in their early twenties, and many seem to have

English names. We find two sad tombstones side by side that show us two climbers with the same last name died together on the same day. Perhaps brothers, both in their twenties when they perished challenging that snow-covered icy mountain.

Dinner that night is in a quaint restaurant near our hotel. I find myself eating a lot of sausages, potatoes, and pieces of dark bread dipped into cheese fondue. The local beer is excellent and thirst quenching. I enjoy it while Becca has her usual wine with dinner. We have a chocolate dessert that we share. It's chocolate cake with hot fudge sauce. Becca looks at me and giggles as we feed each other.

What's the name of that famous cake at the Trellis? Death by Chocolate? What a sweet way to die. Don't the French refer to an orgasm as a "little death"?

La Petite Morte.

This dessert might not look like it, but it tastes a lot like it.

I love chocolate. We both love it. The Swiss know how to do it right. It just melts in my mouth, so luscious and silky. I am addicted to chocolate just like I am addicted to making love to Becca. I can never get enough of her.

The next day we take a cog train up to Gornergrat Mountain. This train is amazing, taking us up the mountain at a steep 47-degree angle. The snow-covered mountains and scenery are breathtaking, and Becca has her camera out again.

We reach the top and realize that Gornergrat is right next to the Matterhorn, I mean, right up close and personal. The Matterhorn, with its striking rocky shape, looks huge even though it's not the tallest mountain in Switzerland.

Unbelievably, there is a restaurant at the top of this mountain. We have our pictures taken with some Saint Bernard avalanche rescue dogs there for just that purpose. I have always loved those dogs, so big and protective yet gentle. The handlers pose them at our feet with the snowy wonderland of the Matterhorn behind us. We finish our photo and I watch another couple step up to have their picture taken with the large dog when I suddenly realize the dog is peeing on its handler's foot. I try not to laugh and see Becca doing the exact same thing. I purchase the photo, and we can pick it up later before getting on the train down the mountain. I reach down to pet the warm soft dogs next to me. They bring brandy and warmth to people unfortunate enough to have been trapped in the icy grip of an avalanche.

It amuses me to think of me being Becca's very own strong Saint Bernard dog to the rescue. I hope I have saved her from the icy avalanche of her ex-husband and lonely life he abandoned her to endure. I know she has saved me from my own avalanche of the cold loneliness of a future without love. Thank goodness I impulsively rescued her that night in the restaurant where I first saw her. That one decision has brought me this incredible life.

I can hardly still believe it is true and not a dream.

We walk around, enjoying the snow-covered mountains all around us. Mount Rosa is pointed out as the highest peak in Switzerland although from this angle, the Matterhorn still looks taller to me. It turns out the Matterhorn is actually part of the African continent, pushed up by centuries of tectonic pressures. I am amazed at that since I have always had an interest in geology.

Lunch is fun in the restaurant looking out the windows at all the snowy white Alpine mountain beauty surrounding us. Becca, of course, has hot chocolate. I, on the other hand, have a local beer with my meal. We enjoy turkey and ham subs with garden salads as our meal and a chocolate chip cookie each for dessert.

After taking the train back down the mountain, we head to the hotel for a sweet late afternoon nap. That night we attend a show at a local restaurant. They specialize not only in good food but also an enjoyable evening of Swiss cultural entertainment. A lot of yodeling, singing, playing music, dancing, and blowing those incredibly long Alpine horns. Becca really seems to be enjoying herself, and I'm glad we got a taste of the local Swiss culture and food. That night I let her fall asleep in my arms, but I know she knows I have plans for the morning.

When she opens her sleepy eyes the next morning, I make sure the only thing filling her vision is my erect cock. I have just the peak for her to climb. After all, we are in the Swiss Alps. There are mountains all around us.

I hope she gets the hint. Thankfully, she does. I find out my wife is an excellent mountain climber. She climbs on quickly and reaches peak after peak. I do everything I can to make sure she is full and satisfied. At last, we both reach the highest summit together, then fall asleep again, exhausted from climbing many hard mountains.

After a late breakfast of omelets, bacon, and toast, I turn in the rental car, and we hop the train to leave Zermatt. We're taking the Glacier Express in one of those glass-dome train cars. It's a five-hour ride across the most beautiful mountain scenery Switzerland has to offer. We sit at a table covered with a white linen cloth and are served a hot lunch of beef tips with gravy, crispy potatoes, and cooked carrots. I try another one of their local beers. Becca orders a "Radler," which is basically beer mixed with Sprite. She doesn't like beer that much, but this she seems to enjoy. I think she does it because she wants to feel as though she's having a beer with me. The train ride is surprisingly enjoyable since it is easy to see all the mountains and valleys surrounding us.

Damn, they do trains really well in Europe, much better than back home.

We end up in Saint Moritz. We check in to our hotel, The Lark, which is right next to a beautiful blue lake surrounded by snow-covered mountains in the distance. We can still see signs from when the Olympics were held here. We walk around the lake, going into town and touring the shops. So far we haven't bought much of anything other than tons of Swiss chocolate.

I notice a jewelry store quite close to our hotel, and an idea pops in my head. Becca's birthday is on the day we fly home, and I want to get her something, obviously. I think a Swiss watch is exactly the right thing. She'll wear it the rest of her life and whenever she puts it on, takes it off, or even glances at it, it will be a reminder of this *time*, our romantic honeymoon, not any other one she's ever been on.

But how do I do this?

We get back to the hotel, and Becca wants to shower and sleep a little. She does seem to want to be in bed a lot. I don't know if it's because of me or unfortunately just the altitude. I tell her that I'm going down to the lobby to email my sister and let her know we're having a good time. That seems a reasonable excuse to get out of the room alone for a while. Becca says fine and goes in the bathroom to get her shower.

I practically sprint out of the room, wanting to get to the jewelry store quickly so that she won't suspect. I hope she stays where I've put her. The thought of actually losing her in a foreign city almost stops me in my tracks. I'll have to get back to her as soon as I can.

The jewelry store has a wide variety of Swiss watches to choose from, and they are supposed to be the best in the world. I look around, hoping something will catch my eye as perfect. And it does. A substantial yet feminine watch jumps out at me. It's gold, so it will match her wedding set.

I don't care how much it costs—wait, maybe I'd better ask. Shit, euros to dollars, dollars to euros, what the hell?

I put it on my credit card, vowing to think about it later. I rush back to the room, finding her curled up for a short nap. I let her nap for a while but then realize that I *have* to wake her up. I admit she gets somewhat pissed at me when I do. I hope she doesn't have a headache from the altitude changes.

Definitely a little grumpy. Maybe I should have let her sleep a little longer. I feel a little guilty and selfish. I need to be considerate of all my wife's needs, not just the needs I need her to need.

"Hey, baby, what're you doing? Are you awake?"

"I was sleeping, you jerk," she says huskily, just barely opening her eyes.

Is she just teasing me or is she serious?

Jerk? I'm not a jerk.

Okay, maybe I should have let her sleep. I just couldn't leave her alone. She looks so beautiful when she sleeps.

"Jerk? Is that anyway to speak to your husband, Mrs. Stevens?"

I am not a jerk about to jerk off. I want her to jerk me off if she wants to. I don't have to do it myself now that I have a wife.

Come on.

What was mine is now hers to do with as she pleases.

Please me, please.

We promised, remember? On Valentine's Day?

"It is when you wake me up from a deep sleep. What do you want, Mr. Stevens?"

Shit, this isn't going well already. Step back, Marine, regroup and then redeploy.

"Well, I was thinking that we could try something I have been thinking about, but maybe not now. Go back to sleep, honey. I'll wake you when it's time to go to dinner. It won't be long now. I am getting hungry."

Umm.

Even though I know better, I can't help being disappointed.

It's our honeymoon, Rebecca. Pay attention to me. I have expectations.

"I'm awake now. Did you need me for something? What do you want?"

"I need your . . . your-r-r-r . . . breasts, but if you don't want to, I'll understand."

HONEYMOON. I repeat. I have certain sexual expectations, you know. Don't you too?

"My God, Michael. You're insatiable. Go take a shower and give me a minute."

Was that a no . . . or a yes? We're on our honeymoon here, Becca. Remember?

I pout just a little but go off as directed. I take a quick shower, barely drying off before I come bouncing out of the steamy bathroom, mirrors completely fogged over, but wanting to give her the full Stevens effect of my muscles dripping with water. Not even a towel around my waist, so there is no possibility of a miscommunication here. I even hope there's a little steam coming off my skin because I took *a hot* shower, definitely not a *cold* one.

I've been thinking that I'd like to see if I can make Becca come just from stimulating her tits. Well, mostly anyway. Never done it before. I've read it is possible. I hope she really is that responsive to me. Maybe she will, maybe she won't, but I want to give it a try, at least once.

I look at her, impassively for once. She slowly gets the message.

"Okay, okay. Come here, Michael."

"Well, don't do me any favors, Rebecca."

Should I give her the watch for her birthday early? Maybe a present will help.

She takes a deep breath, letting it out slowly, "Michael, I love you. What do you want us to do?"

Not sure that sounds enthusiastic, but I'll go with it.

We're both already naked, so that's a step in the right direction. I tell her to sit up against the headboard with pillows behind her back so she is propped up and comfortable. I sit directly in front of her, face to face, putting her legs around my hips and my legs around her. My thighs are holding her thighs wide apart. I mean really open. It might be harder than I thought to stick to my plan. My ready and willing cock sits at the entrance of her moist folds, right there, but not touching her even though everything in me is dying for her.

I'm not going in, I'm not going in. At least . . . not until I get what I want first.

I look her in the eyes before reaching over and cupping both of her breasts with both of my hands at the same time. I start gently kneading, caressing, stroking, pulling everywhere, sometimes on her nipples, but basically all over. Becca's head is falling back slightly, her mouth open and breathing quickly just a bit as she gives herself over to the sensual sensations. I lower my warm mouth to her right breast but keep my hand touching her left breast at the same time.

I suck as much of her soft mound into my mouth as I can all at once. I can't get it all, but I'm trying. I start to use every trick in the book I can think of to try, using my mouth, my lips, my tongue, my fingers, my hand, even my teeth. I pull at her nipples, elongating them between my lips, sucking them hard, and then softly licking them with my tongue. And still my cock just points there at her moist entrance, waiting but not touching yet.

Right there, ready to go. At any time. Just tell me when.

Finally, she starts to moan softly, and her hips start to reach forward for my dick, trying to get me to enter her. Her hips are circling endlessly, and she's bearing down slightly as she tries to get the friction she needs. Looking down, I can see she is flushed, swollen, and glistening already. I think I'm on the right track here. I just keep doing what I'm doing, over and over.

My fingers stroke her down, down on her lower abdomen, close to where I know she wants me to touch her. I touch her with my fingers, drawing endless circles right above her. So close to where we are both longing for me to touch her. I have to start reciting the Periodic Table in my head to keep somewhat in control. I hope she can do this with me because I really want to see and hear her come from just basically her breasts.

They really are magnificent. Pink-tipped and luscious.

Hydrogen, helium, carbon, oxygen, lead, gold, argon, zinc, nitrogen . . . etc.

Her hips really start to move now, and she's panting and groaning for me. She moves, grabs my thigh, and pushes herself hard down right above my knee. Becca rocks hard back and forth on me. She needs that friction because she is so turned on by my attention to her breasts. The sight of such a sexy, sensual woman pleasuring herself on me is too much for me to bear. I am so hot for her, my penis thick and throbbing with need. If she touches me, I will lose control of myself.

"Give it to me, Becca. Give it me now," I almost yell at her urgently.

Suddenly, she rises up a bit, throws her head back, wraps her arms around my head and pulls my face into her cleavage as she moans my name over and over. She is holding me to her lush full chest so hard it's impossible for me to breathe, my nose pressed into her sweet-smelling skin.

"Michael, Michael, Michael! Oh God, that's it. That's it! Feel it with me!" she screams as she comes for me.

Death by suffocation. Sweet shudderings. Such sweet moans and throbbings. I don't mind at all. I could die like this happily. I nuzzle her soft breasts for a moment, before a sense of urgency hits me like a freight train.

While she's still shuddering with intense spasms, I quickly get on my knees, spread her thighs wide, and thrust into her hard. I lean my torso back away from her, using my stomach muscles to control our movements. We both gasp at the same time, her legs spread open in the air as I pound into her. Her hands are cupping my cheek softly, touching my lips gently, and then moving in my hair.

I move my hips about as fast as I can. I have her ankles in my hands holding her in place for me. I grit out between my teeth, "I want you so much, Mrs. Stevens." She thrusts one leg up to my shoulder so I can get at her from a different angle. She screams out loud, I groan deeply, and it's a done deal.

Another mission accomplished to my complete satisfaction. My wife had two orgasms courtesy of me.

Yeah, yeah, yeah for me.

She murmurs over and over again in my arms, "Michael, oh my God, oh my God."

I feel the same way. We are awesome together. What a memorable sexy experience with my wife. I've got to keep a journal or something. This actually works. I didn't know before for certain.

Our last stop on the honeymoon is Salzburg, Austria. It is really not very far across the Swiss and Austrian border, and so I decide this is where we'll finish up our honeymoon. Salzburg has a charming downtown area, and I've managed to get us a deluxe room in the famous Hotel Sacher. We can walk right out of our hotel, cross the bridge over the river, and wander the pedestrian alleys, restaurants, and shops. As we cross the bridge, we notice the iron-link fencing is literally covered in locks. Small ones, large ones, red ones, blue ones, mostly ones that lock with keys.

Like multicolored barnacles.

We continue on, and as we pass the shop windows, I see the same kinds of locks displayed there prominently. I go in to find out what the deal is with the locks. Turns out lovers or married couples buy a lock, secure it to the bridge, and throw the key into the water, therefore symbolizing the unbreakable bond between them. It will never come apart, just like the lock. I love this idea and end up with a small green lock.

Green, like my wife's eyes.

Becca and I go back to the bridge, both of us holding on to the lock as we click it into place. I let her throw the key in the water, laughing as she really heaves it as far as she can into the river below us.

Now there's a little piece of our love, hanging on a bridge in Salzburg forever. Locked together as one.

We spend the afternoon strolling the narrow streets, touring cathedrals, museums, and even visiting one of Mozart's homes. I buy us the famous Mozart chocolate and hazelnut truffles to eat as we continue looking around the city. Of course, I have to kiss her now while the taste of chocolate hazelnut lingers in our mouths. I sweep her in my arms and dip her as I pounce on her open startled mouth. We kiss deeply, with tongues tangling, as I have more of the delicious candy truffle.

I don't care who sees us. I love my chocolate hazelnut–flavored wife.

We have a quick lunch in a unique restaurant in Salzburg. It is actually built and carved into the side of a mountain. I am surprised to discover it is the oldest restaurant in Europe dating back to the 800s, for Pete's sake. Unbelievable to think this space has been used as a restaurant since then. I didn't even think they had restaurants that far back in the past. They serve fried chicken fingers for heaven's sake and a strange Austrian fluffy egg-white dessert. It looks like a full white tit sitting on a pool of raspberry sauce. It tastes good, a peak of pink and white.

That night, Café Mozart, located on one of the main alleys in the pedestrian area, provides us with a dinner of breaded pork medallions and potatoes with gravy. When we get back to our hotel, I make sure we have a piece of the well-known Sacher torte. We share a piece, smirking at the dollop of whipped cream on top. It's basically a piece of really good chocolate cake. It could have used a little hot fudge, in my humble opinion. I feed my wife slowly, first giving her a bite and then me. I love watching my spoonful of cake slide past her lips, seeing her lips close, and hear her moan softly at the sweet taste. I like putting a spoon in her mouth as much as I love spooning her in bed.

We have eaten our way through the Austrian city of Salzburg today.

By the time we finish, I'm aching for our hotel room. It's our last night on the honeymoon before we fly home tomorrow. I wish our honeymoon would never end. Now that we are so close to going home, I actually think about extending our trip to include a visit to Vienna as well. Becca loved the Thanksgiving holiday she once spent there with Kevin and Suzanne.

From what she told me, they went to the Vienna Opera House for a ballet production of *Sleeping Beauty*, toured the summer palace Schönbrunn, visited the Hofburg Palace, Saint Stephen's Cathedral, several Christmas markets, saw stunning massive architecture and building facades during a horse-drawn carriage ride, and the Lippizaner Stallions performance. I would really enjoy watching those graceful white stallions execute such precise prancing movements. General George Patton was involved in them after World War II. Becca tells me the only movie her dad made her go see was *Patton*. Personally, I would love seeing those things with her. She could share with me her memories and favorite things about Vienna.

But our flights are all arranged, so I decide it will be a future trip for us, even including Prague and Budapest. I think I've heard there is a river cruise linking all of those beautiful European cities. I also haven't forgotten I plan on touring England and France extensively with Becca. I want to spend at least three months showing her my favorite places in those two countries.

Tomorrow actually happens to be her birthday as well. I still have her Swiss watch to give her. I should wait until then to give it to her but probably won't make it. I think I'll give it to her tonight after we make love for the last time on our honeymoon. I want it to be on her wrist all day on her birthday as a permanent reminder of this *time* and our love.

When I get her back to the room, I order a bottle of champagne and ask the hotel staff to light the fireplace in our room. It's a comfortable room filled with elegant old European charm. I've noticed that no matter where we stay, the hotels do not believe in top sheets. They all seem to use a similar thick white fluffy duvet as the comforter.

I settle down to spend the evening, making our last memories special. I pour the champagne, slightly surprised when it is pink. We toast our wedding, our honeymoon, our love, and Becca's pink-tipped tits. Pushing her down to the bed, I get out the watch to give her. Her shining olive green eyes are all the thanks I need. I slip it on her left wrist and kiss her open palm. She raises my hand to her mouth and buries her lips into center of my palm, licking it with her tongue before kissing it swiftly.

Just one more thing for her to wear that's from ME. *Now, that should remind her of this special time together. It's a watch, for heaven's sake.*

That night we try some interesting and different positions as we make love. We start out wrapped in each other's arms, simply kissing. This escalates into passionate kissing and grinding against each other, almost dry-humping. I decide to try something different. I ask her quickly if she is willing to do something new. She agrees curiously.

We both stand up next to the side of the bed. Taking her in my arms, I hoist her up against my chest as her arms automatically wrap around my neck to hold me. My hands go under her ass and her legs wrap around my waist. I turn and sit down on the bed with her in my lap. I kiss her, with my head slanted to get the deepest penetration of her mouth that I can. Gently, I push against her until she has no choice but to lean and then fall completely back so that her head and shoulders are on the floor. She is basically leaning against the front of my legs. This is an interesting view of her as I look down at her beautiful body stretched completely down at a slant in front of me.

Because her legs are still around my waist, I am in the perfect position to enter her. Her arms are above her touching the floor in almost a head-standing position. I can get really, really, really deep inside her from this position. I can tell she is enjoying it as much as I am. I think my dick is stroking her G-spot from this angle because she is groaning and moaning and gasping and shuddering in my hands and calling my name breathlessly. I love hearing her whisper her demands and instructions to me.

"Oh God, Michael, just like that, move harder, you're almost there, turn slightly to the right, oh yes, oh yes, that's it, don't stop, please honey, don't stop now. I need you so much. Oh, oh, Michael, that's it, that's it, feel it with me."

I feel the muscles of her pussy start to milk me, clenching rhythmically around me as my wife loses all self-control during her climax. But I am amazed by my own dick. I am nowhere near ready even after sharing in my wife's orgasm. I have the stamina to last, so why not?

Yeah, this is good, but I am an imaginative lover. Before she knows it, I pull her up and back into my arms. This time I throw her into another head-standing position with her legs spread wide on either side. She keeps her balance upside down by leaning slightly on the headboard. I throw one leg over her and straddle her pussy before leaning over to get the angle I need to thrust inside. I am holding on to her so that I don't hurt her neck by slamming her head and shoulders into the bed. My strong shoulders, abs, and arms let me do this easily. This allows me free access to her.

She is in such a helpless position that she can do little more than just take all the pounding dick I am giving her. All I can hear are squeaking noises coming from below which sound very high-pitched and feminine compared to my deep, harsh, almost guttural commands and begging. I beg a lot. It feels and sounds so goddamn sexy to me. I come, she comes, we both come together. I manage to get both of us untangled from one another before we collapse on the bed.

I don't have the strength to pull up the covers to cover us, only to pull my wife close before we pass out in sleep. My last thoughts before I surrender to sweet oblivion are of her and our extraordinary sexual experiences we share together. I love her so much it scares me a bit. To give my heart like this to her is somewhat frightening, yet I can't help it. I hope she loves me as much as I do her, but a little voice in my head tells me that's impossible.

I could care less that the people in the room next to us probably heard us all night long and never got any sleep because of us. At least I didn't hear anyone pound on the wall yelling for us to stop. Hell, yes, we made a lot of noise. Perhaps the sound of our erotic lovemaking turned them on as well. I hope so. I actually like that idea.

Stunningly successful, sensual sex in sexy, snowy Switzerland . . . and Salzburg.

We fly home the next day. Long flight, many movies, holding hands, crowded airports.

It's her first birthday as my wife.

We arrive safely home after the long journey. I haul the suitcases in. We are both exhausted. Even though it is early evening, it is already dark, and I collapse in sleep with my already comatose wife.

I wake up slowly in the dark and glance at the bedside clock. It is almost midnight but still her birthday. Becca is in her favorite sleep position, her face turned away from me and smashed into the pillow with her right knee raised and bent. Her thighs are open.

I prop my head up on my left hand still snuggled against her. My hand wanders under the covers to her ass. I begin gently running my fingers over and over her, caressing the smooth plumpness of her. She sleeps still although she breathes deeply, and her ass seems to rise up a bit for me.

I continue to run my palm over her until it is time for something more.

It is her birthday after all. I want to help her celebrate our homecoming together.

I stealthily slide my fingers in, seeking her moist soft folds. In the dark, my longest finger penetrates her. I stroke her over and over again, feeling the moisture spread within her. I think I can tell the moment when she regains consciousness, moving from dreams to reality. She is waking up to sexual pleasure.

She moans deeply but allows me to continue my mission in the dark. Her right knee spreads apart even further, granting me deeper access I take advantage of quickly and competently. Her hips are moving with the rhythm of my penetrating finger. I slip another finger in to join the lucky one pleasuring Becca.

I am so turned on my dick is begging me for entry. I last as long as I can, only penetrating her wet warmth with my fingers until I give in to its pleading.

I remove my fingers and quickly replace them with my cock, sliding into her from behind. We move together in sexual pleasure over and over, both of us panting and moaning soft words of desire and love. I am about at my breaking point when I feel her dissolve around me in the ultimate pleasure of me inside of her. It feels wonderful, hearing her cry out for me in passion.

I look down and watch my erection slide in and out of her, feeling her soft ass pillow my lower abs as I ram her with my love. The sight in the dimness, the feel of her pussy pulsing around me, and the sound of her urging me on are enough for me to reach my goal. It hits me with stunning strength. I am constantly amazed at the response she can pull from me, thinking every time it cannot get any better than this. Everything I am as a man pours into her. I give her everything I can willingly.

I collapse against my wife's heaving back and kiss her nape and anything else I can reach with my lips. We whisper "I love you" to each other in the dark. I can see the clock before my eyes close in satisfied repose. It is five minutes before midnight. I breathe "Happy birthday, baby" in my wife's ear and kiss it before letting my eyelids droop.

I hear her say, "I will always remember this birthday. It's the best one ever."

I reply, "Your past birthdays are beyond my reach. Your present birthday was celebrated to our satisfaction. All future birthdays will be celebrated in style. Be prepared and anticipate. I like birthday cake and blowing out candles, you know."

Her face is pressed into her pillow as I hear, "Your birthday is coming up, husband. A little over three and a half months from now. I will blow out all your hot candles for you, rest assured. Let me take care of that for you. It will be the birthday celebration to end all celebrations. Anticipate that."

Okay. Wow. I can't wait to turn forty-nine now. Not something to dread at all. Perhaps getting older isn't going to be so bad after all. I will only improve with age, like a fine sweet white wine. My wife is the full-bodied sweet red table wine.

This is the first time we have made love in our house since returning from our honeymoon.

Dark, dark desperate desires fulfilled successfully.

Damn, I'm good.

CHAPTER 29

She Gets My Motor Running

Now that we're home again, it takes us two days to recuperate from all our sexy honeymoon fun.

Who knew sex and sightseeing could be so exhausting?

Although Becca's furniture is great and in place, we still need to buy pieces since my house is bigger. We need a new dining room table and chairs, a buffet, and a kitchen table and chairs. We put her bedroom furniture in one guest room and her guest bed in the third bedroom.

We keep my bed in our bedroom because I'm not giving that up. My mahogany dressers and end tables are classic, so our bedroom is almost complete with furniture. Although I did consider putting the flat screen TV Christmas present from Becca in there, too. But now it's installed in the great room, perfect for watching sports, the news, and movies. I hook up Becca's DVD player to it, so we can watch her favorite love story movies together.

There are still boxes everywhere. We slowly make our way through them, trying to be organized and throwing some things away. Actually Becca does most of it since she gets mad if I put something away, and she doesn't know where I've put it. Becca has a lot of kitchen things, but many of her pots and pans are older. I talk her into getting rid of them, promising her a whole new set of state-of-the-art cookware. She does like to cook and can be pretty good at it, but she likes baking better. I am going to have to watch that because I love chocolate cakes, chocolate chip cookies, and any kind of pie a little too much.

I like desserts, especially ones involving my wife.

We still go out to eat some since I don't want her to be stressed over fixing meals every night. I'm good with a sandwich or salad anyway. I know for sure she makes a delicious vegetable soup, really hits the spot on a cold winter day. Becca already has a full set of china and crystal from her first marriage I am not sure how I feel about us keeping. I don't like her to be reminded of it in any way. I found out she had already ripped up her wedding photo album when Tripp walked out on her. I think she mailed the mangled pictures and album to him. She can have a temper.

Thank goodness that's not still around. I don't want to see such pictures.

Going through boxes, I find out she has an extraordinary amount of clothes and shoes. Having a sister when I was growing up keeps me from not being too shocked. I think she has clothes from decades ago, and it appears different sizes. I don't care if she gains a little weight because I love her curves. A bigger ass is sometimes fun. It seems she never weeds things out and takes them to Goodwill. I try gently to suggest to her this is the perfect time to do so. If she doesn't, I'm going to have to call an architect to design her a bigger closet somehow. Gradually she starts to organize her closet. I let her do it the way she wants. She seems happy when she's done.

Since I am the husband now, I am in charge of all automobile repairs. It is time for both of our cars to have the oil changed. I spend one morning at the BMW dealership getting my car serviced and washed. The afternoon is spent at the Acura dealership in Newport News. It is obvious to me the service department knows Ms. Connelly's car and her quite well. They wonder who the hell I am with her car. It seems okay when I explain we have married. While her car is having its oil changed, I wander into the showroom floor. It seems Becca's TSX is being phased out and replaced by a model known as a TLX. It is simply a gorgeous car: elegant, sophisticated, tough, sporty, and forty thousand dollars. I can see Becca in it, sliding her long legs in the driver's side. Her car is now going on six years old, in good shape, but I vow this will be her next new car when she needs one.

I come home to my wife fixing dinner, a tossed salad with grilled chicken strips. I open a bottle of wine for us to share. The evening is peacefully spent in the great room snuggled on the couch. Becca reads while I watch an old movie. I remember the oil changes today. Old thick oil out, new clear oil in. A car's motor needs to be lubricated to run properly.

Pistons pumping, electric battery filled with power, radiators bursting with hot liquid and steam, sparkplugs sparking.

I think Becca needs her oil changed too.

Becca closes her book and stretches ready for bed.

"Honey, let's take a bath, okay?"

"Yes, I'd like that a lot. Are you ready now?"

"Let's go. I'll meet you in the bathtub, Mrs. Stevens."

We get up and I pick a giggling woman up in my arms and head toward our bedroom. I get us undressed, candles lit, warm water in the tub rapidly. The sight of her sinking into the warm water is soothing, and I join her. We spend time just soaking and soaping each other. I even shave her legs for her, but she won't let me shave my stubble off because she likes it.

Fingers are now wrinkled, so I climb out and help her get dry. I grab the large bottle of Neutrogena bath oil she uses on her legs after shaving. Becca lays on the bed and I tell her face down. I know how she lies down now. Her right knee raised, left leg straight, and hand under her cheek. I take the oil and start to caress her with it on her back, ass, and thighs. The sweet-smelling oil is absorbed completely into her supple skin, making her soft and glowing in the candlelight. She lets me tickle her back for a long time, telling me this is how her mom would put her to sleep when she was small.

She is so relaxed under my hands but not asleep. I ask her to roll over so I can do her front. Becca does and gets into a similar position as before, her left knee raised now, left hand up to her cheek and right hand on the curve of her hip. Taking my time, I slowly oil her throat, her upper chest, her arms, her flat stomach, her thighs, legs, and feet. I love massaging in between her toes as she moans softly. I just tickle her soft skin with gentle strokes, continuing to relax her. She has her eyes closed in complete contentment.

I tickle and tickle, but I don't want her to actually doze off. So it is time for her to not be quite so relaxed. I want her craving the touch of my fingers until she screams for it. Not relaxed but tightly wound up like a spring that will suddenly open. It takes time and patience to get her there, slowly building her up. I watch her every movement, her every sound to tell me how she is feeling. I hear a soft moan now, so I end up oiling her breasts for a long, long time before finally slipping my oily fingers into her moist petals. Her hips circle with the same motion as my hand and in her. She is panting, begging for me, telling me she wants me and that she is so close to coming.

I need to get her there.

Her legs are rigid with the tightness now, and I can barely penetrate her pussy with my fingers. She is squeezing against me and groaning loudly as she moves. Then she stops breathing and holds still, letting me fuck her with my fingers over and over. She is concentrating on the sensations trying to reach the summit of desire. I don't say anything for fear of distracting her concentration. The soft *v* is there between her brows now, and I can feel slight movements inside around my fingers.

All of a sudden her hips surge upward as her body bends in the thralls of passion. I quickly mount her and slide into her slippery pussy. It doesn't take long before I go off like a Texas oil well gushing into the sky. We fall asleep filled with the smell of Neutrogena body oil and sex.

The first Sunday in March, Becca informs me she wants to watch the NASCAR race from Charlotte Motor Speedway on television this afternoon. Car racing is not my favorite sport since all they do is drive round and round. But I pay attention at first as I hear her say the names of many of the drivers. She is watching, but I turn over and close my eyes stretched out on the sofa for an afternoon nap.

I hear the powerful cars racing round a track. Fast muscle cars with incredible engines so loud they roar as they go by. The crowds need ear protection to keep from going deaf from the sound. They are going so fast it is a blur of motion. The skilled drivers are struggling to control the cars, driving inches away from one another as they speed toward a checkered flag waving over the finish line.

Speed. Power. Skill. Courage. Fast reflexes. Pit crew attention. Collisions. Fire possible. Flipping through the air in a spectacular crash.

I dream Becca is a driver of a sleek red Number 46 Ford Mustang (Go Further). I am her Number 48 black muscle car, a Dodge Ram Charger (Ram Tough). We wait at the starting line for the green flag to give us permission to start. The car accelerates slowly, gaining speed to make it around the sloped curves. Push the gas on the straightaways, drafting behind the ass of the car in front. Nudging its bumper just to let the driver know I am close.

Round and round and round the racetrack, hundreds of miles covered in a few short hours. Speeds of 180 mph when possible. We are racing toward the finish line together although she is slightly ahead of me. I want her to beat me there. I am happy to let her win. The checkered flag waves as we cross it neck and neck. We lose all control and collide together in a heated crash of screams and groans.

I wake up disoriented. The Charlotte NASCAR race is almost over, and she tells me Jimmie Johnson is in the lead. I can't shake the dream as it plays over and over in my head.

Gentlemen, start your engines.

At dawn the next morning, I make my dream come true listening to Howie Day's CD. My racy wife lets me drive fast on her track, getting lost in her steep curves. We both win this race together and collide in a spectacular finish. *Collide* by Howie Day starts with the best time of day to make love with Becca.

The dawn is breaking
A light shining through
You're barely waking
And I'm tangled up in you.
I love this song.
Yeah. We collided together wonderfully.

By the middle of March, we have our bedroom and the two guest rooms ready. I think they look great, loving the colors I painted on the walls and the way it's picked up in the bedspreads or comforters. Becca continues to rave over my painting skills all over the house. I am glad she appreciates and notices all my hard work. I enjoyed it, but it was a hell of a lot of work since I am such a perfectionist.

Since the house is almost ready, we are officially open for visitors. Lord knows the woman likes to have company who come and stay. I want them to feel as comfortable in our house with us as they did in hers. I almost thought we were going to have a pajama party with Mackenzie one weekend since they used to have frequent sleepovers.

We invite a friend of Becca's over for dinner one night. Even though they have been friends for a long time, this is the first time we have met. Lyndsey Kymroy is a college professor in town who met Becca when they were both first struggling with the shock of suddenly being divorced. Lyndsey is a very intelligent woman who lives on her own after raising a son and daughter pretty much by herself. Her children are now grown and on their own. I try to get to know her over dinner. After telling her about myself, she seems to open up a bit.

"Michael, did Becca tell you she is a matchmaker? She actually was the one who got my daughter to date the son of one of her teacher friends. They are married now and expecting their first child."

Yeah, we want everyone to be happy. We are matchmaking fools. Keith and Mackenzie come to mind. So far so good on that front.

"Honey, you didn't tell me about that."

"Yeah, that was fun. I just happened to be in the right place at the right time. It was a random suggestion that came true. They did all the work when they introduced themselves and started dating. It was they were ready for it. I am very happy it all worked out."

"Me too. I ended up with a happy daughter, a great son-in-law, and a grandchild on the way. I think I got the best part of the deal. I will be forever grateful you thought of it." Lyndsey smiles.

"I like making people happy. It was such a romantic happy ending. Their wedding was gorgeous. Michael, I told you about it when we first met. It was held outdoors at the country club in Two Rivers. The ceremony overlooked the river. Do you remember me telling you about it?"

"Now that you mention it, I do. I paid attention to what you told me that night very well."

We finish our wine, retire to the great room for more conversation before Lyndsey leaves for the evening.

I like my wife's friends.

CHAPTER 30

I Bet I Can Win in Vegas

I surprise Becca with a weekend flight to Las Vegas, Nevada, which I had Elizabeth secretly arrange for me. There is a direct flight leaving from Newport News International. Two-night package at the beautiful Bellagio Hotel on the strip. I pack a quick suitcase for us both and hide it in the trunk of the car. She has no idea what I have planned when we get up that morning. I tell her I want to take her someplace, so she needs to get dressed because we need to go.

Along the way, she asks me where we are going, but I do not even give her a hint. Her eyes widen as I drive to the airport and get even wider when I park the car in long-term parking. I turn to her with my impassive poker face.

Yes, I have an impassive poker face even though I know I will have to spill the beans now.

"Michael, what are you doing now? Where are you taking me? We are obviously here to get on a plane, right? Or are we meeting someone who has arrived here?"

"We're not meeting anyone. We are flying off for a magical romantic getaway weekend."

"Where? Tell me. You can't keep our flight info hidden from me much longer, so go ahead and tell me."

"I thought Las Vegas would be a hot place to visit together. It is in a desert you know. Much, much better than any other desert I have ever been in though. A real oasis of sin and gambling, I believe I heard. Let's go sin with each other there for fun."

"Sounds like fun to me. I bet I can win at any gambling game they have. Blackjack, craps, roulette, strip poker . . . I can do it all, Marine. Let's play and gamble the weekend away."

"You are in luck, baby. I am taking all requests today. Let me get the suitcase and we will go check in."

Even though we are squeezed together in coach, I let her have the window seat while I am wedged unfortunately in the middle seat. A fairly big sweaty woman sits down next to me in the aisle seat.

Oh no. Don't talk to me, lady. I had plans you have just ruined. I would have had easy access to my wife since we both were so tightly strapped in. She would not have been able to move or get away. Why did that woman have to come? The only woman I want to come near me is Becca.

The flight is fairly quick and direct after we take off from Newport News. Becca reads a magazine while I do a crossword puzzle and rest my eyes a bit. My hand stays locked on her thigh next to me the whole flight. As we cross the vast canyon landscapes below heading into our approach to Las Vegas, Becca keeps her eyes glued to the red rock landscapes below us.

Deep, deep gashes in the earth appear before us, each with hidden treasures at the bottom. The Grand Canyon itself has the magnificent, rapidly flowing Colorado River as its heart and creator. I have always wanted to see it. Maybe someday we can drive out west and take a helicopter tour deep among the canyon walls. I would like that, and I believe Becca has enough of an adventurous spirit she wouldn't be able to resist climbing in the helicopter with me.

We arrive at Sin City in the early afternoon and take a hotel shuttle to the Bellagio. It is a huge beautiful hotel with a large water-filled fountain in front of it. We check in. The lobby alone is so amazing. There are colorful blown glass shapes decorating the ceiling above us, like we are in an aquarium or something. We stand awestruck just looking at all the colors and intricate shapes of the glass.

Our hotel room is large and has a king-sized bed. The shower is a glass enclosure with a bench and two opposing showerheads.

I like that.

I have to stop this chain of thought because Becca is determined to walk the strip. We head out to the chaos below. It is apparent this city never really sleeps. Since it is March, the desert heat has not settled in, so we are fine to walk the sidewalk. Las Vegas is filled with amusement-style casino hotels, a large number of billboards advertising concerts, and other entertainment. Becca says she would like to see Cher at the Caesar's Palace if we can get tickets.

Okay.

I use my phone to reserve us some seats for tomorrow night's performance. We see the hotels inspired by New York City, by Paris, by Venice, and by ancient Rome. Many hotels not only have the required casino but shopping malls inside. The shops in Caesar's Palace are under a domed ceiling that actually makes it seem as though we are outside in a way. The sky changes above us from day to night.

We wander the casino in the Bellagio when we return that night. Slot machines everywhere being fed and stroked by little old men and little old ladies. I have never played the slot machines, and Becca doesn't seem interested in wasting money on them.

Umm.

Slot.

Machine.

Slipping money into the slot.

Pulling down on the lever so that everything spins in front of you.
I like my wife's slot.
I am the machine for her.
She can pull my lever down as fast as she wants.
I will make reality spin out of control, and we will hit the jackpot together.
I like this image. I am good at sexual metaphors. I can make just about anything I see remind me of sex with Becca.

We eat at the hotel's restaurant, a very sophisticated restaurant considering we are near the gambling areas filled with betting tourists. The restaurant is a quiet oasis as we enjoy a first-rate dinner and shared dessert. I am not sure, but I think it is owned by a celebrity chef, so the meals are beautifully presented as well as delicious.

It is dark outside now, so we go out to watch the moving water fountain show at the Bellagio under the stars. The hauntingly melodic music fills our ears as the water shoots high up in a synchronized ballet of movement. The waters sway seductively back and forth, burst upward like geysers, and fall splashing into the pool of water below. All this is timed to coincide with the music. It is a stunning display of water dancing. It is overwhelmingly erotic, and I wrap my arms around my wife as she stands in front of me mesmerized.

I want her to sway for me, her wet hips undulating just like the powerful jets of water. I will shoot to the sky just like these sudden bursts.

As soon as the show is over for now, I gently but insistently lead her back to our room, determined to have a little water show of my own. That two-headed shower and bench are calling to me.

I can do something with that, I know.

Becca tells me she is tired from all the traveling and the walking around town. I suggest a soothing shower before bed. I point out to her how big the glass shower is and how it has two showerheads. We are definitely getting in that shower together. I help her out of her clothes and then quickly strip for her.

Ha ha, get it? The Las Vegas strip? Strip poker?

I only hope I hold the winning hand. I like a sure thing when I play games. I am nothing but a sure game for Becca, but she always makes me work a little to get her. I know she knows she can always say no, and I will stop even though it would kill me.

We climb into the two-headed shower and turn on both. I stand under my nozzle, and she stands under hers, both of us getting wet and washing with the shower gel provided. I am not touching her yet even though my eyes are locked on her every move. I love watching her soapy hands move all over her body as she washes herself clean. I am so busy watching her I basically forget to wash myself at all. I quickly run a soapy washcloth under my armpits and wash my hair and then my chest.

My wife looks like she is done, but I am not done by any means. I turn and take her hand, giving it a quick kiss and bite on the center of her palm before leading her to the stone bench. The shower is misty with steam from the cascading waters. It gives a dreamlike quality to my wife. She said she was tired, so I am going to let her rest. I am more than willing to take the lead this time.

I get on my knees in front of her and spread her thighs apart for me to gain entrance to her. This bench puts her at the perfect height for me. I stare at her, silently asking permission to pleasure her this way. She says nothing, but I see a glimmer of excitement in her eyes before I lower my mouth to her. I grip her wet hips in my hands and pull her forward so that she is leaning at an angle against the cold tile shower wall. I lick and kiss and suck my way around, knowing this part of her very well by now. My tongue endlessly drives in and then retreats over and over.

She is slippery and moving and moaning now. I continue to pleasure her orally, loving the slightly soapy flavor as well as the unique one only she has for me. My cock is swaying like those fountains of water, about to become a geyser just as strong as Old Faithful, the famous geyser in Yellowstone National Park which erupts as a regularly scheduled event. I feel her tremble again my lips, and then she simply dissolves into an orgasmic softness, her woman flesh pulsing as she moans deeply in pleasure.

I knew I could win this game. The best game in town to me. Puts all those casinos to shame. I can be a high-roller player as well as any other man.

Becca is lying against the wall panting when I finally lift my mouth from her. She looks so damn sexy still sitting there like that, and I have an enormous erection either I or she is going to have to deal with. Thank goodness, Becca suddenly takes the lead. She has the strength to trade places with me, so it is now me on the bench with her kneeling between my legs. I am wet all over and actually have drops of pre-cum that have already escaped me. She looks at me first, asking me permission.

I nod frantically yes.

Her mouth closes around me, and I close my eyes briefly as well. But I want to watch her pleasuring me with her warm mouth. Her mouth, her lips, her suction, her tongue, and the movements of her head as she loves me are incredibly sexy to watch. I am turned on not only by the feelings she is giving me but also by the sight and sound of her doing it as well. I am not going to last much longer under such intense erotic attention. I am about to become that geyser of fountaining liquid bursting forth. It is like we are playing Russian roulette. We know I am loaded, but not sure which caress is going to cause my gun to go off and fire a bullet.

I lean even further back against the cold, wet wall and let her have her way with me. I am so close now; she is truly gifted in oral skills. I know it is about to happen, so I am not shocked when I feel it begin. I fall off the edge, letting it wash over and over me.

I am shocked, though, by the strength of it all. I feel lost in it, as if I forget where I am and can only feel Becca's throat move as she swallows all of me. She licks me all over before sliding her talented mouth from me with one last kiss on the tip of my now satisfied and drained dick. We sit there in the shower together on the bench until I am able to get to my feet and turn off the water. We stagger into the bed, and I pull up the covers as we both pass out from sexual exhaustion. Neither one of us wakes up all night long.

We sleep late, late, late the next morning. I call for room-service breakfast, and we eat it in bed, feeding each other fruit and bacon. I never get tired of feeding her. Juicy orange sections, ripe strawberries, biscuits and preserves, chewy bacon; all go in our mouths. When we finally make it to the lobby, I ask the reservations desk how I can rent a car for the day. They make all the arrangements and give us a map as well.

We head out for Boulder City and the Hoover Dam. It straddles the Colorado River on the border of Arizona and Nevada.

Damn, that is one big Dam.

When we arrive, we find the visitor center and buy tickets for the tour of the dam. It is a huge concrete and steel structure, so powerfully strong it is almost too hard to believe it was built by men. I notice a memorial to the construction workers who died, giving their lives for this dangerous concrete wall to be built. The Hoover Dam holds back Lake Mead, and the Colorado River is far, far below. The waters of this river produce the electricity needed by this region.

Becca and I ride the elevator deep into the dam itself. The Hoover Dam is a hydroelectric dam, generating electricity for most of the Southwest. The imposing turbines are there in front of us, working constantly to bring power to everyone around. A very large American flag hangs over them. Our guide informs us of many historical facts and other details concerning the construction and purpose of the Hoover Dam. It truly is one of the man-made wonders of the world.

We continue on exploring the area. I drive us slightly west of the city through neighborhoods. I am surprised to see homes with green grass and blue swimming pools in view from the backyard.

This is a desert. Don't they have to ration water here? I don't know for sure.

I drive west, following the signs to a state park called Red Rocks Canyon. There is a circular road that takes us deep into the canyon. The late afternoon sun makes the red sandstone glow, and shadows outline the strange rock shapes caused by wind erosion. It is a magical place, a landscape like no other. There is nothing remotely like this at home. We are in the West, with all its natural but different beauty.

It is easy to see the rock strata found with these canyons. Becca points it out to me since she loves geology and knows a lot about rocks and minerals. These are sedimentary rocks, once sediments at the bottom of a body of water. Gradually more and more sediments piled up, the water retreated or evaporated, and the sediments were sealed together by pressure and dissolved minerals as the glue. They are fairly soft rocks, easily shaped by the forces of wind and rain and ice and water. It all results in this fascinating canyon unlike anything I have ever seen. Iraq's deserts were stark and the mountains of Afghanistan rocky and forbidding. This place holds the secrets of centuries of time within its rock layers.

We head back to our hotel for dinner and the show tonight. The strip is blazing with colorful lights everywhere we look. It is almost an assault on the senses. So very many colors and lights and huge hotels shaped like pyramids or famous places.

Dinner is a quick bite in the Bellagio, and then we change clothes to attend the concert. I have always loved Cher's voice and even remember the Sonny and Cher Show repeated on television. Becca says Jason once took her to see Sonny and Cher at the Dome in Virginia Beach when they first had a hit song. He wouldn't let her go get an autograph, saying she had to keep him from going down there instead. The concert is fabulous,

Cher's voice lovely, and her intricate costume changes constantly. It is a wonderful evening that is not over yet.

We head back to our room and get ready for bed. Becca has on a pale pink short nightgown, and I am only in my boxers. Not many clothes left to strip off, but it is enough for me. We climb into bed, but I make her sit with her legs crossed as we face each other sideways on the bed. I reach over and find the deck of cards in the nightstand. We are going to play strip poker since we are in Las Vegas. I need for her to gamble and lose all bets. She giggles, telling me she is a card shark from way back. I need to take her seriously.

I chuckle, yeah . . . right.

I deal her five-card stud and wait for her to study her hand. I have two queens, two jacks, and an ace, for goodness' sakes. She lays down two cards, and I replace them for her from the deck. I take one card to replace my ace. Unbelievably I draw another queen, and I have a full house in my hands. Not a full woman yet, but a full house, a potentially winning poker hand. I ask her to place her bet. She bets her panties.

Good.

I bet my boxers.

Good.

All that is left is to reveal our hands. Becca has a two pair but not enough to beat me. She has to hand over her silk panties to me as the winner of this game. She hesitates a bit but then stands up. I am treated to the sight of my woman stripping for me. I catch a brief glimpse of her naked hips before the silk nightgown falls and hides her secrets from me again. It is so tantalizing to know she is going to be without a silken barrier now. I will be free to roam at will.

The panties are slowly, slowly slid down her thighs, to her knees, and then finally around her ankles as she reaches down to take them off. She takes the panties in her hands and shoots them over to me like a slingshot, hitting me in the face with them. I grab them, smell them deeply, and tuck them into the waistband of my shorts. She looks a bit shocked. I now have the silk panties. She is not getting them back.

The music and lyrics to Lady Gaga's hit song "Poker Face" is on repeat in my head.

My, my, my, my poker face.

Time for the second round of poker. She is trying to keep a straight face as she looks at her cards this time. Oh no. She thinks she can beat me this time. She doesn't ask for a single card. Not good for me since I need three new cards to even hope for victory. I bet my boxers again, and she bets her silk nightgown.

Somehow this is not going according to plan. If she wins this hand, I will be naked with nothing left to bet while she will still have that damn nightgown on. I can't let her win. But she does easily since I have nothing worth anything in my cards. I surrender the boxers to her. She grins happily as I am completely naked now. I challenge her to one last game. I have nothing left to lose now, so I am betting myself as the prize.

I deal the cards. We both look at our hands. I have a possible three of a kind but need another king. She is frowning at her cards as if she can't believe what she is seeing. I can tell she is not a happy poker player. She can't hide her thoughts behind an impassive poker face from me. I laugh inside, knowing I am going to win.

I bet I can make her come twice tonight.

She giggles and bets the damn nightgown again. It's all she thinks she has left to bet, but I know better.

Becca requests three replacement cards while I take two.

Yes, I got the king I needed. I now have a three of a kind.

We show our hands to one another. She only has a pair of aces.

I win.

The nightgown comes off as fast as I can throw it across the room as I grab on to my winnings. I enjoyed playing strip poker with her, but now that we are both stripped, I have another game to play in mind.

I spend a great deal of time prepping my wife for the upcoming attractions. I take my time kissing her, and she kisses me back just as passionately. Our hands wander over each other, endlessly caressing and teasing and stroking. When I think she is ready, I surprise her by lying her gently down on top of me, but not face to face. Her legs are straddling my neck. I am turned the other way with my face under her pussy and her mouth above my hard cock. She gets the idea immediately as I feel her take me inside. I thrust my tongue into her sweet moist warmth as the same time.

What an incredible erotic way to make love. Why haven't we done this before?

We know each other very well by now. She knows what I like and need just like I do for her. We both give it our all, wanting to please each other with our love. The only sound are our gasps for air since our mouths are engaged in a very necessary sexual activity. I feel and hear her lose control first, but I am soon joining her as well. We lie down with each other panting and sexually sated. Taking a deep breath, I move us gently into position on the pillows and beneath the covers.

I turn her in my arms, spooning her, and drift off to a sexually satisfied sleep. I remember I promised her two orgasms. But right now we are both so tired. My eyes close.

In the middle of the night, I wake up and need a glass of water. My beautiful wife is completely asleep beside me, her lovely face utterly relaxed in her unconsciousness. I try not to wake Becca, but I need to get to the bathroom for it.

When I come back out and climb into bed, she murmurs my name sleepily and crawls onto me to lay her head on my chest. Slowly, gently, tenderly, intensely, and insistently, I make love to her. Her eyes fly open into my intense gaze as she realizes it is not a dream. I am real and inside her already, moving gently. She was wet and soft for me to enter.

She breathes. "What a wonderfully wicked way to wake up."

I manage to reply, "Yes, I was up and wanted to wake you up too. I am sorry but I just couldn't resist. You are too tempting, my love."

She wraps her legs around me so I can get deeper. Her arms are suddenly around my neck as I grind and then thrust, grind and then thrust. She catches on to my rhythm like an expert.

"What is tempting you now, Stevens?"

"Do you need the entire list of everything about you that tempts me? I am happy to give you the complete list if you so desire."

I am starting to have trouble concentrating on our conversation because I can feel the erotic tension building between us. We are both panting with our mouths open almost kissing but not yet. Our eyes are locked in passion.

"Tell me, tell me how I tempt you, my love. I desire you and want to know. I can tell you everything that is so masculine about you it calls to the deep-down feminine part of me. I cannot resist you. I am like those poor addicted gamblers below in the casino, endlessly filling the slot machines with hopeful nickels, hoping to hit the jackpot. I am obsessed with you and only you."

I groan out everything I love about her sexually. My throat is tight around the words as I struggle to hold on for her. She is not quite there yet.

I breathe seductively. "I am the one with the hopeless addiction to you. I love your smell, not only the natural feminine smell of an aroused woman waiting for me to love her, but you. Your scent changes. Sometimes it is just a clean, natural sweetness. Other times your perfume subtly reminds me of vanilla. My mouth waters from that alone."

I continue strangled with building desire. "Your soft face, the texture of your hair, the taste of your mouth is forever part of me now. I love feeling your breasts caressing my chest when I am on top of you. Your waist fits my hands. And below the waist is a true wonderland of tastes and textures. I cannot get enough of you. I want to die making love to you, my heart stopping when I come inside of you one last time."

"Not tonight, honey. This is nowhere near our last time together. I am so close, Michael. Are you? Help me get there," she groans brokenly.

"Don't worry about that. I bet I can, over and over. Let me in. Let me give you everything I have inside just for you. Feel it. Let go, let it happen, just surrender."

Her eyes flutter close as she concentrates on the physical sensations building steadily inside her as I make love to her. I leave her alone as she frowns with that soft *v* between her brows. I kiss it gently but no longer whisper to interrupt her total concentration. She groans, straightens her legs stiffly suddenly, and then holds her breath. I feel it happen for her and hang on for all its worth.

She simply melts around me, shuddering and bucking up under me. She moans my name breathlessly, and I lose the bet I had with myself I could thrust another ten strokes. I make it four before going off like a jackpot, lights flashing and loud noises. We are in Vegas after all. I bet I could win and I did. Two orgasms belong to me tonight in sinful Las Vegas. I bet her I could deliver them to her, and now I have kept my promise. I do not go back on a bet. I have sinned my very best.

I win. It was an honest bet, and I am an honorable man. I keep my bets. Especially to her.

The flight home the next morning isn't so bad. We laugh, remembering our Las Vegas gambling adventure. I bet neither one of us will forget it ever.

Las Vegas was an adventure to experience with her since I am willing to risk it all. I am more than willing. I took the risk that night when we met. I am a risk taker, and it has made me the happiest of married men.

Thank you, God.

I hit the jackpot when I first saw her face.

CHAPTER 31

March Madness in the Mountains

Days pass by at home. The following week after our Vegas weekend, Jason and Elizabeth call and invite us to spend a long weekend with them in Bristol, a small southwestern town nestled in the mountains on the border of Virginia and Tennessee. I enjoy the drive to the Appalachian

Mountains and the journey south through the Shenandoah Valley. Interstate 81 is filled with trucks and state police.

I set the cruise control, refusing to get a ticket. Cruise control controls speeding since I can have a lead foot at times. My car is so smooth and easy to drive it is easy to forget how fast I am driving. All I have to do is steer and avoid the trucks. It's basically a six-hour drive, and we fill it listening to CDs and talking. She has a huge bag filled with quite a lot of CDs. I enjoy her taste in music.

I usually want to listen to our wedding CD. I enjoy the memories it evokes in me. The sexy rendition of "Crazy in Love" from the hotly romantic *Fifty Shades of Grey* movie just about causes me to steer off the interstate. My right hand is firmly clamped around my wife's thigh, my fingers close to her core but never moving closer. I am driving after all. I can drive one-handed. The miles slip away.

We arrive in Bristol, Virginia. Jason and Elizabeth have a lovely home, and we end up in the basement guest room. Jason has a big-screen television in the basement and seems perfectly content as long as he controls the remote. They show me Bristol, and we drive by the famous NASCAR Bristol Motor Speedway. The next thing I know, Becca is talking about car racing and her favorite drivers. She likes Jimmie Johnson because she thinks he is cute.

Damn it. She thinks he's cute?

Shit. Is there nothing she doesn't know about sports?

I suddenly realize that is why she watches so many sports. She watches for the cute, sexy male athletes. Jimmie Johnson, Peyton Manning, Phil Mickelson, Adam Scott, David Beckham, Michael Phelps, the Olympic swimmer, etc.

Fuck! How the hell do I compete with that?

Damn it, damn all to hell.

She says she always watches the Daytona 500 and the Indianapolis 500 as well.

I give up.

I start to worry about male actors now. Is that why she buys certain movies? Because of the male star?

I try to think what DVDs she has. Ryan Gosling in The Notebook; Channing Tatum in Dear John and The Vow; Zac Efron in The Lucky One; Russell Crowe in LA Confidential, A Good Year, and Gladiator; Alex O'Loughlin in the Moonlight TV show; Robert Pattinson in all five Twilight movies; Ryan Reynolds in *The Proposal*; Keanu Reeves in *The Lake House*; and Jamie Dornan in *Fifty Shades of Grey*.

Fuck, Fuck, Fuck.

There are so many of them. Did she make herself come imagining these athletes and actors? There must be something about each one of these men she desires. She had been all alone, a woman obviously filled with desires yet unable to find the man to satisfy them in her.

God Damn It.

Yeah, it's definitely a pattern here. I guess it helped her while she was alone for the past fifteen years since there was no real man for her to love.

But damn, I am her fantasy man now. She better be fantasizing about me and only me. I'm the one here, not those athletes and actors she has never met. I'm real, not them. Don't fantasize about strange men, baby. Fantasize about me making love to you. I will do everything I can to make all her fantasies come true if she'll let me. I can be as sexy and romantic as all those guys in the movies. I pay attention to what they do and what they say. I don't want her to even briefly picture another man while I am making love to her. Me and me only.

Shoot!

I just look at her, wondering what else I can do. I think she can tell by the look in my eyes I am a little mad and upset at her. She looks back at me, frowning, as she tries to figure out what I am thinking. I can see the question in her eyes. She knows me, but she doesn't know how well I know her. I'll make sure tonight is a night she will remember and fantasize about the next day. I know I will.

I am the fantasy man come true for her just as she is the fantasy woman for me.

We spend Saturday driving to Damascus and riding bikes down the Creeper Trail, an old train railbed whose tracks have been removed. That evening we meet a couple who are friends with Jason, Elizabeth, and Becca. John and Dorothy join us for dinner at a charming restaurant in Abingdon called 128 Pecan. We are seated on a cute outdoor porch at a small table for four. As I get to know them, I realize they are highly intelligent, fascinating people, each with their own varied interests. I enjoy the evening, eating a delicious pecan encrusted trout. Becca has crab imperial.

No dessert for her. Yet.

The conversation is lively, and I learn that Dorothy loves to read and has done extensive research into ancestry backgrounds. She seems to love to do that, and her research was even used on a television show in which celebrities found out about their ancestors. John is a retired college professor who is very interested in writing. One of his haikus is going to be inscribed on the wall of a Washington DC Metro Station when it is finally completed. John and Dorothy seem to have gotten to know Becca over the years as she visited Bristol. I hope I passed the test as her new husband.

After we get home, it is still early enough to catch some of the NCAA college basketball games on television. Becca, Jason, and I settle in the basement in front of the big-screen TV. Elizabeth heads upstairs to her bedroom to read before going to sleep. The tournament has reached the Final Four. Becca is pulling for Duke University, but both Jason and I believe Kentucky will take the whole tournament. University of Connecticut has already eliminated North Carolina.

Damn, she obviously understands basketball too. There is no sport I can teach her about.

Hockey, no.

Skiing, no.

Cricket? Maybe. But I don't understand the appeal of that either.

She pays attention to the NCAA Tournament action between college teams but seems to care nothing for professional NBA games.

Me neither.

Kentucky wins the basketball game.

Yes.

It will be Kentucky versus UConn in the final game Monday night.

That night, we make love in the basement guest room. Jason and Elizabeth's bedroom is two stories away from us. I feel sure they can't hear anything so far away. I get undressed and join my fantasy wife in bed. I hardly give her time to get comfortable before I make my sexiest move on her. I crawl down to the foot of the bed and grab her right foot. I start by running my index finger up and down the length of her foot. It tickles her, and she tries to pull her foot away from me, but I have a tight grip on her ankle. My lips and teeth follow the same path and then my tongue in long wet strokes. I really have to hold on to her foot tightly because she can't keep it still.

Basketball game coming up. I can shoot with the best of them. I hope I don't dribble though. Well, not from my mouth anyhow.

She is staring down at me, watching my mouth on her foot. I swoop down on her big toe, sucking it into my mouth deep and hard. She gasps and tries to pull away, but I don't let go. I do everything to her toes that she does to my cock when she gives me a blow job. I can see her start to squirm and twist her hips. She is panting slightly and trying to get away from me.

Oh no, ref. No penalty shot for me.

I read somewhere sucking her toes goes straight to her groin like a live wire. I enjoy this foot fetish for a while, but then I need to change tactics. I kiss my way up her right leg, up her thigh, right next to her moist smooth folds. I go back and repeat the journey on her left leg.

I dribble my ball down the court, looking for an opening to score a goal from behind the foul line. No harm, no foul. I spy a weakness in her defense around the net. I drive toward her basket, intending to dunk my ball as soon as possible. A real slam dunk. Two points for me. Swishhhh.

By now, Becca's thighs are wide open for me to my utter delight. I spend a little time worshipping her sweet pussy, but then have to feel her with more than my lips and tongue. I swiftly impale my wife, holding my chest and head up with my arms on either side of her. I use my strong stomach muscles to dive deeper and deeper into her with each stroke. She wraps her legs tightly around me, grabs hold of my ass, and digs her nails into me, trying to pull me even deeper. Those nails are sharp. Then she moves her long legs from around me and closes them around me. I feel as though she is trapping me inside her.

I decide to lay up before the ball is passed back to me. I am shooting a three-pointer into her net.

Instead of thrusting, we begin a grinding rocking motion against one another. The feeling is so different for us both. I give it to her with the best of my ability until we both lose complete and utter control together. It is as if I can feel both of our climaxes within my own body. I'm groaning, unable to speak past the tightness in my throat, as she screams my name when she comes violently for me. Thank God we're in the basement guest room, instead of the upstairs third bedroom.

The game is over with my overwhelming slam dunk into her net. I hit my hand on her rim, but the ball goes in the basket satisfyingly.

Goal, point, game over. Fantasize about that, Mrs. Stevens.

You were with me, and I was the man who made you lose control.

Me.

I am your very own fantasy man come true for the rest of your life.

We leave the next morning for home. We need to get home in time for tonight's NCAA tournament final game. Becca puts in different CDs to listen to during the six-hour drive. I set cruise control again and listen to the romantic soundtracks from *Last of the Mohicans*, *Pride and Prejudice*, and *Somewhere in Time*.

The days go by, and I start to notice my wife's naturally husky voice is sounding a bit different. Slightly hoarse and husky. She sounds like she has a stuffy nose. Nasally congested. She starts sneezing frequently and tries to blow her nose although her nose is so stuffed up it isn't working well.

Allergies, maybe?

The pollen is everywhere now, coating our cars in yellow. But I come to the conclusion my love is really sick. She has a head cold. Sinus pressure. She's miserable.

Oh no, is it a sinus infection requiring a trip to the doctor for stronger medicine than I can purchase at CVS Pharmacy? I am not a doctor after all.

I am then treated to the full effect of an ill, miserable wife. She is frustrated and moody with sickness.

Headachy.

Uh oh.

No headaches, please.

"Oh goodness, Michael, I can't breathe. My head is killing me."

"What can I get you, honey? Take some aspirin for the headache, and it will go away soon. Do we have any nasal spray? Let me take you to your doctor. I think it's a sinus infection. You need an antibiotic to make it go away."

"Don't be silly. It's just a head cold. It will run its course. I just need to wait it out. Just, just leave me alone. I'm a runny, stuffy mess and I don't feel well. Could you go to the store and get me more tissues? I'm running out. Get Puffs with the lotion. My nose is getting sore, red, and irritated."

"I'll go get them for you. But if this infection settles into your throat and lungs, I am picking you up and hauling you to the doctor's office no matter what you say. I promised to take care of you, and I'm not going to let you stop me."

"Just go get the Puffs, Michael. I'll be fine in a few days."

I do as she asks, a little glad to get away. A sick Becca is a sight to behold, and she is grumpy. Gradually, the sinus pressure is relieved as she blows and blows and blows her nose.

Wow.

Thank goodness that's over. She doesn't handle being sick very well. I don't handle her being sick well either.

After I know she is completely over her sinus infection, I decide my wife needs to visit the doctor anyway. I am now Dr. M. G. Stevens, wanting to give Mrs. Stevens, the patient, a thorough physical examination.

"Becca, come here, honey. I am in the bedroom." I yell for her.

She comes in and asks me what I want. She is busy in the kitchen and a little pissed at being interrupted.

"I'm not sure you are totally well yet. I think you need to see the doctor to make sure. Come into my clinic here and have a seat on my examination bed please."

I can see the light dawn in her eyes as she figures out I want to play doctor.

"Yes, Doctor. Should I get undressed first before I lie on the bed for my exam?"

"Uh, uh, uh, yes please. Disrobe for me. I need to be able to see all parts of your body. I am not sure where you are sick so I need to look carefully."

She watches me as I watch her slowly remove all of her clothes. Watching her remove her lace peach-colored bra and panties is almost too much for me.

I need to exam all of this loveliness in front of me.

Becca lays down on the bed and waits for the doctor. I strip frantically, getting caught in my jeans when I forget to take my shoes off first. Finally, Dr. Stevens is ready to begin the examination.

"Mrs. Stevens, I am going to exam your ass today. Please scoot over and make room for me."

She does, and I lie down on the bed beside her with the pillows propped up behind me. My stethoscope is ready and willing to be used now.

I gently pull her to me but have her straddle my hips with her knees bent on each side. She is facing my feet. I just hope she is wet enough for me to enter her. I have her lift up and impale her pussy on me. Her back and ass are right there in front of me, easily within reach. She doesn't move on me as she adjusts to the feeling of me inside her. I wait until she is ready.

I place my hands on the cheeks of her ass and grab on. I can reach forward and continue to stroke and tickle her ass.

"Mrs. Stevens, the sickness appears to be located in your full ass. I am going to massage it out of you. I know you will feel so much better very soon. Trust your doctor to know what is best. I have been giving you exams for quite some time now. I am experienced with this sort of sickness. I will take good care of you."

"Yes, Doctor, please take very good care of this patient. I am quite sick. I want to feel better. I know you will make sure I take all my medicine."

Yes, take it all.

"Your ass appears quite round today. Can I help you move it?"

"Absolutely, sir."

I grab on and she starts riding me, bouncing up and down urgently. I hang on; the sight of her smooth ass and curved back is all I can see. We both enjoy the exam until she reaches around and masturbates herself to a fulfilling climax. I am about to explode. But suddenly I realize she has left me and is turning around.

"Doctor, Doctor, I need to swallow my medicine now. Do you have it ready for me?"

I strangle out the words that I have her medicine coming right up now.

Open wide for a more than a spoonful of liquid cure. Get ready. I'm ready now.

Her mouth engulfs me, and I erupt like a fire hose spraying water at a burning building. She moans as she swallows her medicine greedily. I am done, so done. She was an excellent patient, and I am the luckiest doctor.

I wonder if she could be my nurse sometime. I could use some tender loving care.

One afternoon I came home to women in our house discussing window treatments, blinds, curtains, and drapes. There were swatches of fabric lying everywhere as Becca tried to make a decision. I left all of this to her, trusting in her good taste. When they were all installed, I was shocked at what a difference it made in the look of the rooms. It was like the final touch that was needed. I am glad our windows are now covered even though we still have plenty of light. I like the privacy I now feel. I like privacy. I don't want all my neighbors knowing everything there is to know about me and my wife.

I come into the kitchen one early evening in the spring. My wife is preparing us dinner. I can smell parmesan chicken roasting in the oven, and I quickly determine we are having a salad as well. Becca is standing at the granite countertop, chopping carrots on the wooden cutting board.

I see she has the large knife in her hand as she slices the large, round, orange carrot she has in her grip into tiny round disks of chopped carrots. Carrots are very good for eyesight, I believe. She has on a white button-down blouse and a fairly tight jeans skirt. Not flowy but snug on her ass. Barefoot in the kitchen fixing me food. But she is unfortunately armed. She has a sharp knife in her hand.

Obviously I am highly trained in disarming an armed opponent. The Marines trained me how to approach stealthy with every move planned in advance. That knife needs to go. It is in the way.

I approach her. "Hey, my love, it smells great in here. The smell alone drew me to the kitchen. My mouth is watering. I love your parmesan chicken. How much longer before it is ready to eat?"

She glances at the timer with its so obviously red digital numbers. "Forty-five minutes. I am fixing a tossed salad too."

"I can see that. Do you need any help chopping vegetables?"

"No I got it. Could you get me the cucumber from the fridge, please?"

"Sure."

I find the damn cold cucumber. She has finished chopping carrots and is now about to add slices of cucumber to our salad. I have to watch impotently as she makes very quick work of the long, fat cucumber.

Is she done chopping now? What other round, long, thick vegetable do I need to watch being sliced and diced under my wife's sharp knife?

I watch as Becca grabs the salad bowl and throws all the pieces of vegetables in it along with the lettuce and other salad fixings. No dressing yet since we have to wait to eat.

Lubricant on lettuce leaves too long can cause wilting of said leaves.

I like creamy ranch dressing the most, but she prefers oil and vinegar. The salad bowl is placed in the refrigerator to stay cold until we can eat later.

Excellent.

She now has nothing left to occupy her until the timer on the oven dings. I am under the gun. Minutes ticking by. The added pressure of a clock makes me consider my first move. I am not exactly subtle.

My cock is springing up, so I spring it on her.

It is spring after all.

Becca goes to stand at the sink to wash her hands. I come up right behind her and nuzzle the nape of her neck. She hums happily as she reaches to turn the water off. I encircle her with my arms, my aching dick pressed against her ass, my palms reaching and gently stroking her breasts. I love feeling the gradual change come over her as I can get just a hint of nipple erection.

She leans into me, enjoying my touch. I take this as the go-ahead, all-clear sign. I reach up and slowly undo each button of her blouse until I can pull it open to expose her lacy underwire bra made of sheer white fabric. White blouse, white bra. I wonder if her panties are white too. I will find out momentarily. Right now I have a bra to get past.

I cup her breasts, still pressing my chest against her back and breathing in her ear, kissing occasionally and licking occasionally. I find the front closure I like. Snap. The bra comes open, and I have now have full access to my disarmingly charming wife's tits. My mouth is watering, and I have to swallow, but this is a hand action now, not a mouth one. I massage her full breasts at will. We are both breathing faster now. But it is not enough for either of us. Regions below our belly buttons are demanding service and attention.

My hands drop to her skirt. I slowly begin to slide it upward. She has to scoot a bit to help me, but we manage to get the tight denim skirt up above her ass and bunched around her waist. I discover a tiny white thong covering my wife's essentials. Barely. I lean slightly, grab them, and pull them down to her ankles. She only steps out of one side.

I feel her spread her thighs for me, and I press my aching cock against her entrance but do not thrust. Her left arm comes up and reaches for my hair. I have my right hand on the curve of her ass, my left hand still massaging her left tit. I realize I am getting a little rough with my grip, so I force myself to calm down and cup her gently instead.

We continue to play like this for a few more breathless moments. She is still pressed against the sink. She leans forward slightly, spreads her thighs further, lifts her ass, and reaches around behind her to grab my erection. I realize she is guiding me home, and I do as she asks, thrusting in gently but insistently. We are both leaning forward as I start to move in her, pulling and pushing at her pussy. She is gasping now and moaning "Oh, oh, oh, oh" over and over. Her right fingers are suddenly massaging her pussy from the front as I penetrate from the back.

I am joining her in encouraging words, but can only get out "Yes, yes, yes, yes." Neither one of us has an extensive vocabulary at the moment. Sentences are beyond us now.

She's matching me thrust for thrust. The kitchen is getting hot from the heat of the baking chicken in the oven and us. I wonder wildly how much time I have left on the oven timer but can't be bothered to look at the moment. I am in my wife so that is all I can concentrate on.

I feel and hear her reach it. She screams my name and dissolves around me with intense rhythms of her internal muscles as they grip me. I thrust past all of that and give in to the pleasure bursting out of me. All I can do is hold on to her as the last of my orgasm fades slowly away. We stand there silently enjoying the feel of me still inside her, our bodies pressed together against the sink counter.

I slide out of her tenderly. I am dripping out of her. Grabbing a washcloth, I quickly get it wet with warm water. I turn her and pick her up on the granite countertop. Her skirt is still up around her waist.

"Mrs. Stevens, you are a bit of a sloppy mess now due to me. Let me help you with that. Spread your legs. I need to clean you up a little. I won't hurt you. The cloth is warm. Let me."

She is still turned on, I can tell, but it is very sensitive right now. I gently wipe her pussy up trying to get all of me off her. Now that she is clean, I need to make sure I got most of it. I decide to taste her to find out for sure.

I spread her thighs with my hands on her knees before getting at pussy level. She has caught on to my plan since she is not stupid.

My mouth presses to her and my tongue thrusts. She is still sensitive from her climax, so I give her time to adjust to the new sensation of a wet tongue instead of a hard dick. My wife tastes of a combination of us both. Not sure about this, but there is enough of her taste to enable me to go on. She smells like sex as my nose is pressed tightly against her. I could do this all evening. Unfortunately all good things must come to an end. She is leaning back on her elbows, now completely submissive, and allows me to carry on. I do so willingly.

She is gasping and moving, but not there yet. I penetrate her with my middle finger all the way and find her G-spot. That obviously feels good to her as she suddenly stops moving to concentrate on the physical sensations. I have my way with my wife. She comes for me and for me alone, gushing in my rapidly licking mouth.

I hear the timer on the stove go off loudly. It just doesn't let up. It buzzes, my wife is buzzing, and I am buzzing. We three are buzzing. I give all of us time to calm down before I reach over to turn off the damn buzzing timer. The chicken is hot and ready to eat now. I find now that my sexual appetite has been appeased, I can actually enjoying eating my chicken dinner. I'm hungry.

Umm, maybe a late-night snack or sinful dessert will need to come my way later on.

Becca seems to gain a little control as she gently questions me, "Dinner is hot and ready for you. Are you still hungry?"

"Yes, Rebecca, although I just enjoyed a unique appetizer, I find I have room for baked chicken and tossed salad."

"Coming right up, sir." She scoots forward and jumps down off the counter into my embrace. She giggles happily.

"Do we have anything for dessert tonight, my love?"

"I've bought some caramel sauce and vanilla ice cream. I have some wet nuts, whipped cream, and cherries. How about a caramel sundae? Is that good for you?"

Yes, you are very good for me and to me.

"Yes, that sounds good. Thank you. A sundae on Sunday for me."

She laughs at the quick wit. "You're welcome. I like surprising you with sweet treats."

Surprise me then with sex.

"But you, wife, are the sweetest treat of all."

Again, I am thankful for window treatments that provide a measure of privacy. Nosey neighbors knowing our business are not a just a nuisance but also an impossibility now. I love making love to my wife whenever and wherever she will let me have her.

It's what we do together all over our house. Every room, every surface, every day if I can.

CHAPTER 32

Fun Fucking with Food

Late that afternoon, I receive an urgent text from my wife while she is out. She is shopping for dinner, it seems.

> **M. At Fresh Market. What would you like for dinner tonight? Let me know and I'll get it for you. Bx**

> B. You know what I like by now. Steak. T bone would be fine for tonight. MX

Ha ha! A big piece of meat with a big bone. Damn. She is only talking about groceries. I, on the other hand, am not.
  I chuckle out loud. Another text quickly arrives, typed by the quick fingers of my loving wife.

> Anything else to go with that steak, Mr. Stevens? Bxx

> I'd like a hot, baked potato tonight, please. I want you hot as well, Mrs. Stevens. Covered in butter and slippery, just like that potato. M XOX

Why do I only get a few small kisses from her? I know she can do better than that. I send her big kisses and a big hug!

> M. I don't know about the butter, but I can promise the hot. Too hot for you to even take a bite and swallow without getting burned. Do you want me slippery? Bxxx

Damn, my wife is quick-witted. She figured out I was talking about something else entirely. Does she want to play this seductive game with me?
  The way her mind works fascinates me. I can barely keep up with her.
  What can I say now? Still small kisses from my wife. Three only. Obviously not enough for me. I always want more.

> B. I like hot, melted butter. I'll take my chances. The hotter the better. Especially on my baked potatoes. Slippery is fantastic as long as it is in all the right places. Sour cream can be good as well. Get some. M XOXOX

Damn, she sent me small kisses. Three. Small. Kisses. Doesn't she even notice my hugs and kisses to her?

> M. I don't care that much for sour cream on my potatoes. Creamy good, sour, not so much. Hot, melted, slippery

> butter makes my mouth water. Umm, feeling a little hot here. B XXX

Why doesn't my wife ever send me a hug? I love her big kisses, but shoot, a hug is nice, too, you know. I don't get it. I send her hugs. As big as I can.

> B. I know you are hot. Butter is . . . well, butter. Slippery and greasy. I could do something with that. Do I get dessert, too? MXXXXOOOO

> M. What kind of dessert do you want tonight? I am looking at a vast selection here. BXXXX

Umm. Four big kisses this time.

> Rebecca, you know my favorite dessert by now. Do I have to tell you again? You must not be paying very much attention to my wants and desires. M XXXXXOOOOO

Sending her five big kisses and five big HUGS. PAY ATTENTION.

> M. What do you really want tonight for dessert? BXXXXX

Still no hug from her. How can I get one?

> Hot Wife. I want chocolate cake covered in fudge frosting with you hugging me while I eat all of it by myself. Michael XOXOXOXOXO

On the surface, our texts back and forth to each other are about groceries and dinner tonight. But I am losing my mind, the sexual connotations blatantly obvious to me. It seems my wife wants to play a bit later. I can picture her there in Fresh Market texting me with her fast fingers on her cell. Umm. Fast fingers. Memories of my wife's fast fingers suddenly fill my mind. I shake them off. Focus and concentration needed now. I am not going to let her win.

> Hot Husband. I think that can be arranged to your specifications. Will do my best to find the most perfect chocolate cake with fudge icing in Williamsburg. Your loving wifeOOOOOOOO

Looks like I'm not even getting any more kisses now. Well, if she can withhold them from me, then I am not giving them to her. Until, of course, she is here and in person. Then I'll give her as many as I can.

> My LOVING WIFE. If you don't get home soon, I may be forced to eat dessert first, skipping dinner altogether. Mr. Stevens, Mrs. Stevens' loving husbandXOXOXOXOXOX

> I'll be there ASAP. I want a little piece of your dessert, too, you know. Will you share with me? I like chocolate very much.

Now where did the hugs go again? Should I give up on hugs and kisses from her?

> I think you can actually have a big piece of my chocolate dessert if you ask me nicely. Say please.

Please . . . please me.

> I promise to please you as much as I can, Michael. That's as nice as I can get.

> You are the nicest wife I've ever had. OH, wait, the only wife I've ever had. I remember now. M

> I'd better be your only wife, Mister. See you shortly. Be ready for dinner and dessert. You're cooking. Get the grill hot. I want a nice big piece of tender meat to chew on and swallow tonight. Sound delicious to me. I like steak. I want mine well done tonight. Well done, and still hot. Be careful when you cook it, Michael. It must be tender and moist.

Damn, she is clever with the sexual double entendres. Of course, I interpret her statements sexually. I'm about to laugh out loud. Looking forward to dinner with my wife tonight.

Umm, I'll show her a piece of tender meat. I have just the thing. I know she'll enjoy it. She certainly knows what to do with it.

But I can't let her win now.

> Mrs. Stevens. You are giving me heart palpitations. Stop it. I love to eat my steak juicy and slightly rare. A rare delicate flavor. I like mine just a little pink inside. Mouth-watering and delicious. So tasty it just seems to melt in my mouth. Drive safely and get home, so we both can have steak and dessert tonight. Mr. Stevens (You may need to call an ambulance for me if you keep this up.)

> But I like keeping it up, Michael. Please let me. It's so much fun to tease you. Come on, big boy. Let me keep it up. Becca

Damn, my wife is clever. I'll show her big and up. I'm breaking out in a sweat over a few texts. Imagine how I will feel once she actually gets here.

What do I say now? I need to stop her before I have a heart attack. This all started with a simple question about what I wanted for dinner. I am now in over my head.

> I can tease you as well, you know. Come home, my love. I'll show you how good I can be at teasing you, too. I'm starving now. Can't wait to eat. Hurry.

Please.

> Ok. Whatever you want, my love, my sweetheart, my very own Prince Charming.

Thank God. Get yourself home safely, Mrs. Stevens. I can't wait to see you.

> Rebecca. I LOVE YOU! COME HOME TO ME! NOW!
> Michael

> Michael. I LOVE YOU MORE!! I'M COMING! NOW!
> Rebecca

Now that's what I want to see and hear. She took the words right out of my mouth.

> B. NOT POSSIBLE FOR YOU TO LOVE ME MORE THAN I LOVE YOU. M

Point for me. I win.
I hear the buzz of an incoming text. It's a long one.
Shoot, I thought I had won. But maybe not yet. I am assuming I won a bit prematurely.
Umm.
Do NOT like the sound of that at all.
Premature is not a habit I want to have.

> M. Yes, Mr. Stevens, after everything you said, I am definitely in the mood for a nice, fat, big, juicy steak. I don't usually eat my steak medium rare but I think I might give it a try tonight. Just as long as it is hot and well cooked. You know I do enjoy a good piece of meat occasionally. I'll bring one home and you can fix it for me. I can't wait. Hungry now. On my way home to you. See you soon. B XOXOX

Damn, damn. I was sure I had won, but she's broken me. I give up. I can't keep up with her. Utter defeat and willing surrender to her. I am about to actually break out into silly giggles. She amuses me constantly.
What the hell do I say now?

> B. I'll see what I can do for you. My wish is to make you happy, wife. I know you will enjoy the enormous, tender, juicy steak tonight. I can be a very good chef. It will be cooked to your exact specifications and hot. Medium

rare, well done, it really doesn't matter to me as long as you are happy when you're done eating dinner. I want you feeling satisfied and full. Be careful driving home. But hurry. I'm ready for dinner and my dessert. Hungry too.
M XXXXXX

So there, Mrs. Stevens. I wait, but she doesn't respond. So maybe I won after all. I just hope she is actually driving now. Don't let her text and drive. She needs to concentrate on driving home to me.

When she gets home, she acts like nothing happened, but she seems to be smiling slightly and fighting off a giggle. I decide to keep her happy and giggling. We put away the groceries so we can fix dinner a little later. The chocolate cake with fudge frosting is left on the granite counter.

We have time since it is late afternoon. I act as though it is a normal late afternoon, spent watching mindless television and piddling around the house. I go back into our master bedroom and take off my clothes, pull the comforter and sheets back to the foot of the bed, and call for my wife.

She had been in the kitchen chopping tomatoes, cucumbers, and carrots for the evening salad. She comes in, looking a little irritated at having been interrupted and summoned. Thank goodness that expression changes when she sees me.

"What are you planning on doing, Marine? Are you inviting me to play, or is this a solitaire game on your part?"

"I think we both can play as partners in this game. Come here. You have on too many clothes. Let me help you with that."

I see the curiosity build in the depths of her eyes as she walks over and stands in front of me. I am sitting on the edge of the bed, and I pull her into the space between my open legs. Reaching forward, I glance upward at her before undoing the button on her shorts and slowly pulling down her zipper. She is looking down at me under her lashes. When her shorts are loose, I slide them down her legs to her ankles. She steps out of them gracefully, and I throw them across the room.

Next, her button-down blouse. I raise my hands to the button at the top and begin to undo each button down her front until I can pull both sides of her blouse open. She has on a lacy taupe-colored underwire bra and matching tiny string panties.

Okay, I like what I am finding so far.

I pull her arms out of her sleeves and throw that blouse across the room as well. Now she is standing there in front of me in just her bra and panties.

I pull her to the bed and prop her up against the pillows leaning on the headboard. Then I leave her alone, heading for the kitchen and a cake with fudge frosting. I grab it and head back to our bed and my waiting willing wicked wife. She looks at me as I set the cake on the nightstand.

"It took me forever to find a cake with fudge frosting as you requested. I hope you appreciate all my efforts to satisfy all requests from you."

"Yes, my love, I think fudge will be fun to fuck with. What do you think?"

"Honestly, darling, I'm not sure what to think. I've never been intimately acquainted with fudge, only you."

"I think you, me, and the fudge frosting are going to become very intimate with each other in the very near future."

"You do seem to like to play with food, honey. Any particular reason for this?"

"I think it's because I like to eat food, just as much as I like to taste you and for you to taste me. I think this afternoon we should eat at the same time. Are you interested, Mrs. Stevens?"

"Just show me how, Mr. Stevens. What do you plan to do?"

Good question. I will be happy to show you my plan of attack, my love.

"Don't worry, Becca. I know I said I was going to have my chocolate fudge cake all by myself. However, I've changed my mind. I love you, so we can share it. I want to share everything with you."

I reach over and uncover the chocolate cake. The frosting is thick and creamy. Taking a deep breath, I stick my finger in it and gather a large dollop. I look at Becca before smearing it all up and down my erect penis. She doesn't say anything but hums slightly in the back of her throat. I gather more fudge on my finger before turning to my wife.

My intentions are quite clear. This frosting will be smeared lovingly on her pubic folds. She leans back and enjoys my smearing fingers.

Now then.

I need to get us into position. I maneuver her until I am lying beside her with my mouth between her thighs and her mouth between my legs. It is though we both time our erotic attacks at the same exact moment.

This is outstanding.

It is almost too much to bear from the very start. To feel the pleasure of tasting and exploring my wife at the same time she is doing it to me as well is an overload of sexy sensations. We both make it last for as long as we can.

Thank fuck she comes in my mouth first, allowing me to fully enjoy her orgasm. I love feeling her melt in my mouth tasting of fudge icing. Amazingly, she manages to keep licking and sucking me all the way through the climax, although she is gasping and moaning with the pleasure of it all. I stay in position next to her, letting her finish me off. I could last like this forever.

But then suddenly I just can't. My fudgy dick explodes in her mouth, draining me completely. When I am able, I roll over to her side and pull her close. Tipping her head back with my hand wrapped around her jaw, I kiss her deeply, tasting the icing still. We are both a fudgy mess on our lips.

It took us both a while, but the dessert was delicious.

She is the icing on my cake, just the right amount of sweetness.

I make sure my wife is full and satisfied.

With me.

We didn't actually have the steak dinner until later.

Since the house is ready for visitors, we invite Keith and Mackenzie for dinner Saturday night. I am in charge of grilling pork chops outside on the patio while Becca fixes the baked potatoes, Caesar salad, and peach pie. She sets the table with a lace tablecloth, china, crystal, silver, a spring flower centerpiece, and candles. It is too damp to eat outdoors, so it appears we are having a romantic dinner for four in the dining room.

I do as I am told and grill juicy, tender pork chops. Not a burned one in the bunch. My mind wanders a bit, thinking of the peach pie she is baking in the oven. It smells outstanding whenever I go in the house. Becca says it is her favorite fruit pie. She bought whipped cream to put on top of it when she serves it.

Umm.

She likes sweet juicy peaches. A lot.

My sweet peach of a wife always orders peach ice cream from Brewster's Ice Cream Parlor when they have it. She likes peach ice cream. Plus, I remember the whipped cream experiment on our wedding night.

Peaches and cream, like my wife's beautiful skin. What can I do with peach ice cream?

Umm.

An image of my wife blindfolded with me feeding her delicious peach ice cream comes to mind. I love feeding her, watching her open her lips for me before slipping the spoon into her luscious mouth. The sight of that really turns me on. Her lips closing around the spoon and the sound of satisfaction from the back of her throat are suggestive and so erotic to me. I need to remember this. I will go by Brewster's tomorrow morning and get a pint of their creamy peach ice cream. I think it's a plan for tomorrow night. We have peach pie and whipped cream for dessert tonight, but peach ice cream is the plan for tomorrow.

A peachy festival.

Keith and Mackenzie arrive around six, bringing a bottle of Riesling with them. We start with baked brie covered in a mixed berry jam in the great room and then move to the dining room for dinner. Conversation among the four of us is smooth and relaxed.

Keith asks, "Tell me again how the two of you met, Michael."

"Well, it wasn't long after I moved here. I saw her across a restaurant and couldn't take my eyes off her. One thing led to another, and I ended up being her knight in shining armor, fending off the odious advances of a delusional ex-husband. It took me a while, but I wore her down and we've been together ever since. She absolutely made me work to get her."

"Gosh, Michael, how can I compete with that? Mackenzie, do I need to protect you from your ex-husband? I'd be happy to do so for you if it means we end up as happy as Michael and Becca."

Umm. Does he mean happy for the rest of their lives? Married too?

Mackenzie seems a little stunned by Keith's question but recovers when she says, "No, I don't need protecting. He is just a self-centered jerk. But karma has intervened. He is now paying the price, having to live with his second wife, the bitch from hell."

We enjoy our dinner, exclaiming over my juicy, tender chops.

Pork is the new white meat, don't they say in commercials?

And the sweet, still hot from the oven, peach pie is the perfect way to end the evening. I pile the whipped cream on mine and smile at my wife. She absolutely knows what I am remembering as she smiles back at me.

I have plans with a creamy peach dessert. I'm just anticipating it for tomorrow night.

Keith and Mackenzie leave at ten, promising to invite us over as well.

Since Becca and I spend time together cooking in the kitchen, I have really come to appreciate the sensual temptations of preparing good food and eating it. Food is beautiful and engages the senses. The sight of it in front of me, the mouth-watering scent of a well-cooked meal, the textures and tastes of the food as I put it in my mouth to enjoy it. I love sharing a meal with Becca, and we have both learned new foods from each other.

Needless to say, I enjoy the peach ice cream with my wife the next evening. I think she did, too. We end up with sticky sheets and have to strip the bed and change it before we can go to sleep.

I don't mind. It was worth it. Peach-flavored ice cream sex for me.

I think she likes strawberries too. Strawberry season is May. I love a good strawberry shortcake. Juicy strawberries, sponge cake, and whipped cream. I suddenly have an image of Becca as my very own strawberry shortcake. Maybe someday I'll consider tasting strawberry-flavored pink nipples.

Where can I put the shortcake?

Umm.

Whipped cream, definitely, but not sure where the cake will end up on my wife's delectable body.

Perhaps later I will decide where the cake goes.

CHAPTER 33

Sensual Spring Flings

    Two days later, I decide my wife needs to be rewarded for all her hard work in turning my big empty house into our home. I stop by Boyer's Jewelers and pick up a pair of two-carat diamond earrings for her. Her ears are pierced, and I like the look of these glittering earrings. They are classy and timeless in their simplicity.

When I get home, I find Becca is still gone, playing canasta with her friends. I take advantage of the situation, getting everything ready. I want to surprise her with the diamond earrings, so I set up a little treasure hunt for her to enjoy with she gets home. I start placing yellow Post-its all over the house, beginning with the front door and put them everywhere. Each Post-it is numbered and tells her where to go next. I plan on sending her from room to room, searching for the next Post-it. I and her earrings are the treasure waiting for her at the end of the hunt.

I wait for her (naked, of course) in the bedroom, hoping she will follow directions. I hide the diamonds under the pillow beneath me.

When I hear her come in the house, she calls out, "Michael, where are you? What are all these Post-its?"

I yell back, "Follow the clues, honey. Please."

It takes her quite a while since I went a little crazy overboard putting the damn things all over the place. Thank goodness, I numbered them. Finally, she is standing in the doorway, looking at me. I'm perched up on the pillows, happily waiting with my arms behind my head.

Yes, I am the treasure chest, hiding diamonds for you.

"Michael, I enjoyed hunting all your clues. They led me to you and here you are, apparently happy to see me."

It's quite clear I am glad to see her at lust, uh, last.

"Honey, this last note says I need to ask you for my treasure. What exactly are you surprising me with today, Marine?"

"I have many surprises for you, baby. Come here and search me. The treasure is here just waiting for you."

It takes her a little while to search. Her hands seem to be everywhere all at once. I struggle against her tickling fingers and try to stay on top of the hidden earrings. But she is so distracting. I almost forget about the damn diamonds before she finally finds them under my pillow. She squeaks when she sees them, throws her arms around my neck, and kisses me repeatedly in thanks. I find out she has on a baby-blue-colored underwire demi-cup bra that hooks in the front with a matching tiny thong. There is stitching on the bra cups that resemble vines covering her nipples. A matching cluster of vines covers the slightly damp apex of her thighs. That's all I need to see before I roll over on her and have her my way and she has me her way.

Judging from her response, I think she loves the earrings and me, of course.

Fixing the house up has kept us busy and happy. We tend to argue over little things at times, but I can usually get what I want after a while.

I know I still have that tendency to give orders, and I try not to dominate every situation. Control is important to me, but I learn to give some of it to her. I guess it's just all part of us living together. We go furniture hunting for the dining room table and buffet first. The ones we have been using are her old ones from when she was married to the asshole. Cheap oak. I definitely need that table and buffet to be replaced. Since we're not in a hurry, we can go to many different stores to search for just the right pieces.

We even visit antique stores because I like all the ornate carved details found on some of the older pieces of solid furniture. Charley's Antique Store has a beautiful mahogany set I see as soon as we enter the store. I watch Becca carefully to see if she is drawn to it as well. I catch her sparkling eyes as they trace over the table, chairs, and matching buffet.

Well, okay then.

We quickly make all the arrangements necessary to have the set delivered to the house. I find I really like that dining table. It is big and strong and sturdy. A heavy table. It may be a bit hard, but I don't think Becca notices when I lay her across the table one night. I have my slightly wicked way with her and will never forget how she looked all stretched out for me. Stunning and sensual. I am a bit shocked she let me, but I overcome her natural hesitation by blasting her with all my charms. I'll never think of that sturdy mahogany table in quite the same way again. It isn't the same as a soft bed. I hope she wasn't too uncomfortable although she didn't seem to mind.

After all, I had her trapped between a hard mahogany wood table and my equally hard as wood cock.

She wasn't getting away and didn't even try. It will be an interesting memory to have when we sit down to eat in the dining room.

I am very pleased about how many places we have now christened in our house. It is no longer big and empty. I've enjoyed my wife in our king-sized bed, the tub and shower in the adjoining bath, the kitchen counter, the sofa in the great room, on the carpeted floor in front of the fireplace there, on the dining room table, and against the wall and desk in my study.

I am hoping when the weather is warm enough at night, I can make love to her outside on the padded patio furniture. It must be dark and the middle of the night, though. I love seeing the adventurous sexual side of her. She is surprisingly willing although she makes me go through the motions of persuading her. As long as it is private between us, she has no problems. I feel the same way about her. I don't want to share the intimate sight of my wife coming for me with anyone else. That's for me to see and enjoy alone.

Our days and nights are filled with activities and friends. Sometimes we have company when Jason and Elizabeth come to visit, Keith and Mackenzie, Sara and Roger, Anne and Bill, or Courtney stops by while visiting her brother who also lives here.

Saturday morning I come in after working in the yard. I have been planting my wife a rose garden like the one her dad lovingly tended during her childhood. The rose bushes are in a line along the split rail fence separating our yard from our neighbors. I have planted a peace rose, of course, a dark red rose called Mr. Lincoln, the beautiful white Kennedy rose, and a unique lavender-colored rose. I have looked up on the Internet how to plant and care for these roses. I hope they bloom for us all summer long. I will present her with bouquets of roses I grew for her myself.

I am sweaty and exhausted so I take a quick cooling shower and then flop onto the sofa to cool off. Becca is sitting in her big stuffed chair with her laptop in her lap, doing something. She is always on it, typing e-mail, looking things up on Google, Facebook, Twitter, or YouTube. I turn over to close my eyes but don't actually fall asleep.

I hear Becca squeak a bit then type rapidly. Next, I realize she has made a phone call on her cell. Her voice is very quiet as she talks, as she thinks I am asleep and doesn't want to disturb me. I can barely tell, but it seems she has called for tech support on her computer. I guess there is a problem, but let her handle it. I hear her softly speak, missing some of it but getting most of what she says.

"Okay. Hi. Who are you? Daniel? Where are you? Oh really? What do I need to do first? Okay. I can do that. Turning it off now. . . . Okay, back on. Please wait. Welcome. Start normally. Okay. What do you want me to type? Okay. Yes. I did. Okay . . . click on download, right? Accept. Oh, I see. . . . You now have control of the pointer up on my laptop. This is strange to watch you move it around in there. . . . Go ahead. I can't stop you now. Explore away and find the problem, please . . . I need it fixed. . . . Wait, go slow, slower . . . I see . . ."

I am struggling against laughing out loud. Thank goodness my face is turned toward the sofa like I am sleeping. But I lose the battle with smiling as I hear her try to fix the problem.

"Why did you click there? It said upload drivers.... I need protection, please. Virus and malware. I let it run out. Stupid, I know.... I don't know what I am doing. Okay. Thanks.... Put that on it for me. Good, that sounds like it will last forever.... No, it's not too much for me.... Wow, what is that? Gosh, it's really deep in there, isn't it, hidden among everything.... I didn't know you could go so deep.... So that's the problem? Yes... I don't know how that got there. I didn't download that. I did not put that there. Maybe it came like that.... What did you say? More RAM? What is that?... No, I don't think I need more.... Are you sure I need more than that?... Okay then, go ahead. Just do it. Just... yeah, it's all right. Go on."

"Now what about that thing?... Well, please get it off my laptop... I'm watching... I see you trying to make it go away, but it's just not working no matter how many times you click on that button.... Why won't it go away? Take it off it.... You have to get it off, I can't get it off by myself, you know.... You're the expert, not me.... Can you make it faster please? It's so slow sometimes.... Thanks.... The hard drive?"

"You need me to remove my battery....Oh no! I am not taking it out. Yes, I am plugged into the electricity. What? Where is it?... I have never done that before. Okay, I am turning over. The rocker switch?... Okay. Oh, something just landed in my hand. It is long and heavy. Is that the backup battery?... Wow, do I need a new one of those? Ok, good.... So you need to look around now without my battery being in. Go ahead, look away.... I am watching you though. I see your pointer moving everywhere.... Gosh, you are fast.... How do you know which buttons to click on?... Wow, where are you now? This is really deep, isn't it?... I did not know there was so much stuff installed on it. And this is on my hard drive right?"

"Okay, thanks, that's good.... I have plenty of memory left. What is that you keep trying to delete but it won't let you?... Root something... I see. No matter what you do it is just not leaving... What is it? More protection. Why does it need to go away?... What harm is it doing?... Oh, too many layers of protection can slow things down?... Okay, I see now. It is in the way... I didn't do anything. It must have come like that.... Too powerful for you to handle, huh? Now what do we do?... Okay. I'll call them. Help me.... Okay. I see the 1–800 number. Don't leave me though, Daniel... I will call them on my home phone while you

stay on the cell.... Okay, listen in case I need help. It's ringing now....
Don't go away now. I need you to stay with me."

I listen as my wife talks to some poor guy in Colorado about how she needs this thing taken out of her laptop. She wants him to do it or tell her how to do it. Obviously he will be getting his own hard-on listening to her husky voice tell him what she needs him to do for her. I am about to die. It is all I can do to stay facing the sofa and pretending to be asleep. This conversation is damn entertaining and suggestive. My wife cannot help herself. She gets herself in these positions. I am surprised she is not giggling, but she is remaining calm and professional on the phone.

Finally, it appears that the problem has been taken care of sufficiently. She hangs up one phone and turns back to Daniel, the young patient computer geek.

"Daniel, it's me again. Are you still there?... Okay. I think it is gone. Go ahead and look to be sure it is really gone and not still hidden deeply in there.... Okay. Yes, I am watching.... I am amazed at your skill, young man. You really seem to know what you are doing.... How did you learn at such a young age? So no classes, just fooling around by yourself?... Okay. I see. It is just repetition, clicking over and over again.... That's how you know which buttons to click on and what to make go away.... Well, you are good. I am impressed by you. I am so incompetent when it comes to technology.... I never had to deal with protection issues before.... The tech guys at school took care of all that nonsense for me.... Yes, I see that panda.... So that is my protection, right? Is it a good one?... And forever, it will last forever right? Okay, that is good.... I don't have to think about it anymore. I know I will be safe with that."

"You're finished with me now? Because I am done.... Great.... Wait, though, my battery is still out.... How do I get it back in?... Okay, that is easy for you to say.... It should just click into place right? Okay.... No, it isn't. No, it is not. It won't stay in... Darn. Let me try again.... No, it fell back out in my hand.... How do I do this?... Hold the rocker switch back?... Okay, I am trying again.... No, now it is half in and half out.... Stuck.... Oh gosh. I can't get it in and now I can't get it out of there..."

She giggles. "Daniel, you are going to have to come here, pull it out, and then put it in yourself.... I cannot do it.... I'm kidding.... I know you are in Florida, for goodness' sakes. I am joking. . . . Oops, it fell out again. . . . I guess I am going to have to take it to Best Buy and let them put it in for me. . . . Or maybe my husband can get it to stay in. . . . He is good at that. Yes, I am married. Happily. . . . But he is asleep now, so I will ask him to help me later. . . . It's ok, I'll figure it out somehow on my own."

"Okay, that's all I have. . . . Are you finished now? . . . I see. . . . Get out of my laptop then. Okay. Thanks again, Daniel. Yes . . . I will call you back if I have any more problems. . . . I appreciate everything you did for me. . . . You're very patient and give good directions. Easy to do what you want me to do. . . . Yeah, really easy. . . . Okay. I enjoyed talking to you too. . . . It was a pleasure. . . . Take care, Daniel. Bye now."

I lay there listening to my wife get the poor tech support guy to fix her laptop. She wasn't laughing or giggling; she was dead serious with the geek computer genius extraordinaire named Daniel. Probably some smart-ass young man who knows all there is about computers and video games since that is all he ever does. Becca obviously has the phone number of tech support on her cell, so she has done this before. But I struggle not to laugh out loud as I listen to her sexually suggestive conversation. I wonder if Daniel has a hard-on where he is on his end of the line, listening to my wife's husky voice. I know I do. Hopefully young computer geek Daniel is four or more states away in Florida or Colorado or some place. He had better not be close to my wife.

She belongs to me.

When she is done, I turn over and open my eyes. I have managed to compose myself as I ask her, "Did you get it done?"

"Yeah, no worries. Crisis mode with laptop averted. It's all good now."

"Good baby, I'm glad to hear you are so competent with computers."

"Not really. I try to learn though by watching when they take over."

"Yes, it is strange how someone in a different state can take control like that."

"I know it is necessary but I always end up feeling a little personally invaded afterwards."

"I know. Me too. Glad it is over, honey. I am proud of you for handling it alone."

"I can handle a lot of things alone if you will let me.

"But I do have one last problem, Michael."

"What is it? Can I help you with it?"

"Yes, I hope so. My battery is out. It needs to be put back in. Do you think you could do it for me?"

I get up and go over to her. She hands me the battery and the HP. I slip it into place and hear a satisfying little click. It is done for her. Easy.

"Oh, sweetie. Thank you. I couldn't do it. I tried several times, but you know me and my fumbling fingers."

"I like your fumbles. Your fingers are very special to me. You can fumble on me anytime you want."

"Okay, I cannot resist the urge to fumble."

"Later. Later, you can use your fumbling fingers on me, and I will return the favor in spades. Wait for it. I am coming for you later. That's a promise you can be sure I will keep. I swear."

"Later, baby. I will show you some new technological advances specifically designed with you in mind. You and you alone, Stevens. Only you."

"I am anticipating it. Tonight can't come soon enough, and neither can I."

"I will be coming with you as well. We will come together."

"I don't mind one at a time, but together is certainly something to strive for as well. I like watching you come and enjoy that fully before I lose my mind."

"I know you like to watch. Me. Come. For. You."

"It is endlessly fascinating and arousing to me."

"I make no promises of coming tonight."

"Not a concern of mine. I will get you there if it takes all night."

"Promises, promises. We shall see if you can deliver on it later."

"Okay. I surrender. Delivery will be on time and hard."

"Not a package marked 'fragile'?"

"No, not fragile. Strong and hard."

"How strong? How hard?"

"I may have to show you now if you keep questioning my ability to deliver my goods promptly."

"You are slow today. That is exactly what I have been trying to get you to agree to, prompt delivery now and not later."

My wife's eyes are twinkling with humor and wickedness. I know she knows I know she knew exactly what she was saying the whole time. She is full of sexual innuendos, double entendres, and husky-whispered promises of sensual delights. I cannot get enough of her no matter how I try. She beguiles me with her quick wit, the way her mind works, the slight sarcasm of her voice, her giggling and laughter, and her stunning sexuality. I am in awe and completely and totally enthralled in her powerful magical web. I will die remembering her giggle. It is the sweetest sound in the world and turns me on all the time.

I rush over and throw her over my shoulder. I hear her gasp and giggle as she struggles, but I am heading down the hall to the bedroom. I am trying to make it to the bed, but I then I have to stop and have her pinned to the hall wall. I strip her pants and panties off, unzip myself, grab her hands linked in mine over her head, and part her thighs by thrusting my thigh in between. She spread a bit further, granting me access to her internal secrets. She is already whispering her demands, and I try to follow all directions as given.

I explore and fix Becca's real laptop for her. I drive into her with my own hard drive. It's a complicated, technical job, but someone has to click the right buttons, so everything works smoothly and downloads quickly. Her HP laptop is my Hot Pussy as far as I am concerned. She tears her right hand out of mine and helps by keeping her fingers stroking her touch pad to make my pointer go where she wants it to go. I like being her tech expert and fix everything I can lay my hands on in her internal hard drive. She is mine.

Click. Click. Click the right button.

I install her HP laptop with RAM memory, more than she will ever be able to use.

No charge.

I feel her clench around me in rhythmic shudders that surprise us both by their strength. And I lose myself, burying my dick inside her and burying my face in the curve of her neck. As I come for her, I murmur words of love and desire I have only ever said to her. Only for her and only to her.

My wife, my love, my sexual partner for life.

We collapse on the floor panting.

One night by the end of the week, I realize it has actually been a couple of days since we've made love together. I can't believe I've let the time slip away from me. I'd have it every night and every morning, with occasional middle-of-the-night or afternoon delightful surprises if I could. But we've been busy with stupid stuff that needed to be done, and sometimes life just gets a little in the way.

I have been remiss in my duties as the husband and vow to make it right tonight. Later, after an enjoyable evening just hanging out, we both climb into our big soft bed. We lay there together with her head on my shoulder and my arm around her, gently caressing her back. I am desperately trying to figure out how to make my first move.

Before I can, I begin to realize that my wife is slowly, but intently, letting me know she has missed me as much as I have missed her. Seems she has made her first move first.

Soft sweet kisses rain down on me, first on my mouth, my face, my eyes, my neck, my shoulders. Her hands caress my hair, my chest, and my stomach. I can see she is as turned on as me, wanting what I want just as much. She softly whispers words of love to me. I let her take the lead for a while, enjoying the loving attention. But when she works her way south, I know I need something different tonight even though I usually really love making love to her mouth.

I slide around, getting off the bed and standing next to it. I reach over and pull my wife into the position I want. She's lying in front of me so I can take her legs and pull them up and around my waist. I have to lift her hips high in my hands to get her where I want her to be. My fingers dig a bit into her ass as I hold her tightly.

Seeing her like this makes me so ready. I know I should really check first to see if she is wet enough for me, but I hope she is since she was kissing me for so long. I push my aching cock into her slowly but soon lose myself in the sensations of having her all around me. Since her hips are still in the air, she can't find any purchase other than to squirm in my tight but loving grip.

The image of a beautiful open peace rose flickers in my mind, its petals edged in pale pink, the center still hidden among its gentle folds yet enticingly there. No thorns to mar its beauty. No need for protection anymore.

Becca's shoulders and head are the only thing touching the bed as I have my hands under her ass, holding her up to me. She really can't do much but take everything I'm giving her. And I give it all to her, everything that is inside of me. I hold on as long as I can, wanting so badly to let her go first.

I start to think I'm not going to make it, wondering wildly what I can think of to help me last. I am getting tired of state capitals and the Periodic Table. I think about reciting the preamble to the Constitution or maybe the

Gettysburg Address. How much of that can I remember? I learned it in fifth grade, for heaven's sake.

Seeing Becca and feeling her make me have to recite it in my head from scratch to help me hold on to some stamina.

Four score and seven years ago, our fathers brought forth upon this continent . . .

Finally, I feel the beginnings of the stirrings of her climax. She's moaning and staring up into my eyes, as she feels all the wonderful pleasure sweep through her over and over. It's suddenly all too much for me to handle anymore. I lose all control of myself, loving her intensely and wanting nothing more than to be close to my wife. It's one of the strongest climaxes I've ever experienced before I lower my wife's hips to the bed and collapse on top of her, panting for every breath I can take. Of course, I am starting to feel that same way every time I make love with my wife. Each time I am stunned by the response she can bring out in me.

I have absolutely lost track of all of her orgasms by now. We may be in the triple digits by now although I am not sure. I lift my head slightly to gaze into my wife's beautiful olive green eyes. I want to see if she is as filled with the wonder of our love as I am. And unbelievably, I see it there too . . . in her eyes. She feels it as deeply as I do, this lightning-bolt connection we have to one another. It's everything to me.

Do other men love and lust after their wives like I do? We have such strong feelings for one another I can't get enough of her. I can't, I can't stay away. She is always loving with me, always available, always sweet and desirable. Sometimes I have fun trying to convince her to go along with my plans. I enjoy a sexy challenge. She makes me work for it. Failure is not an option. I can be very persuasive and persistent.

Of course, I do not present any challenge to her if she initiates intimacy. I am a done deal, as far as she is concerned. Since I want her all the time, it is usually me making the first move although not all the time. I often surprise her in the kitchen while she is cooking. I make sure I turn off the stove before I lift her up on the granite counter, spread her thighs roughly apart with my hands, and get on my knees between them, so that my mouth is at the perfect level for her.

Panties come flying off, pushed aside, or torn by my eager fingers. I can always buy her more silk panties. It is such a thrill when she is the first to come on to me. I love knowing she wants me as much as I do her. She will also get on her knees for me after trapping me against the counters. Her sexual abilities in that department continue to leave me breathless and amazed.

That night, I hold her in my arms just as much as she holds me. We sleep, murmuring our love to each other in sleepy whispers, wrapped up in one another, and unable to let go of each other even while we sleep. I always wake up wrapped around her or touching her in some way. She is my last thought before sleep and the first thing I see when I open my eyes the next morning.

It's just the best way to wake up ever.

As the days warm up, I spend more and more time outdoors, enjoying the yard work, believe it or not. Becca joins me sometimes, but it is not really her thing although she has definite opinions about what she likes or doesn't like.

One day, when she comes out and sees me working, she comes over and runs her hands all up and down my back, reaching up under my T-shirt. I turn and chase her as she runs squeaking toward the house. I easily catch her with my arms around her waist, pulling her up and off her feet easily. The next thing she knows I have her flat down on the patio chaise lounge chair, and I am half-laying on top of her.

Can I get away with making out with her in the backyard in the middle of the day?

Damn, sometimes I have a one-track mind.

She looks so cute trying to get away from my tickling fingers, giggling. I start to put my hand up her blouse trying to get to her skin to really tickle her.

"Michael, Michael, stop, stop, stop tickling me." She struggles, twisting and giggling between every word. She is breathless as she pleads to me. As she feels my hand reaching higher, she suddenly realizes my intentions have changed. I'm not in the mood to just tickle her anymore. Her breasts are right there.

I want much more.

"But, Mrs. Stevens, I love to hear you laugh and giggle. You can tickle me anytime, anywhere, and anyway you want. I like to be tickled. Give it your best shot. I'm not as ticklish as you are. Go ahead, I dare you. Touch me. Tickle away."

"Stop, stop it, Michael. I mean it, stop. I'm not tickling you. We're in public, for goodness' sakes. I know we're in our own backyard, but anyone could come out or look outside their windows. It's the middle of the day in broad daylight. I prefer them not to see us making love. That's private for us alone."

Looking around, I realize I had better stop before we or at least I get carried away. I know she's right. The neighbors are just too close, and there are many windows in sight.

I sigh resignedly before telling her, "I'll get you later, Mrs. Stevens. It's a promise. Count on it."

And I do that night. When it's dark and no one can see us. I always keep my promises to her. Patio sex outdoors under the stars.

Fun, fast, forceful fornication for us. I am gifted in all things technically challenging whether it is my wife's laptop or her lap.

CHAPTER 34

Charming Southern Hospitality

Elizabeth calls us one night in the middle of April right after Easter. She's a travel agent and finds all kinds of deals. Turns out she has information about spending several days in Charleston, South Carolina. Becca used to live there when she was married to the asshole and still loves the place. I frown, thinking I'm not sure I want to go there. I don't want her reminiscing about being married to him.

There's a bed and breakfast in downtown Charleston called Number 2 Meeting Street Inn. It's on the Battery overlooking the Ashley River, and Tripp never took her while they lived so close. She tells me she has always wanted to stay there because the inn is so romantic looking. She says it has beautiful porches, curved porticos, and looks like a wedding cake to her. It is possible for both Jason and Elizabeth and us to stay there for a few days. I agree, wanting to make her romantic dream come true. It sounds like fun to me. I've never been there before.

On a Saturday in late April, we drive down south Interstate 95 toward Charleston, South Carolina. Jason and Elizabeth will meet us there late this afternoon. I have my GPS, but Becca knows the way already. As I drive south, I look over and realize she has on the two-carat diamond earrings I gave her in the treasure hunt. They sparkle sweetly in her earlobes, and I smile slightly, liking the sight of something I've given her on her. Two-carat diamond studs. I chuckle a little out loud, thinking that sounds about right to me.

I'm her own personal stud, and those glittering diamond earrings should remind her of it whenever she wears them. She brings sparkle to my life, making it clear to me those earrings are perfect for her. I hope they tell her everything in my heart.

We listen to Britney Spears sing "Toxic," "I'm a Slave for You," and "Hold It Against Me." Nelly Furtado offers "Promiscuous," "Maneater," "Do It," and "Say It Right." The Black Eyes Peas songs "I've Got a Feeling" and "My Humps" make me very aware of my own feelings and my wife's nearby humps as I drive, enjoy the music, and take note of the sexually suggestive lyrics of these songs playing in our car.

I can't wait to check in to the romantic Inn.

It takes us hours and hours and hours, an easy drive made enjoyable by our conversation and music, but we arrive there at four o'clock in the afternoon, checking into our room at the Number 2 Meeting Street Inn. The Inn is as utterly charming as she remembered, sitting gracefully on the Battery facing the Ashley River and Charleston Harbor and surrounded by live oaks and palmetto trees in the distance.

When the bellboy opens our door for us, Becca actually gasps softly. It has a four-poster rice bed with carvings up and down each post. The room itself is decorated in Southern plantation style. It's lovely, and I know we'll enjoy the nights we spend there.

Jason and Elizabeth arrive shortly, and we all go out for a stroll along the Battery harbor. The point of the Charleston Peninsula is where the Ashley and Cooper Rivers flow together to form the harbor. Becca points out Fort Sumter in the distance. She is a bit of a Civil War buff, having been raised by a father who took the family to battlefields all over the state of Virginia as fun vacations. She knows so much about it, all the interesting little details that make history come alive. I am reminded again how smart she really is.

I delight in all of her stories, loving her more and more. There is always something new for me to learn about her. The palmetto trees and live oaks in the little park along the Battery are beautiful, with the iron cannons and shot still in place, pointing toward Fort Sumter out in Charleston Harbor.

The four of us go to dinner at a quaint little elegant restaurant called 82 Queen. It is on Queen Street, of course. We sit outside under the live oaks, draped with little white lights. Becca orders a barbecue sauce–covered shrimp and grits. We go through the whole grits argument again as she tries to get me to eat her grits. It has become our own version of the old comedy routine, "Who's on First?"

I've never been much of a grits fan, but she practically inhales her plate when the food arrives. She forces me to taste them this time with various threats to my life, and thankfully I find these grits to be a lot tastier and creamier than I remember. I end up with a wonderful steak covered in a creamy Jack Daniels whiskey sauce and crispy hash brown potatoes.

After dinner, we walk up and down lovely, tree-lined Meeting Street, enjoying the beautiful architecture, flowers, and intricate iron gates of the homes there. I really like the style of architecture here. The houses have multiple side porches called piazzas with a front door that actually opens the first floor piazza instead of the house itself. Evidently this is so the houses can make the most of the ocean breezes. It can be quite hot and humid in Charleston in the summer. It's already warm in April, with the scent of soft spring flowers in the gardens and window boxes. The azaleas are in bloom all over the city, creating a riot of bright colors.

We pass a huge mansion on the way back to the inn. Becca says it is called the Calhoun Mansion. I can see the most beautiful two front doors I have ever seen sparking in the entrance to the house. They are made of cut glass and like the entrance to heaven. My wife says it was named after John Calhoun, one of the fiery architects of Southern succession. It was also used in several movies although it is privately owned. It is available for tours during the day.

It's dark by the time we get back to our room, and we soon go to sleep together under crisp, sweet-smelling sheets. We touch each other with love as we drift into dreamland.

Butterfly kisses. Butterfly kisses across my shoulders and neck. I dream . . . and dream, just drifting away. It's the middle of the night, pitch-black dark. Soft, warm, sweet butterfly kisses on my face, my lips, under my chin . . . then my neck and the curve of my throat as it meets my shoulder. Butterfly kisses now on my chest. Warm. Moist.

I drift . . . sweet kisses on my stomach. Butterfly kisses . . . I roll over to my back and fall away. Butterfly kisses. Feels so good, so good. More and more and more and more. On me. Butterfly kisses and warm breath. So many butterflies all around me.

Kiss, kiss, kiss, kiss, over and over on me. I dream the most delicious dream, breathing deeply in my sleep. Butterfly kisses, all around me, everywhere. I can't get away from them . . . I don't want to. Warm, warm, wet suction. I groan softly still asleep, trying, trying to get comfortable. But those kisses follow me.

Many and many butterfly kisses, barely touching me, yet I feel every one of them. I'm engulfed in those sweet kisses. The warmth of them. I can't, I can't get enough of those kisses. I breathe deeply, moaning softly, my heart is beating slow and deeply in my chest. Gentle, soft, smooth, tight . . . butterfly kisses on me. I reach out in my dream, not knowing what's going on. I dream and dream and dream, drifting gently but intently toward a goal. So good, so good, too good.

Suddenly, waves of pleasure sweep through me over and over, in the dark, I'm dreaming . . . of coming passionately into my wife's mouth. Sudden blinding passion and lust. What's . . . happening? Was that real or a dream? My eyes open, but it's so dark. Am I awake or asleep? I feel gentle after shakes trembling through my body and realize I'm gasping softly. It's utterly dark, and I can't see a thing. I am so disoriented, not sure where I am.

Becca is suddenly next to me in the dark comforting me and murmuring "Shhhh" as she pulls my head down to her chest and wraps her warm soft arms around me.

"Go back to sleep, honey. You had a dream. I'm right here. You're safe in my arms. I love you."

I drift away in her arms, dreaming once more of butterfly kisses.

The next morning, I wake up to my wife's sparkling, smiling, olive green eyes. I receive a sweet good-morning kiss. She seems very happy for some reason. I think she must be happy because we're together in such a romantic place.

I have the strangest feeling, memories in the dark, right on the edge of my consciousness. I guess, I guess it must just be a dream I can't shake. Images almost surfacing but still remaining lost. Not sure, feeling confused, so I don't say anything to her. Did I? Did we? No, I think I would remember, but something is definitely elusively there. I can't quite put my finger on it.

Surely I would remember making love with my wife. I'm not going to sleep through something like that, am I? A feeling. A memory. A loving touch, kisses, and then total surrender. My wife's warm mouth. A memory of extreme pleasure flooding through me drifts through my mind.

I take a deep breath and let it out slowly, trying to calm down my suddenly beating heart. What's wrong with me? I can't seem to solve the mystery of why I feel this way. Did something happen last night? I feel it. There's something I should be remembering. I just know it.

Not knowing what to do about it, I grab my wife's hand and lead her into the shower. We don't have time for anything other than a quick shower since we're meeting Jason and Elizabeth on the porch for breakfast. We soon enjoy a delicious homemade breakfast with real china teacups, bacon, omelet, and strawberry jam on my biscuit. I can tell Becca's brother and sister-in-law also enjoy the finer things in life.

Becca has a plan for the day. She has certain places and activities already in her mind, evidently wanting to share them with us. We end up following her around town like three little ducks on the express tour of Charleston. We walk through the Market, something like a flea market to me, but the items are really high-quality instead of cheap.

There are women there selling homemade straw baskets woven from the local marsh grasses. They are intricately made and quite lovely. Becca says Charleston is well-known for the straw baskets and that it is a dying skill as fewer and fewer children take it up from their parents. Next thing I know, my hands and arms are filled with all of her purchases for our home. We now have a straw basket. I have to go back to the car to get rid of it all.

We take a carriage tour of Charleston, riding in a horse-drawn surrey with the fringe on top. The guide, dressed in a Confederate costume with a red sash around his waist, is delightful and full of local knowledge. He points out the earthquake bolts on most of the older homes. Turns out Charleston is on an active fault and has had severe earthquake damage in the past, as well as hurricanes, of course. The horse-drawn carriage takes us past Rainbow Row, the line of pastel-colored town homes for which the city is famous.

We have Planter's Punch at the Planter's Club. Its recipe is dark rum, lemon juice, Grenadine syrup, and bitters, as the official cocktail that originated in Jamaica many years ago. I have to keep Becca from having two of those drinks. We eat dinner at Magnolia's. The tasso ham gravy and grits here seem to be the reason why she wanted us to eat at this particular restaurant. I realize she is trying very hard to share with me all of her favorite things. When we return to the inn, we sit on the porch with wine and watch the fireflies twinkle under the trees in the garden. I feel so relaxed and enjoy watching my wife have a lovely evening.

The next day finds us on the Civil War Tour of Charleston, or, as they would say, the War of Northern Aggression. We start by touring the Edmondson-Alston house on the Battery. Turns out P. G. T. Beauregard watched the bombing of Fort Sumter from that upstairs piazza. It's a lovely Charleston townhome with antique furniture and paintings on the walls.

After paying our admission, the guide tells us to wait out on the side bottom piazza. There are plenty of benches there and a view of the lovely blooming garden. My eyes are immediately drawn to a strange contraption on the piazza. It is a long, long board that slightly dips in the middle, held on each end by wooden posts on curved rockers. I ask about it, wondering what on earth it is. I am told it is a joggling board, quite popular in the 1800s. The guide urges us to sit on it and bounce, believe it or not.

We try out the joggling board on the side porch. The board bends and rocks back and forth as we sit on it. Becca mounts the board in her short shorts, and I climb on facing her at the other end of the board. I balance myself on it carefully as it moves slightly under my ass. I am straddling the thing just like my wife. We are far away from one another. This was once used by engaged couples as a way to sit close to one another as they jogged the board up and down gently. It certainly is hard to stay on it without ending up practically on each other's laps.

Bouncing up and down sliding toward each other is definitely a bit erotically suggestive. It mimics the movements of two lovers straddling each other in passion or even a woman sitting sidesaddle on a horse as she rides it. We bounce and slide slowly toward one another. The gentle bounce and slide is inevitable. I can't fight the slide. We are gradually getting closer and closer to one another, ending up pressed against each other face to face in the middle of the board.

Umm. Sidesaddle. A mental image of my wife sitting on my dick intimately inside her but with both her legs on one side, perhaps with one leg bent at her knee as she rides me up and down like her very own stallion. I like this image very much. I like to be ridden by Becca as often as she desires. Does this position work? Will it be pleasurable or slightly uncomfortable for one of us? I file this image away for later possible research. I am willing to give it a try to see if it works.

By this time Becca and I have bounced suggestively toward one another. Another few bounces and we will be groin-to-groin bouncing against one another straddling that damn flexible board. We are in public, surrounded by Becca's family and other tourists watching us. Perhaps I need to stop bouncing. Becca is giggling but I put a stop to it.

I climb off the board and tell Jason and Elizabeth to give it a go as I give my hand to my blushing wife to help her dismount. Jason laughs and refuses to get on the damn board. He holds up in hands in protest, but Elizabeth looks somewhat disappointed. No one else mounts it. I guess Becca and I have provided the necessary explanation of what a joggling board is for. I picture nineteenth-century Southern women with bare asses under their large hoopskirts bouncing away delightedly with their suitors facing them on the board. I am shocked that it seems to have been quite common to own one of those joggling boards.

Then we head over to the visitor's center for Fort Sumter. We tour the museum and buy tickets for the boat ride over to the fort. It was a very enjoyable boat ride across the harbor, and the fort was interesting as well. What a war that was. Sudden and harsh, pitting brother against brother, family against family, and friends against one another. From my perspective, since I know a lot about warfare myself having been in one, it stuns me in its primitive brutality.

I try to get Becca to understand the battle, even giving her some details about ones I was in as well. She listens to me intently, her eyes wide as she hears about some of my near-miss experiences. I tell her things I've never really told anyone else, how frightening it all was now that I look back.

I know that I never expected to make it out of there alive. I didn't think I'd live to be forty.

She reaches for my hand, and I can see she is thinking how glad she is that I am now safe and with her. I feel the same way.

After the fort tour, we take a break to eat lunch at Poogan's Porch in downtown Charleston. The creamy she crab soup topped with brandy here is the reason. Poogan's Porch specializes in unique low-country cuisine. I end up with a shrimp and pasta dish while Jason has a low-country dish called Frogmore Stew. It doesn't really have frogs in it, just boiled shrimp, corn, new red potatoes, and Italian sausage flavored with Old Bay Crab Seasoning. It looks so good I actually wish I had ordered it as well although my meal was perfectly delicious. Becca promises to make it for us when we get home. Before I leave, I find out this restaurant is also known for its ghost, a lady dressed in black that appears on the upstairs balcony at times.

Who knew?

After lunch, we cross the huge Cooper River Bridge, driving to a place called Boone Hall Plantation. It's a beautiful plantation-style mansion with tall white columns and a long driveway stunningly flanked by many live oaks. It turns out they used the house in several movies filmed in the area including *North and South*, *Dear John*, and *The Notebook*, starring Patrick Swayze, James Reed, Channing Tatum, and Ryan Gosling as each movie's male romantic leads, respectively.

I think I remember them as being romantic movies as images flicker through my memory. They were about loves that lasted a lifetime. Since I'm all about that now, I decide Becca and I will have to have a movie night when we get back home. I want to see if I can spot Boone Hall in those movies. When I mention it to her, she says she already has DVDs of all of them.

We finish the afternoon by touring Drayton Hall, the only surviving Georgian plantation left on the Ashley River through the city. Dr. Drayton was able to save his home by warning Sherman's Union soldiers that they had smallpox at the house. Quarantined. The soldiers passed by without burning it, scared to get closer because of the disease. It was all a lie, of course, and quite clever.

The large, elegant plantation mansion was saved. By the time we're all done, I think Becca has exhausted us all. We troop back to the inn to enjoy our last evening here. I just want a quiet evening with my wife in our room.

Making love to her. In Charleston, South Carolina. In charmingly Southern Number 2 Meeting Street Inn on the Battery facing the Ashley River.

That night, we're lying together wrapped up in each other's arms quietly. I'm considering how to make my move and what I want us to do when I suddenly get the shock of my life.

Becca whispers to me, "Show me, Michael, show me how you make yourself come. I want to watch you. I want to see."

What the FUCK did I just hear? Okay, this isn't exactly the quiet loving evening I had in mind.

I struggle to get any words out. "Baby, I . . . I . . . no. I don't . . . don't want you to see me like that."

She just continues to look at me intently but tenderly. "But I might learn something that will pleasure you. Something I don't know. Show me. I showed you me, now you show me you. It's only fair."

"Honey, believe me, you already know how to pleasure me. There is nothing else left to learn. And . . . and . . . it's different with you than me. You are . . . exquisite to watch. You're my everything, my dreams come true. Baby, men are different. I don't want you to see."

I know I want to give her anything she wants, but this . . . this, I don't think so. No. Not happening.

"Michael, don't you know I crave intimacy with you? I want to know everything there is to you. All your facets. There is nothing too intimate or shocking that you can do. I love you and I want you. Show me, please."

Fuck it. She's throwing my own words back at me. She thinks she's being clever. How am I going to get out of this? She means it. Where the hell did she get this idea from, anyway? Think, Stevens. Think logically.

"Honey, I . . . I . . ."

I know I won't be able to stop if I tell her the truth. I have no filter, no control where she's concerned. I can't hold back my thoughts and feelings from her. It's been like that since the very beginning.

And then the words rush quietly out of my mouth as I try to explain. "Men are . . . animals, baby. I'm an animal. I don't want you to see that side of me. It's not beautiful like you are. It's . . . harsh, and raw, and brutal, and done. A means to an end. I've done that shit enough. All those times in the service, all the times I was lonely and alone. Years. You're the dream come true. I love the way we are together, not the way I am without you."

Her eyes are soft, shining olive green into my gray ones. I can see her thinking over my words. She finally sighs and seems to give it up.

Thank God.

"Okay, Michael. I'll let it go for tonight. But don't think you're off the hook, Stevens. I won't forget. Remember you're mine, as much as I am yours."

Damn, that's what it says on our wedding rings. She's going to hold me to that promise, I know. This woman is smart, I'll give her that. She knows she has me wrapped around her little finger and anything else I can get my hands on. She knows I want to please her as much as I can. I am afraid she hasn't really let it go, knowing she never forgets anything and can be the most stubborn woman I know.

I fear I am ultimately doomed. Not sure how I'm ever going to get out of this. I've got to wipe that thought out of my wife's head and heart. Umm. I've got to think, but then those olive green eyes are there, tantalizing me with all sorts of possibilities.

My wife never ceases to amaze me. She surprises me, shocks me, delights me, and bewitches me. I do my best to make sure she totally understands how much better we are together than apart. How much I never want to be without her, a lonely Marine alone in a damn desert, dreaming and dreaming of the fantasy he believed would never come true. Not for him, not really. The chance seemed too remote, too impossible to obtain. Especially then. But it was the only thing giving me a reason to keep going, keep fighting, to keep alive somehow.

Now that the elusive desert dream has unbelievably come true for me in my wife's soft embrace, I don't think Becca really understands the depth of my feelings for her, how overwhelming they are to me as well. I am determined she gets it. Deep down inside of her, so that she can't have any room for doubts.

I'll never leave her, never abandon her to a long and lonely life like her asshole ex-husband. I would sooner die than leave her. I need her to feel secure in my love and safe always. I slowly but steadily make my point, getting my way, but making sure she gets hers as well. I don't let her sleep at all that night. I don't care how damn tired we are the next day. She can sleep when we get home. I finally let her fall asleep in my arms in the predawn hours.

Hopefully, I made my point. I certainly tried hard enough. Gave it my best shot. Sidesaddle sex has suddenly become one of my favorite lovemaking positions. It definitely works.

Becca has to struggle a bit to stay on the bucking bronco below her, but she manages just fine, like an experienced rodeo rider. She stays on much, much longer than the customary eight seconds most professional bull riders last. It actually made it more fun for us both. I have found I love exploring new sexual positions with her. I never have been so erotically adventurous before, but I have a good imagination. She is willing, so I am willing.

It's not like I have ancient Chinese sex memorized or anything. I have never researched the Kama Sutra although I have heard of it. What's in there? Illustrations? Drawings and directions? I have never been one to watch much pornography although it was readily available while I served, particularly overseas. Many of my Marine buddies were hooked on it.

Sure I enjoyed watching X-rated porn stars performing, but it was an ultimately empty experience instead of deeply satisfying. Stupid plots and dialogue, only enough to get the actors from one sex act to the next. It was obvious no love was being felt or even faked, only a fleeting mechanical sexual pleasure. They were simply actors acting, going through the motions of sexual intimacy in front of a camera, designed for men and women, I guess to masturbate to as they watched in the privacy of their own bedrooms. Porn is a successful industry after all.

I am still able to be shocked and horrified to a degree by some of it. Some BDSM practices I just don't get the point of them really. I have never been interested in experimenting in that direction at all. It simply isn't part of me. I feel no need for it. And thank goodness, neither does my wife. Not sure what I would do if she wanted me to spank her, handcuff her, or whip her with a belt or something. Even though I would want to please her with everything I have inside me, I don't think I could actually do it to her. Fine for some people, but not us.

Not me. Never. No pain for either of us while we make love.

Making love is sweet pleasure, not pain. Sure, there are aspects of domination and surrender but only in the sweetest, loving ways. I love dominating her in bed, making her give in to my will, my instructions, my needs. Her sweet surrender knocks me to my knees. I also love it when she dominates me as well, and I give in willing, in total compliance to anything she desires. All she has to do is look the right way, and I give in completely.

I could get off watching porn, but I enjoyed erotic photos of women in men's magazines far better. Those magazines were all I had sometimes, punctuated by brief sexual relationships I had no real interest in ever pursuing beyond a physical one. I can hardly remember them now, just a blur of nameless, faceless women with female body parts. But even better for me, Becca truly is that fantasy woman come true for me. Right off the centerfold spread of *Playboy* magazine. I can actually touch her, kiss her, enter her, and make love to her.

She's real and she loves me. I know it. I feel it every day, every hour, every minute, every second.

Fucking amazing. Really unbelievable to me.

The next morning, we have breakfast with Jason and Elizabeth out on the wide porch before they head back home. Delicious sausage and biscuit gravy. I think Jason can see how happy Becca is and that he is finally able to relax and trust me. I've decided Becca and I are going to take the opportunity to also see Savannah while we're this close. It's only a two-hour drive south along the coast. Becca knows the way.

On the drive along the coast, Becca pulls out a CD. I don't recognize the singer at all. Unfortunately, I have not heard of Tori Amos before, but Becca says she loves her songs. I listen, liking the sound of her voice as I drive. One particular song comes on.

My wife says, "Honey, this is my favorite song on this CD. It is called 'Sleeps with Butterflies.' Listen to the words. I think you will like it if you pay close attention to the lyrics."

I do as she asks, wondering why. I hear the song begin with the first stanza, but the chorus that is repeated stands out to me.

I'm not like the girls that you've known
But I believe I'm worth coming home to
Kiss away night
This girl only sleeps with butterflies

The erotic dream in the Meeting Street Inn pops suddenly in my head. So it was not a dream after all. It was real. This is Becca's way of telling me she made love to me that night. I turn and look at her. I can tell by the look in her eyes and the blinding smile on her face that I am right, so very right. I smile back, not knowing what to say now. But then I realize I need no words. She knows.

I drive south. To Savannah, Georgia.

If Charleston is the queen of Southern cities, then Savannah is her hot, younger, single sister. A magical princess, like in a fairy tale. Real Southern royalty.

CHAPTER 35

Hot Savannah: We Need Ice to Cool Off

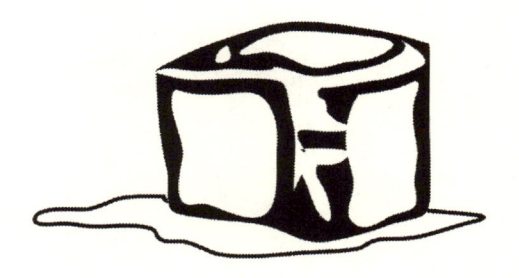

We start by going to visitor's center and park the car. There we find a trolley that takes us all around the city, allowing us to get on and off as we desire. All we need is the sticker that proves we have paid for the privilege. It's easy and a good way to see everything and hear about it as well. The city is laid out in an organized grid of streets with many, many park squares filled with live oaks, fountains, and monuments.

Riding around the city on the trolley gives us a chance to enjoy the beautiful Southern architecture found here. The townhouses are delightful, details like dolphin or big mouth fish drain spouts and intricate iron gates. Hidden gardens are treasures between the homes.

The colorful azaleas are also in bloom here as they were in Charleston. We see park benches in the squares, just like the one made famous in *Forrest Gump*. Tom Hanks sitting on the bench talking to strangers as they wait for the bus.

My mama told me," Life is like a box of chocolates. You never know what you're gonna get."

Bite into all chocolate-covered truffles to find the sweet surprise inside. Caramel, nuts, fruit fluff, hazelnut cream, whatever. I never miss any opportunity to eat sweets. All too tempting for me. I give in to the temptation easily, not worrying about future consequences, only the immediate satisfaction that is found in a good candy treat. My wife is the candy treat I crave always. I can't ever say no to her. I don't have the willpower and strength to deny either of us. Why should we when it is so damn good between us, and I think I am in heaven every day and every night?

But the most stunning thing about this city is its countless squares, filled with those beautiful, somehow mysterious and timeless live oaks and spooky Spanish moss. It dangles from the oak trees everywhere, making the city look like a magical, mystical place. Becca tells me Charleston used to have a lot of it as well but lost most of it when Hurricane Hugo blew through in 1989. It's still growing back there slowly. I remember seeing some of it while in Charleston, but Savannah is full of it. I enjoy the way it looks.

Spooky danglings hanging down from the oak branches above us. This slightly isolated beautiful city surrounded by the river and marshes is like a scene in the movie Gone with the Wind. The Spanish moss raining down from twisted thick oak branches above my head makes it especially dreamlike. Like a misty elusive dream. I am reminded of that sexually erotic dream I had in Charleston. It was a real dream, but also reality at the same time. I know I came in my sleep, brought on by my wife's nocturnal ambush and butterfly kisses.

We stop and get off the trolley to tour several homes. We visit the home of Juliet Gordon Howe, the woman who started the Girl Scouts. Next, we see the house Sherman stayed in when his troops occupied the city. The desk where he wrote the famous note giving Savannah to President Lincoln as a Christmas present is still there.

Becca seems especially excited to visit the Mercer House, the scene of a gruesome murder. Turns out a movie was made about it called *Midnight in the Garden of Good and Evil*. Another movie for me to watch now I've been there, this one starring John Cusack and Kevin Spacey. It seems to me to be the perfect descriptive title for Savannah. This place is unique. She tells me she already has a copy of the DVD, so it will be easy to do when we get home.

We hop back on the trolley and have a quick lunch at the Pirate House. This old tavern actually once hosted pirates and was the inspiration for Robert Louis Stevenson's *Treasure Island*. Lunch is a delicious combination of seafood. My fried seafood platter is great, and Becca seems to really enjoy her crab cakes. We are entertained by costumed pirates wandering the restaurant while we eat.

I check us into the towering modern waterfront Hilton, obviously right next to the river. I am even able to get us a room on the riverside. It's a lovely water view from our small balcony. We spend the early evening strolling along the Savannah River and going in all the quirky shops along the waterfront. They are all housed in the old cotton warehouses lining the river. We eat a late dinner sitting outside one of the restaurants and watch the boats sailing up and down the river as we eat the local seafood. Almond-coated broiled flounder for me and creamy crab imperial for my wife.

The humid, sultry, warm air of Savannah just never seems to let us cool off. It's hot here. I'm hot and my wife is hot. I could cut the humidity with a knife. It's almost hard to breathe, feeling my lungs struggle a bit with all the moisture in the air. It's still only April.

I decide a little cooling down is in order before we both melt tonight.

Returning to the hotel, I leave Becca in the room while she showers and gets into her silk nightgown. She wears one just in case we have to leave the hotel room suddenly, I think. Just as long as she doesn't put on any panties, I can keep it out of my way. Obviously, they would have to go. I go down the carpeted hallway and get a big bucket of ice.

Stopping at the drink machine, I purchase us a couple of soft drinks. Getting back to the room, I find that Becca isn't out of the shower yet. I pour some iced drinks to cool us down. When Becca gets out, I'm sitting on the bed. I pat it next to me, indicating that she should join me. She scoots up next to me, and I hand her the iced drink. She looks at me gratefully.

"Gosh, Rebecca, it's hot here. Savannah is a hot place. Are you hot, too, sweetheart? You look a little flushed to me. I feel really hot. Touch me. Feel how hot my face is."

She gently strokes my bristly cheek, saying, "I know. I can't believe how hot it already is here. It's still only late April. It must be unbearable in the summer. I feel better now that I've had a shower. Why don't you get one, too? You'll feel better after you get that sticky feeling off your skin."

She's looking at me expectantly, not really catching on as fast as I would like. She thinks this is just going to be a normal evening.

"I think I have a better idea about how I can cool off."

She looks at me surprised yet curious. She doesn't know what I have in mind to help us both cool off.

Now, how do I do this? I have never been a bondage kind of guy. Whips and chains and floggers and handcuffs are not my thing at all. Pain has no appeal for me, and I certainly don't ever want Becca to be afraid of me or associate anything remotely painful with our lovemaking. I'm not into anal toys or any of that shit.

Not interested at all. I am what I think to be a normal guy with normal feelings and desires. I can be intense, I know. Not that I think those people who are into that are not normal or something. It is simply that I don't get it.

Pleasure and pain are completely different to me. I can't ever see hurting her or wanting her to hurt me either. It's just that I love her so much. I would never want her to be scared of me or uncomfortable. No pain ever associated with me loving her. I guess maybe some of that stuff is supposed to actually feel good to some people, but I never want to find out. I was raised in the South, for pity's sake. Not even remotely curious.

My parents taught me to be a gentleman and treat women with respect. My mother would have skinned me alive if she ever got an inkling that I was treating a woman with less than respect. I would never have been able to face the look on Mom's face if I had. But Becca did let me blindfold her on our wedding night. She enjoyed the whipped cream, peach ice cream adventure, and the hot fudge all over me, for that matter.

It was a little harmless fun, I thought. She could even blindfold me sometime if she wanted too. I think I'd actually enjoy that. Not so sure about being restrained myself, but I trust her so I'll give it some thought. The idea of me not being able to get away from her suddenly sounds rather interesting to me. We'll see. Umm. Later. But for tonight, I need to cool my wife off. She's just too hot for me. Maybe ice and tying her down loosely aren't that far off the mark.

I look around the room, trying to decide how to proceed. I notice her pink silk robe draped across the end of the bed. It has a nice long sash.

Reaching down, I pull it from its loops and run it through my fingers slowly. Becca is watching me intently, wondering what is going through my mind. She doesn't say anything.

"Do you trust me, Mrs. Stevens?"

She does not answer as quickly as I would like.

She has to think about it first? I thought we were past all that.

Finally, she answers softly, "Yes." She's hesitant, though. Her eyes widen, wondering what possible little game I have in store for her now.

I grab her thighs, gently sliding her down flat onto the bed, her head on the pillows. I stare into her eyes, making she is still okay with this. Pulling her wrists above her head, I wrap the silk sash around her wrist loosely but not so loose that she can get out. I take the other end of the sash and tie it to the headboard of our bed. She is now tied to the bed, unable to get away from me. Her eyes tell me she's not afraid, only curious. She knows I would never hurt her. She's safe with me always. I find I like having her where I want her and feel sure she's going to stay there.

I slide her pink silky nightgown up and up, until it's to her neck. I like my wife in pink. I am momentarily distracted by pink silky nipples as well. Pink pouty hard buttons. Two of them just waiting for me, like little tightly furled rosebuds of desire. I want to feel them blossom in my mouth so I spend a little time doing so before getting on with other slightly sinfully seductive plans.

She is lying there naked for me, so beautiful and so hot. I think briefly about covering her eyes with her gown as well, but then I decide I want her to watch me with the ice. We definitely need to cool down. Keeping my eyes locked on her, I get undressed quickly before straddling her hips.

"Are you okay, honey? I think I know just the perfect way to cool you off, Mrs. Stevens. Are you with me? Trust me, this is going to be fun."

Reaching over to the nightstand, I grab a piece of ice. I can see she has now figured out my plan. I raise my eyebrow at her, silently asking permission. She nods slowly but doesn't really look that sure of herself. Taking my time, I start with her nipples first. I want them hard for me, and I think ice might do the trick.

I run the hard piece of ice over and over her again. She twists and tries to get away from the cold, but I can see her nipple come to attention rapidly. I treat her other breast with the same care. Those two erect nipples feel so good under my tongue and in my mouth. By now the ice cube is about gone, and I grab another one.

"Michael, Michael, the ice is so cold it feels as though it burns."

"I know baby. Just relax. The ice is melting. Feel it. Melt for me too."

This time, I run the ice up and down the center of her stomach, letting it melt as it glides across her skin. I end up with the cube melting into a pool of cool liquid in her navel. I run my tongue over her, licking up all the moisture, capturing it before it can roll down her sides in drips. She starts to moan and twist just a little. It's cold and burning, and she's trying to pull away from the coldness and the strange burn at the same time.

I think I'm ready to proceed to even warmer flesh now. The new ice cube makes its way south, heading for warm, moist folds in which to melt. I tease her clitoris repeatedly with the ice, never too long or too much sensation for her to handle. I don't want her to feel pain, only teasingly cool pleasure.

When I push the remaining small sliver of ice slightly into her, she bucks up under me, trying to get away. She can't get away because the silk sash holds her to the bed. By this time, there is no more ice cube. Her heat has melted it all away in my fingers.

Vanilla Ice, the rapper, would be proud of me. I have my very own "Ice Ice Baby."

Since my fingers are already now where I want them to be, I take full advantage of the moist situation between her thighs. I caress her over and over again. She moans, but somehow I can tell she's just not getting there. I decide on a different course of action now that the ice has melted. My fingers were getting a bit frostbitten anyway. They are numb on the ends, and I don't like losing my sense of touch. I'm not feeling the least bit cooled off, and I know she isn't. I have definitely lost my cool. I can feel the heat flooding my body, making me slightly feverish.

Warm to the touch. Like a fever in my blood and body.

Getting off her, I flip her over, so that now she is on her chest facing down on the bed. I lift her hips up, guiding her into a position on her knees. This is trickier than I thought since she is still tied to the bed. I try to figure out how to give her what we both need. Since I've overcome her natural shyness, Becca has really started to enjoy oral sex as much as I do.

It has become one of the top three most requested activities. I need to somehow get my mouth under her. I lift her and slowly slide my way under her until she is straddling my neck. She's almost where I want her. Since her arms are tied to the bed, they are stretched over my head, her full breasts dangling right there above my eyes.

Damn. My mouth starts to water.

Taking her hips gently into my hands, I lift her until she is basically sitting on my face with her sweetness right at my mouth. Her wet smooth folds are all I can see. I press my mouth into her, licking and sucking. My nose could practically fuck her; I am so pressed into her. She is all I can feel, all I can taste, all I can smell. I'm really good at this, so it doesn't take long before she is pulsing and gushing all around me, her head thrown back and eyes closed, groaning for me. I slide out of my position carefully but as I fast as I can.

Getting behind her, I tell her to hold on to the headboard and bend slightly over for me. I know she's wet enough now for me, so I bury myself in her from behind. Skin to skin, my skin touching her inside. She is still shuddering from pleasure. I don't give her time to come down from it.

Pounding into my wife, I feel her unbelievably reach another shuddering climax before I just can't control myself anymore. We both fall on the bed, gasping. I gently untie my wife from the bed and pull her into my arms, holding her as we both try to calm our hearts and breaths.

I feel like such a man, the luckiest man. I am completely tied to this woman. Wrapped tightly in her spell. Yep, Savannah is a hot, hot, hot city. We're definitely coming back someday.

I feel content and satisfied as we drive Interstate 95 back north to Virginia. We listen to several CDs on the way north. Madonna's songs include the cute "Crazy for You," and sweetly romantic "Cherish." Becca pulls out a Janet Jackson one next. I enjoy listening to the sultry voice on the sexually suggestive songs "That's the Way Love Goes," "Any Time, Any Place," and "Love Will Never Do Without You." Katy Perry's "I Kissed a Girl," "Teenage Dream," and "Firework," just about do me in. I enjoy the lyrics a little too much, fantasizing my way up the interstate.

I realize I am becoming aroused by the music and lyrics. I wonder absentmindedly if my wife would be up for some car sex if I can find a secluded place to park. She is reading with her hand on my right thigh. I concentrate on driving instead of sex. I need to get us both home safely. I realize my foot is pushing just a bit too hard on the accelerator, no doubt because of frustration. I set cruise control because there are state troopers everywhere in South Carolina and North Carolina. I drive past a crazy tourist place called South of the Border, if I can believe that. We can't get home fast enough for me.

I want her in our bed, showing me her own type of Southern hospitality.

I certainly had a fantastic time, touring two of the most beautiful, gracious southern cities. I think Becca really enjoyed showing me all the places she loves. Nice to be gone, but equally nice to get home. Our house is now a home because of her. We finally get there at sunset. I look over at her as I turn into our driveway and switch off the car. I smile, remembering our icy play in Georgia.

I liked the ice. Playing with cold. Coldplay. Umm. The band with lead singer Chris Martin. I will have to pick up a current CD or greatest hits.

"Did you have a good time in Charleston and Savannah, Mrs. Stevens?"

"Yes, I did Mr. Stevens. They are two of my favorite cities. I'm glad I was able to show them to you. Did you have a good time, too? Which southern city did you enjoy the most?"

Yes, most definitely. I enjoyed the fuck out of each charming city. I am after all a Mississippi-born man from the Deep South. I feel at home south of the Mason–Dixon Line as well as in the southern regions of Becca. She is the true southern city of my dreams. Hot, beautiful, secret gardens; stunning architecture; unique scents; and true hospitality. The whole Southern experience all wrapped up in my beautiful wife.

I am lucky, lucky, lucky.

The South shall rise again.

"Oh, baby, there is no way I can decide that. They are both beautiful cities, each with their own unique attractions. You can't compare the two. I love them both. I can see why you wanted to share them with me. I always have a good time when I'm with you. That's a given. I'm very easy to please, you know." I assure her.

She leans over and whispers against my mouth before we get out of the car, "Good. It pleases me greatly to please my husband, you know."

I kiss her a sweet, welcome-home kiss, getting slightly carried away, in our own car, in our own driveway, in our own home.

Home once more. I enjoyed our sexy Southern adventure, but home is equally nice.

CHAPTER 36

Sizzling, Steamy Summer Sex

"Always in My Head" by Coldplay is now my favorite song on the CD I listen to in my car all the time. I hardly ever change it, just letting it repeat over and over again. All of the songs in the CD are great. I learn them by heart. They are the soundtrack of my summer. We attend Pungo's Strawberry Festival in Virginia Beach and buy pints of fresh strawberries. That night I am strawberry shortcake.

May comes to a warm close with Memorial Day weekend. It is the unofficial start of summer. Since we both are very patriotic, we set out

American flags and watch the old World War II movie *The Longest Day*. Becca's dad and his brothers served in the military during the war. Her dad was in the army in France and Germany, another uncle served in Africa, and another in the navy in the Pacific Theater. Becca says she, Jason, and Elizabeth sometimes talk about traveling to Europe and following her dad's old battle map when he was part of the Battle of the Bulge. Now that we are married, I hope the four of us can do that trip possibly next year if Elizabeth can make all the arrangements for us.

We have recently gained a new neighbor who just moved in a week ago to the brick two-story house next door. We decide to invite him over for a Memorial Day cookout on the patio so we can get to know him. He seems to be our age and alone with no family. I go over to invite him. His name is Brandon Randolph, who moved here from West Palm Beach, Florida, although he says he is originally from New England. A true Connecticut Yankee. He moved south to escape the cold, icy winters up north. Then he headed to Virginia for a happy medium between the two.

Brandon strolls over from his backyard to ours, bringing a bottle of white wine from Saude Creek Vineyards in New Kent County. He is a little over six feet tall with salt-and-pepper hair and a neatly trimmed mustache and beard. Becca has already set the table and brought out bowls of tossed salad and pasta salad as well as ice tea glasses and empty wine glasses. I open the bottle, fill our glasses, and we get to know each other, settling into the chairs to talk and watch the sunset over the river. I am close enough to the grill that I can keep an eye on the ribs.

Brandon seems comfortable with us from the start. He defers to me and is kind and gentlemanly with Becca. His eyes tell me he thinks she is gorgeous, but he doesn't cross any line. He can't seem to take his eyes off her. I understand that condition. But his eyes are admiring her, not lusting. I can tell Becca likes him too as they start to tease each other a bit. She makes fun of him being a Yankee and he teases her about being a Southern belle.

Yeah, my wife is really Scarlett O'Hara, for sure. She is a true Southern woman. Being a true Southern gentleman from Mississippi lets me know we are made for each other.

They both have the same sense of humor, making little statements that can be interpreted in many different ways sexually but never obscene. It is funny to listen to the quick exchange of observations. We all laugh together easily. I realize I like the way he explains things clearly, patiently, and competently. He seems like a very intelligent guy. His voice is calm and seductive. Even I pick up on the seductiveness of his voice—and I'm a guy. I can see Becca hears it too, the sensual sound of his words.

Umm. I hope my wife thinks my voice is seductive sounding too.

I will have to find out later if she is just as affected by my seductive deep male voice.

He tells us he spent many years in the U.S. Navy, primarily serving on submarines.

What is that bumper sticker I saw?

"Submariners do it deep."

Umm.

Not around my wife, he doesn't.

I am deeply impressed because it takes a certain type of man and a special courage to spend months under the ocean in such an ultimate stealthy weapon of mass destruction. He has done that with his life, but once he got out of the Navy, he spent his time as a computer technician, helping people who have infected home personal computers. He really seems to enjoy his job now. He says he gets to help people, it's fun, never boring, and challenging mentally. He gets to speak to people all over the country when they call for his help.

Brandon admits he has never been married. He must be fairly well off financially if he chose to buy a home in Two Rivers. He has bought a home that doesn't quite fit his life yet. It tells me he has hope of changing that because I did the exact same thing. He's alone in a new town, just like I was not too long ago. I know precisely how he feels. I wonder briefly if Becca has any single woman friend we could introduce to him Lyndsey Kymroy pops in my head. I see Becca looking at him and I know, I just know, she is thinking the same thing. I vow to ask her about it later in bed.

Well, maybe after that. I may not be thinking about Brandon quite then. She continues to hold my attention completely so that I can't think of anything else if she is close to me.

Becca is the peace rose I have in my hands. I have removed all thorns from those long-stemmed roses. I have to uncover her special secret core petal by soft petal. I can't rush it. I love what I know about her now and realize it will take me my lifetime to learn all her hidden secrets. I look forward to removing every single petal. Yellow tinged in pink.

By now I have finished grilling the barbeque ribs, and we sit down to eat. Becca asks Brandon if he plays golf. He says he loves to play and has his own clubs. I suggest he join the country club so we could start to play golf occasionally. This is great as far as I can tell. He seems like a great guy, a nice man to have next door, and someone I could enjoy knowing as a friend. Becca says she wishes she could come play too but knows she would slow us down. She took golf in college, played some with the asshole, and used to have her own set of golf clubs. She sold them when she needed money after being deserted that summer fifteen years ago.

I tell her, "Becca, honey, I'll be happy to play with you. Let me take you to get your own set of clubs. It doesn't matter if you can't play to me. It will just be fun. Believe me, I hack away at my shots often. Brandon will see if he has to spend time with me on the golf course here. I may scare him away."

Brandon quickly speaks up, "No one can be worse than me. I have just taken up the game. I am still learning how to play. I am the one who will be embarrassing myself on the fairways, not you, Becca."

Becca replies, "I usually could hit my ball straight. Not far enough to lose it, but somewhat straight. I never hit it so far that I lost sight of my pink golf ball. In college, we went to play golf in Newport New Deer Run golf course. Our professor gave us yellow golf balls. It was fall, and the fairways were covered with yellow leaves. We lost our golf balls the whole time. It was hard to spot the yellow ball among all those yellow leaves. I have used pink balls ever since when I played."

Brandon and I chuckle at the image this funny story gives us. She must have searched everywhere for her balls.

Pink lady golf balls. Pink balls. Pink. Balls. Becca's round tits pouting with dusky pink nipples tantalize me. I love sucking those nipples, licking, softly biting them with my teeth, never causing her pain though. Maybe she will let me taste her tonight. She seems to be quite attached to the idea that she only uses pink balls when she plays golf. I will show her pink balls if she wants. I am quite attached myself.

"So no slicing to the right? Or a hook to the left? Baby, that's great. I want to play with you. We'll see. We could hack our way around the course as a threesome."

Wait, wait. What am I agreeing to here?
Not sure about a threesome.

Golf yes, otherwise no, over my dead body.

"Michael, could you explain to me sometime about the different clubs? I am never sure which club I should select."

My clubs. All the time. No one else's clubs. Doesn't matter which one, I have the perfect one for you.

"No worries, honey. I'll help you with your club selection. It's easy. I'll even customize your golf grips for you. It makes it easier to handle the club."

Grips are damn important. Handle carefully.

Brandon says softly, "A good grip makes all the difference."

The thought of my wife's hands wrapped around the handle of a golf club just about makes me laugh.

Brandon says, "I have trouble driving the ball. My short game is better, and I am an old champion at Putt Putt. Watch out for me on the greens."

"Yeah, I like to putt too. It's so satisfying when my ball actually goes in the cup. Not that I make a birdie, a par, or a bogey. I hit the ball so much there is no golf term for it. Triple, triple, triple, double, double bogey. I lose track of how many times I stroke the ball," she replies easily.

Yes, I like making sure my ball goes in the hole as well. Stroke my balls too.

"I have trouble keeping up with my strokes as well," I look at my wife, daring her to go there.

As many strokes as you can handle, wife.

"If we do play, I will try to keep score instead of not paying attention to the game. I can write a tally mark for each stroke for you if you want," murmurs my wife.

Brandon chuckles softly, trying to keep a straight face. I am fighting the same battle, but my wife seems to be keeping her calm expression as if she is simply discussing the weather instead of a hot golf game of many strokes of my driver or my three iron.

I have many different irons and large-headed drivers at my disposal in my personal golf bag.

Becca tells Brandon about the three times she actually went to the practice rounds at the Masters Golf Tournament in Augusta, Georgia. Jason, Elizabeth, and she have journeyed south to wander the green fairways of Bobby Jones's creation. She mentions the Augusta National Clubhouse, the large oak tree behind it where everyone meets, the soft manicured grass, the perfect putting greens, the Amen Corner, the Butler Cabin, the Eisenhower tree that no longer exists and cheap pimento cheese sandwiches. She laughs about following Phil Mickelson and Adam Scott all over the course one day. Evidently the other golfers held no interest for her that day.

Goddamn it. Millionaire golfers showing up again. Phil is married but Adam I am not sure about at all. He is like a goddamn model with Australian accent and everything.

Shit.

We finish dinner as the stars come out. Becca goes in the house to bring out a strawberry shortcake decorated with whipped cream and blueberries.

A real red, white, and blue dessert. Patriotic for Memorial Day.

Of course, dessert was delicious. I am particularly glad to see there are plenty of strawberries, blueberries, and whipped cream left over. I remember playing with strawberry shortcake.

That is so going to happen tonight. I vow. She is going to be covered in red strawberries, blue blueberries, and white whipped cream. Becca just doesn't know it yet. I want a patriotic dessert because I love my country. It's Memorial Day, and I am a veteran of a war. I deserve a red, white, and blue celebration of my own.

After dessert, Brandon lingers for a while before making his polite thanks for a wonderful evening, new friends, looking forward to us playing golf together, and good-night. Both of us respond honestly liking Brandon and telling him to come over whenever he needed or wanted us. I watch him wander alone through the darkness to his own backyard and his own big empty house. He was fun, funny, and a gentleman who never said an impolite word during our discussion of a golf game. I am looking forward to having a friend live so close by.

Who does my wife know for him? I must remember to ask her. Are any of her PEO friends single and available? I think of Keith. Now that he and Mackenzie are inseparable, maybe he knows an ex-girlfriend or someone.

Lyndsey Kymroy is my first choice for Brandon, but I will find out if Becca thinks so as well.

Becca and I will find someone for him so he can be as happy as we both are. I like him, and I am looking forward to getting to know him better. He will be a friend that has nothing to do with my time in the Marines, only this new life with my wife.

I take my wife in the French doors, sweep her up in my arms, and grab the rest of the strawberry and blueberry shortcake before hauling it all to the master bedroom.

Red, white, and blue dessert for me to enjoy on a memorable Memorial Day weekend.

America is a beautiful country, unlike any other place in the world. We are not perfect, but we always try to do the right thing if at all possible. Spanish American War, World War I, World War II, Korean Conflict and even the disaster that was the Vietnam War were wars fought for the good of the opposed.

Desert Storm in Kuwait and the War against Terror fought on the foreign shores of Iraq and Afghanistan started after we were attacked on our own soil by cowardly terrorists who only wanted to kill innocent men, women, and children instead of real armies made of real soldiers. I know those murderers are in Hell and not Heaven with a bunch of virgins as a reward for committing suicide along with mass murder.

Oh beautiful
For spacious skies
For amber waves of grain
For purple mountain majesties . . .

It is a patriotic holiday after all. I served my country well, and I served my wife very well.

CHAPTER 37

Blow Out My Birthday Candle

My birthday is June 1. I don't want much this year, but I am pleasantly surprised to see my wife has planned a little intimate celebration of her own in honor of my birthday. We spend a quiet day together, just enjoying each other's company. For dinner that night, she surprises me with some premium steaks from the Fresh Market. I grill them outside on the patio, making mine medium rare and hers medium well. She doesn't like much pink in her meat. We have steamed broccoli and boiled potatoes smothered in butter and cheese.

For dessert, Becca stopped by the Trellis and ordered me a Death by Chocolate cake of my very own. It's a huge seven-layer chocolate cake covered in fudgy frosting. It's intense chocolate, rich, and decadent. She comes out, singing to me softly and expects me to blow out the single gold candle. I am also surprised when she hands me a small wrapped gift.

I open it eagerly since I really rarely receive presents. Inside are silver cuff links from Colonial Williamsburg, engraved with our entwined initials M and B. She says she wants to see me wear them the next time I get dressed up in my tux and her in an evening gown to go dancing or out for a nice dinner. I know these are the only cuff links I will ever wear from now on.

Then she startles me when she pulls out another wrapped box. I find a golf shirt and tee time reservation at the Golden Horseshoe Golf Course, the course I played after she accepted my proposal. Wow. I really liked my birthday this year, never having had anyone take the time to celebrate with me before since I was a child. Becca makes it memorable for me.

Later that night, we get ready for bed. I wash up first, brush my teeth, and climb into bed while Becca gets ready. She seems to be in the bathroom for quite some time. I am dozing off when I realize she is in bed with me. She has on a completely sheer light blue teddy that snaps together at the crotch and barely covers her breasts.

She suddenly produces a black blindfold left over from our flight home from our honeymoon. She doesn't say anything, waiting for me to nod in agreement. I hesitate a moment, knowing I have never done this before, but I'm willing to please her. She lifts my head gently to place the blindfold over my eyes, and I am completely blind. I lay back on the pillow, listening and wondering what she has in store for me on my birthday.

I feel her lift my hand to her lips and kiss my palm. Then she wraps something around my wrist and ties it tightly though not tight enough to hurt me. My arm is lifted above my head, and I realize she is tying me to the wrought iron bars of our bed's headboard.

Uh oh.

I am lying there blind, naked, and tied to the bed. I can feel my erection bounce upward in welcome. One arm is tied to the bed, but she leaves my right arm free.

What's next?

"Honey, what are you going to do with me now?" I ask her softly.

"Why, Mr. Stevens, I am giving you your last birthday present."

"What is it? I'm curious. I can't see it. I can only feel, hear, taste, and smell it. Please tell me what my present is."

What does she have in store for me?

"Me, Mr. Stevens. Your birthday present is me. Listen to me and feel me."

"I will. Do I get to taste and smell my present as well?"

"Perhaps later if you are a very good boy and do as I say."

I'll be very, very good, the most obedient of all boys.

"I think you have me at a disadvantage here. It seems to me I have no choice but to do as you say. I'm tied to the bed."

"I know. I am enjoying seeing you like this, so helpless to me. I can do whatever I want to you, and you really can't stop me."

"Go ahead, Mrs. Stevens. Go ahead."

She leans over and whispers to me, "I plan on it."

I feel her get off the bed and leave me. Where the hell did she go? I listen carefully. I feel as though I am alone, and the waiting is killing me. Suddenly I feel the bed dip as she gets on next to me. I lie there still for her, having trouble breathing. She doesn't say anything, but I know she is there. I can smell the scent of her hair not far from my face. I begin to feel what reminds me of soft feathers running all over my chest and stomach.

What? It is so soft, barely touching me.

I begin to picture the feather duster from the kitchen. I think I am right. Becca runs the feathers all over my torso. She stops suddenly, and then I feel the feathers run up my legs from my feet to my thighs. It stops before reaching my erection. I am so hard I know the veins are standing out on my penis.

I am panting, waiting, anticipating the soft brush of feathers on me, over and over again. She never says a word, she doesn't touch me, only the feathers. Finally, when I am about to beg for it, the feathers tickle my dick. I am losing my mind, feeling the softness, yet wanting much, much more. The feathers disappear.

I feel her grab my right hand in hers holding it tightly. Her other hand gently strokes the palm of my hand tickling me. She caresses all over my hand, the back and between each finger. Then I feel her tongue trace the exact same places, kissing and nipping my palm, kissing my knuckles, and licking in between each of my fingers. It is as though my hand is hotwired to my groin. I gasp when I feel her pull my entire thumb in her mouth, sucking gently. She does the same thing to each of my fingers. By this time, I am about to come from my hand alone.

I know my cock is erect, willing, and waiting, but she is ignoring that part of me for now. She gently places my palm on her breast, holding me to her as I massage her tenderly. Then she is gone. I hear and feel her get behind me after she pulls me into a sitting position.

She is kneeling with her legs on either side of my ass, her breasts against my back. I feel her reach around and put her hand under my chin to tilt my head all the way back. She rises up above, and suddenly her open mouth swoops down on me, her nose to my chin. She is kissing me upside down. Her tongue dives deeply inside, and I surrender to it willingly.

I feel her reach around my side and grab my hard-on tightly. She begins stroking me rapidly up and down my length with a firm grip, and I die in pleasure. She is pressing her pussy against my ass and grinding against me to get the friction she needs to come. I am moaning as loud as she is.

Oh, just like that, that's perfect. Keep going, don't stop, please don't stop.

I feel her come closer as she suddenly crawls around in front of me and pushes me back down on the bed. She places her lips on just the top of my cock, sucking hard on me as she continues to pump me. I am gasping and bucking my hips in absolute mind-blowing pleasure, feeling and hearing my wife but unable to see her. I enjoy my wife's excellent blow-job skills.

She can help me blow out my forty-nine birthday candles anytime she wants.

I cry out when her hand and mouth leave me. I hear a soft snap and believe she has unsnapped the crotch of her teddy for me. But then swiftly, she impales herself on my entire length, leaning over me and crushing my mouth with hers in a deep, deep kiss that I feel all the way to my toes.

I am moaning and panting under her kiss, feeling her move up and down on me intensely. It is just too good to be true. I can't stop the feelings that wash over me. There is nothing else in the world but the feel, smell, taste, and sound of my wife loving me with her body and heart. In the darkness, I can only imagine how we look together locked in the act of lust and love. I cry out in utter pleasure.

"Becca, my love, my angel. I'm yours."

"Michael, I love you, I love you. Give me you. Give me all of you."

"Oh, baby. I'm so close, so close." I can barely get the words out.

"I know. I can feel it. Soon, baby, soon. Don't worry, I'll get you there."

My right hand is still free. I have been kneading her breast, but now I reach down between us and touch both of us where we are joined together as one. I stroke my penis as she raises up and tease her as intimately as I can. She groans loudly, panting and frantically moving on me. I wish I could see her, but the darkness is complete. I can only imagine the sight of her while I pleasure both of us.

It is too much.

I am about to lose control when I feel her stiffen and grind down on me in her orgasm. She screams for me so loudly that it sends me over the edge into pleasurable oblivion. I let loose, coming fiercely into her moist tightness, hoarsely yelling out loud a moan that seems to burst out of me. She collapses on me, and I hold her with my one arm as we slow down from such physical releases.

I'm speechless. My wife never ceases to beguile me with her charms. I am enslaved to her by my love for her.

Slowly, Becca reaches up and takes the blindfold from my eyes. I blink rapidly as my eyes adjust to the dim candlelight filling our bedroom. She then stretches upward to untie the silken rope holding my wrist to the bed. All I can do is look at her, and she stares back at me.

I think we have shocked each other with the sexual intensity of that experience together.

Now that I am free, I pull her close into my arms and then reach down for the covers. I am utterly spent and so is she. She snuggles into me, kisses my chest, and closes her eyes.

I hear one last thing before sleep claims me.

"Happy birthday, Michael."

"Thank you, baby. I am now officially one year older."

"No worries Marine. Like a fine wine, you improve with age."

I sing in my head.

Happy birthday to me, happy birthday to me, happy birthday to me . . . happy birthday to me.

Becca is watching me with love clearly shining from her sparkling olive green eyes.

It was my happiest birthday ever.

Becca blew me away with her birthday gift to me this year. If turning forty-nine was this mind-blowing, I wonder what will happen when I am turning fifty next year. That will be a milestone birthday. I realize I no longer mind getting older as long as I know I will spend the rest of my life with Becca Stevens.

CHAPTER 38

What a Trip to Ireland

In the middle of June, I surprise my wife with an eight-day bus tour of Ireland, one of my favorite countries, since I have an Irish background. Turns out she has a predominantly English heritage. Ireland is a beautiful country, absolutely covered in all of the amazing shades of green. I find I love showing my beautiful wife the world, and since she loves to travel as much as I do, I plan on us doing it frequently.

We've now been together a year on June 10th, and I want to mark the occasion with something memorable. We can easily afford it, so why shouldn't we go to celebrate the first time I ever saw her? In my mind, it is easily as important as the day I made her officially mine.

Thank goodness I rescued her that day. Look at everything that has happened to me because of that one split-second decision.

The flight takes us from Norfolk to Newark and then across the Atlantic Ocean to Shannon Airport in Limerick, Ireland. It's a bus tour with other people mainly from the States and Australia. After checking in to our hotel, we set out to wander the Irish streets. Spotting a large stone castle in the distance, we gradually make our way there. It's King John's Castle, left over from the Norman conquest of Ireland. Judging from the look of the castle, it is easy to see these Norman soldiers took their conquest very seriously. They were not kidding around. It commands an imposing defensive position within the surrounding city.

The fortress is a massive gray stone and forbidding in its towering strength. It must have scared the shit out of everyone in the area, leaving no doubt about who was in charge now. We tour the castle, listening to the historical interpreters with their interesting lyrical Irish accents. I love that accent, almost wishing I spoke with it too.

We also spend time going through the Norman cathedral next door to the castle. It, too, is massive and forbidding for a place of worship. It is surrounded by a cemetery with tall Celtic crosses as tombstones. There is nothing soft about that cathedral. Returning to the hotel, I make sure I make love with my wife before we fall asleep. I want this trip to be romantic for her. I want her memories to last our lifetime.

I love my wife's shining, green eyes gazing at me deeply as I make love to her.

The bus tour takes us on a drive all around the country. Narrow, narrow, narrow country roads bordered by gray stone walls. Field of dug-up blocks of peat used to heat homes and pastures filled with sheep or cattle. Small Irish towns with Irish pubs advertising Guinness. Some larger cities along the coasts. It becomes obvious that there are castles, cathedrals, and abbeys everywhere we look in Ireland.

We stop at beautiful Kylemore Abbey, a stone home that once became a Benedictine Abbey for nuns. It is in a beautiful location, surrounded by trees and mountains and the most reflective, still lake I have ever seen. The structure once belonged to a married couple. The wife died young and suddenly, and the grief-stricken husband built her a small mausoleum on the grounds to keep her near to him, even in death.

I can understand how he must have felt.

Irish stew, scones with clotted cream and strawberry jam, cabbage and potatoes, oatmeal with Irish whiskey, gallons of Guinness, Bailey's Irish cream and mead... etc. We work our way around the country, staying in hotel after hotel. They all seem to have that damn curved shower and white fluffy duvets with no top sheet. Galway, on the coast, is a beautiful town with excellent street entertainment and the best lemon gelato in the world.

I get to play a round of golf at the hotel on the northwestern coast of Ireland. I hack my way around the open-style golf course, not used to courses without real clearly marked fairways. I feel as though I'm lost in the middle of an undulating grassy field, trying to find the hole to sink my ball in. I swing my iron clubs all over the open course.

Yeah. I know. Golf in Ireland. I like to sink my balls into holes.

In Northern Ireland, Belfast is fascinating with its impressive museum dedicated to the RMS *Titanic*, a ship built there by the local massive shipyard that has been building ships for over a century now. We wander the museum, stunned and saddened by the stories of that horrible shipwreck. There is one display that mentions a woman that was rescued from the sinking. She was a nurse and ended up on the *Lusitania* when it went down not long after. Unbelievably, she survived again, leading me to think she needed to stay off all damn ships. She had the good luck to live through two horrendous shipwrecks but seemed to bring bad luck to everyone else on board. I wonder if she ever sailed again.

The bus takes us to Dublin, the capital of the Republic of Ireland. We spend the day touring a castle, a cathedral, a museum housing the famous Book of Kells, and an old stone prison.

That night, I am surprised to see our hotel room actually has a tub, a fairly big tub at that. Thank goodness we don't have to slip and slide in a dangerous shower again tonight. I am thinking that tub looks big enough for both of us. After a little convincing, I tempt my wife into joining me. Becca puts her hair up before climbing into the warm water with me. We sit facing each other in the tub, with our legs entwined. I wash her foot lazily, massaging her heel and toes.

I wonder briefly if I should suck her big toe into my mouth. I think it is supposed to feel good, hotwired to her groin.

"Mrs. Stevens, tell me, are you wet for me now?"

Are you really, really wet?

"Michael, I'm wet all over. I'm sitting in a tub up to my neck in warm water. Haven't you noticed? I'm right in front of you."

"I'm not sure. You don't look wet enough to me. Come closer, Rebecca. Let me find out for sure how wet you are all over."

Wet in all the right places. Let me check.

"From what I can see, Mr. Stevens, you are just as wet as I am."

"Oh, no, not yet, not all over me. There is a special warm wetness I am looking for. Come here."

"My God, Michael! Will you ever get enough? There's not much room for me to move in this tub, you know."

"No. I'll never get enough. Not of you. Never. I have a lot of lost time to make up for. I spent way too many years alone in that damn desert in Iraq and the mountains of Afghanistan. The only thing that got me through it was doing my job, day after day. Just doing my job as a Marine. And the dream of something better one day in the future. Something to give me a reason to be alive. You're that for me. You give me what I need deep down in my soul. Give a man a break, honey. Come here now. Next to me. Close. There is plenty of room for you in my lap."

We end up sloshing and splashing just about all of the water out of the tub before we're both done. I don't care what the maids think when they find that bathroom after we leave tomorrow morning. It's a flooded mess. Wet towels everywhere.

Becca was wet everywhere I searched.

We finish the bus tour by rounding the southern coast before returning to Limerick for our last night and flight home the next day. As a farewell dinner, we are treated to a real live medieval dinner in a real medieval castle called Bunratty. We have to eat with our fingers and everything. Soup from a small bowl and barbeque ribs. The banquet hall is covered in tapestries, and we are brought food by medieval serving wenches in low-cut dresses. The musical entertainment is wonderfully medieval, and we head back to our hotel, having thoroughly enjoyed our vacation to Ireland.

The flight back home from Shannon Airport was long even though we could sleep in first class. We slept some and watched movies to kill the time. It was good to finally be home, but I am glad we made those memories. It takes us several days to recuperate from all our fun again.

My Irish eyes are definitely smiling. Sweet, sweet Irish memories and sparkling, olive green eyes. One of the many shades of green found in the beautiful country of Ireland.

CHAPTER

39

A Gorgeous Game of Golf

The days warm up gradually as we begin to enjoy the summer months. Not long after we got back from Ireland, Becca decides we need to visit the Virginia Living Museum in Newport News. We pack a picnic lunch since she says they have an outdoor area with tables. It's a delightful little museum, and I end up learning more about the state of Virginia. It has unique exhibits that clearly explain the differences between the Tidewater, Piedmont, and Appalachian Mountain Regions. There is even a wooden nature walk behind the museum.

We have a pleasant afternoon trying to find the animals that are in their enclosures. It is surprisingly hard to find the fox, the fawn, or the wolves because they seem to blend in with their environment. Becca and I race each other to see who can spot the animals first as we walk the entire wooden trail. We finish with our picnic eating outside on wooden picnic tables nestled among the trees. I like eating outside, and I love a picnic with my wife.

We spend several lazy days just messing around the house. I decide I need to make good on my promise to take her golfing with me. We purchase her a set of good golf clubs and the blue bag she picks out. Me, Becca, golf bags, golf clubs, drivers, golf balls, tees and gloves, and a beautiful golf course with wide fairways to hit.

Let's go play golf together.

I can't wait to see her grip her iron clubs, swing her hips, and putt her way around the course at Two Rivers with me. It matters only that she has fun, not that she is any good.

Brandon wants to come with us, so we make a tee time for us three to play. Maybe between Brandon and myself we can manage to get Becca around all eighteen holes. I rent us a golf cart and put the bags behind us. My wife has to drive the cart, so we head out for the first tee with Brandon close behind us.

Brandon and I tee off and hit the fairway close together. We drive a bit further up to the red ladies tee box. I watch Becca head up there with her pink ball in hand. She looks damn sexy in her cute little golf outfit. I am afraid all I can concentrate on are her long legs and perky breasts swaying under the knit material of her golf shirt. She grabs the driver, and I almost tell her to not use that club. She swings and misses the ball. She swings and misses again. One more time.

I can see she is getting a bit frustrated but still willing to try. I gently suggest she try the three iron instead since she is having trouble with such as large club head. This time she actually hits the ball, an actual golf shot down the center of the fairway. It doesn't go far, but it is surprisingly straight. She giggles and heads back to me to drive the cart. We head down the cart path.

Brandon and I are only along for the ride. We are both focused on making sure she has a great time. We hit our balls quickly and get out of her way. None of us bothers to keep score. Becca is hitting the ball frequently since it just doesn't travel as far as ours. When we get to the green, she has really has a decent short game and chips her ball up on the green. We all land on the putting surface, and I remove the flag from the hole. Since her ball is the farthest from the cup, she gets to putt first. She told me she likes Putt Putt and does not hesitate to strike the ball. She doesn't read any break in the greens. Sometimes her putt goes in, and sometimes it breaks off in a different direction.

The three of us spend a delightful summer afternoon chasing pink balls all over the golf course. I buy us sodas from the cart girl when she comes by us with a cooler full of drinks. Pink balls are going everywhere. I end up in the woods, the marsh grasses, and beyond the cart path searching for my wife's pink balls. Brandon finds several for me as well. She is a really good sport about it and jokes about her pitiful golf skills.

I think she is doing great. We are going to have to get her signed up for real golf lessons with the pro at the clubhouse. Just watching her grip her club, kneel to pick up her ball, and lean over to place her tee and ball for her drive are enough to make me have a great time on the course. Brandon seems to enjoy himself as well, making as much fun of his own game as Becca does about hers. However, he is a natural on the golf course, making it look easy. I am glad I am not actually paying close attention to our scores because as usual I would be losing.

Pink balls flying everywhere, pink lips, pink nipples under her golf shirt, and pink secret places for me to drive my balls into straight down the fairways.

I show Becca my balls when we get home. My golf club is hard and made with a titanium shaft. She grips it like I taught her. I tee up my ball for her. As she strokes me, she leans over and nuzzles my balls, caressing them over and over. The combination is heavenly. I enjoy her attention to my uniquely male body parts. We are made so very differently, and I relish in our differences, realizing how perfectly we fit together.

Male and female. Together as God meant us to be.

Before I can drive my big driver home, Becca surprises me by swinging her legs over me, straddling my hips swiftly. She rises up a bit so I can get my tee into position before slowly impaling herself down on my titanium shaft. Now she grips me with her internal muscles instead of her hands.

She just sits on my for a moment, staring down at me and running her fingers teasingly on my lower abdomen.

She gently traces the hairs of my happy trail as they lead to where we are intimately joined. I feel her rhythmically contract and release, contract and release her muscles, voluntarily controlling the muscles inside her pussy. The feeling is incredible as she mimics the way she milks my dick during her climaxes. I close my eyes and enjoy this special ecstasy. I am shocked at how hard her internal muscles can actually grip me.

She has been doing her Kegels.

Becca leans back slightly as she reaches down to masturbate herself on me. I grip her hips as I watch spellbound as she closes her eyes and gets lost in sex. I watch avidly for the changes that come over her, the expressions, the breathing, the blush, the alternating movements. She sometimes frowns in concentration, sometimes smiles, sometimes throws her head back on her straining neck. I watch as she grinds on me, rocking back and forth deeply, then suddenly bouncing up and down. I stare at our bodies where they are intimately joined. I can catch a glimpse of the shaft of my cock as it enters her before she slides back down. Even the sight of her smooth folds pressed against my groin is erotic.

Damn, we look hot together.

Soon it appears she is getting close to coming on me and I wait, holding my breath and holding on to my control. But then she seems to lose it as it melts away from her. She slowly stops moving on me, and her eyes open as she gazes down on me with a hot expression in her eyes. We are still joined.

"Honey, you feel so good on me. I could stay inside you like this forever. What do you need me to do? I'm here. Tell me."

Becca leans over me and kisses my mouth without replying at first. She places both her palms on my cheeks and holds me in place while she devours my mouth with her tongue. It fills my mouth, thrusting and then retreating. She is leaning over me, her full tits right there softly teasing me with those pouting hard nipples. I grab on to her pink balls and caress them as they fill my palms with their feminine softness.

Becca's mouth is at my ear, kissing, sucking my neck, under my jaw, my mouth, my cheeks, my eyes, my nose. She whispers to me as she begins to pump her hips up and down on me. Her hands hold my face in place gently.

"Husband, I love you, I love you. You feel hard inside me, touching me in places I have deep inside. Love me, honey. I want to feel you lose control under me. I need you to. Let it come out. Feel me all around you, loving you with all of me. There is nothing else in the world right now but you and me together in love. I want to feel it erupt from you. Give me all of you. Please, please, please give it to me now."

By this time, I am barely holding on, my hands that had been cupping her dangling breasts move to her ass. Her firm globes fill my palms, and I grab them tightly as she pounds her hips on me. I am lost in the sensations, feeling the one woman I love in this world all over me. I can't help myself. I want to watch, I want to keep my eyes locked on hers. But I am suddenly overwhelmed with an orgasm I just can't stop, a tidal wave of pleasure and emotion.

I am coming first, not Becca, but I can't stop it; it is too much for me. Becca's open mouth suddenly swoops down on my lips as I groan out her name over and over and over. I have nothing left to give her, but I still have an incredibly aroused woman wrapped around me intimately. She is panting and moaning my name against my mouth, and I feel her fall off the edge of her own pleasure.

Thank fuck.

Her hips move frantically as she strains to feel every last throbbing pleasure before completely collapsing in my arms. Neither one of us can breathe or speak anymore. My hands hold her ass, and I am still inside my wife, softening slowly in her wet warmth. Now that we are done playing this round in bed, I feel as though I have competed in a four-day professional golf tournament.

Someone present me with a tournament trophy, please. The Masters silver trophy will do just fine. I deserve it and so does my wife for her excellent skills. My score is under par for the course. Becca has joined the ranks of a golf professional in my opinion.

"I love you, Mrs. Rebecca Connelly Stevens. I will play golf with you anytime."

Play anytime, anywhere. Play a round on me. My treat.

"And I love you, Mr. Michael Gable Stevens. I enjoy playing with your club and balls as well."

My nuts are my balls and my dick is my driver, my three iron, my pitching wedge all rolled into one.

"Inform me when you want to reserve a tee time on my own personal course."

Personally and intimately yours. Lifetime erotic country club privileges. Exclusive.

"I don't know, Mr. Stevens. Golf is an expensive sport. Can I afford to play a round on your lovely course?"

"I can give you a very special discount price. One just for you. No one else gets to play my eighteen-hole course but you."

A full round.

"But darling, playing eighteen holes takes at least four hours, doesn't it?"

"You can take as long as you need to play a round of my golf. It is entirely up to you. There are no foursomes behind you to make you rush. You don't need to wait and let other players play through. It is up to you how long you play."

Play for hours, please.

"I like playing golf with you. I find the fairways fit my swing perfectly. It is easy to stay straight and not veer off to the left or right. You know I love to chip and putt. It is so satisfying when I stroke my pink ball into the hole on the green."

A straight stroke is needed. Hit the ball and follow through.

"I am going to buy you a lifetime membership at my country club. We can play there as often as you like. A regular tee time. What do you think, my love? Should I reserve a time for us?"

I am taking reservations for the rest of our lives. All requests immediately granted.

"Yes, I believe so. My golf game won't improve if I don't practice often. Make our tee time for every morning and every night as well. I need to practice my swing and putting skills."

That's it. I lose it. I burst out laughing. She grins at me, knowing she won. She beat me again.

"I give up, I give up, I give up. I can't keep up with you honey. You have beat me, and I surrender to your superior quick wit. I don't know what to say now. I have exhausted every sexually suggestive golf metaphor I can think of for now."

"There is nothing else for you to say, my love, except that you love me. That's all I need for you to say. And that I won."

"That's easy. You won. I love you."

I believe we doze off like this, before I feel her slide off me to cuddle next to me in sex-induced sleep.

Who knew the slow, skillful, steady game of golf could be so exciting? Golfers have to control every part of their bodies consciously in order to make a successful shot. The very beat of their heart, their breathing, their emotions, and mental clarity; all are necessary for them to succeed. I find I have a real appreciation of the game of golf now. It is not just a simple pastime. It is a game that can be enjoyed my whole life.

"Paradise" by Coldplay.

I have died and gone to paradise.

CHAPTER 40

Mountain Meadow Mating

I do try to think of different activities we can do together to make summer fun. I decide a day trip to the Blue Ridge Parkway in the mountains might be enjoyable. I like the drive, looking at the beautiful mountains and stunning valleys below. Becca puts together some lunch for us to take because we love to picnic.

I drive us up Interstate 64 heading northwest past Richmond. It is about a two-and-a-half-hour drive. I put in a CD I made with Keith of all of my favorite U2 songs. Becca says she loves them too, and we obviously have been to Ireland now. We ride and listen to "One," "Beautiful Day," "City of Blinding Lights," "With or Without You," "Ordinary Love," "Sweetest Thing" and "Electrical Storm." I hold Becca's hand linked with my fingers on my right thigh as I drive one-handed up to the Blue Ridge Mountains and Parkway.

The scenic views of the Shenandoah Valley start to appear in front of us. I get off the interstate at the top of Afton Mountain and follow the signs to the parkway. I pay the park's entrance fee, and we slowly drive the curvy mountain road. I stop at scenic overlooks so Becca can take pictures. We find a fairly short hiking trail through the mountain woods and follow it until we reach the tall, thin waterfall at the end. I'm starting to get hungry now, so when we reach the car, I suggest we find a place to picnic soon.

I continue to drive down the parkway, looking for somewhere suitable. I see a small parking area with one other car and think this might do. Maybe we can find a grassy meadow in which to spread the soft blanket. We walk a little ways from the car following the trail, with me carrying the picnic basket. I am starting to give up hope, but then we come upon a secluded grassy meadow. Looks good to me.

Spreading the blanket on the grass, Becca gets out the food as we flop down on the cloth. I dive into my turkey, lettuce, and tomato sandwich since it is way past my lunchtime now. It doesn't take either of us long to finish eating; I think she was as hungry as I am. Maybe it's this mountain air. I take her in my arms and place her head in my lap so that I can play with her hair. I'm feeling relaxed with the sun on my face and my love near me so that I can touch her.

She reaches up suddenly to my hair saying, "Michael, there is a leaf caught in your hair. Let me remove it. Lean down, please."

I look at her, murmuring back to her, "Mrs. Stevens, you have just a little mayonnaise on the corner of your sweet lips. Let me remove that for you."

Slowly I lean over to lick my way across her lips, removing all traces of the mayonnaise that really wasn't there. I am wondering what else I can remove from my lovely wife's body when gradually I become aware that my wife has turned her head slightly and seems to be pulling my zipper to my shorts down.

Umm. I guess she has something amorous in mind on this warm summer afternoon in the mountains.

She catches me a bit off guard, which is rare for me. Next thing I know I feel her soft lips around my still-soft penis. She makes a low sound in the back of her throat as she feels me grow longer and thicker in her mouth. I think she likes to do this to me, making me big and hard for her, alive. It doesn't take long before I am, finding myself gently thrusting my hips slowly, as I just can't hold still under her warm mouth. The warm summer sun, the breeze, and her warmth are all around me, filling me with warmth as well.

Suddenly I feel the coolness around me as my wife takes her mouth away, giving me one last kiss. She makes her intention clear as she slips off her shorts and panties but keeps her top and bra firmly in place. I'm still fully clothed with just my zipper down and dick up.

God, I hope we are far away from whoever was in that other car in the parking area. I don't want them suddenly showing up to spoil anything.

That thought swiftly leaves my mind as she gets on top of me and mounts my aching, lonely, cool dick. The suddenness of her move sliding down on me makes me gasp. She looks down at me with love clearly shining in her eyes. I know that look, knowing I look the same to her. Becca just sits there on me, all around me, not in any hurry. I slip my hands under her top and feel up her breasts, stroking her soft mounds gently but repeatedly. I'm about to try to get my fingers up and under her lacy bra.

She leans slightly over and reaches for her wine glass.

Umm. She's thirsty. Now? Right now?

After taking a large sip, she bends over me and places her opening lips on mine. Cool, slightly sweet wine pours into my mouth, and I swallow greedily and lick her wine-flavored lips.

I like this wine tasting. Give me more, please. I am drunk with love and lust for you.

She then leans over my chest and nuzzles close to me with her lips at my ear. She begins to move her hips and whispers to me at the same time. She tells me how much she loves me, wants me, needs me, desires me, how good I feel to her. I am overwhelmed by love for this woman, only this woman.

For once I let her do all the talking, only whispering quietly, "Oh, baby. You feel so good, don't stop, don't stop loving me."

She makes me feel like such a masculine man, the luckiest man in the world. The sun is shining in my eyes as I enjoy my wife's erotic attentions.

We both start to move faster and faster in one another, reaching and striving toward that ultimate goal of bliss in one another. I love her so much, and that thought is all it takes to push me right over the edge. I groan out her name as I shudder under her, losing all of my self-control.

I feel Becca stiffen and throw back her head, moaning repeatedly as she follows me into her own pleasure. I would never have forgiven myself if I hadn't made sure my darling wife wasn't feeling as satisfied as me.

Thank goodness.

She leans down on my heaving chest and buries her face in my neck as she tries to control her breathing. I feel her lips kissing my neck, under my chin, my cheek, my eyes, my nose, and finally my mouth. We lay together in a beautiful mountain meadow enjoying the outdoors, the natural beauty surrounding us, and each other.

I love the mountains of not only Virginia but my wife as well.

A lovely duet between Gavin McGraw and Colbie Caillat called "We Both Know" comes to my mind. I sing the words with them in my head as I hold my wife close.

We both know, our
Own limitations, that's why we're strong
Now that we've spend some time apart
We're leading each other out of the dark

CHAPTER 41

Just Call Me Worry Wart

Becca comes home one afternoon after shopping for a while by herself. She made a few purchases at Dress Barn and bought me some new clothes at Belk's as well. I like that she picks up things for me because she has great taste and seems to know what looks good on me. She seems rather preoccupied while she wanders around putting things away.

I can't quite put my finger on it, but something is bothering her. That little *v* that forms between her eyebrows is definitely there. I wait patiently, hoping that she will tell me on her own. I even give her the perfect opportunity for us to talk, but she keeps everything bottled up inside her. It starts to drive me crazy, my imagination conjuring up all kinds of problems. We make it through dinner, but she still seems a bit lost in her own thoughts.

All evening long, she sits with me in the great room reading her book quietly while I watch a golf tournament. She is busy and preoccupied but still makes comments about the players. It is obvious she knows quite a lot about the game and the professional players. Becca says she used to go to the Kingsmill Golf Tournament held in Williamsburg.

Good grief. Still more to discover about this woman.

She has seen many of the top players in person—Tiger Woods, Phil Mickelson, Rory McIlroy, and even Jack Nicklaus. She mentions Phil a little too much for my piece of mind. It seems she has a bit of a celebrity crush. I start to worry about competing with millionaire golfers before remembering he is happily married with daughters. Not sure I would have had a chance otherwise.

I'm still curious how she seems to know so much about sports. So I ask her about it.

"Honey, you amaze me with how much you know about so many different sports."

"I don't know, Michael. Sports were always on television so I paid attention. My brother and father were very patient explaining things to me. Football is actually my favorite. Daddy was a big Redskins fan when I was a girl. I wanted to watch the games with him, but I didn't understand."

"He told me to pick an offensive and defensive player to watch specifically. I chose Chris Hanburger, number fifty-five, outside linebacker for the Redskins. Slowly I could pick up on what was happening during the game. I even got Chris's autograph when he retired since he lived in Hampton. He was inducted into the NFL's Hall of Fame not long ago."

She pauses, remembering when she was a child. "I watched baseball games, NASCAR, basketball games, soccer matches, bike racing, and tennis with Daddy and Jason. I pay attention during the NFL playoffs, the Super Bowl, the Final Four NCAA tournament for college basketball, Wimbledon, the Masters, British Open, PGA tournament, the U.S. Open, the 1976 Miracle on Ice Hockey game between the U.S. team and the Russians at the Lake Placid Winter Olympics, Daytona 500, Indianapolis 500, the Triple Crown horse races, the Tour de France, the Summer and Winter Olympics, and the World Series."

She pauses and then continues. "Over the years, I have learned about many of the athletes in all those sports. It is more fun when I know their names and can recognize them by sight. I admit I don't care much for soccer, though, because I really get bored just watching them running around kicking a ball. So that's about it. I enjoy it. Over the years I have learned about a lot of athletes, teams, coaches, and stadiums. I would like to see the Redskins play at FedEx Field though someday."

"I am glad you do, honey. I think you know more about sports than I do. I try my best to keep up with you."

I continue to watch the tournament as she reads, glancing up at the golf on the television from time to time. Even though she still looks down at her book perched in her lap, her eyes often lose focus. I can see she is not really reading. Her focus and concentration are shot.

"Becca, what's wrong, honey? I can see that you're upset about something. Tell me what it is, please."

Whatever it is, I can fix it. I promise. Tell me. Let me.

She glances at me out of the corner of her eyes, "It's nothing, baby. Really. I'm a silly woman, that's all. I let my imagination run away with me."

"What do you mean? What happened?"

My imagination is in overdrive. Did something bad happen to her? I need to know.

She takes a deep breath and lets it out slowly, but still doesn't say anything. I wait, and wait, and wait. Still she says nothing. Long moments pass. I can see by her eyes that she is trying to figure out what to do, what to say. She seems to be considering every option.

Doesn't she know by now that she can tell me everything? No secrets between us. She can say anything to me . . . except telling me that she is leaving me, of course. I never want to hear her say those words to me. Never, never tell me that. I am losing my mind.

"Did . . . did I do something to upset you?"

Her eyes flash to mine in an instant. "Of course not, darling."

"You're starting to worry me to death. Whatever it is, I'll take care of it. We'll deal with it together."

"You make me feel so loved, Michael. So safe. It seems I have gotten used to how intense you can be at times. Now, it just makes me feel loved." She smiles at me gently.

"Then tell me so I can help. I'm quite good at rescuing you, you know."

"I remember," she whispers softly.

And then the words start stumbling out of her mouth. "I just . . . felt funny today. I don't know how to explain it. A feeling. Like I was being watched or followed in some way. Like I could feel a stare on my back. I can't put my finger on it. I never saw anyone that scared me, it's just the hairs kept standing up on my arms. Goosebumps, even. It must have just been my imagination and I'm being silly. I know I couldn't wait to get out and into the car with the doors locked. I don't know why I felt like that, but it made me panic. Stupid. Who would be watching me? That's ridiculous."

I can see she is trying to convince herself that nothing happened, and it was all in her mind. I'm not so sure, and I refuse to take any chances. That night in bed as she's falling asleep, I tell her over and over that no crazy stalker's ever going to get near her because I'm there.

"I'll protect you, baby. I'm big and strong, you know."

She giggles slightly. "But who's going to protect you?"

"Honey, I'm big and ugly enough to protect myself. I have fast hands, haven't you noticed yet?"

"I have to admit I have noticed your fast hands, Mr. Stevens. Although I'm not sure they are as fast as they used to be."

"Are you kidding me? My hands are as fast as they've ever been. Do I need to give you a demonstration, Rebecca?"

Say yes. I am definitely fast. Never doubt me, honey.

"Yes. Please. Show me your fast hands. I need proof."

And with that, I distract her away from her worries with my fast hands. However, believe me, I won't forget. Somehow I have the uneasy feeling this isn't going to go away. Something doesn't feel right. She's not the type of woman to imagine things.

I remember that silver Mercedes with the dark-tinted windows, someone sitting in it at night and knowing without a doubt now someone was there watching Becca's place. I saw it several times at night in her parking lot. Too many damn times for my peace of mind.

Once I even started to go over to it and confront whoever was inside to find out what the hell was going on. But the headlights suddenly came on as the car turned and sped out of the lot before I could reach it. I haven't seen it at our house now that Becca is living with me, but I have not forgotten about it.

It worries me. I plan on keeping an eye out for all silver Mercedes cars with dark-tinted windows.

CHAPTER 42

Beach Blanket Bingo in a Bikini

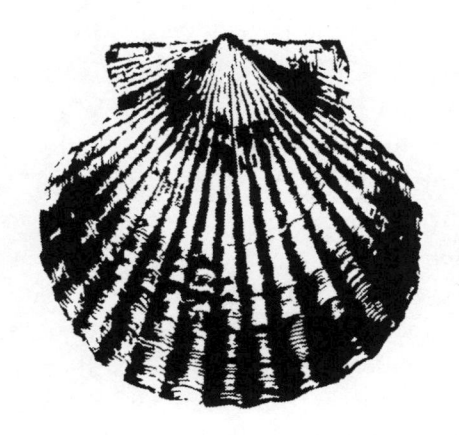

Over the next few days, everything seems to be settling down into normal routines. We're still looking for the right kitchen table and chairs, and since it's the summer, it seems as though I have endless yard work.

We spend three days at a beach cottage in Kitty Hawk at the Outer Banks. Becca looks so damn cute all the time in her bathing suit or a pair of shorts. I spend the time trying to keep my hands on her as much as possible. Thank goodness for sunscreen. She needs it as much as I do since the last thing I want is for us to get sunburned so that we can't touch each other. We spend lazy days at the beach, tour the Wright Memorial, and drive down to Hatteras for the day to see the lighthouse.

Since our rented cottage is right on the ocean, we go for long walks, picking up seashells. We are alone on the beach as the sun sets over the Sound to the west. I talk her into getting into the waves with me. We both have on our swimsuits, so she agrees. Her bathing suit has been a distraction for me all the time we've been lying on the beach. It's a beautiful aqua blue color, two triangles covering her full breasts, and a small bikini bottom that barely is decent. I love seeing her that way, but not that crazy about every other guy on the beach being able to see so much of her. Her skins tans evenly since I am very careful to keep her covered in sunscreen all day.

Becca reads. I nap. We walk. We people-watch. We pick up shells. We talk to the surf fishermen. We swim. We listen to the battery-operated boom box I brought with us. I play a CD I made with some of our favorite songs. We listen to "I Want You to Want Me" by Cheap Trick; "Amazed" by Lonestar; "Chasing Cars," "Read My Mind," "You're All I Have," "Chocolate," "Make This Last Forever," "Called Out in the Dark" by Snow Patrol; "My Life Would Suck Without You" and "Dark Side" by Kelly Clarkson; "Cool" and "An Early Winter" by Gwen Stefani; "How to Save a Life" by The Fray; "Simply Irresistible" by Robert Plant; "You and Me" and "Everything" by Lifehouse; "Umbrella" and "Diamonds" by Rihanna; "Halo" by Beyoncé; "We Belong Together" by Mariah Carey; and "First Love" by Jennifer Lopez.

I love music and the lyrics.

The afternoon goes on until it is now early evening, and the beach has cleared out except for us. My wife is engrossed in her romance novel. I wonder if it is a hot, sexy read for her. It's still quite warm as the sun sets slowly, and I am sweating and crusted with sand.

I grab my wife's hand and pull her up. We're going in. The ocean water is cool at first, but it doesn't take long for us to adjust to it. I stay close to her, jumping the waves together. It doesn't take me long before I get her pressed up against me, her arms and legs wrapped around me and my hands under her ass, gripping her.

I look around to be sure no one is there to see us before I slip both my swimming trunks, and her bathing suit bottoms off under the water. I hold them tightly so we don't end up losing them in the ocean. I don't want us walking half-naked back to our beach cottage.

The salty coolness of the ocean contrasts with the sudden warmth I feel when I enter my wife. She holds me as tightly as I am holding her, rocking against each other to find that special friction necessary. My hands grip her ass as I move her back and forth on my length. I lose my control slowly, forgetting everything but my love close to me.

Wanting, wanting so much to get as close to her as I can. I stare into her eyes, knowing my eyes are dark and dilated with passion. She closes her eyes to me as she starts to feel it sweep through her, that incredible pleasure we find in each other. I groan gutturally as I feel my own intense orgasm come to me, giving her my heart and soul in the Atlantic Ocean.

"Oceans" by Coldplay will always remind me of our water adventure.

After spending these several days at the beach, we return home. In the car driving up Route 168, Becca pulls out two CDs by a singer named Dido. She has a sweetly seductive edge to her voice. Becca is even softly singing the lyrics along with her. I like three songs in particular. "I've Got Sand in My Shoes" is appropriate for our situation at this very moment. "White Flag" is about heartbreak, but "Here with Me" speaks to me the most. Becca sings the chorus.

I won't go
I won't sleep
I can't breathe
Until you're resting here with me.

That night when Becca comes to get into bed, she drops her silk robe on the end of the bed and pulls down the covers. I see the unbelievable sexy tan body of my wife. She glows with a golden tan skin, but my favorite parts of her are her tan lines around her breasts and hips.

Somehow the contrast between tan and white pale skin is so erotic. It is as though it marks the areas of her body that are for me only. I get to enjoy them; no one else sees those pale parts but me. They are hidden places clearly defined now by her tan lines. Her pale breasts tipped with rosy nipples outlined by surrounding tan skin are like a bull's-eye target in my eyes. I can't help myself. I have to explore all those private areas so temptingly pale for me to enjoy. She looks so damn seductive, all tan and pale and with pink, erect nipples.

I am waiting for her to join me in bed, propped up on the pillows and watching her climb in with me. She pulls up the covers and turns to hug me to her. I turn out the light so that we are in candlelight. And that's it. The dim light makes her tan appear darker, and the pale areas glow white.

Easy for me to see.

I enjoy exploring all the hidden places of my wife's body, places I now know intimately like the back of my hand. Pale glowing white skin, dusky pink tips pouting with desire, and smooth wet secret deep places in the dark. All of it. I wonder briefly if she likes me brown as well, my torso, legs, and back tan, but my hips and ass still white.

I like summer when my wife has a tan.

For the next couple of days, I start to notice that we receive a few phone calls where no one says anything when I answer, but I can tell there is someone there on the line listening. No one answers, only hanging up after I repeatedly say hello. I try not to worry Becca, telling her it could be kids or telemarketers, perhaps. But she answers a couple of them as well as me. I get caller ID and refuse to let her answer the phone unless we recognize the number. But basically we enjoy normal days, normal activities together.

In late June, Becca proceeds to tell me she received a phone call from her college friends in Lexington. She is planning on driving to the mountains to stay with her friends Pauline and Julia just for the weekend. Her friend Tricia from Clifton Forge will be there as well as Courtney. It's a yearly girls' weekend.

Pauline has a small camp next to the Jackson River and a party boat that she takes out on Lake Moomaw for swimming, fishing, tubing, and jet skiing. The girls also go kayaking on the river as well. Pauline has two RV campers for everyone to sleep in actual beds. I know I'm being silly, but I am not happy about her going. I don't want to be left behind even though I know she's going no matter what.

"Michael, I am going to spend time with my girlfriends. We do this every year, and I am not going to miss it."

"But are you sure you'll be safe? I'm not sure I like the idea of you staying in the woods and going out on the water."

"Don't be ridiculous. It's fun. We have a great time. It's not dangerous. I wouldn't do that."

"Becca, I don't think you should go."

"Michael, you're not stopping me. I'm going no matter what you say. I'm sorry, but that is the way it is going to be."

"You don't care what I think?"

"That's not true. But you're being unreasonable. I'm an adult. Yes, we are married, and I care about what you think. However, you cannot order me around. I am your wife, not someone you command."

"But, but..."

"No buts, Michael. I'm going. I love my friends, and I love spending time with them. I only get to see most of these girls once a year. We were close in college, all majoring in elementary education. I just need for you to understand and let me go and enjoy some time with them. You should be happy for me."

"Can I... can I come with you? It sounds like a lot of fun for me. I've never been Jet Skiing before. And I have always wanted to go kayaking."

"No, you can't come with me. It's a girls' weekend. None of the girls, except Courtney, are married and it will make them feel awkward having you there."

"Don't you want me to meet your friends? I would love to meet them."

"Michael, you're making me mad now. End of discussion. Leave it alone. You're not getting your way. I'm going and that is that. It's over. I'm leaving on Friday and I will be back late Sunday."

She thinks a moment. "Why don't you plan something? What about a golf weekend with Keith? Brandon? The two or three of you could have fun, maybe Myrtle Beach or something. I know there are many cheap golf courses there. You could drive down together on Friday or Saturday morning and get an inexpensive motel room. Play golf as much as you can."

She tries to tempt me with seafood.

"Get a seafood dinner at a calabash seafood restaurant. It's great in Myrtle Beach. It would keep you busy and not moping around here while I am gone. Think about it. Call Keith. Call Brandon. Make it happen, Stevens. Go do something with your friends while I am with mine. It's only for one weekend. It will be okay."

Okay, that didn't exactly work out the way I wanted. I can't order her to do what I want all the time. I know she needs her own life to some extent. It's me that has the problem. All right. I'll give Keith and Brandon a call. I feel sure they'll agree.

I manage to make it through the weekend and have a great time playing golf with Keith and Brandon. Myrtle Beach is cheap, and we can't get enough of that calabash seafood they have there. Becca comes home on Sunday, full of stories about how she fell out of the kayak and got dragged over the rocks in the Jackson River, trying to hold on to the kayak so that it didn't get away from her. She shows me her bruises to prove it.

Oh no. I knew she would get hurt.

But she doesn't seem to care and just laughs about it, telling me how silly she had looked. She said she was laughing so hard, Pauline and Tricia had to practically haul her out of the water, dragging her and the kayak over slippery moss-covered river rocks. It was funny to her. She keeps laughing about it, thinking how she must have looked, all wet and bedraggled. She is thankful the kayak didn't drift away from her reach.

The girls ate picnic foods like hamburgers, potato salad, and pasta salad, while sitting next to the river in a small screened-in hut. They built a campfire and stayed up late talking and laughing, remembering when they all were in college together.

The next morning, Pauline took them out on her party pontoon boat and even let Becca steer for a while. They jumped into Lake Moomaw near the dam and floated on rubber tubes under their arms. Julia even took Becca on the back of the Jet Ski, screaming fast over the lake.

It means a lot to her to keep these friendships alive. I know I'll see those girls at homecoming this fall at the college. We both have a great weekend with our friends. I need to give her the space and time to enjoy herself, sometimes without me. The bottom line is I want her to be happy, and if letting her spend time with her friends does that, then I am happy. I can let her have fun, sometimes without me.

I know I can.

Now that she is back home with me, I quickly make sure she understands how much I missed her this weekend apart. She has no choice as I pick her up in my arms, stride down the hallway, and throw her onto the bed. She squeaks in surprise as I grab her, pull her panties and shorts down swiftly, and turn her over face down on the bed. I quickly rid myself of my jeans and boxer shorts before grabbing her ass and pulling it up for me.

I hope she is ready for me as I thrust into her from behind. Her glorious ass is right there for me to enjoy. I gradually increase the intensity, depth, and speed of each thrust inside her. Both of us are grunting with each movement of my dick within her. Neither of us can form words; all we can do is feel the buildup of passion and emotion.

I love my wife so much as I pound my love into her over and over. She begins to stiffen a bit under my hands, and I feel her tremble inside. It grows and grows until both of us are stunned. Waves and pulses of pleasure flood through her, and she screams for me and only me. I lose all of my ironclad control, flooding her with my own pleasure. We collapse together, and I pull out of her, rolling over to her side. I put my arm across my eyes as I struggle to control all heartbeats and breaths. Becca's chest is heaving up and down as she attempts to calm down her body.

I missed her. I never want to be apart from her for very long. She missed me too.

CHAPTER 43

Tripp, the Asshole Ex

Becca leaves Tuesday in the early afternoon for her once-a-month lunch with the PEO ladies. Believe it or not, they're meeting at the Second Street Bistro, eating outside on the patio by the street. She's gone for several hours as normal, but when she returns, nothing is normal. She rushes into the house, visibly upset, and I tell she's been crying on the drive home.

"Michael, oh Michael! I saw Tripp! He was at the restaurant today. We were sitting outside, and I had my back to the main part of the restaurant. I knew I kept feeling that strange awareness of being watched. I don't know how long he was there behind me. He could have been there the whole time I was. When I saw him, he was sitting in a booth, just staring at me. He made me so uncomfortable. I absolutely couldn't wait to leave. It was all I could do to sit there and wait until we had all finished lunch and paid for it."

"Did he talk to you at all?"

"No, he only sat there the whole time staring at me. I could feel his eyes constantly on my back. I was so startled by it all I could barely walk past him to go out the door. He just kept staring and even turned and watched me leave. He didn't say anything, thank goodness. I don't think any of my friends noticed anything was wrong, but I left as fast as I could. Oh, Michael, I think perhaps he's moved back here! I'm scared, baby. What do I do? What can I do to make him stop?"

"Okay then. Don't worry. He won't get near you again. I'll find out for sure where he is living now."

It's clear to me now that Tripp had been the one watching Becca that day at the mall. I know she's not someone who lets her imagination run wild. I think of the silver Mercedes with dark windows in the dark, and now it all makes sense to me. He's the damn fucker that was sitting in that car night after night outside of my woman's house.

I feel certain Tripp has been watching Becca for a while now. Ex-husband now turned sick stalker. It seems he still is not willing to let her go.

As soon as I can that afternoon, I call my attorney and explain the situation to him. He suggests I call a private investigator in town and gives me his recommendation. I do, and the PI assures me it is a simple request to find out where that asshole is living now. I want him watched. If he's watching my wife, I'm damn well going to watch him back. I find out that evening that yes, he is living in Williamsburg out in Stonebridge Apartments on Richmond Road.

So the fucker really is back. When will he finally leave us alone? He's delusional if he thinks he's getting her back.

The private investigator reminds me that I really can't do anything legally yet. He hasn't touched her, threatened her, or said much of anything to her. I have nothing on which to base a restraining order.

Frustrating. I feel so impotent, not being able to fix this. But I won't forget and will be constantly aware. I am used to paying attention to everything around me after patrolling the streets in Iraq and Afghanistan.

A couple of days go by with nothing untoward happening. There are evening concerts in Merchants' Square once a week. The Air Force Heritage Band from Langley AFB is playing tonight, so we get out our chairs and head down there. The concert starts at seven, so we have to get there a little early to put our chairs in place because it gets crowded fast.

We invite Brandon to come with us since this is his first summer in Williamsburg and didn't know about the free entertainment. Becca and I find room for our chairs over on the side, not far from the Cheese Shop. I go in to pick us up ham and turkey sandwiches and soft drinks, so we have a little picnic of our own before the show.

It's a perfect summer evening for a concert, and the band does not disappoint, playing a lot of current and past music we all recognize. We're enjoying the concert, and it lasts for a good hour and a half on a beautiful summer evening that is surprisingly pleasant.

Between songs, I glance around at the crowd, surprised at how many people are now here. Some are standing nearby along the sidewalks because not everyone shows up with a chair. I catch just a glimpse of a familiar face, coldly realizing that Tripp is standing there among the bystanders. He is staring intently at my wife.

Fuuuccccckkkk!

I start to get up to confront him, but he immediately shifts his eyes to mine when he sees I'm staring right back at him. I think I see a slight smirk on his face before he turns angrily and disappears among the crowd. I stand impotently, wanting to chase that smug bastard down, but not wanting to leave Becca alone.

Who knows if he might double-back and grab her or something before I can get to her? I don't know what he wants or what he might do. I take deep breaths, trying to calm down and think logically. It has all happened in a split second, and I don't think Becca has realized anything other than the fact that I stood up so suddenly, I almost knocked over my chair.

I sit back down, making sure Becca doesn't know anything. I don't want to worry her anymore. I glance at her and she seems fine. But I know I didn't fool Brandon. He noticed my reaction and is on high alert just like me. He might not know what I saw, but he could tell I wasn't pleased. He is protective of Becca in his own kind and gentle way.

But I vow I will hurt that fat prick someday.

I hire the private investigator to keep tabs on Tripp as much as he can. I swear I will not be lulled into a false sense of security. I know sooner or later he's going to make a mistake, and I'll get him. Even though she hasn't forgotten, I think Becca is almost relaxed, having convinced herself he'll leave her alone. I don't have to wait long as it turns out.

It is now the Fourth of July, and Becca and I spend it in Colonial Williamsburg. There is a small hometown parade made up of middle-school bands, marching Boy Scouts, little girl baton twirlers, riders on horseback, the Shriner's Club motorcycles and classic cars. By six in the late afternoon, we head to the lawn in front of the Wren Building on William and Mary's campus. The local hospital sponsors a hot dog, hamburger, and ice cream festival to raise money for charity. We buy a ticket each and enjoy eating out and watching the other people, so many dressed in red, white, and blue. There are games for the children to play as well.

Colonial Williamsburg is full today of patriotic Patriots.

In the evening, I go back to the car and get our lawn chairs so we can get a good spot for the fireworks. They start at nine-thirty after it gets dark enough to enjoy them. We find the perfect location and settle down to wait. As I am sitting and enjoying the darkening skies and stars popping into view, I glance around at the crowd of people around us and realize I am staring at Becca's ex-husband Tripp. He is behind us with a clear view.

Staring.

I have had enough of seeing him too often near my wife. I don't hesitate and rush to confront him. Before five seconds pass, I am standing in front of him.

He's becoming a creepy stalker, for sure. I can't believe there he is again, too close to my love. He just can't seem to give it up. Is he obsessed with her? That he used to have her and now he can't?

"What are you doing here? I won't have you near Becca. Go away and leave her alone. Stop watching her and get away from us. If I have to, I will take out a restraining order against you. I'm not joking. Stay away, or I will do everything I can to make you leave her alone. She doesn't want to have anything to do with you anymore. She is not married to you and she's mine now."

Tripp doesn't back down, saying, "There's nothing you can do. I am here simply waiting to see the Fourth of July fireworks tonight. I can stand wherever I want. You can't stop me. It's a public place, and I haven't talked to her or bothered her at all. Go ahead, call your lawyer, and threaten me all you want. I can do what I want. I'm not breaking any law."

"Don't mess with me, or I will make sure you regret it. Mark my words. Go find somewhere else to watch the fireworks. Now."

I stand there threateningly until he finally turns and leaves, disappearing into the crowd and the darkness. When I return to Becca, she is upset because she witnessed our exchange even though she was too far away to hear our words.

"What happened? I didn't know why you suddenly got out of your seat. At first I couldn't see who you were talking with because it was dark, and you were blocking my view. I couldn't believe it when I caught a glimpse of Tripp. Did he say what he was doing?"

"He is just here to see the fireworks. I didn't like him being here near us, so I asked him to leave. Eventually, he did."

I try to calm her down and tell her he is gone. She doesn't know why he was here. I can't really relax and enjoy the fireworks display since I can't help scanning all the people around us. I was glad when the evening was over, and I could take her home.

A week later, one evening in mid-July, Becca says she wants to go to the College Bookstore to pick up some books she has ordered. I say I'll take her because I don't want her going by herself when it is almost dark. We park in the lot behind the Cheese Shop and walk over to the bookstore. I soon lose sight of her as she goes to retrieve and purchase her books. I know from experience that she will be wandering the store for a while.

I glance over the military history books, killing time until she comes to find me. She knows where to find me. Time goes by until it seems to me she is taking a little too long tonight to come and get me. The store is actually about to close. I stand up, walk to the center aisle, and start scanning for the sight of her. I start to walk, looking down each side aisle. Then I hear a noise, the sound of a struggle, coming from ahead of me in the next side aisle.

Recognizing my wife's voice immediately, I hear her cry out, "Let me go! Stop! Stop it! Let go of me! You asshole! No, no, stop!"

I race forward, turning the corner as fast as I can. I spot Becca struggling to get away from Tripp, his hand clamped tightly around her wrist. She twists and turns, trying to get him to release her.

He's looking at her wedding rings and snarling at her. "You married the bastard? *You fucking married him?*"

Becca is screaming and kicking and slapping and scratching as hard as she can as she struggles against his grip.

No one touches what is mine! Come on, Becca, stick your knee up hard in his crown jewels.

He looks up and spies me racing toward him menacingly, the intense rage clear in my eyes.

He dares to touch my wife, hurting her. I've got to stop him, get Becca safely out of his hands.

He roars at me furiously. "*You're* the fucking bastard that is always around her, always in my way. Always fucking there, touching her, kissing her. I want you gone, you bastard. She's mine. I had her first!" He swiftly lets go of Becca as she throws herself in my direction. I step between them, protecting her.

And unbelievably, I suddenly see a quick glimpse, a flash of steel before Tripp stabs me hard, twice in my left shoulder. It happens so fast, and I really wasn't expecting that. I hate that he's caught me slightly off guard. I should have been better prepared. I train for this. It surprises me that he has a knife. He has shown premeditation by coming prepared with a weapon. I have no weapon with me other than my martial arts training and strength.

He's stronger than I thought, but I'm faster. Not even feeling my shoulder, I quickly disarm him, wrenching the knife out of his hand by twisting his wrist backwards, punching him hard in the jaw before throwing my leg around and kicking him brutally on the side of his head with my boot. I'm so fast that I don't think he knows what hit him.

My elbow comes up to block his ineffectual punch. I push my fingers, hard into the pressure point on his chest, making him swiftly pass out without warning. It's actually all over in a heartbeat. I am feeling stunned by the suddenness of his attack and my response.

He slumps to the floor heavily, cracking his skull sickeningly against the metal bookcases and then the stone tiles as he falls. I stand over him, holding him down with my knee in his chest, but he's unconscious, blood pouring out of his matted skull. It's forming a puddle beneath his head.

I stand up, turning to see if Becca is okay. She has her hand pressed to her mouth, trying not to scream as she stares as me in horror. I look down and realize that I am covered in blood, my chest slick with it.

Where did that all come from?

"Oh my God, oh my God! Somebody call 911, call 911! Michael, Michael, are you okay? Sit down, baby, please. I'll help you. You're going to be fine. Stay with me, look at me, stay with me, honey. I'm here, I'm here with you."

I can hear the complete panic in her voice. Suddenly we're surrounded by people, but I can't think about that. I see yellow spots before me and feel faint before I can sit down like Becca said to do. She has her sweet arms around me, trying to ease me down to the floor gently. All I can see is her worried, beautiful green eyes as she holds me close.

Everything goes dark in front of me, fading away, and I'm gone, falling, lost in the deep, thick, dark fog. Utter darkness descends upon me. Gone.

CHAPTER

44

Holy Hell! I'm Hospitalized!

Flickering images, drifting. The feel of soft hands touching me, stroking my face, my cheeks, running fingers through my stubble.
I sleep in darkness.
Gentle whispers. "Baby, I miss you. Come back to me. Wake up for me. Open your eyes and let me see you. I'm here, honey. Know that I am right beside you. I love you, Michael, I love you so much. I need you

here. Open your eyes. I haven't left you. I'm holding your hand. Can you feel me?"

I can't open my eyes, falling deeper and deeper into the darkness.

Hands touching me, turning me, touching my shoulder. It aches; don't touch me. Sharp pains, then cooling hands. Ice chips between my lips. It seems as though I can feel a needle prick my arm. My shoulder really hurts.

Ouch. I dream, confused and alone.

"Michael, Michael, can you hear me? I don't know what to do without you."

Voices in the distance, in the fog surrounding me. I think I recognize that voice. Its huskiness calls to me, willing me to wake up somehow.

"Doctor, how much longer? How long before he wakes? Please tell me, I need him to wake up."

I struggle but can't shake the fog.

I slowly open my eyes, squinting through narrowed eyes, swallowing, not knowing where I am, confused and disoriented.

Thirsty, too thirsty. Do I have to pee? Umm. Can't think about that right now.

I'm in a strange room with light green walls and a light behind me on the wall above my head. I gradually realize I'm lying in a hospital bed, my head slightly elevated. There seems to be a thick bandage covering my left shoulder.

I can feel Becca's hand in mine. My wife's hand, the hand I'd know anywhere. She's sitting in a chair next to my bed, with her head down on the bed next to my chest. One hand is under her cheek, pillowing her head. I can hear her breathing softly, her eyes closed in sleep.

I frown at her when I notice she doesn't look so good. Never thought I'd say it, but she's pale, too pale, with dark circles under her eyes and a worried frown on her face even while she's asleep. That soft *v* is between her eyebrows. I want to kiss it away. Her clothes are rumpled, and she looks unkempt. She's a bit of a mess.

I peel my hand out of her grip and place it gently on her hair, running my fingers through the soft strands. She stirs, jerks up, and suddenly her green eyes fly open, staring at me.

"Michael, oh baby, you're awake. Finally. I've been so worried and missed you so much. Thank God you're back with me now. I don't know

A Real Love At Last

what to do without you. I never want to live without you. God, if you had, if you had died, I'd die, too. I'm so glad to see you, my love."

Yes, apparently I am awake now and no longer dreaming in a misty fog.

"What . . . happened? Where are we? Why are we here? It's all a bit of a blur, baby. I can't really remember. What happened to me?"

She looks at me intently before replying, "You're in Sentara Hospital now, darling. We were in the College Bookstore two nights ago. Do you remember that? I was wandering around the store, looking at books when suddenly Tripp was in front of me. I didn't see him until he was there right in front of me. I didn't know what he wanted, why he seemed so mad. He was furious with me, I think, because it was the anniversary of when I married him. No clue what he wanted. I married him on July 12, that same day. Maybe that is why he came looking for me. I don't know how he found us. I can't imagine that he was somehow following me, but he appeared without any warning."

She pauses briefly and then continues. "When he saw my wedding rings, he seemed to snap somehow and grabbed my left wrist and started screaming at me. I tried to get away, but he was too strong. It was all so sudden, and I couldn't believe what was happening. He just seemed to come out of nowhere. One minute I was alone, and the next thing I knew he had a tight hold of my wrist and was yelling at me for marrying you after he saw my rings."

"I guess there was no way he knew we had gotten married before that night. I certainly never told him because I haven't talked to him since we finalized the divorce with our lawyers. He was hurting me, squeezing my wrist so hard. I slapped him with my free hand and tried to scratch my nails down his face. I was kicking and screaming as loudly as I could."

"You came running, and before I could even realize what was happening, Tripp stabbed . . . he stabbed you twice in your left shoulder with a knife. I had no idea he had a weapon hidden somewhere. I didn't see it until it was too late. You knocked him out, but then passed out, from the sudden blood loss, I think. I tried to catch you when you fell, but you're so heavy. I managed to get you to the floor, but blood was pumping out of your shoulder in spurts by then."

"Michael, there was suddenly . . . so much blood, I couldn't stop it with my hands. It all happened so fast, like a blur. I think I went a bit into shock, unable to really process what had happened. I can't believe he actually stabbed you. I have really misjudged him all these years. I just didn't think he was capable of such violence. Suddenly there were people all around us. I was holding your head in my lap while they called for help."

Becca closes her eyes as she remembers. "There was just so much blood. People tried to give me their scarves to put over your wound, to try and stop the bleeding. The fire station is just around the corner, so it wasn't long before medical help arrived. The police were called since it was a stabbing. I guess they talked to people who saw what happened after I started screaming."

"Thank goodness the ambulance came quickly and took us here to the hospital. When we got to the emergency room, the doctors finally came out and told me you needed immediate surgery since Tripp had sliced one of the major blood vessels in your shoulder. You've been unconscious ever since. It's been a nightmare."

Serious surgery? Seriously? Shit.

"How long . . . how long have I been out? And can I have something to drink? I'm really thirsty. I need some water."

"Two days, honey. I've been here with you the whole time. I never left you alone. The longest two days of my life. I've been so worried about you." She brings me ice chips, saying she doesn't know if I am allowed to have a glass of water yet.

I hope she asks the nurse soon because I am really thirsty. I need a big glass of cold water.

I struggle to think clearly. "Where is Tripp? Did they take him to jail for attacking us? Were the police called? Did they arrest him?"

She takes a deep breath, holding it before slowly exhaling. "From what I could tell, they transported him here to the hospital the same time as us. I really wasn't paying much attention since all I could focus on was you. I knew they took him into the emergency room."

She looks at me gently. "Yesterday, a police officer came to talk to me here. He wanted my statement about what happened. I told him everything, even all the incidents we've had with him. I found out he was severely injured. Evidently from traumatic brain injury, I guess, when he cracked his skull on the floor. He may also have hit it on the sharp edge of the metal bookcases as he fell. No one has told me. There was a lot of blood on him, under his head and on the floor. I tried not to look. I was too concerned about you, darling, to pay close attention to what was happening to him."

"The police have been investigating. Of course, there are no legal charges since he attacked you first. It was obviously self-defense. I believe he will be arrested and taken to jail when he is well enough to be released from the hospital. I guess we will have to go to court to testify against him. He's gone, Michael. He will be in jail soon. He's gone. It's over. Don't worry anymore. I'm glad it is over."

I look back at her, trying to process all this information. I only remember bits and pieces, images in my mind. Maybe I'll remember more later. All I really feel is a deep sense of relief. I wasn't trying to hurt him badly, only enough to protect Becca. It was an accident on my part.

I am not sorry he was arrested and placed in jail, not sorry he's unable to be free. He did stab me twice and obviously had planned it out since he came equipped with a knife. Somehow he must have found out where we lived and followed us to the bookstore that night. Finally, he's gone out of our lives. Hopefully, time in prison will teach him to leave us alone.

I grab Becca's hand back in mine, feeling stronger by the minute. "Let's go home. Take me home, baby. I want to go home with you. Now."

"Honey, you just woke up; they're not going to let me take you home yet. You need to recuperate here at the hospital where the nurses can take care of you. You've lost a lot of blood. I know you must be weak. The doctors operated on you. You need blood and an IV to bring up your fluids. You've had a morphine drip. The nurses finally removed it this morning."

"You can take care of me, honey. You're all I need to get better." She nods, but I know I won't get my way, not yet. I resign myself to more time in the hospital and following doctors' orders.

I realize I have to hold her, hold my wife. "Come and lay down here next to me. I need to have you closer. There's room. Come on."

She hesitates, not sure if she is allowed in my hospital bed, but then slips off her shoes and gently stretches out next to me on my right side. I can hold her with my right arm as she settles into the crook of my arm. I can see she's being very careful around the bandage on my left shoulder.

The song "How to Save a Life" by The Fray, from the television show *Grey's Anatomy*, runs through my mind. This show is a medical drama about doctors at a hospital in Seattle, Washington. It seems fitting to me to have that song on repeat in my confused brain. Someone apparently had to save my life. And I know Becca has already saved it as well.

I hold her, just breathing and relaxing in the knowledge that she is close to me with her head on my shoulder and her hand on my heart, feeling it beat strong and steady. This is one of her favorite spots; I can stay like this forever. I'm feeling better by the minute.

She reaches up and puts her hand on my face, cupping my cheek and running her fingers through my stubble gently. I know she loves to do that. I love for her to touch me, feeling her touch the rough yet soft bristles. I reach up with my left hand, wincing a bit with a sharp pain, but it's bearable.

I can stand a little discomfort for what I have in mind. It's so worth it.

I am awake, it's all over now, and my wife is in my arms.

Could it be any better?

I gently begin to run my fingers over and over her cleavage, stroking between her breasts, across her nipples, and cupping her fullness. I need to feel her, to feel that connection we have and know that I am alive. I'm about to slide my fingers inside her blouse when she suddenly giggles and tries to twist away from my hand.

"Michael. Michael. My God, you're insatiable. Stop. Get a grip. We're in the hospital. The door is open. The nurses or doctors can come in at any time. You just had major surgery, for goodness' sake. What am I going to *do* with you, Stevens? Rest, please. You need to wait. Get well first."

"I've been resting, evidently for two days now. I need to feel you and know we are safe together. And as for what you can do with me, well, . . . *anything* you want, Mrs. Stevens. Remember?"

"Yes, yes, I remember. Right now I want you to cooperate and get well. I need you home with me ASAP, Marine. I want you strong and well again."

I am released two days later.

A little surgery can't stop me from living my life. From loving her.

CHAPTER 45

River Walk in San Antonio, TX

By the first part of August, I am feeling much, much stronger. We have been contacted by the police again, and statements have been taken not only from us but also from other witnesses in the bookstore that night. I contact my lawyer, but the wheels of justice move slowly. We simply wait to see what will happen next, not knowing if we will have to go to court and testify against Tripp.

He was denied bail and is in regional jail. I hope he has plenty of time to ponder his situation and actions. I have no real ill will toward him, but I am very, very glad he is unable to get to us again. I am still shocked he took his obsession as far as he did. Perhaps he will regret the way he has treated a very lovely woman who once loved him.

Since I like to show my wife off, I decide we need to go to Texas for some Western fun. She seems delighted when I tell her my plans. Elizabeth makes our flight and hotel reservations for three days in San Antonio. We fly out of Norfolk International Airport and have to change planes in Atlanta before landing in San Antonio.

The Marriott's hotel shuttle takes us to our hotel on the city's famous River Walk. The small river that runs through the middle of the city is lined with Tex-Mex restaurants, hotels, cute stores, and even a small amphitheater for live concerts, dancing, and other entertainment. We check in our room.

Becca immediately wants to tour the Alamo, the mission that was the site of a horrible thirteen-day siege between Texas independence patriots and the Mexican army in 1836. Again, my wife astonishes me with her never-ending historical knowledge. She knows about this battle very well.

We walk from our hotel to find the stone mission of the Alamo. From old movies, I expected it to be out in the middle of nowhere. It actually is on a busy street, looking small surrounded by modern buildings. The Alamo itself is still standing with very little of the protecting walls left around it. There is a beautiful green garden behind it with lovely bushes and old trees.

We approach the large wooden front door. Becca points out the historical marker which restates Col. William Travis's letter asking for reinforcements that never came for him. We see the line drawn in the sand, now in the permanent sidewalk, where anyone who wanted to leave before the Mexican army lay siege to them could. William Travis, Jim Bowie of the famous Bowie knife, and Davy Crockett all died here, defending the Alamo and fighting for Texas independence from Mexico. These men are revered in San Antonio.

We tour the museum inside. They have plenty of displays about the famous battle as well as artifacts such as Crockett's long rifle. These men were vastly outnumbered, 136 defenders versus the whole Mexican army. The fact they lasted as long as they did is amazing. We find out they were all killed when the Mexican army overran it. Davy Crockett died defending the front door. The Texans rallied after it using "Remember the Alamo" as their battle cry. The Mexicans were defeated in a quick battle at San Jacinto. The Mexican General Santa Ana was caught disguised as a woman trying to escape.

After the tour, we stop and go in small Western jewelry stores across the street. Becca sees a pair of turquoise and silver earrings I can tell she likes. I immediately buy them for her as a memory of our visit here. Next, we head back to the River Walk. We take the touristy boat tour, which travels the lazy river and ends up back where we started. It is beautiful and peaceful to float the narrow winding river at the heart of San Antonio.

By this time I am hungry for dinner. We find a restaurant with umbrella-covered tables right next to the river. I order a large beef-and-cheese burrito while Becca wants guacamole.

Eww.

The waiter rolls out a tray on wheels and stops at our table. The wooden bowl is filled with avocadoes. He proceeds to make a show of fixing her guacamole from scratch. When he is done, Becca claps and gives it a try. She loves the fresh taste of the prepared dish.

"Open your mouth, Michael. I want you to try this."

"No, thanks."

Nope.

"Are you sure? It's really good. It's good for you, too."

"I've heard that, but I'll pass."

"You won't even try it? Why not?"

"Honey, not so crazy about slimy green food."

"It's not slimy. Not at all. It's creamy. There is a difference."

"Looks slimy to me."

Green slime.

"Have you ever tried it before?"

"Well, no, actually. I never have."

Nope.

"This is your chance. I try new experiences with you all the time."

Umm. What other new things can I have her experience with me?

"I know. It is one of the many things I love about you, my love."

"Then trust me. You do trust me, don't you?"

What?

"Yeesss."

"Open up those sexy lips of yours, Marine. I want to put something in your mouth. Let me."

I don't know about this.

"Gosh, honey, does it have to be slimy green avocadoes that you want to put into me? I can think of many other things I would like to taste in my mouth."

I trust her, but I know I am done for. She is stubborn and is not giving up until she makes me put that green slime in my mouth.

"You don't believe me then. I wouldn't make you eat something that tastes disgusting. I love it and I want to share with you. Come on, brave Marine. Show me some of that courage I know you have inside of you."

There is no way out of this situation. I am going to have to eat the damn guacamole.

"Okay, Mrs. Stevens. I surrender. I trust in your good taste. Let me have it so I can get this over with and enjoy the rest of my dinner."

Okay. Just do it quickly so I can swallow it whole.

She looks at me, thinking. I watch her take a triangular corn nacho chip in her hand and scoop the green slimy stuff on it. She raises her hand with the sample up close to her mouth and then shockingly leans over very close to my mouth. The guacamole-laden chip is millimeters from each of our lips. I get her idea now. We are taking bites of the chip from opposite sides so that our lips meet in the middle. Maybe this won't be so bad after all.

She watches me as I stare at her. She nods slightly, and our mouths open simultaneously. I close my eyes to block out the sight of slimy green mess. We both bite down at the same time. Our mouths fill with the guacamole and crunchy chip but meet when our lips touch.

I don't care we are dripping it down between us. I chew and swallow with her and then kiss her flavored mouth. It's a unique flavor, unlike anything I have ever tried before. It is creamy, and the crunch of the nacho contrasts in my mouth.

She is kissing me back passionately; neither one of us the least bit concerned about the boatload of tourists cruising by us on the river. I hear a few wolf whistles and encouragements but don't stop kissing my wife until we can no longer breathe.

So there, Mrs. Stevens. I am brave enough to take you on. Go ahead. Bring it.

Nighttime descends as we make our way back to our hotel. The River Walk sparkles with colorful lights and bustling activities. We are both tired as we prepare for bed and pass out completely before I can even think.

The next morning I wake up my wife with her very own Western bull-riding contest. The symbol for San Antonio is the bull. They can be found all over the city, different colors and styles decorating them. Statues of bulls with curved sharp horns guarding street corners and businesses.

I am as strong as a bull. She grabs on to my horns and rides away.

After a late start that morning, we head over to the old elegant Menger Hotel for breakfast. It is where Teddy Roosevelt stayed while gathering his Rough Riders for the Spanish–American War in Cuba back in 1898. Supposedly Robert E. Lee also stayed there when he was an engineer in the U.S. Army. It has a stunning old carved massive dark wood bar in a room off the lobby. The bartender points out a bullet hole in the wooden wall near the bar. Evidently, things got a bit rough there with the Rough Riders.

We wander around, viewing a movie about the siege of the Alamo and then taking a trolley ride around the city. The river meanders back and forth like a snake through San Antonio. The Spanish settlers built several stone missions along the banks of the river.

We get off to tour one such mission. It has the full protective stone wall in place with the mission itself tucked safely inside. The Spanish priests were in the awkward position of wanting to bring religion to the local Indians, using them as almost slaves, and protecting themselves from the Comanches at the same time. We wander the stone walkways, admiring the arches and intricately carved Rose Window in the mission church itself. There is actually a wedding in progress in the church, so we do not go in. This is still an active religious denomination among the locals.

We take the trolley back to our hotel after stopping at two more missions. I suggest a very late lunch, early dinner. We end up at a fun restaurant on the River Walk and enjoy tacos and beer. For dessert, we order a vanilla ice cream fudge sundae and share it.

The mall connected to our hotel is a regular mall but has stores with Western jewelry, crafts, and cowboy boots. I realize people here actually wear cowboy hats and boots regularly. We look at the selection, amazed at all the styles and colors. My wife tries to get me to try a pair on, but I refuse. I wonder briefly if I should buy her a pair since she seems interested. Becca, naked except for cowboy boots with squared off toes and blocked heels, comes to my mind. I can almost imagine those cowboy boots on my shoulders.

Umm. Does she want some boots?

I watch her.

Yes, apparently she does. Not sure where she will wear them in Virginia, but okay.

I call the clerk over to get her fitted. She picks out a pair of brown leather ones with carvings designed on the top. She tries them on and walks back and forth across store for me to see and her to feel. Becca is surprised that they are comfortable on her feet. I purchase them immediately.

Since we ate so late in the day, we head back to the room in the Marriott to relax for the rest of the evening. We talk, get in our pj's we use when in strange hotels, and watch some movies on television. One movie after the other. It is late now and time for bed.

It takes me a while but I manage to get those cowboy boots on her again. Her nightgown is thrown off like a lasso. Before she can get away, I have her in position, and those cowboy boots are the only thing she has on. I pull them up on my shoulders next to my ears and enjoy my wife's shocked but delighted expression. We enjoy riding each other for most of the night before our Western rodeo is over.

Ride 'em, cowboy. Ride 'em, cowgirl. We both stay on much longer than the eight seconds of professional rodeo riders.

When we're done, we both burst out laughing and can't stop.

Two of Randy Houser's country songs play in my head the whole time as we make love in the Western town of San Antonio, Texas.

"Like a Cowboy." "Boots On."

I like my wife in her cowboy boots and nothing else. Riding my big cock bare-assed. Maybe I will pick up a pair of cowboy boots for me too. No spurs.

CHAPTER 46

Tied Up in Knots? Not Me!

Summer comes to a close with near misses by Atlantic hurricanes out spinning up the coast. August is hot and humid. Labor Day weekend finally arrives. I labor all day on the yard while Becca labors in the house. We spend some time laboring together.

Work, work, work. Isn't Labor Day weekend supposed to be a workless weekend?

It can be hard labor outdoors. I end up quite dirty and sweaty. But I quite enjoy the fruits of my labor. I am her husband, and it is my job to keep her happy, in all ways. I never need a day off or a vacation from this job. I will work at it all night long if I have to in order to make sure my wife is satisfied with the yard, the house, and me.

After both of us spend Sunday afternoon working in the house and yard, I join her in our shower to get some of the dirt and sweat off. As we dry off in the master bathroom, I treat my wife to her first orgasm on Labor Day weekend.

I stand in front of us with her fingers locked in mine above our heads. I have my back to the large bathroom mirror, and I know she can see our reflection in the mirror. She can see the muscles of my shoulders, back, ass, and thighs. I make love to her, watching her eyes as she watches my movements.

I hold her tightly as she shudders and almost falls with the force of her climax. I give her a little time and then pull her makeup chair in front of the mirror facing to the side. She sits obediently.

"What do you have planned next, my love?"

"Watch and see, honey. I will be right back."

I go in the bedroom and pull open her top dresser drawer. I grab a long blue silk scarf and come back to her.

"Baby, do you want to play some more? This time is for me, if you don't mind. Are you fine with that?"

"I see you have my scarf. What are you going to do with that, Mr. Stevens?"

"If you don't like this, please tell me, and I will stop immediately, okay?"

"You have me quite curious now, Marine. What is the scarf for?"

"Please put your hands behind the chair and link your fingers. I am going to loosely tie your wrists together. If you feel uncomfortable being unable to use your hands, tell me right away. It's okay. But I thought I'd like to make love to your mouth only, no hands from you. Your mouth, Becca."

"All right, honey, no hands. Tie away."

She places her hands behind the chair and links them together. This position pushes her breasts forward temptingly. I gently tie her wrists together wrapping the blue scarf around them before tying a big bow. She is ready and waiting.

"Are you sure, baby? I won't hurt you. I will be very careful, I promise."

She nods as she looks at my erection right in front of her face. I lean forward, and she gives me a hello lick. Her lips open for me. I slowly enter her warm mouth gently. I place my hands tenderly on her hair and begin to move very, very slowly. Her mouth slides back and forth on me. I turn and watch us in the mirror.

The sight is extremely erotic as I watch her orally give me pleasure. I watch me slide in and out of her lips. I last as long as I can, never thrusting or hurting her. The steady pace is getting harder and harder to control, but I never vary it, never slowing but never increasing either. Her hands are behind her; only her mouth is touching me.

My eyes are locked on our image in the mirror. I can tell she is enjoying doing this for me as she hums and moans in the back of her throat. The feeling and pressure builds inside, and I reach down and grab the base of my penis tightly as it continues to move in and out of her mouth gently but insistently.

It catches me by surprise, the sudden surge of pleasure as it bursts out of me. I hold her head still as I come, spurting everything I have into her welcoming mouth. I groan in pleasure as she swallows and licks me clean. To watch it all in the mirror, every moment of pleasure is seared into my consciousness forever.

I slide gratefully out of her and lean over the counter to catch my breath. She stands up for me to untie her wrists and then pulls me into a full body hug, whispering, "I love you."

We collapse into bed spooning, satisfied with our work this Labor Day weekend. I have worked her over, and she worked her magic on me. I never need time off from this job as her loving husband.

The house and yard are now exactly as we both want, ready for the colorful autumn. Becca says it is her favorite time of the year. She loves to watch the leaves change from green to yellow, red, and orange. We watch football, go on hikes in Newport News City Park, visit Lee Hall Mansion's wine festival, and enjoy the lovely Occasion for the Arts in Colonial Williamsburg and the Fall Festival in Newport News. We drive to a pumpkin patch on the Middle Peninsula to pick out our pumpkin for the front porch and later as a Halloween jack o' lantern.

By mid-October, we drive up to the Skyline Drive to see the colorful fall leaves drop at the tops of the Blue Ridge Mountains. We follow the curving scenic mountain road all the way to Luray. The soundtrack from *Phantom of the Opera* accompanies us. I wonder if it is still playing on Broadway in New York City. Maybe we can fly up there one weekend and enjoy the musical. Possibly *Jersey Boys* too. I will try to remember to look it up on the Internet when we get home.

I follow the signs that lead us to the famous Luray Caverns. Becca has toured these limestone caverns many times, but I have never seen them. She even took her class there once on a field trip. I purchase tickets before we follow the guide down the stairs into the cavern. We are down in the cool air of an underground limestone cave.

It is well lit with an easy-to-walk-on concrete path, handrails, and steps to climb. I am amazed at the colors of the limestone stalactites, stalagmites, and full columns surrounding us. The pale pink, rusty red, gray shades, and tan of the limestone shapes blend seamlessly from one color to the next.

We enter a large chamber deep within the cool cavern. It is huge, dominated by a tremendous column of limestone. It looks like an enormous thick candle made of limestone with streams of rock wax dripping down its sides everywhere. The guide explains that lovers often get married in this open space below ground. I am shocked when I hear strange music start to play, like an organ in church. The sounds are being produced by tiny hammers striking different-sized stalactites and stalagmites to make them vibrate. It is a magical eerie sound produced by nature.

Around the third weekend in October, we have our first, real, serious disagreement. I am surprised when Becca informed me she is going out. I ask where, but I guess I shouldn't have done that. She is halfway out the door with her car keys dangling in her hand. She murmurs she is going to see Woody. Then she is gone, leaving me confused and frankly fuming.

Who the hell is Woody? A man or a woman?

I hope Woody is a man but . . . maybe not?

A man named Woody is not someone I am comfortable with my wife seeing.

A woman called Woody is . . . downright terrifying.

I have no idea where Becca is going, who she is going to be with, and when she will return. It is hours later when her car pulls back in the driveway.

I am now royally pissed at her.

She comes in and says she will fix dinner in a little bit. No mention of her afternoon appointment if that was what it was.

With some person named Woody. Damn.

I wait until after dinner and help her clean the kitchen. When we are done, we go into the great room for the evening news and Becca's book.

I cannot stand it a moment longer.

"Honey, who is Woody?"

Yes, tell me who this Woody you spent the afternoon talking with is to you.

She hesitates but then says, "He's my financial advisor."

Okay. Finances. I handle the finances for the most part. Woody is a man, damn it, I guess.

"Why do you need a financial advisor?"

"I have some investments of my own. I have been taking care of them since Tripp left. Woody helps me, and it was time for a review."

What kinds of investments? IRAs? Stocks? Bonds? Mutual funds?

"Is his company in Newport News, Hampton, or Williamsburg?"

"It's down in Newport News."

"What did he say?"

"Everything's fine."

"Becca, I would like to meet him. Please call and set up an appointment for us both to talk to him."

I want to see this Woody fellow myself.

"No."

"No?"

What?

"No."

"Goddamn it, Becca, don't you say no to me. I am your husband, and I promised to take care of you. I need to know what is going on."

I don't like secrets between us. I am an open book. She knows it all and then some.

"No, you don't. It is my money and my business. I can handle it. Don't cuss at me. Stay out of my business."

"Your business? Everything about you is my fucking business. So we are not equals in our marriage. I gave you my name, my heart, my love, my soul, my money. It is all for you. But now I find it is different with you. I have changed my will in case something were to happen to me. We do not have a pre-nup, so if God forbid you divorce me, you can have every cent. I won't need it if you are gone."

"I just . . . I just want to have control of the money I tried so hard to save on my own. And you know I hate it when you use the word 'fucking.'"

I'm sorry. I don't want to be the kind of husband who cusses at his wife. It is just I am not used to this defiance from her.

"I get it. This is your real backup plan. You don't trust me deep down to take care of you. You think I will leave financially ruined like your asshole ex. That just isn't going to happen. But I see I cannot force you to trust me. It saddens me that you feel like this. I trust you with my life. Give me the same privilege."

She takes a deep breath. "It's not that I don't trust you. I don't know why I kept it a secret from you. I just need to, that's all. Now leave it alone. It is my business. I'm sorry, but that is the way I feel."

She has left me no choice now.

There is nothing left for me to say. I clam up, refusing to talk. She clams up, refusing to talk. I look at the nightly news but don't hear a thing. She looks at her book but doesn't ever turn a page. She is not really reading at all.

I am stubborn and so is she. Neither one of us wants to be the first to give in. The evening passes in total silence. I am a little shocked she is taking it this far, but I am not giving in. I am the hurt party in this. She hurt me, not the other way around. It is up to her to give in and apologize.

She gets up quietly and goes back to the bedroom to go to bed. I check the doors and make my way to join her. I am faced with a closed door and a pillow and blanket on the floor in front of it.

Apparently, she is really pissed.

Suddenly, it strikes me as funny. I chuckle softly. The last thing I need is for her to think I am laughing at her. I can't believe she has actually thrown me out of our bed.

Now what do I do? Do I knock? I wonder if the door is locked.

I try it quietly and find out yes, it is locked.

Fuck.

I am going to have to sleep in another room or evidently she wants me on the damn sofa.

To hell with this.

I knock.

No answer.

I knock.

No answer.

I feel as though she has me all tied up in knots.

I know she is in there and she can hear me.

"Becca, let me in. This has gone far enough. Now let me in."

"No!" I hear.

Shit. I try to be gentle and understanding.

"Honey, I'm your husband. I love you. Please let me in. I need to sleep with you. Please."

"No, I don't want to tonight. Go find someplace else to park your nosey ass."

So I am nosey. I thought she liked my ass though.

"I was not being nosey. I was being concerned. There is a difference."

"Don't be all full of masculine logic. You know I hate it when you do that. I am emotional right now. It is best if you just leave me alone. Give me some time and I will get over it eventually."

"How long do you need? A half hour? An hour?"

Please let it be over soon so I can sleep with her in our bed.

"Oh, go away. I need all night. Just go sleep somewhere else and let me calm down. I will think better tomorrow."

I knew she was going to say that. She wouldn't have put the bedding out if she was intending otherwise.

I don't know what to say.

"All right. But this is first time we haven't sleep together in many, many months. I will not be sleeping. If you change your mind, please come find me. I need to hold you to fall asleep, you know."

"I know. But not tonight, please. I'm sorry. Not tonight."

"I love you. Please stop being mad at me for trying to do my job as your husband. I can't take it when you push me away."

It breaks me so much.

"I love you too. But I have said all I am going to say to you tonight. Good night. I will see you in the morning."

And that's it. She is done and gone.

Gwen Stefani's song "Early Winter" starts to play in my memory. All I can recall at the moment is Gwen's voice singing the main chorus.

The sun's getting cold, it's starting to snow
It looks like an early winter for us
It looks like an early winter for us
An early winter . . .

Yes, it might say autumn on the calendar, but it is a damn cold winter in my home right now.

I take my nosey, lonely ass back to the great room where at least there is a television. I have my pillow and a blanket. I prepare myself for a marathon of late-night talk shows and movies. I don't sleep at all, actually a bit shocked at what is on television in the middle of the night.

It just serves to make me miss my wife even more. I have been banished to the cold, lonely great room and an uncomfortable-to-sleep-on couch.

I spend time on my laptop, watching the music video for *"Locked Out of Heaven"* by Bruno Mars. I can relate.

'Cause your sex takes me to paradise
Yeah, your sex takes me to paradise
And it shows, yeah, yeah, yeah
'Cause you make me feel like I've been locked out of heaven

Around six in the morning, as the sun brightens the eastern sky, I go and stand in front of the bedroom door and listen with my ear pressed against it.

No sound or movement from within her fortress.

I slide down the wall opposite the door to await my wife. I sit and stare at the door.

I am tired.

My eyes droop once, then twice, then down in sleep.

Becca finds me at eight asleep in front of the door. I wake up to her arms helping me to my feet. She embraces me and kisses me softly before taking me into the room and tucking me in under the covers.

I am at last back where I belong.

She climbs in and spoons herself against me so I can relax and sleep. She says nothing, other than a very soft "I'm sorry."

Our fight is over.

We go to see Woody, the financial wizard extraordinaire, the very next week. He works for Financial Command in a new office off of Canon Boulevard near the Marriott Hotel in Newport News. I like him and feel much better about Becca's nest egg of which she is justifiably proud. I can tell they like and know each other very well. Becca asks him about his wife and two boys who are into extreme water sports. He teases her about retiring from teaching. It is clear he knows she didn't like it anymore and is glad she is out from under all that pressure. They laugh a lot and tease each other, but he also covers a great deal of her portfolio, pointing out that it is diversified nicely.

I think about letting him handle things for me as well.

October comes to a close, and on the Friday before Halloween, Becca tells me we are going on a Ghost Walk in Olde Towne Portsmouth. It is a lovely tree-filled neighborhood on the Elizabeth River, filled with homes from the 1700s and 1800s. We park and go to Trinity Church for the start of the tour. Our guide has a lighted lantern as we follow him through the church cemetery and then down the narrow sidewalks of Olde Towne.

As we pass the Confederate monument dedicated to the Portsmouth boys who fought and died for the South at the Battle of Malvern Hill, I suddenly see Yankees ahead. In the middle of Court Street, we are stopped by men on horseback dressed as Union soldiers. They do not want us to pass. Portsmouth was largely occupied by the North during the War Between the States. Finally we are allowed to pass.

We follow the guide down the narrow dark streets, stopping at certain houses to hear the ghost story from that particular location. The people telling the stories are dressed in period costumes. They are actors and actresses from the Wells Theater, and they know exactly how to tell a scary story.

We hear about ghosts wandering the operating room in the Naval Hospital, ghosts running up and down stairs, standing at the foot of someone's bed, slamming doors, and the ghosts of escaped slaves on the Underground Railroad as they tried to hide in the underground sewers below the city.

All in all, we enjoyed at least a dozen different spooky ghost stories before ending up in a small park hidden between the houses on Middle Street. We are then treated to iced sugar cookies and a hot paper cup full of apple cider ladled from an iron cauldron over an open fire.

Fun, fun, Halloween-type fun.

The next evening, we pass out candy to the young costumed trick-or-treaters who come knocking at our door on Halloween night.

Coldplay's "Ghost Stories" is a beautiful song. I like the idea of our spirits continuing on after we die. Not necessarily as ghosts, but souls forever in heaven together.

I receive a phone call from my lawyer concerning Tripp's attack. Turns out he has plea-bargained his charge of malicious wounding. He waves his rights to a jury trial and is found guilty as charged. He is sent to prison for the next five years and fined as well.

Becca cries a bit on hearing the news, sad that it has come to this for someone she thought she loved once, but mostly she cries in relief that the ordeal is finally over.

One Saturday in November, my wife surprises me with airline tickets to Asheville, North Carolina, in the western Smoky Mountains of that state. I am not sure what she has planned. I have never been to the western part of North Carolina.

We end up staying at the gray fieldstone built Grove Park Inn. Becca has us booked for a room on the exclusive top floor. We even need a special code to get the elevator to reach our floor. Not only is the room elegant in a mountain kind of way, but we are treated to a free happy hour before dinner that night.

Becca has a tee time arranged for us tomorrow morning and rented golf clubs. We set out on a crisp clear autumn morning, making tracks in the dew still on the fairway grass. The colorful mountains of North Carolina are all around us. We laugh and giggle our way around the course, losing many golf balls along the way. Becca's balls are often in the water, and mine hide in the trees. But we persevere until we finish all the holes. We stop at the 19th Hole Clubhouse for a refreshing drink.

That afternoon we tour the grand French-style chateau known as the Biltmore Estate. It is a lovely home filled with countless rooms, libraries, a formal dining room, fireplaces, a bowling lane, an exercise room, and the downstairs servants' quarters needed to run such a huge home. The structured gardens are still blooming somewhat, and we buy an ice cream cone of the Biltmore's own variety of ice cream produced at the dairy on the property.

Delicious dinner back at the Grove Park Inn with my endlessly funny, clever, and quick-witted wife. That night I make sure she gets the full treatment of Northern Lights courtesy of me. I explore all the northern regions of her body above the Mason–Dixon Line known as Becca's belly button. By the time I have explored the Northern Territory well, she is urging me to head south. Since I am from the South, I oblige my Becca's request. Below the border I go.

She is a true Southern belle, and I make sure I ring her bell loudly over and over again. She clangs with a sweet musical tone.

North Carolina. North. Yeah. North Carolina is a southern state with a northern name.

The song "*Northern Lights*" by Cider Sky comes to mind. It is from the *Breaking Dawn Part 2* soundtrack. Becca loves to listen to that soundtrack in her car frequently.

I want to fly, fly into this beautiful life
I think it would be nice with you

I want to fly into this beautiful life, I think it would be nice with you
With you, with you, with you.
Yes, definitely. Yes.
I agree wholeheartedly with the song's lyrics.

CHAPTER 47

Cinderella's Castle

    We make it through Thanksgiving with the family once again visiting. I am filled with such gratitude this year, thankful for my lovely wife and surrounded by her family and friends. December is a blur of Christmas preparations beside the normal Grand Illumination fireworks that signal the start of the holiday celebrations of Colonial Williamsburg.

I have a Christmas celebration of my own planned for us. It is now the one-year anniversary of my proposal and her acceptance. We are going to Germany for a quick week of sightseeing before Christmas. We make sure everything is ready for the holidays because we will not be returning until two days before Christmas Day.

We fly across the ocean and land in Frankfurt, Germany. It is not hard to make our way to a picturesque German town next to a river called Heidelberg. Becca and I check in to our hotel and spend the day wandering the pedestrian main street and ending up touring the castle up on the hill. It looks over the town of Heidelberg with imposing dominance.

I love looking in all the little shops downtown. European cities do a great job of preserving their cities' historic centers by closing them off to vehicle traffic. The center then becomes an oasis of past calm protected from modern hustle and bustle. Heidelberg is great, and we enjoy eating in a charming German restaurant before returning to sleep.

Over the next few days, in a rented car, we make our way around the country and tour whatever we fancy. Rottenberg is a medieval walled city that delights Becca. We find a Christmas shop where she purchases a German ornament to put on our tree when we get home. The narrow streets and alleys, the pastry shops filled with tempting desserts displayed openly in their windows, the town square with its town hall, and plenty of tourists wandering around just like we are. A town crier beckons us to the center of the city for the clock tower performance.

Munich is fascinating. Becca says she remembers the Summer Olympics that were held there in the seventies. I remember those Olympics because of the senseless terrorist attacks on the Israeli athletes in the Olympic village. She keeps mentioning the gold-medal-covered swimmer Mark Spitz, a little too much for my comfort. I can swim too, you know.

I will show her my strokes tonight. I can breaststroke, backstroke, freestyle, dog-paddle if I have to. I think a little swimming competition is in order.

Dachau, the remnants of the German concentration camp, is right outside of Munich. Becca is interested in World War II because her dad and uncle served. She wants to see it even though I do not. It is a horrible place. The iron gates alone piss me off. It says "Work Shall Set You Free." It is simply cruelty at its finest. I struggle with this as we tour the museum, the barracks, and even the damn ovens.

How did this happen?
Germany is a wonderful country, with beautiful scenery and warm, friendly people. I come up with no answers. It just doesn't make sense, but war is senseless.
I know that for sure.
The tour of Dachau takes us to the early evening. We find a restaurant and a modern hotel for the night.
The swimming demonstration went quite well. I dove into the deep end and proceeded to stroke my way back and forth the length of the pool. I enjoyed the breaststroke the most, but I think Becca liked the freestyle on me. I tried hard to win, but Becca was with me neck and neck in the competition. We both touched the edge of the pool at the same time and tied for the win.
A gold medal performance for us both.
More than one gold medal.
Two each.
No silver or bronze for us.
I drive us south toward Bavaria. The landscape changes and becomes more mountainous. The small towns we visit are filled with delightful buildings, decorated with whimsical paintings and intricate carvings. Just beautiful. We meander, stopping to stay at elegant restaurants, eating lots of German potato salad and sausages, drinking beer out of the biggest steins I have ever tried to drink from. We visit the small Christmas markets set up in town squares and drink a hot red wine drink called Gluvine. One evening it starts to snow slightly as we walk around in this holiday wonderland.

That night we have our own snow-covered holiday celebration. Vanilla-ice-cream-covered peaks and valleys. The snow melts rapidly under the heat we generate between one another. I am not happy about sleeping in sticky sheets, but it is the price I have to pay. She is a delicious vanilla-flavored dessert. There is nothing plain about vanilla. It goes with everything.

I drive further into the German Alps. And then we find what I have been looking for: Neuschwanstein, King Ludwig's mountain castle. The castle that Walt Disney based Cinderella's castle on for his resort in Florida. We check in to a charming hotel in the small town nestled beneath the towering fairy-tale castle.

The next day, after a late start since I have to play Prince Charming fitting a shoe on Cinderella, we eat a leisurely breakfast. We wander the small city and buy tickets for the castle tour. A horse-drawn carriage takes us up the steep and winding narrow road leading to the castle. It is quite a lovely castle with turrets and secret passages and ornately decorated rooms.

Ludwig bankrupted the country to build himself several castles. He was a strange guy who ended up strangely dying. It is a murder mystery German royalty–style. Perhaps the German people had to stop his out-of-control spending somehow.

Becca loves the castle and buys souvenirs. We have a little lunch there in the castle's café. I love how happy she is, seeing a real royal castle hidden like a secret jewel among the mountains. When we return to our hotel, I purchase a framed watercolor print of the castle in winter. It will hang in our great room as a reminder of our German adventures.

We spend the night in our small inn beneath the castle. From our hotel room window, we can see Neuschwanstein with a clear full moon in the dark evening sky. In the opposite direction is another massive castle, this one belonging to King Ludwig's parents. It is lit at night.

We get ready for bed and turn out the lights. It is virtually pitch-black dark in our room, only the very faint glow of moonlight to help me distinguish any shapes at all. Becca is curled up on her side spooning me. I hear and feel her sigh happily as she relaxes. She whispers to me how much she enjoyed seeing the real Cinderella castle and that Germany is a beautiful country. I can hear her, feel her, smell her, but barely, barely see her. I find it strangely erotic that she is there with me in the dark, like a dream.

She wiggles her ass against me, trying to get comfortable but having quite an effect on me. I know what magic lies close at hand. I do not need a fairy godmother to turn her into a princess because she already is that for me.

I have just the magic wand necessary to make her feel like a true princess.

I hold her close, whispering to her how much I love her, my lips touching her ear. My tongue starts to explore the soft curves found there, and I breathe warmly into her right ear. I bite her ear lobe sparkling with the diamond earrings I gave her. She is covered in my diamonds; her ears and her hands proclaim she is mine.

I nuzzle the nape of her neck, the curve of her jaw, and the place where her throat meets her shoulder. She is starting to breathe a bit faster, and suddenly she turns, and her open mouth finds mine in the dark. Her neck is arched under my hand as I lift her chin so I can kiss her even more deeply.

By now, her fingers are running through my hair and massaging my scalp. I am starting to ache with desire, having long since become thick and rigid. My cock is knocking at her ass. She lifts her right leg slightly to give me access to her warmth between her thighs.

I press home, loving the feel of her engulfing me in moist heat. We rock together, slowly at first but then with more urgency as it becomes more and more intense. To feel everything and yet see very little is an amazing sensory experience. Because we are so deeply in the dark, the touch, the smell, the sound, and the taste become overwhelming. I can't keep quiet.

"Princess, oh baby, let me love you. This is where I belong, right here with you like this. You make me feel complete when we are together. I can never get enough, be deep enough, find the words to tell you the depth and strength of my love for you. Tell me you love me. Let me feel your body tell me you love me. Come for me, I need to feel you inside trembling for me and me alone. I love you."

She is moaning, gasping, and moving rapidly against me. I don't think she is capable of speech at this moment. I reach around and massage her wet folds over and over and over. She is lost in the sensations, reaching deeper and deeper inside to find that special place of total surrender to me. My fingers dip deeply inside her.

I feel her begin to flutter inside and fall over the edge. She stops moving against me as she holds her breath, and I bury myself in her to the absolute hilt of my now magic wand, trying to find the magic words and spell to make it all happen for her.

She is almost there.

I murmur quickly, "Please baby, I am about to lose all control. Come now!"

I hear her scream my name, and she violently thrashes in my arms. I feel my orgasm rush up inside me, and I spurt over and over inside her in a glorious release of physical bliss. We lose ourselves in our mutual sexual pleasure, knowing we are made for one another.

The glass slipper fits perfectly, proving she is my true love forever. The erotic image of my wife's long legs ending in a pair of crystal-clear high-heel slippers comes to mind. I mentally wrapped them around my neck and dive into her, charming her with all the charms I possess. A real damn Prince Charming just for my sweet Becca. *The fairy tale come true.*

"Oh, honey, I love you so much. You are my loving husband, the prince of my heart and soul. I adore you. I love being your wife and lover. I never knew such happiness would ever be possible for me. It is stunning to me. I am afraid I will wake up and find you were just a dream. A fantasy of the perfect man made just for me."

"Never going to happen, Becca. You are my dream come true. If this is a dream for us both, I hope we never awake from it."

I am her Prince Charming in the flesh. She is my real love, my princess, my Cinderella. Not a fairy tale at all. It's magic.

"True Love" and "Magic" by Coldplay are the perfect songs for this perfect moment.

CHAPTER 48

Real Love at Last—Really!

It's the middle of December, and we wake up to a cold, snowy Saturday morning. It is beautiful outside with the light dusting of snow sparkling like ice diamonds. It is a good day to stay in and watch movies. By the afternoon, we have had lunch and settle down on the sofa to watch a movie on DVD. We have steaming cups of hot chocolate with marshmallows and a piece of Dove milk chocolate at the bottom as a sweet surprise. They do that in Europe.

Becca picks *The Notebook,* starring Ryan Gosling as the perfect man who loves for a lifetime. It is a sweet, sweet movie, and she points out Charleston in the background, Boone Hall, and the Calhoun Mansion used as settings. Ryan's character is trying desperately to make the love of his life remember their love story. They had a unique way of meeting each other and fell in love over the summer but then are ripped apart from one another by circumstances. They slowly find their way back to each other after years apart.

My wife is wrapped in my arms and leaning against me with her legs on the sofa, knees slightly bent. I start caressing her and slip my right hand up her blouse to draw soft circles on her stomach as she enjoys the romantic movie. By now I am pretending to watch the movie because all my attention is on the sexy woman leaning against me. My fingers reach up and cup her right breast, finding a bra in the way. I check it out and can unsnap the front enclosure with one hand. Okay then, breasts exposed now. My palm caresses her pink peaks gently until I feel that little tight bud extend for me.

Oh yes.

She is breathing a bit faster now but otherwise is still focused on the movie. My left hand slowly descends upon her until it reaches the elastic waistband of her yoga pants. Thank goodness it is elastic. Sliding my fingers inside, I head straight for the hot pussy I know is there waiting for me, with knees slightly raised and apart for me. I find it and love how she feels for me. The Grand Canyon of red folds and deep gashes with a hidden treasure deep down inside if I can just go deep enough. I keep caressing her pink-tipped mounds like they are the Rocky Mountains just for me to climb.

I am getting so turned on now. She is as well and is starting to move her hips and sigh deeply as she grants me access to her secret woman places. It is simply amazing to me the differences in our bodies. I am hard and she is so soft; I melt into her. Her softness pillows me all over, and I just want to settle myself into her and ride away deep in her love. I want those legs around me and my cock moving inside her now. I reluctantly move both my hands away from her and hear Ryan passionately declare, "I want you, all of you . . ."

I gently slide from behind her and make sure she is comfortable before pulling her yoga pants down and off her. I swiftly remove the top and dangling bra so that she is completely exposed to me. She settles back staring at me as I unzip and pull out my aching cock. Her legs spread, and I see her smooth, waxed pink pussy wet and glistening for me in invitation. I can't resist lowering all of me onto her sweet softness and settle in deeply. Her breasts pillow me, and her ass is two globes of softness in my hands as I slide my hands under her hips. She can't get away now.

I push and grind and push and grind and thrust and slide my dick over and over into her cleft, that deep dark tunnel made for me, the tunnel of her love for me. Her legs are around me as she sticks her fingernails in my ass, holding me and making me go as deep as possible in her. I hear her breathing change as she gets closer and closer and closer to the pleasure we find in one another, only her, only me all the time. I groan out promises, and directions, and desires, and love to her in her ear as I pound my hips like a piston inside her. My head is buried in the curve of her neck, my lips sucking like I am marking her with hickeys. She won't like that, so I aim for her mouth instead and thrust both my dick and my tongue in her warm wetness at the same time.

She moans under my kiss and starts to come wildly, clenching her pussy around me tightly and then quaking inside like an earthquake rumbling through her intimate places. I feel the shudders and aftereffects subside before I erupt into a volcano of molten sperm and desire, exploding over and over inside her. I am rock-hard and spurt hot lava everywhere. I remember seeing the volcano on the Big Island of Hawaii erupt with red lava pouring into the sea and exploding as it suddenly cools. The only thing that hardens when it cools rapidly off igneous rocks like granite and the lovely black volcanic glass called obsidian.

I am an igneous rock formed from my earthy wife. I am hard to her soft. We fit together perfectly. I get hot when I am hard, not cold. It is amazing how she can do this to me: turn my penis into a hard thick shaft of granite just for her. I love my wife. We dissolve into tender kisses as I relax onto her soft pillowing body. I could stay inside her forever, locking inside her. She whispers she loves me.

I am complete, completely done and completely happy, and completely in love with the love of my life. I am the happiest of all men. She beguiles me, fascinates me, makes me laugh at the way her quick mind works, and I will die remembering her giggle. I will never get tired of that sound, the most important sound in the world to me. I want her happy, and she is when she is being clever and devilish and somewhat wicked.

I turn and see the end of the movie, when the couple dies together after a lifetime of love. I know they are in heaven together. I pray it will be true for us too.

Jason and Elizabeth call to wish us happy holidays, but they do not come for Christmas this year. Since I am here and Becca is not alone anymore, they have flown to California to spend it with their daughter Kelsie. We get to have a lovely Christmas Eve alone together.

Late afternoon Becca presents me with a shopping list. It appears I am being sent on a mission of the greatest importance. I need to obtain supplies from the Fresh Market for tonight's Christmas Eve dinner. I look at the list quickly. It is not hard, no mission impossible. I can do this. I head out the door and drive directly to the Fresh Market. I quickly obtain all the listed items but pick up a few of my own.

Fresh Market has an extensive display of orchids. I see a flower studded with many large pink blossoms dripping down its stem like a waterfall. The darker pink center folds mesmerize me.

Umm. So blatantly obvious and erotic. It looks like the secret places in a woman. Not subtle like the peace rose at all but very exposed for me to see. I buy one to give to my wife. I want it on the nightstand next to our bed.

I head home also equipped with a bottle of Frosty Dog wine from Chateau Morrisette. We eat a lovely dinner sitting at the dining room table. Dessert consists of chocolate chip cookies. We head to the great room to listen to some music. Gradually, I get my wife into a prone position under a ready and passionate me in front of the blazing stone fireplace.

I pretend to be Santa coming early with a sack full of presents I need to drop down her chimney. There is a definite fire burning in the fireplace as we make love in front of it in the great room. I glance at the beautiful orchid I placed earlier on the marble hearth before looking down at my erection thrusting into Becca's personal pink orchid.

It gets hot in here.

We leave chocolate chips cookies out for Santa before going to bed on Christmas Eve.

Christmas Day comes in a flurry of family, friends, dinner, and presents presented lovingly to one another. I give Becca a five-carat-total-weight diamond tennis bracelet she loves and lets me put it on her right wrist. She has her diamond engagement and wedding ring on her left hand and the gold Swiss watch on it as well. Now the diamond tennis bracelet decorates her right wrist.

Both arms covered now. Good. I like her sparkling with my diamonds.

She surprised me on Christmas night with a digital camera, large numbers of pale-white pearl necklaces, big red silk ribbons and large green velvet bows, and her naked body. I am allowed to take erotic pictures of my wife for me alone to enjoy. Suddenly I am Mr. Professional Photographer issuing orders of how I want her to pose. She is willing and does whatever I say. I pose her on our bed, in the bath, draped across the dining room table, propped with knees slightly spread on the granite kitchen counter, and lying in front of the fire in the great room.

I have a great deal of fun arranging the pearls on her, the red ribbons, and the big velvet bows. She is stunningly photogenic. I photograph her with long strands of pearls everywhere, silky red ribbons decorating her pussy, or just her tits and a big green velvet bow on her perky heart-shaped ass. She is a Christmas miracle to me.

Wow. I am rendered speechless for once at the sight of her posing for me. I go crazy snapping picture after picture. I must have taken hundreds.

I spend the evening downloading the images on my laptop for me to enjoy whenever I want. I particularly like the photo I chose as my desktop background. The pale glistening pearls are dripping sensually from Becca, a soft gleam against her skin. I think it is as good as any photo I have seen in a magazine. My wife is a natural model, posing easily in front of me. Her eyes shine with love and humor, and I capture that look in the photo.

She is a seductive vision of pale skin, pink nipples, and the shine of the pearls. I decide I will have to get her a real pearl necklace, maybe a three-strand choker or a long necklace that will fall into her cleavage, for her birthday on the 21st of February. I make sure I make love to her tonight, unwrapping the great big red bow that covers her. She is my Christmas present and hope for the future as well. It is a special Christmas night. We hardly sleep at all.

After the Christmas madness is all over, we invite Sara and Roger up for a New Year's Eve cookout. Courtney and Chris have their own plans in Roanoke, and we are all skipping First Night on campus. It is a surprisingly mild late-December day and not too cold to spend time on the backyard patio. I think Sara and Roger both have finally come to the conclusion that I am not about to desert Becca and leave her heartbroken.

They have recently returned from a strangely exhausting tour of the Baltic Region of Europe. They visited Bulgaria, Macedonia, Albania, Croatia, Serbia, Bosnia, Kosovo, and Turkey. Maybe more, I don't know. I think she said they went to eleven countries within a short time, a whirlwind of Baltic countries. Sara was saddened by the destruction still apparent in Sarajevo from the war almost twenty years ago. She said it made her sad because she remembers Sarajevo was a lovely city that once held a Winter Olympics.

We grill salmon steaks and corn on the cob for our meal and eat outside, enjoying wine and the mild late-December evening. Sara and Roger leave before dark so they will get home without problems and drunks on the interstate. They call after fifty minutes to let us know they arrived safely. It is a running joke between them. Roger always arrives on time, and Becca seems to get home faster than he thinks she should if she was driving the speed limit as directed. They constantly challenge each other about driving Interstate 64.

We sit together enjoying the silence and watching the sun turn the night sky into streaks of peach, orange, turquoise, and red. I look at my beautiful wife, reflecting on all the changes we have been through in our journey together so far. We have both fallen deeply in love with one another, for the first time and the last time in our lives.

I look forward to our future as one. I get up and put on a Mariah Carey CD in the background. Our Bose speaker system is excellent, and we listen to music all the time. I hear Mariah sing my all-time favorite song of hers, "We Belong Together."

"Mrs. Stevens, what is your New Year's resolution for tonight? Do you have something you want to change in the New Year?"

"No, Mr. Stevens, there is absolutely nothing I need to improve in my life for the coming year. I resolve only to love you with all my heart."

Excellent resolution.

"That is very good to hear. I have a New Year's resolution though. Do you want to hear what it is?"

"Oh no. Does it involve me? Is there something I need to change to make you happy?"

"Honey, it is my resolution, not yours. I resolve to never let you slip through my fingers again."

You are a slippery, slippery woman.

"But I like slipping through your fingers."

"No, I remember when you slipped away from me for a long whole week. I almost committed suicide. No more Week from Hell for me. It was all I could do to get you to give me a second chance. I almost gave up all hope. You are not going to be slippery again. I intend to keep my fingers on you tightly now."

Just as tight as I want your fingers on me.

"Oh, honey, I am already slippery for you. Come let your fingers discover just how slippery I am. I will show you my secret places you can slide into. Now please."

Soon, I promise. I will show you an unforgettable, rocking New Year's Eve. Thank you, Dick Clark, the master of all New Year's Eves. Just call me Dick as well. He will be intimately involved in all celebrations at midnight tonight.

"Becca, I am shocked! I can't believe you said that. I never know what is coming out of your mouth from one moment to the next. I am serious. You are not getting away again. I will never forget the hell you put me through when we first met. I had to work really, really hard to get you back in my life. I really didn't think you would let me in."

"I like you to work hard. Really hard. Work to get me tonight. I am not easy, you know. I don't give it up to anyone who happens to come along. Only you, my love."

You had better not be giving it up to anyone but me, your fucking husband. I have the legal rights to you now. I plan to exercise all my legal rights. You are my wife now. Get used to it.

Besides, I am already hard for you. Pay attention. Look at me. I want you with my heart, soul, and body.

"Okay, I can see you have a one-track mind tonight. Remind me about that when the clock strikes midnight on a new year. I have a big ball that needs to be dropped, just like in Times Square. Let's ring in the new year my way."

Ring, ring. Multiple rings. She is wearing two diamond wedding rings from me. They never leave her finger.

"Desperately, I'm looking forward to you ringing my bell tonight at midnight, my love."

"No worries. I plan on ringing it all night long."

I know you are a true Southern belle. Swing for me. Let my iron clanger hit the inside of your bell over and over. No cracks like the Liberty Bell, though.

"Promises, promises, Marine. The question is can you deliver?"

Is she kidding me? I always deliver my package to her on time and dependable. I am the fucking FedEx deliveryman, always prompt and reliable.

"I promise you will be pleased with my delivery later tonight. Anticipate the arrival of my package for you. Handle with care. Open it gently, my love."

"So a true New Year's Eve gift to celebrate the coming year. Will you be coming as well? I plan on coming to this special party also. Let's make it a date. I dare you. I don't think you have any surprises left for me now. I have your number, Marine. Count on it."

She sits there grinning at me, daring me to beat her now. I can't really think of what to say.

I surrender once again to her superior power of witty speech and sexual innuendos. She is simply too quick-witted for my poor sex-obsessed brain to cope with tonight. Yes, yes, a thousand times, yes. We are both coming to the party at midnight. Another New Year to celebrate our still new life together. We have been married almost a year now. A year of amazing experiences.

I hoist my squirming, giggling wife up and head indoors. On the way through the kitchen, I grab the opened bag of red- and green- and silver-wrapped holiday Hersey's Kisses. I have plans for these chocolate kisses. And a bottle of our favorite pink champagne and two fluted glasses.

We end up in the bedroom where I toss my giggling wife onto our bed, where she bounces upon landing. She pretends to try to get away, but she is laughing so hard she really can't get any words out. I pull her ankles down so she is lying on the bed with her head on the pillows. She still has on her jeans and sweatshirt. These have to go.

I take a moment to light the bedside vanilla-scented candle and turn on the wedding music CD I love so much.

I look at her, daring her to move with my eyes. She nods in agreement and watches as I stand up and strip my clothes off rapidly.

First me naked, now her.

I pull her up into a sitting position and gently raise her sweatshirt up and over her head. Her pink sheer bra pushes her pink pouting nipples proudly upward just waiting for my panting mouth. I slide her bra straps down each arm so she is now strapless.

Umm.

I like this.

Perhaps I will leave this a little bit longer.

I push her back onto the pillows and reach for her zipper on her tight jeans. Open so I can pull down her jeans. I have to explore her belly button for a while before I need to get those damn jeans off and out of my way. It is not easy to slide them down her hips. They are tight, but she lifts her hips for me.

After a few awkward moments, I manage to get them off her, finding the absolutely tiniest pink silk thong I have ever had the pleasure of meeting. There is barely a triangle of pink protecting her private area in the front, and the back is only thin straps which do not cover her magnificent ass at all. I like this underwear set tremendously. I leave both her bra and her thong in place.

Grabbing the bed of holiday-wrapped Hershey's Kisses, I decide my wife needs a little added sparkle for New Year's Eve. After all, there are fireworks all over the world to celebrate the coming of the new year. I plan to celebrate our coming as well.

Becca is lying there just watching me, curious and expectant but silent. She likes chocolate just like me.

I pour both of us pink champagne, and we toast the coming year and her tits. I always make sure they are toasted. The pink bubbling drink matches her pink lingerie.

We are so color-coordinated it is scary. Who knew the lingerie would be as pink as her pink nipples and the pink champagne? I like pink on my wife. The yellow peace rose edged in gentle pink comes to mind. My wife's petals also blush pink. I need to see that now.

I begin by placing two red Hershey's Kisses on each of her nipples, balancing them in place. She needs to keep them in place. I can see she is catching on rapidly. I will not make it easy on her. She has to stay still, and I plan on making it hard for her. To stay still, that is.

My thick dick is already making itself hard for her. It obviously needs to pop its cork tonight. Soon.

A silver Hershey's Kiss goes in her navel. It fits the slight indentation there perfectly like a diamond sparkling on her. I plan on keeping Becca covered in diamonds of every kind while we are married. She wears my diamond wedding bands, diamond earring studs, and now the diamond tennis bracelet.

Perhaps I should give her a diamond necklace instead of the three-strand pearl choker I thought of at Christmas.

Umm, wait.

The diamond necklace can be for our one-year anniversary on the 14th of February, followed by the pearl choker for her birthday on the 21st.

Good. I like this plan. More jewelry to mark my possession of her.

Back to my red-and-silver-decorated wife. Obviously her pussy needs several green Kisses. I place three of them there in a cluster. She is now decked out for the holiday.

Red, silver, green. Hershey's Kisses.

I start by kissing her so gently that all Kisses stay in place. She is starting to breathe a little faster now, and the Kisses on her breasts are trembling, but her bra helps keep them in place. I reach over and unwrap one red Kiss on her right nipple. I pop the breast-shaped chocolate kiss in my mouth and let it dissolve. My wife is allowed to share just a little when I give her a chocolate-flavored deep kiss. She moans and licks my lips.

"Baby, I want my own Kiss. Unwrap one for me too, please."

"Of course, my love. Chocolate Kiss coming right up just for you."

I take a moment to pull down the cup of her pink bra from her right Kiss-less breast. Her nipple is now exposed to me, a hard, tight pink flower bud. I worship it for a moment or two, causing my wife to squirm a little. Oh no. The red Kiss on her left breast trembles but does not fall off, thank goodness.

I reach over and unwrap red Hershey's Kiss number two. I take the Kiss in my mouth between my lips and lean over Becca's mouth to share. She takes a bite as we both dissolve into chocolate-flavored kisses. I reach over and expose her left nipple now. She is pushed up by her underwire bra and exposed to my wandering lips and fingers. I can tell she is getting very turned on by now, but we have a lot of Kisses left to go. Silver and green still in place.

I make fairly quick work of the silver navel situation because both of us will not last much longer. All that is left now are three green Kisses in her pussy. Green like my wife's eyes although her eyes are more olive than festive holiday green.

Becca is pleading with me by now. She is trying to stay still but wants me inside her. The damn Hershey Kisses are now in her way, as well as mine. I unwrap all three Kisses. I pop one in my mouth, chew, and swallow. I pop the second one in Becca's mouth and watch as she chews and swallows. The third unwrapped chocolate Kiss has a place to go. It gets nestled in my wife's tempting slit between her legs. Her folds hold it in place.

I lean back to admire its special location just a moment before I pounce on it with my mouth. Becca bucks up in surprise and, I hope, passion. I lick and chew and swallow and basically end up with a chocolate-smeared mouth and a slightly chocolaty pussy. I try to lick as much of it as I can before I enter her. She gasps in a deep-throated way. Her breathing changes rapidly to shallow pants as she is drawn closer and closer to her coming climax.

"Baby, baby, baby, stay with me, stay with me. I'm here inside you, loving you deeply. Let's do this together tonight. I love you. Are you close? I am, so very close to you. Give it to me, all of you now. Feel it with me, feel it, feel it, just let go now, oh baby, please soon, now please, now please, now please."

Intense sexual pleasure sweeps through us both as we moan each other's names in ecstasy. It barely takes any time at all before we are ringing in the coming new year, each of us going off with a bang, so to speak. We didn't actually wait until midnight for me to drop my ball in her Times Square and ring her little pink bell, my Southern belle of a wife. But I think we both see shooting fireworks lighting the night sky with brilliant flashes of colorful sparks. My mind conjures the image of sparks falling gently to earth and going out gradually like twinkling lightning bugs.

I know I feel the sexual spark that seems to hold us together as a couple still desperately in love and in lust with one another. It still burns so strongly. I know she feels it too.

As usual, I hear music and lyrics in my head as I relax. "My First Love" by Jennifer Lopez.

I wish you were my first love
'Cause if you were the first
Baby, there would be no second, third, or fourth love
Woah, oh, oh, oh

We lay there holding each other closely for hours before it really is midnight. We kiss to seal the deal of a hopeful and loving new year to face together. I hear a few random fireworks go off outside with an actual bang, someone celebrating in their backyard using fireworks purchased from some roadside shack in North Carolina.

Happy New Year to us both.

I can't take my eyes off her. As usual, I blurt everything all out in a rush of feelings and emotions. I want her to know how much I look forward to the future spent with her. I am her happy husband whose sole purpose in life is to keep her happy as well.

"I love you, Mrs. Stevens. With all my heart and soul. I want you safe by my side always. I'd be nothing without you. I am completely and utterly under your spell. I couldn't get away even if I wanted to. I know our love is real. It was real from the moment I first saw you. I know everyone thought it was too quick, but not for me. I had already waited a lifetime for you. That's why I couldn't get to you fast enough that night. And I know your love for me is real. Do you know how I know, baby?"

She looks at me lovingly.

I know that look now. I've seen that look in her eyes now for quite some time. It feels as though my life began when I first saw her walk into the Second Street Bistro that night we met. She must see it reflected back to her in my eyes as well.

"How do you know, Mr. Stevens? Tell me. I need to know how you know for sure."

"Because I know you *really* love me, you *really* want me, you *really* need me, and you *really* lust after my body. That's how I know for sure, Rebecca."

"Sounding rather . . . sure of yourself there, Michael. No doubts, right?"

"I am sure. Positive. No doubt in my mind. There better not be any in yours either. I'm as sure of your love for me as I am of my love for you. There's nothing you can do about it. I told you I'm not going anywhere. You can trust me. You're stuck with me for the rest of your life. Get used to it."

I realize our love is a mature love. We are not teenagers swept away by passion's first temptations. We are not young twenty-something adults trying to find our way in the world of careers and families. I liked my thirties, but I enjoy the maturity that has come to me in my forties. I know what I want and need in my life. I had searched for it for many years and gave up on it many times.

I didn't think it was possible for a man like me. I had been unlucky so far and had begun to believe that real love, like in books and movies, was simply an unattainable dream, a fantasy perpetuated by the media and fairy-tale stories. I think Becca had given up as well since I know her first husband was not the real love of her life. Because that is now me. I occupy that unique space in her life and I am never, ever giving it up. I'd die first.

She breathes so softly out the words that I can barely hear her. "I love you, Michael Stevens. I desperately need you, desperately want you, and desperately love you with all my heart. I am yours, and you are mine. Until death do us part. We promised each other."

"And I love you, my darling. Until death do us part. I promise."

She promises tenderly. "I vow never to forget we share a once-in-a-lifetime kind of love. You are my real love, and I am yours, my darling."

She takes my hand in hers and tenderly kisses each of my knuckles. I feel the warm caress of her moist lips and tongue before she turns my hand over and buries her lips against the center of my palm. My cupped hand holds her cheek softly before I raise her knuckles to my lips.

"My love, for as long as we both shall live."

And maybe not even then. Our love is real, and it's forever. And if what I believe is true, I'll be with my Becca for eternity. The real thing. I think I can finally breathe now. Deeply and completely. Like my love for her. Really, real love.

Cue Chris Brown's song "Forever." The musical soundtrack of our lives.

Tonight is the night to join me in ecstasy
Feel the melody in the rhythm of the music around you, around you
I'm gonna take you there,
I'm gonna take you there

Becca is my beautiful, soft yellow peace rose, her petals edged in blushing pink, endlessly captivating in her beauty, softly seductive in her secret places, an open blossom glorying under the warmth of our love, and no need for protective sharp thorns any longer. She is never kept from me. Becca is mine, forever more. I am hers. We are one.

The End.

Victoria Leigh Gabriella

July-November 2014

Williamsburg, VA

Twitter: vlgabriella

Facebook: A Real Love at Last

Author's notes

This book is a work of fiction, not an autobiography, about a couple who find real love in their forties. They are no longer teenagers like in *Twilight* or twenty-somethings like in *Fifty Shades of Grey*. However, some characters exist only in my imagination while others were inspired somewhat by my family, friends, and acquaintances. No names are exactly the same. Michael is a figment of my overactive imagination, based on absolutely no one I have ever met. In my mind, he looks a bit like the actor Max Martini or maybe Daniel Craig (?)

Becca is based loosely on me, but she is not me. She is the me I wish I had been in the past, the me I wish to be but can't be now, and the me I hope for in the future but realize is now impossible. She is Jennifer Connelly; I wish I looked like her. *Haha!* Stunning woman in her forties.

The places, cities, states, countries, athletes, sports, actors, singers, and songs are my favorite things. I have traveled to each of them. I watch the athletes and love the actors in my favorite movies. The songs are absolutely my favorite ones, and I listen to them all the time. The music videos for each can be found on YouTube.

The historical places and facts explained are the best I can do from my poor memory. I love history and am a Civil War buff just like Becca. My middle name is Lee, after Robert E. Lee, and my grandfather and uncle were named Jefferson Davis Garner. I am from the South.

My favorite restaurants are true, but do not think it is always possible you can order the meals I write about from their actual menus. (Sometimes)

I have very sweet memories of my Daddy working on his rose garden in my childhood backyard, especially after he retired. The peace rose was as described. It was stunningly large and right outside my bedroom window. It is absolutely the queen of all roses in my opinion, and it is my favorite, a lovely shade of soft yellow and pink on the same petals.

My pen name will be Victoria Leigh Gabriella since my first name is Vickey, and I always wished it had been Victoria; my middle name is Lee, so now Leigh; and my last name Garner starts with a G like Gabriella, which rhymes with Cinderella. Gabrielle was a favorite student of mine years ago.

There is only one person who has been on this journey with me almost from the start: a young, smart, and funny woman named ReBecca Richardson. She is wonderful, smart, and kind, and she never reminds me I am thirty years older than she is. She is my hairdresser with tattoos and purple streaks in her hair at times. She is a writer and listened to me when I told her of a dream I couldn't forget. I had started to write it down to get it out of my head. She encouraged me, edited and revised my first few pages, and gave me ideas for a direction to go toward. It just grew and grew and grew over about six weeks. This is it.

Thank you for reading. It has been an amazing adventure for me. I am sorry it is over. I hope you think it is sweet, sexy, funny, erotic, and too good to be true.